J.M. COETZEE

J.M. Coetzee's work includes *Waiting for the Barbarians*, *Life & Times of Michael K*, *Disgrace*, *The Childhood of Jesus* and *The Schooldays of Jesus*. He was the first author to win the Booker Prize twice and was awarded the Nobel Prize in Literature in 2003.

D1627697

David Higham Associates
FILE COPY
Publication Date:_____

Also by J.M. Coetzee

Dusklands
In the Heart of the Country
Waiting for the Barbarians
Life & Times of Michael K
Foe
White Writing
Age of Iron
Doubling the Point: Essays and Interviews
The Master of Petersburg
Giving Offense
Boyhood
The Lives of Animals
Disgrace
Stranger Shores: Essays 1986–1999
Youth
Elizabeth Costello
Slow Man
Inner Workings
Diary of a Bad Year
Summertime
The Childhood of Jesus
(with Paul Auster) Here and Now: Letters, 2008–2011
(with Arabella Kurtz) The Good Story
The Schooldays of Jesus
Late Essays: 2006–2017

J.M. Coetzee

Scenes from Provincial Life

VINTAGE

1 3 5 7 9 10 8 6 4 2

Vintage
20 Vauxhall Bridge Road,
London SW1V 2SA

Vintage is part of the Penguin Random
House group of companies whose
addresses can be found at global.
penguinrandomhouse.com

Penguin
Random House
UK

Copyright © J.M. Coetzee 1997, 2002, 2009,
2011

J.M. Coetzee has asserted his right to be
identified as the author of this
Work in accordance with the Copyright,
Designs and Patents Act 1988

First published in Vintage in 2018
First published in hardback by Harvill
Secker in 2011

Boyhood was first published in Great
Britain by Secker & Warburg in 1997;
Youth was first published in Great Britain
by Secker & Warburg in 2002;

and *Summertime* was first published in
Great Britain by Harvill Secker in 2009.
They were revised for republication
in 2011

penguin.co.uk/vintage

A CIP catalogue record for this book is
available from the British Library

ISBN 9780099555674

Grateful thanks to Faber and Faber Ltd
and the estate of Samuel Beckett for
permission to quote from *Waiting for Godot*

Typeset by Palimpsest Book Production
Limited, Falkirk, Stirlingshire

Printed and bound in Great Britain by
Clays Ltd, Elcograf S.p.A.

Penguin Random House is committed
to a sustainable future for our business,
our readers and our planet. This book is
made from Forest Stewardship Council®
certified paper.

In memoriam D.K.C.

Author's note

The three parts of *Scenes from Provincial Life* have appeared before as *Boyhood* (1997), *Youth* (2002), and *Summertime* (2009). They have been revised for republication.

I would like to express my thanks to Marilia Bandeira for assistance with Brazilian Portuguese, and to the estate of Samuel Beckett for permission to quote (in fact to misquote) from *Waiting for Godot*.

Contents

Boyhood

One

They live on a housing estate outside the town of Worcester, between the railway line and the National Road. The streets of the estate have tree-names but no trees yet. Their address is No. 12 Poplar Avenue. All the houses on the estate are new and identical. They are set in large plots of red clay earth where nothing grows, separated by wire fences. In each backyard stands a small block consisting of a room and a lavatory. Though they have no servant, they refer to these as 'the servant's room' and 'the servant's lavatory'. They use the servant's room to store things in: news-papers, empty bottles, a broken chair, an old coir mattress.

At the bottom of the yard they put up a poultry-run and install three hens, which are supposed to lay eggs for them. But the hens do not flourish. Rainwater, unable to seep away in the clay, stands in pools in the yard. The poultry-run turns into an evil-smelling morass. The hens develop gross swellings on their legs, like elephant-skin. Sickly and cross, they cease to lay. His mother consults her sister in Stellenbosch, who says they will return to laying only after the horny shells under their tongues have been cut out. So one after another his mother takes the hens between her knees, presses on their jowls till they open their beaks, and with the point of a paring-knife picks at their tongues. The hens shriek and struggle, their eyes bulging. He shudders and turns away. He thinks of his mother slapping stewing steak down on the kitchen counter and cutting it into cubes; he thinks of her bloody fingers.

The nearest shops are a mile away along a bleak eucalyptus-lined road. Trapped in this box of a house on the housing estate, there is nothing for his mother to do all day but sweep and tidy. Every time the wind blows, a fine ochre clay-dust whirls in under the doors, seeps through the cracks in the window frames, under the eaves, through the joints of the ceiling. After a daylong storm the dust lies piled inches high against the front wall.

They buy a vacuum cleaner. Every morning his mother trails the vacuum cleaner from room to room, sucking up the dust into the roaring belly on which a smiling red goblin leaps as if over a hurdle. A goblin: why?

He plays with the vacuum cleaner, tearing up paper and watching the strips fly up the pipe like leaves in the wind. He holds the pipe over a trail of ants, sucking them up to their death.

There are ants in Worcester, flies, plagues of fleas. Worcester is only ninety miles from Cape Town, yet everything is worse here. He has a ring of fleabites above his socks, and scabs where he has scratched. Some nights he cannot sleep for the itching. He does not see why they ever had to leave Cape Town.

His mother is restless too. I wish I had a horse, she says. Then at least I could go riding in the veld. A horse! says his father: Do you want to be Lady Godiva?

She does not buy a horse. Instead, without warning, she buys a bicycle, a woman's model, second-hand, painted black. It is so huge and heavy that, when he experiments with it in the yard, he cannot turn the pedals.

She does not know how to ride a bicycle; perhaps she does not know how to ride a horse either. She bought the bicycle thinking that riding it would be a simple matter. Now she can find no one to teach her.

His father cannot hide his glee. Women do not ride bicycles, he says. His mother remains defiant. I will not be a prisoner in this house, she says. I will be free.

At first he had thought it splendid that his mother should have her own bicycle. He had even pictured the three of them riding together down Poplar Avenue, she and he and his brother. But now, as he listens to his father's jokes, which his mother can meet only with dogged silence, he begins to waver. Women don't ride bicycles: what if his father is right? If his mother can find no one willing to teach her, if no other housewife in Reunion Park has a bicycle, then perhaps women are indeed not supposed to ride bicycles.

4

Alone in the backyard, his mother tries to teach herself. Holding her legs out straight on either side, she rolls down the incline towards the chicken-run. The bicycle tips over and comes to a stop. Because it does not have a crossbar, she does not fall, merely staggers about in a silly way, clutching the handlebars.

His heart turns against her. That evening he joins in with his father's jeering. He is well aware what a betrayal this is. Now his mother is all alone.

Nevertheless she does learn to ride, though in an uncertain, wobbling way, straining to turn the heavy cranks.

She makes her expeditions to Worcester in the mornings, when he is at school. Only once does he catch a glimpse of her on her bicycle. She is wearing a white blouse and a dark skirt. She is coming down Poplar Avenue towards the house. Her hair streams in the wind. She looks young, like a girl, young and fresh and mysterious.

Every time his father sees the heavy black bicycle leaning against the wall he makes jokes about it. In his jokes the citizens of Worcester interrupt their business to stand and gape as the woman on the bicycle labours past. *Trap! Trap!* they call out, mocking her: Push! There is nothing funny about the jokes, though he and his father always laugh together afterwards. As for his mother, she never has any repartee, she is not gifted in that way. 'Laugh if you like,' she says.

Then one day, without explanation, she stops riding the bicycle. Soon afterwards the bicycle disappears. No one says a word, but he knows she has been defeated, put in her place, and knows that he must bear part of the blame. I will make it up to her one day, he promises himself.

The memory of his mother on her bicycle does not leave him. She pedals away up Poplar Avenue, escaping from him, escaping towards her own desire. He does not want her to go. He does not want her to have a desire of her own. He wants her always to be in the house, waiting for him when he comes home. He does not often gang up with his father against her: his whole inclination is to gang up with her against his father. But in this case he belongs with the men.

Two

He shares nothing with his mother. His life at school is kept a tight secret from her. She shall know nothing, he resolves, but what appears on his quarterly report, which shall be impeccable. He will always come first in class. His conduct will always be Very Good, his progress Excellent. As long as the report is faultless, she will have no right to ask questions. That is the contract he establishes in his mind.

What happens at school is that boys are flogged. It happens every day. Boys are ordered to bend over and touch their toes and are flogged with a cane.

He has a classmate in Standard Three named Rob Hart whom the teacher particularly loves to beat. The Standard Three teacher is an excitable woman with hennaed hair named Miss Oosthuizen. From somewhere or other his parents know of her as Marie Oosthuizen: she takes part in theatricals and has never married. Clearly she has a life outside the school, but he cannot imagine it. He cannot imagine any teacher having a life outside school.

Miss Oosthuizen flies into rages, calls Rob Hart out from his desk, orders him to bend, and flogs him across the buttocks. The blows come fast one upon another, with barely time for the cane to swing back. By the time Miss Oosthuizen has finished with him, Rob Hart is flushed in the face. But he does not cry; in fact, he may be flushed only because he was bending. Miss Oosthuizen, on the other hand, heaves at the breast and seems on the brink of tears – of tears and of other outpourings too.

After these spells of ungoverned passion the whole class is hushed, and remains hushed until the bell rings.

Miss Oosthuizen never succeeds in making Rob Hart cry; perhaps that is why she flies into such rages at him and beats him so hard, harder than anyone else. Rob Hart is the oldest boy in the class, nearly two years older than himself (he is the youngest); he has a sense that between Rob Hart and Miss Oosthuizen there is something going on that he is not privy to.

Rob Hart is tall and handsome in a devil-may-care way. Though Rob Hart is not clever and is perhaps even in danger of failing the standard, he is attracted towards him. Rob Hart is part of a world he has not yet found a way of entering: a world of sex and beating.

As for himself, he has no desire to be beaten by Miss Oosthuizen or anyone else. The very idea of being beaten makes him squirm with shame. There is nothing he will not do to save himself from it. In this respect he is unnatural and knows it. He comes from an unnatural and shameful family in which not only are children not beaten but older people are addressed by their first names and no one goes to church and shoes are worn every day.

Every teacher at his school, man or woman, has a cane and is at liberty to use it. Each of these canes has a personality, a character, which is known to the boys and talked about endlessly. In a spirit of connoisseurship the boys weigh up the characters of the canes and the quality of pain they give, compare the arm and wrist techniques of the teachers who wield them. No one mentions the shame of being called out and made to bend and being beaten on one's backside.

Without experience of his own, he cannot take part in these conversations. Nevertheless, he knows that pain is not the most important consideration. If the other boys can bear the pain, then so can he, whose willpower is so much greater. What he will not be able to endure will be the shame. So bad will be the shame, he fears, so daunting, that he will hold tight to his desk and refuse to come when he is called out. And that will be a greater shame: it will set him apart, and set the other boys against him too. If it ever happens that he is called out to be beaten, there will be so humiliating a scene that he will never again be able to go back to school; in the end there will be no way out but to kill himself.

So that is what is at stake. That is why he never makes a sound in class. That is why he is always neat, why his homework is always done, why he always knows the answer. He dare not slip. If he slips, he risks being beaten; and whether he is beaten or whether he struggles against being beaten, it is all the same, he will die.

The strange thing is, it will only take one beating to break the spell of terror that has him in its grip. He is well aware of this: if, somehow, he can be rushed through the beating before he has had time to turn to stone and resist, if the violation of his body can be achieved quickly, by force, he will be able to come out on the other side a normal boy, able to join easily in discussion of the teachers and their canes and the various grades and flavours of pain they inflict. But by himself he cannot leap that barrier.

He puts the blame on his mother for not beating him. At the same time that he is glad he wears shoes and takes out books from the public library and stays away from school when he has a cold – all the things that set him apart – he is angry with his mother for not having normal children and making them live a normal life. His father, if his father were to take control, would turn them into a normal family. His father is normal in every way. He is grateful to his mother for protecting him from his father's normality, that is to say, from his father's occasional blue-eyed rages and threats to beat him. At the same time he is angry with his mother for turning him into something unnatural, something that needs to be protected if it is to continue to live.

Among the canes it is not Miss Oosthuizen's that leaves the deepest impression on him. The most fearsome cane is that of Mr Lategan the woodwork teacher. Mr Lategan's cane is not long and springy in the style most of the teachers prefer. Instead it is short and thick and stubby, more a stick or a baton than a switch. It is rumoured that Mr Lategan uses it only on the older boys, that it will be too much for a younger boy. It is rumoured that with his cane Mr Lategan has made even Matric boys blubber and plead for mercy and urinate in their pants and disgrace themselves.

Mr Lategan is a little man with close-cropped hair that stands upright, and a moustache. One of his thumbs is missing: the stub is neatly covered over with a purple scar. Mr Lategan hardly says anything. He is always in a distant, irritable mood, as though teaching woodwork to small boys is a task beneath him that he performs unwillingly. Through most of the lesson he stands at the window staring out over the quadrangle while the boys tentatively measure and saw and plane. Sometimes he has the stubby cane with him, idly tapping his trouser-leg while he ruminates. When he comes on his inspection round he disdainfully points to what is wrong, then with a shrug of the shoulders passes on.

It is permitted for boys to joke with teachers about their canes. In fact this is one area in which a certain teasing of the teachers is permitted. 'Make him sing, sir!' say the boys, and Mr Gouws will flash his wrist and his long cane (the longest cane in the school, though Mr Gouws is only the Standard Five teacher) will whistle through the air.

No one jokes with Mr Lategan. There is awe of Mr Lategan, of what he can do with his cane to boys who are almost men.

When his father and his father's brothers get together on the farm at Christmas, talk always turns to their schooldays. They reminisce about their schoolmasters and their schoolmasters' canes; they recall cold winter mornings when the cane would raise blue weals on their buttocks and the sting would linger for days in the memory of the flesh. In their words there is a note of nostalgia and pleasurable fear. He listens avidly but makes himself as inconspicuous as possible. He does not want them to turn to him, in some pause in the conversation, and ask about the place of the cane in his own life. He has never been beaten and is deeply ashamed of it. He cannot talk about canes in the easy, knowing way of these men.

He has a sense that he is damaged. He has a sense that something is slowly tearing inside him all the time: a wall, a membrane. He tried to hold himself as tight as possible to keep the tearing within bounds. To keep it within bounds, not to stop it: nothing will stop it.

Once a week he and his class troop across the school grounds to the gymnasium for PT, physical training. In the changing room they put on white singlets and shorts. Then under the direction of Mr Barnard, also attired in white, they spend half an hour leapfrogging the pommel horse or tossing the medicine ball or jumping and clapping their hands above their heads.

They do all of this with bare feet. For days ahead, he dreads baring his feet for PT, his feet that are always covered. Yet when his shoes and socks are off, it is suddenly not difficult at all. He has simply to remove himself from his shame, to go through with the undressing in a brisk, hurried way, and his feet become just feet like everyone else's. Somewhere in the vicinity the shame still hangs, waiting to return to him, but it is a private shame, which the other boys need never be aware of.

His feet are soft and white; otherwise they look like everyone else's, even those of boys who have no shoes and come to school barefoot. He does not enjoy PT and the stripping for PT, but he tells himself he can endure it, as he endures other things.

Then one day there is a change in the routine. They are sent from the gymnasium to the tennis courts to learn paddle tennis. The courts are some distance away; along the pathway he has to tread carefully, picking his steps among the pebbles. Under the summer sun the tarmac of the court itself is so hot that he has to hop from foot to foot to keep from burning. It is a relief to get back to the changing room and put on his shoes again; but by afternoon he can barely walk, and when his mother removes his shoes at home she finds the soles of his feet blistered and bleeding.

He spends three days at home recovering. On the fourth day he returns with a note from his mother, a note whose indignant wording he is aware of and approves. Like a wounded warrior resuming his place in the ranks, he limps down the aisle to his desk.

'Why were you away from school?' whisper his classmates.

'I couldn't walk, I had blisters on my feet from the tennis,' he whispers back.

He expects astonishment and sympathy; instead he gets mirth. Even those of his classmates who wear shoes do not take his story seriously. Somehow they too have acquired hardened feet, feet that do not blister. He alone has soft feet, and soft feet, it is emerging, are no claim to distinction. All of a sudden he is isolated – he and, behind him, his mother.

Three

He has never worked out the position of his father in the household. In fact, it is not obvious to him by what right his father is there at all. In a normal household, he is prepared to accept, the father stands at the head: the house belongs to him, the wife and children live under his sway. But in their own case, and in the households of his mother's two sisters as well, it is the mother and children who make up the core, while the husband is no more than an appendage, a contributor to the economy as a paying lodger might be.

As long as he can remember he has had a sense of himself as prince of the house, and of his mother as his dubious promoter and anxious protector – anxious, dubious because, he knows, a child is not meant to rule the roost. If there is anyone to be jealous of, it is not his father but his younger brother. For his mother promotes his brother too – promotes and even, because his brother is clever but not as clever as he, nor as bold or adventurous, favours him. In fact, his mother seems always to be hovering over his brother, ready to ward off danger; whereas in his own case she is only somewhere in the background, waiting, listening, ready to come if he should call.

He wants her to behave towards him as she does towards his brother. But he wants this as a sign, a proof, no more. He knows that he will fly into a rage if she ever begins to hover over him.

He keeps driving her into corners, demanding that she admit whom she loves more, him or his brother. Always she slips the trap. 'I love you both the same,' she maintains, smiling. Even his most ingenious questions – what if the house were to catch fire, for instance, and she had time to rescue only one of them? – fail to snare her. 'Both of you,' she says, 'I will surely save both of you. But the house won't catch fire.' Though he mocks her for her literal-mindedness, he respects her dogged constancy.

His rages against his mother are one of the things he has to keep a careful secret from the world outside. Only the four of them know what torrents of scorn he pours upon her, how much like an inferior he treats her. 'If your teachers and your friends knew how you spoke to your mother . . .,' says his father, wagging a finger meaningfully. He hates his father for seeing so clearly the chink in his armour.

He wants his father to beat him and turn him into a normal boy. At the same time he knows that if his father dared to strike him, he would not rest until he had his revenge. If his father were to hit him, he would go mad: he would become possessed, like a rat in a corner, hurtling about, snapping with its poisonous fangs, too dangerous to be touched.

At home he is an irascible despot, at school a lamb, meek and mild, who sits in the second row from the back, the most obscure row, so that he will not be noticed, and goes rigid with fear when the beating starts. By living this double life he has created for himself a burden of imposture. No one else has to bear anything like it, not even his brother, who is at most a nervous, wishy-washy imitation of himself. In fact, he suspects that at heart his brother may be normal. He is on his own. From no quarter can he expect support. It is up to him to somehow get beyond childhood, beyond family and school, to a new life where he will not need to pretend any more.

Childhood, says the *Children's Encyclopaedia*, is a time of innocent joy, to be spent in the meadows amid buttercups and bunny-rabbits or at the hearthside absorbed in a storybook. It is a vision of childhood utterly alien to him. Nothing he experiences in Worcester, at home or at school, leads him to think that childhood is anything but a time of gritting the teeth and enduring.

Because there is no Wolf Cub pack in Worcester, he is allowed to join the Boy Scout troop though he is only ten. For his inauguration as a Scout he prepares himself punctiliously. With his mother he goes to the outfitter's to buy the uniform: stiff olive-brown felt hat and silver hat-badge, khaki shirt and shorts and stockings, leather belt with Boy Scout clasp, green shoulder-tabs, green stocking-flashes. He cuts a five-foot stave from a poplar tree, peels off the bark, and spends an afternoon with a heated screwdriver burning into the white woodflesh the entire Morse and semaphore codes. He goes off to his first Scout meeting, the stave slung over his shoulder with a green cord that he has himself triple-braided. Taking the oath with a two-finger salute, he is by far the most impeccably outfitted of the new boys, the 'tenderfeet'.

Boy Scouts, he discovers, consists, like school, of passing examin-ations. For each examination you pass you get a badge, which you sew on to your shirt.

Examinations are taken in a preordained sequence. The first examin-ation is in tying knots: the reef knot and the double reef, the sheepshank, the bowline. He passes it, but without distinction. It is not clear to him how one passes these Boy Scout examinations with distinction, how one excels.

The second examination is for a woodsman's badge. To pass, he is required to light a fire, using no paper and striking no more than three matches. On the bare ground at the side of the Anglican church hall, on a winter's evening with a cold wind blowing, he assembles his heap of twigs and scraps of bark, and then, with his troop leader and the scout-master observing, strikes his matches one by one. Each time the fire does not take: each time the wind blows out the tiny flame. The scout-master and troop leader turn away. They do not utter the words, 'You have failed,' so he is not sure that he has in fact failed. What if they are going off to confer and decide that, because of the wind, the test was unfair? He waits for them to come back. He waits for the woodsman's badge to be given to him anyhow. But nothing happens. He stands by his pile of twigs and nothing happens.

No one mentions it again. It is the first examination he has failed in his life.

Every June vacation the Scout troop goes on a camp. Save for a week in hospital at the age of four he has never been away from his mother. But he is determined to go with the Scouts.

There is a list of things to take. One is a groundsheet. His mother does not have a groundsheet, is not even sure what a groundsheet is. Instead she gives him an inflatable red rubber mattress. At the campsite he discovers that all the other boys have proper khaki-coloured groundsheets. His red mattress at once sets him apart. That is not all. He cannot bring himself to move his bowels over a stinking pit in the earth.

On the third day of the camp they go swimming in the Breede River. Though, at the time when they lived in Cape Town, he and his brother and his cousin used to catch the train to Fish Hoek and spend whole afternoons clambering on the rocks and making castles in the sand and splashing in the waves, he does not actually know how to swim. Now, as a Boy Scout, he must swim across the river and back.

He hates rivers for their murkiness, for the mud that oozes between his toes, for the rusty tin cans and broken bottles he could step on; he prefers clean white sea-sand. But he plunges in and somehow splashes across. On the far bank he clutches the root of a tree, finds a foothold, stands waist-deep in sullen brown water, his teeth chattering.

The other boys turn and begin to swim back. He is left alone. There is nothing to do but launch himself back into the water.

By midstream he is exhausted. He gives up swimming and tries to stand, but the river is too deep. His head goes under. He tries to lift himself, to swim again, but he has not the strength. He goes under a second time.

He has a vision of his mother sitting on a chair with a high, straight back reading the letter that tells of his death. His brother stands at her side, reading over her shoulder.

The next he knows, he is lying on the riverbank and his troop leader, whose name is Michael but whom he has been too shy to speak to, is straddling him. He closes his eyes, filled with well-being. He has been saved.

For weeks afterwards he thinks of Michael, of how Michael risked his own life to plunge back into the river and rescue him. Each time it strikes him how wonderful it is that Michael should have noticed – noticed him, noticed that he was failing. Compared with Michael (who is in Standard

Seven and has all except the most advanced badges and is going to be a King's Scout) he is negligible. It would have been quite appropriate for Michael not to have seen him go under, even not to have missed him until they got back to camp. Then all that would have been required of Michael would have been to write the letter to his mother, the cool, formal letter beginning: 'We regret to inform you . . .'

From that day onward he knows there is something special about him. He should have died but he did not. Despite his unworthiness, he has been given a second life. He was dead but is alive.

Of what passed at the camp he breathes not a word to his mother.

Four

The great secret of his school life, the secret he tells no one at home, is that he has become a Roman Catholic, that for all practical purposes he 'is' a Roman Catholic.

The topic is difficult to raise at home because their family 'is' nothing. They are of course South Africans, but even South Africanness is faintly embarrassing, and therefore not talked about, since not everyone who lives in South Africa is a South African, or not a proper South African.

In religion they are certainly nothing. Not even in his father's family, which is much safer and more ordinary than his mother's, does anyone go to church. He himself has been in a church only twice in his life: once to be baptized and once to celebrate victory in World War Two.

The decision to 'be' a Roman Catholic is made on the spur of the moment. On the first morning at his new school, while the rest of the class is marched off to assembly in the school hall, he and the three other new boys are kept behind. 'What is your religion?' asks the teacher of each of them. He glances right and left. What is the right answer? What religions are there to choose from? Is it like Russians and Americans? His turn comes. 'What is your religion?' asks the teacher. He is sweating, he does not know what to say. 'Are you a Christian or a Roman Catholic or a Jew?' she demands impatiently. 'Roman Catholic,' he says.

When the questioning is over, he and another boy who says he is a Jew are motioned to stay behind; the two who say they are Christians go off to assembly.

They wait to see what will happen to them. But nothing happens. The corridors are empty, the building is silent, there are no teachers left.

They wander into the playground, where they join the rag-tag of other boys left behind. It is marbles season; in the unfamiliar hush of the empty grounds, with dove-calls in the air and the faint, far-off sound of singing, they play marbles. Time passes. Then the bell rings for the end of assembly. The rest of the boys return from the hall, marching in files, class by class. Some appear to be in a bad mood. 'Jood!' an Afrikaans boy hisses at him as he passes: Jew! When they rejoin their class, no one smiles.

The episode disturbs him. He hopes that the next day he and the other new boys will be kept behind again and asked to make new choices. Then he, who has clearly made a mistake, can correct himself and be a Christian. But there is no second chance.

Twice a week the separation of sheep from goats is repeated. While Jews and Catholics are left to their own devices, the Christians go off to assembly to sing hymns and be preached to. In revenge for which, and in revenge for what the Jews did to Christ, the Afrikaans boys, big, brutal, knobbly, sometimes catch a Jew or a Catholic and punch him in the biceps, short, vicious knuckle-punches, or knee him in the balls, or twist his arms behind his back till he pleads for mercy. 'Asseblief!' the boy whimpers: Please! 'Jood!' they hiss back: 'Jood! Vuilgoed!' Jew! Filth!

One day during the lunch break two Afrikaans boys corner him and drag him to the farthest corner of the rugby field. One of them is huge and fat. He pleads with them. 'Ek is nie 'n Jood nie,' he says: I am not a Jew. He offers to let them ride his bicycle, offers them his bicycle for the afternoon. The more he gabbles, the more the fat boy smiles. This is evidently what he likes: the pleading, the abasement.

From his shirt pocket the fat boy produces something, something that begins to explain why he has been dragged to this quiet corner: a wriggling green caterpillar. The friend pins his arms behind his back; the fat boy pinches the hinges of his jaws till his mouth opens, then forces the caterpillar in. He spits it out, already torn, already exuding its juices. The fat boy crushes it, smears it over his lips. 'Jood!' he says, wiping his hand clean on the grass.

He chose to be a Roman Catholic, that fateful morning, because of

Rome, because of Horatius and his two comrades, swords in their hands, crested helmets on their heads, indomitable courage in their glance, defending the bridge over the Tiber against the Etruscan hordes. Now, step by step, he discovers from the other Catholic boys what a Roman Catholic really is. A Roman Catholic has nothing to do with Rome. Roman Catholics have not even heard of Horatius. Roman Catholics go to catechism on Friday afternoons; they go to confession; they take communion. That is what Roman Catholics do.

The older Catholic boys corner him and quiz him: has he been to catechism, has he been to confession, has he taken communion? Catechism? Confession? Communion? He does not even know what the words mean. 'I used to go in Cape Town,' he says evasively. 'Where?' they say. He does not know the names of any churches in Cape Town, but nor do they. 'Come to catechism on Friday,' they order him. When he does not come, they inform the priest that there is an apostate in Standard Three. The priest sends a message, which they relay: he must come to catechism. He suspects they have fabricated the message, but the next Friday he stays at home, lying low.

The older Catholic boys begin to make it clear they do not believe his stories about being a Catholic in Cape Town. But he has gone too far now, there is no going back. If he says, 'I made a mistake, I am actually a Christian,' he will be disgraced. Besides, even if he has to bear the taunts of the Afrikaners and the interrogations of the real Catholics, are the two free periods a week not worth it, free periods to walk around the empty playing fields talking to the Jews?

One Saturday afternoon when the whole of Worcester, stunned by the heat, has gone to sleep, he takes out his bicycle and cycles to Dorp Street.

Usually he gives Dorp Street a wide berth, since that is where the Catholic church is. But today the street is empty, there is no sound but the rustle of water in the furrows. Nonchalantly he cycles past, pretending not to look.

The church is not as big as he thought it would be. It is a low, blank building with a little statue over the portico: the Virgin, hooded, holding her baby.

He reaches the bottom of the street. He would like to turn and come back for a second look, but he is afraid of stretching his luck, afraid that a priest in black will emerge and wave to him to stop.

The Catholic boys nag him and make sneering remarks, the Christians persecute him, but the Jews do not judge. The Jews pretend not to notice. The Jews wear shoes too. In a minor way he feels comfortable with the Jews. The Jews are not so bad.

Nevertheless, with Jews one has to tread carefully. For the Jews are everywhere, the Jews are taking over the country. He hears this on all sides, but particularly from his uncles, his mother's two bachelor brothers, when they visit. Norman and Lance come every summer, like migrating birds, though rarely at the same time. They sleep on the sofa, get up at eleven in the morning, moon around the house for hours, half-dressed, tousled. Both have cars; sometimes they can be persuaded to take their sister and her boys for an afternoon drive, but they seem to prefer passing their time smoking and drinking tea and talking about the old days. Then they have supper, and after supper, play poker or rummy until midnight with whoever can be persuaded to stay up.

He loves to listen to his mother and his uncles going for the thousandth time over the events of their childhood on the farm. He is never happier than when listening to these stories, to the teasing and the laughter that go with them. His friends in Worcester do not come from families with stories like these. That is what sets him apart: the two farms behind him, his mother's farm, his father's farm, and the stories of those farms. Through the farms he is rooted in the past; through the farms he has substance.

There is a third farm too: Skipperskloof, near Williston. His family has no roots there, it is a farm they have married into. Nevertheless, Skipperskloof is important too. All farms are important. Farms are places of freedom, of life.

In among the stories that Norman and Lance and his mother tell flit the figures of Jews, comic, sly, but also cunning and heartless, like jackals. Jews from Oudtshoorn came to the farm every year to buy ostrich feathers from their father, his grandfather. They persuaded him to give up wool and farm only with ostriches. Ostriches would make him rich, they said. Then one day the bottom fell out of the ostrich-feather market.

The Jews refused to buy any more feathers and his grandfather went bankrupt. Everyone in the district went bankrupt and the Jews took over their farms. That is how the Jews operate, says Norman: you must never trust a Jew.

His father demurs. His father cannot afford to decry the Jews, since he is employed by a Jew. Standard Canners, where he works as a book-keeper, belongs to Wolf Heller. In fact it was Wolf Heller who brought him from Cape Town to Worcester when he lost his job in the civil service. The future of their family is bound up with the future of Standard Canners, which, in the few years since he took it over, Wolf Heller has built up into a giant of the canning world. There are wonderful prospects in Standard Canners, says his father, for someone like himself, with legal qualifications.

So Wolf Heller is exempted from the strictures on Jews. Wolf Heller takes care of his employees. At Christmas he even buys them presents, though Christmas means nothing to Jews.

There are no Heller children at school in Worcester. If there are Heller children at all, they have presumably been sent to SACS in Cape Town, which is a Jewish school in all but name. Nor are there Jewish families in Reunion Park. The Jews of Worcester live in the older, greener, shadier part of the town. Though there are Jewish boys in his class, he is never invited into their homes. He sees them only at school, brought closer to them during assembly periods, when Jews and Catholics are isolated and subjected to the ire of the Christians.

Every now and again, however, for reasons that are not clear, the dispensation that allows them freedom during assembly is withdrawn and they are summoned to the hall.

The hall is always packed. Senior boys occupy the seats, while boys from the junior school crowd the floor. The Jews and Catholics – perhaps twenty in all – thread their way among them, looking for space. Hands surreptitiously snatch at their ankles, trying to trip them.

The *dominee* is already on the stage, a pale young man in a black suit and white tie. He preaches in a high, sing-song voice, drawing out the long vowels, pronouncing every letter of every word punctiliously. When the preaching is over, they have to stand for the prayer. What is it proper for a Catholic to do during a Christian prayer? Does he close his eyes and move his lips, or does he pretend not to be there? He cannot see any of the real Catholics; he puts on a blank look and allows his eyes to go out of focus.

The *dominee* sits down. The songbooks are handed out; it is time for the singing. One of the women teachers steps forward to conduct. 'Al die veld is vrolik, al die voëltjies sing,' sing the juniors. Then the seniors stand up. 'Uit die blou van onse hemel,' they sing in their deep voices, standing to attention, gazing sternly ahead: the national anthem, their national anthem. Tentatively, nervously, the younger boys join in. Leaning over them, waving with her arms as though scooping feathers, the teacher tries to uplift them, encourage them. 'Ons sal antwoord op jou roepstem, ons sal offer wat jy vra,' they sing: we will answer your call.

At last it is over. The teachers descend from the platform, first the principal, then the *dominee*, then the rest of them. The boys file out of the hall. A fist strikes him in the kidneys, a short, quick jab, invisible. 'Jood!' a voice whispers. Then he is out, he is free, he can breathe fresh air again.

Despite the menaces of the real Catholics, despite the hovering possibility that the priest will visit his parents and unmask him, he is thankful for the inspiration that made him choose Rome. He is grateful to the Church that shelters him; he has no regrets, does not wish to stop being a Catholic. If being a Christian means singing hymns and listening to sermons and then coming out to torment the Jews, he has no wish to be a Christian. The fault is not his if the Catholics of Worcester are Catholic without being Roman, if they know nothing about Horatius and his comrades holding the bridge over the Tiber ('Tiber, Father Tiber, to whom we Romans pray'), about Leonidas and his Spartans holding the pass at Thermopylae, about Roland holding the pass against the Saracens. He can think of nothing more heroic than holding a pass, nothing nobler than giving up one's life to save other people, who will afterwards weep over one's corpse. That is what he would like to be: a hero. That is what proper Roman Catholicism should be about.

It is a summer evening, cool after the long, hot day. He is in the public gardens, where he has been playing cricket with Greenberg and Goldstein:

Greenberg, who is solid in class but not good at cricket; Goldstein, who has large brown eyes and wears sandals and is quite dashing. It is late, well past seven-thirty. Save for the three of them, the gardens are deserted. They have had to give up their cricket: it is too dark to see the ball. So they have wrestling fights as if they were children again, rolling about on the grass, tickling each other, laughing and giggling. He stands up, takes a deep breath. A surge of exultation passes through him. He thinks: 'I have never been happier in my life. I would like to be with Greenberg and Goldstein forever.'

They part. It is true. He would like to live like this forever, riding his bicycle through the wide and empty streets of Worcester in the dusk of a summer's day, when all the other children have been called in and he alone is abroad, like a king.

Five

Being a Catholic is a part of his life reserved for school. Preferring the Russians to the Americans is a secret so dark that he can reveal it to no one. Liking the Russians is a serious matter. It can have you ostracized. It can have you sent to jail.

In a box in his cupboard he keeps the book of drawings he did at the height of his passion for the Russians in 1947. The drawings, in heavy lead pencil coloured in with wax crayons, show Russian planes shooting American planes out of the sky, Russian ships sinking American ships. Though the fervour of that year, when a wave of enmity against the Russians suddenly burst out on the radio and everyone had to take sides, has subsided, he retains his secret loyalty: loyalty to the Russians, but even more loyalty to himself as he was when he did the drawings.

There is no one here in Worcester who knows he likes the Russians. In Cape Town there used to be his friend Nicky, with whom he played war games with lead soldiers and a spring-loaded cannon that fired matchsticks; but when he found how dangerous his allegiances were, what he stood to lose, he first swore Nicky to secrecy, then, to make doubly sure, told him he had changed sides and now liked the Americans.

In Worcester no one but he likes the Russians. His loyalty to the Red Star sets him absolutely apart.

Where did he pick up this infatuation, that strikes even him as odd? His mother's name is Vera: Vera, with its icy capital V, an arrow plunging downwards. Vera, she once told him, was a Russian name. When the

Russians and the Americans were first set before him as antagonists between whom he had to choose ('Who do you like, Smuts or Malan? Who do you like, Superman or Captain Marvel? Who do you like, the Russians or the Americans?'), he chose the Russians as he chose the Romans: because he likes the letter, r, particularly the capital R, the strongest of all the letters.

He chose the Russians in 1947 when everyone else was choosing the Americans; having chosen them, he threw himself into reading about them. His father owned a three-volume history of World War Two. He loved these books and pored over them, pored over photographs of Russian soldiers in white ski uniforms, Russian soldiers with tommy guns dodging among the ruins of Stalingrad, Russian tank commanders staring ahead through their binoculars. (The Russian T-34 was the best tank in the world, better than the American Sherman, better even than the German Tiger.) Again and again he came back to a painting of a Russian pilot banking his dive-bomber over a burning and devastated German tank column. He adopted everything Russian. He adopted stern but fatherly Field Marshal Stalin, the greatest and most far-sighted strategist of the war; he adopted the borzoi, the Russian wolfhound, swiftest of all dogs. He knew everything there was to know about Russia: its land area in square miles, its coal and steel output in tons, the length of each of its great rivers, the Volga, the Dnieper, the Yenisei, the Ob.

Then came the realization, from the disapproval of his parents, from the puzzlement of his friends, from what they reported when they told their own parents about him: liking the Russians was not part of a game, it was not allowed.

Always, it seems, there is something that goes wrong. Whatever he wants, whatever he likes, has sooner or later to be turned into a secret. He begins to think of himself as one of those spiders that live in a hole in the ground sealed with a trapdoor. Always the spider has to be scuttling back into its hole, closing the trapdoor behind it, shutting out the world, hiding.

In Worcester he keeps his Russian past a secret, hides the reprehensible book of drawings, with their smoke-trails of enemy fighters crashing into the ocean and battleships sliding bow-first under the waves. For drawing he substitutes games of imaginary cricket. He uses a wooden beach bat and a tennis ball. The challenge is to keep the ball in the air as long as possible. For hours on end he circles the dining-room table patting the ball in the air. All the vases and ornaments have been cleared away; every time the ball strikes the ceiling a shower of fine red dust descends.

He plays entire games, eleven batsmen a side each batting twice. Each hit counts as a run. When his attention flags and he misses the ball a batsman is out, and he enters his score on the scorecard. Huge totals mount up: five hundred runs, six hundred runs. Once England scores a thousand runs, which no real team has ever done before. Sometimes England wins, sometimes South Africa; more rarely Australia or New Zealand.

Russia and America do not play cricket. The Americans play baseball; the Russians do not appear to play anything, perhaps because it is always snowing there.

He does not know what the Russians do when they are not making war.

Of his private cricket games he says nothing to his friends, keeping them for home. Once, during their early months in Worcester, a boy from his class had wandered in through the open front door and found him lying on his back under a chair. 'What are you doing there?' he had asked. 'Thinking,' he had replied unthinkingly: 'I like thinking.' Soon everyone in his class knew about it: the new boy was odd, he wasn't normal. From that mistake he has learned to be more prudent. Part of being prudent is always to tell less rather than more.

He also plays proper cricket with whoever is prepared to play. But proper cricket on the empty square in the middle of Reunion Park is too slow to be borne: the ball is forever being missed by the batsman, missed by the wicketkeeper, getting lost. He hates searching for lost balls. He hates fielding too, on stony ground where you bloody your hands and knees every time you fall. He wants to bat or bowl, that is all.

He courts his brother, though his brother is only six years old, promising to let him play with his toys if he will bowl to him in the backyard.

His brother bowls for a while, then grows bored and sullen and scuttles indoors for protection. He tries to teach his mother to bowl, but she cannot master the action. While he grows exasperated, she quivers with laughter at her own clumsiness. So he allows her to throw the ball instead. But in the end the spectacle is too shameful, too easily seen from the street: a mother playing cricket with her son.

He cuts a jam-tin in half and nails the bottom half to a two-foot wooden arm. He mounts the arm on an axle through the walls of a packing case weighed down with bricks. The arm is drawn forward by a strip of inner-tube rubber, drawn back by a rope that runs through a hook on the packing case. He puts a ball in the tin cup, retreats ten yards, pulls on the rope till the rubber is taut, anchors the rope under his heel, takes up his batting position, and releases the rope. Sometimes the ball shoots up into the sky, sometimes straight at his head; but every now and again it flies within reach and he is able to hit it. With this he is satisfied: he has bowled and batted all by himself, he has triumphed, nothing is impossible.

One day, in a mood of reckless intimacy, he asks Greenberg and Goldstein to bring out their earliest memories. Greenberg demurs: it is a game he is not willing to play. Goldstein tells a long and pointless story about being taken to the beach, a story he barely listens to. For the point of the game is, of course, to allow him to recount his own first memory.

He is leaning out of the window of their flat in Johannesburg. Dusk is falling. Out of the distance a car comes racing down the street. A dog, a small spotted dog, runs in front of it. The car hits the dog: its wheels go right over the dog's middle. With its hind legs paralysed, the dog drags itself away, yelping with pain. No doubt it will die; but at this point he is snatched away from his perch at the window.

It is a magnificent first memory, trumping anything that poor Goldstein can dredge up. But is it true? Why was he leaning out of the window watching an empty street? Did he really see the car hit the dog, or did he just hear a dog yelping, and run to the window? Is it possible that he saw nothing but a dog dragging its hindquarters and made up the car and the driver and the rest of the story?

There is another first memory, one that he trusts more fully but would never repeat, certainly not to Greenberg and Goldstein, who would trumpet it around the school and turn him into a laughing stock.

He is sitting beside his mother in a bus. It must be cold, for he is wearing red woollen leggings and a woollen cap with a bobble. The engine of the bus labours; they are ascending the wild and desolate Swartberg Pass.

In his hand is a sweet-wrapper. He holds the wrapper out of the window, which is open a crack. It flaps and trembles in the wind.

'Shall I let go?' he asks his mother.

She nods. He lets it go.

The scrap of paper flies up into the sky. Below there is nothing but the grim abyss of the pass, ringed with cold mountain peaks. Craning backwards, he catches a last glimpse of the paper, still bravely flying.

'What will happen to the paper?' he asks his mother; but she does not comprehend.

That is the other first memory, the secret one. He thinks all the time of the scrap of paper, alone in all that vastness, that he abandoned when he should not have abandoned it. One day he must go back to the Swartberg Pass and find it and rescue it. That is his duty: he may not die until he has done it.

His mother is full of scorn for men who are 'useless with their hands', among whom she numbers his father, but also her own brothers, and principally her eldest brother Roland, who could have kept the farm if he had worked hard enough to pay off its debts, but did not. Of the many uncles on his father's side (he counts six by blood, another five by marriage), the one she admires most is Joubert Olivier, who on Skipperskloof has installed an electric generator and has even taught himself dentistry. (On one of his visits to the farm he gets toothache. Uncle Joubert seats him on a chair under a tree and, without anaesthetic, drills out the hole and fills it with gutta-percha. Never in his life has he suffered such agony.)

When things break – plates, ornaments, toys – his mother fixes them herself: with string, with glue. The things she ties together come loose, since she does not know about knots. The things she glues together fall apart; she blames the glue.

The kitchen drawers are full of bent nails, lengths of string, balls of tinfoil, old stamps. 'Why are we saving them?' he asks. 'In case,' she replies.

In her angrier moods his mother denounces all book learning. Children should be sent to trade school, she says, then put to work. Studying is just nonsense. Learning to be a cabinet-maker or a carpenter, learning to work with wood, is best. She is disenchanted with farming: now that farmers have suddenly become rich there is too much idleness among them, too much ostentation.

For the price of wool is rocketing. According to the radio, the Japanese are paying a pound a pound for the best grades. Sheep-farmers are buying new cars and taking seaside holidays. 'You must give us some of your money, now that you are so rich,' she tells Uncle Son on one of their visits to Voëlfontein. She smiles as she speaks, pretending it is a joke, but it is not funny. Uncle Son looks embarrassed, murmurs a reply he does not catch.

The farm was not meant to go to Uncle Son alone, his mother tells him: it was bequeathed to all twelve sons and daughters in equal portions. To save it from being auctioned off to some stranger, the sons and daughters agreed to sell their portions to Son; from that sale they came away with IOUs for a few pounds each. Now, because of the Japanese, the farm is worth thousands of pounds. Son ought to share his money.

He is ashamed of his mother for the crudeness with which she talks about money.

'You must become a doctor or an attorney,' she tells him. 'Those are the people who make money.' However, at other times she tells him that attorneys are all crooks. He does not ask how his father fits into this picture, his father the attorney who did not make money.

Doctors are not interested in their patients, she says. They just give you pills. Afrikaans doctors are the worst, because they are incompetent as well.

She says so many different things at different times that he does not know what she really thinks. He and his brother argue with her, point out the contradictions. If she thinks farmers are better than attorneys, why did she marry an attorney? If she thinks book learning is non-sense, why did she become a teacher? The more they argue with her the more she smiles. She takes so much pleasure in her children's skill with words that she concedes every point, barely defending herself, willing them to win.

He does not share her pleasure. He does not think these arguments funny. He wishes she would believe in something. Her sweeping judgments, born out of passing moods, exasperate him.

As for him, he will probably become a teacher. That will be his life when he grows up. It seems a dull kind of life, but what else is there? For a long time he was going to become an engine-driver. 'What are you going to be when you grow up?' his aunts and uncles used to ask. 'An engine-driver!' he would pipe up, and everyone would nod and smile. Now he understands that 'Engine-driver' is what all small boys are expected to say, just as small girls are expected to say 'Nurse'. He is no longer small now, he belongs to the big world; he will have to put aside the fantasy of driving a great iron horse and do the realistic thing. He is good at school, there is nothing else he knows of that he is good at, therefore he will stay on at school, moving up through the ranks. One day, perhaps, he will even become an inspector. But he will not take an office job. How can one work from morning to night with only two weeks' holiday a year?

What sort of teacher will he make? He can picture himself only dimly. He sees a figure in sports jacket and grey flannels (that is what men teachers seem to wear) walking down a corridor with books under its arm. It is only a glimpse, and in a moment it vanishes. He does not see the face.

He hopes that, when the day comes, he will not be sent to teach in a place like Worcester. But perhaps Worcester is a purgatory one must pass through. Perhaps Worcester is where people are sent to be tested.

One day they are assigned an essay to write in class: 'What I do in the mornings.' They are supposed to write about the things they do before setting off for school. He knows the kind of thing he is expected to say: that he makes his own bed, that he washes the breakfast dishes, that he cuts his own sandwiches for lunch. Though in fact he does none of these things – his mother does them for him – he lies well enough not to be found out. But he goes too far when he describes how he brushes his shoes. He has never brushed his own shoes in his life. In his essay he says you use the brush to brush the dirt off, after which you use a rag to coat the shoe with polish. Miss Oosthuizen puts a big blue exclamation mark in the margin next to the shoe-brushing. He is mortified, prays that she will not call him out in front of the class to read his essay. That evening he watches carefully as his mother brushes his shoes, so that he will not get it wrong again.

He lets his mother brush his shoes as he lets her do everything for him that she wants to. The only thing that he will not let her do any more is to come into the bathroom when he is naked.

He knows he is a liar, knows he is bad, but he refuses to change. He does not change because he does not want to change. His difference from other boys may be bound up with his mother and his unnatural family, but is bound up with his lying too. If he stopped lying he would have to polish his shoes and talk politely and do everything that normal boys do. In that case he would no longer be himself. If he were no longer himself, what point would there be in living?

He is a liar and he is cold-hearted too: a liar to the world in general, cold-hearted towards his mother. It pains his mother, he can see, that he is steadily growing away from her. Nevertheless he hardens his heart and will not relent. His only excuse is that he is merciless to himself too. He lies but he does not lie to himself.

'When are you going to die?' he asks his mother one day, challenging her, surprised at his own daring.

'I am not going to die,' she replies. Her voice is gay, but there is something false in it.

'What if you get cancer?'

'You only get cancer if you are hit on the breast. I won't get cancer. I'll live forever. I won't die.'

He knows why she is saying this. She is saying it for him and his brother, so that they will not worry. It is a silly thing to say, but he is grateful to her for it.

He cannot imagine his mother dying. She is the firmest thing in his life. She is the rock on which he stands. Without her he would be nothing.

His mother guards her breasts carefully in case they are knocked. His very first memory, earlier than the dog, earlier than the scrap of paper, is of her white breasts. He suspects he must have hurt them when he was a baby, beaten them with his fists, otherwise she would not now deny them to him so pointedly, she who denies him nothing else.

Cancer is the great fear of her life. As for him, he has been taught to be wary of pains in his side, to treat each twinge as a sign of appendicitis. Will the ambulance get him to hospital before his appendix bursts? Will he ever wake up from the anaesthetic? He does not like to think of being cut open by a strange doctor. On the other hand, it would be nice to have a scar afterwards to show off to people.

When peanuts and raisins are doled out during break at school, he blows away the papery red skins of the peanuts, which are reputed to collect in the appendix and fester there.

He absorbs himself in his collections. He collects stamps. He collects lead soldiers. He collects cards – cards of Australian cricketers, cards of English footballers, cards of cars of the world. To get cards, one has to buy packets of cigarettes made of nougat and icing-sugar with pink-painted tips. His pockets are full of wilting, sticky cigarettes that he has forgotten to eat.

He spends hours on end with his Meccano set, proving to his mother that he too can be good with his hands. He builds a windmill with sets of coupled pulleys whose blades can be cranked so fast that a breeze wafts across the room.

He trots around the yard tossing a cricket ball in the air and catching it without breaking his stride. What is the true trajectory of the ball: is it going straight up and straight down, as he sees it, or is it rising and falling in loops, as a motionless bystander would see it? When he talks to his mother about this, he sees a desperate look in her eyes: she knows things like this are important to him, and wants to understand why, but cannot. For his part, he wishes she would be interested in things for their own sake, not just because they interest him.

When there is something practical to be done that she cannot do, like fixing a leaking tap, she calls in a Coloured man off the street, any man, any passer-by. Why, he asks in exasperation, does she have such faith in Coloured people? Because they are used to working with their hands, she replies.

It seems a silly thing to believe – that because someone has not been to school he must know how to fix a tap or repair a stove – yet it is so different from what everyone else believes, so eccentric, that despite himself he finds it endearing. He would rather that his mother expected wonders of Coloured people than expected nothing of them at all.

He is always trying to make sense of his mother. Jews are exploiters, she says; yet she prefers Jewish doctors because they know what they are doing. Coloured people are the salt of the earth, she says, yet she and her sisters are always gossiping about pretend-whites with secret Coloured backgrounds. He cannot understand how she can hold so many contradictory beliefs at the same time. Yet at least she has beliefs. Her brothers too. Her brother Norman believes in the monk Nostradamus and his prophecies of the end of the world; he believes in flying saucers that land during the night and take people away. He cannot imagine his father or his father's family talking about the end of the world. Their sole goal in life is to avoid controversy, to offend no one, to be amiable all the time; by comparison with his mother's family his father's family is bland and boring.

He is too close to his mother, his mother is too close to him. That is the reason why, despite the hunting and the other manly things he does during his visits to the farm, his father's family has never taken him to its bosom. His grandmother may have been harsh in denying the three of them a home during the war, when they were living on a share of a lance corporal's pay, too poor to buy butter or tea. Nevertheless, her instinct was right. His grandmother is not blind to the dark secret of No. 12 Poplar Avenue, namely that the eldest child is first in the house-hold, the second child second, and the man, the husband, the father, last. Either his mother does not care enough to conceal this perversion of the natural order from his father's family, or else his father has been complaining in private. Whatever the case, his grandmother disapproves and does not hide her disapproval.

Sometimes, when she is caught up in a quarrel with his father and wants to score a point, his mother complains bitterly about her treatment at the hands of his family. Mostly, however – for her son's sake, because she knows how close the farm is to his heart, because she can offer nothing to take its place – she tries to ingratiate herself with them in ways he finds as distasteful as her jokes about money, jokes that are not jokes.

He wishes his mother would be normal. If she were normal, he could be normal too.

It is the same with her two sisters. They have one child each, one son, over whom they hover with suffocating solicitude. His cousin Juan in Johannesburg is his closest friend in the world: they write letters to each other, they look forward to holidays together at the sea. Nevertheless, he does not like to see Juan shamefacedly obeying his mother's every instruction, even when she is not there to oversee him. Of all the four sons, he is the only one who is not wholly under his mother's thumb. He has broken away, or half broken away: he has his own friends, whom he has chosen for himself; he goes out on his bicycle without saying where he is going or when he will be back. His cousins and his brother have no friends. He thinks of them as pale, timid, always at home under the eye of their fierce mothers. His father calls the three sister-mothers the three witches. 'Double, double, toil and trouble,' he says, quoting *Macbeth*. Delightedly, maliciously he echoes his father.

When she feels particularly bitter about her life in Reunion Park, his mother laments that she did not marry Bob Breech. He does not take her laments seriously. Yet at the same time he cannot believe his ears. If she had married Bob Breech, where would he be? Who would he be? Would he be Bob Breech's child? Would Bob Breech's child be him?

Only one piece of evidence remains of a real Bob Breech. He comes across it by chance in one of his mother's albums: a blurred photograph of two young men in long white trousers and dark blazers standing on a beach with their arms around each other's shoulders, squinting into the sun. One of them he knows: Juan's father. Who is this other man? he asks his mother. Bob Breech, she replies. Where is he now? He is dead, she says.

He stares hard into the face of the dead Bob Breech. He can find nothing of himself there.

He does not interrogate her further. But, listening to the sisters, putting two and two together, he learns that Bob Breech came to South Africa for his health; that after a year or two he went back to England; that there he died. He died of consumption, but, it is implied, a broken heart may have contributed to his decline – a heart broken because of the dark-haired, dark-eyed, wary-looking young schoolteacher whom he met at Plettenberg Bay and who refused to marry him.

He loves to page through his mother's albums. No matter how indistinct the images, he can always pick her out from the group: the one in whose shy, defensive look he recognizes himself. In her albums he follows her life through the 1920s and 1930s: first the team pictures (hockey, tennis), then the pictures from her tour of Europe: Scotland, Norway, Switzerland, Germany; Edinburgh, the fjords, the Alps, Bingen on the Rhine. Among her mementoes there is a pencil from Bingen with a tiny peephole in its side allowing a view of a castle perched on a cliff.

Sometimes they page through the albums together, he and she. She sighs, she says she wishes she could visit Scotland again, see the heather, the bluebells. He thinks: My mother had a life before I was born, and that life still lives in her. He is glad, in a way, for her sake, since she no longer has a life of her own.

His mother's world is quite different from the world of his father's photograph album, in which South Africans in khaki uniform strike poses against the pyramids of Egypt or against the rubble of Italian cities. But in his father's album he spends less time on the photographs than on the fascinating pamphlets interspersed among them, pamphlets dropped on the Allied positions from German aeroplanes. One tells the soldiers how to give themselves a temperature (by eating soap); another pictures a glamorous woman perched on the knee of a fat Jew with a hooked nose, drinking a glass of champagne. 'Do you know where your wife is tonight?' asks the subtitle. And then there is the blue porcelain eagle that his father found in the ruins of a house in Naples and brought back in his kit-bag, the eagle of empire that now stands on the mantelshelf in the living room.

He is immensely proud of his father's war service. He is surprised – and gratified – to find how few of the fathers of his friends fought in the war. Why his father rose to no more than a lance corporal he is not sure: he quietly leaves out the *lance* when he repeats his father's adventures to his friends. But he treasures the photograph, taken in a studio in Cairo, of his handsome father sighting down a rifle barrel, one eye closed, his hair neatly combed, his beret tucked in regulation fashion under his epaulette. If he had his way it would be on the mantelshelf too.

His father and his mother disagree about the Germans. His father likes the Italians (their heart was not in the fight, he says: all they wanted to do was surrender and go back home) but hates the Germans. He tells the story of a German shot while he was squatting on a privy. Sometimes, in the story, it was he who shot the German, sometimes one of his friends; but in none of the versions does he show any pity, only amusement at the German's confusion as he tried to raise his hands and pull up his pants at the same time.

His mother knows it is not a good idea to praise the Germans too openly; but sometimes, when he and his father gang up on her, she will leave discretion behind. 'The Germans are the best people in the world,' she will say. 'It was that terrible Hitler who led them into so much suffering.'

Her brother Norman disagrees. 'Hitler gave the Germans pride in themselves,' he says.

His mother and Norman travelled through Europe together in the 1930s: not only through Norway and the highlands of Scotland but through Germany, Hitler's Germany. Their family – the Brechers, the du Biels – is from Germany, or at least from Pomerania, which is now in Poland. Is it good to be from Pomerania? He is not sure.

'The Germans didn't want to fight against the South Africans,' says Norman. 'They like the South Africans. If it hadn't been for Smuts we would never have gone to war against Germany. Smuts was a skelm, a crook. He sold us to the British.'

His father and Norman do not like each other. When his father wants to get at his mother, in their late-night quarrels in the kitchen, he taunts her about her brother who did not join up, but marched with the Ossewabrandwag instead. 'That's a lie!' she maintains angrily. 'Norman was not in the Ossewabrandwag. Ask him yourself, he will tell you.'

When he asks his mother what the Ossewabrandwag is, she says it is just nonsense, people who marched in the streets with torches.

The fingers of Norman's right hand are yellow with nicotine. He has a room in a boarding house in Pretoria where he has lived for years. He makes his money by selling a pamphlet he has written about ju-jitsu, which he advertises in the classified pages of the Pretoria News. 'Learn the Japanese art of self-defence,' says the advertisement. 'Six easy lessons.' People send him ten-shilling postal orders and he sends them the pamphlet: a single page folded in four, with sketches of the various holds. When ju-jitsu does not bring in enough money, he sells plots on commission for an estate agency. He stays in bed till noon every day, drinking tea and smoking and reading stories in Argosy and Lilliput. In the afternoons he plays tennis. In 1938, twelve years ago, he was the Western Province singles champion. He still has ambitions of playing at Wimbledon, in the doubles, if he can find a partner.

At the end of his visit, before he goes back to Pretoria, Norman takes him aside and slips a brown ten-shilling note into his shirt pocket. 'For ice cream,' he murmurs: the same words every year. He likes Norman not only for the present – ten shillings is a lot of money – but for remembering, for never failing to remember.

His father prefers the other brother, Lance, the schoolteacher from Kingwilliamstown who did join up. There is also the third brother, the eldest, the one who lost the farm, but no one mentions him except his mother. 'Poor Roland,' murmurs his mother, shaking her head. Roland married a woman who calls herself Rosa Rakocka, daughter of an exiled

Polish count, but whose real name, according to Norman, is Sophie Pretorius. Norman and Lance hate Roland because of the farm and despise him because he is under the thumb of Sophie. Roland and Sophie run a boarding house in Cape Town. He went there once, with his mother. Sophie turned out to be a large blonde woman who wore a silk dressing gown at four in the afternoon and smoked cigarettes in a cigarette-holder. Roland was a quiet, sad-faced man with a bulbous red nose from the radium treatment that had cured him of cancer.

He likes it when his father and his mother and Norman get into political arguments. He enjoys the heat and passion, the reckless things they say. He is surprised that his father, the one he least wants to win, is the one he agrees with: that the English were good and the Germans bad, that Smuts was good and the Nats are bad.

His father likes the United Party, his father likes cricket and rugby, yet he does not like his father. He does not understand this contradiction, but has no interest in understanding it. Even before he knew his father, that is to say, before his father returned from the war, he had decided he was not going to like him. In a sense, therefore, the dislike is an abstract one: he does not want to have a father, or at least does not want a father who stays in the same house.

What he hates most about his father are his personal habits. He hates them so much that the mere thought of them makes him shudder with distaste: the loud nose-blowing in the bathroom in the mornings, the steamy smell of Lifebuoy soap that he leaves behind, along with a ring of scum and shaving-hairs in the washbasin. Most of all he hates the way his father smells. On the other hand, he likes, despite himself, his father's natty clothes, the maroon cravat he wears instead of a tie on Saturday mornings, his trim figure, his brisk way of walking, his Brylcreemed hair. He Brylcreems his own hair, cultivates a quiff.

He dislikes visiting the barber, dislikes it so much that he even tries, with embarrassing results, to cut his own hair. The barbers of Worcester seem to have decided in concert that boys should have short hair. Sessions begin as brutally as possible with the electric trimmer scything his hair away on the back and sides, and continue with a remorseless snick-snack of scissors till there is only a brush-like stubble left, with perhaps a saving cowlick at the front. Even before the session ends he is squirming with shame; he pays his shilling and hurries home, dreading school the next day, dreading the ritual jeers that greet every boy with a fresh haircut. There are proper haircuts and then there are the haircuts one suffers in Worcester, charged with the barbers' vindictiveness; he does not know where one has to go, what one has to do or say, how much one has to pay, to get a proper haircut.

Six

Though he goes to the bioscope every Saturday afternoon, films no longer have the hold on him that they used to have in Cape Town, where he had nightmares of being crushed under elevators or falling from cliffs like the heroes of the serials. He does not see why Errol Flynn, who looks just the same whether he is playing Robin Hood or Ali Baba, is supposed to be a great actor. He is tired of horseback chases, which are all the same. The Three Stooges have begun to seem silly. And it is hard to believe in Tarzan when the man who plays Tarzan keeps changing. The only film that makes an impression on him is one in which Ingrid Bergman gets into a train carriage that is infected with smallpox and dies. Ingrid Bergman is his mother's favourite actress. Is life like that: could his mother die at any moment just by failing to read a sign in a window?

There is also the radio. He has outgrown Children's Corner, but is faithful to the serials: Superman at 5.00 daily ('Up! Up and away!'), Mandrake the Magician at 5.30. His favourite story is *The Snow Goose* by Paul Gallico, which the A Service broadcasts again and again, by popular request. It is the story of a wild goose that leads the boats back from the beaches of Dunkirk to Dover. He listens with tears in his eyes. He wants one day to be faithful as the snow goose is faithful.

They perform *Treasure Island* on the radio in a dramatized version, one half-hour episode a week. He has his own copy of *Treasure Island*; but he read it when he was too young, not understanding the business of the blind man and the black spot, unable to work out whether Long John Silver was good or bad. Now, after every episode on the radio, he has nightmares centring on Long John: about the crutch with which he kills people, about his treacherous, sentimental solicitude for Jim Hawkins. He wishes Squire Trelawney would kill Long John instead of letting him go: he is sure he will return one day with his cutthroat mutineers to take his revenge, just as he returns in his dreams.

The *Swiss Family Robinson* is much more comforting. He has a handsome copy of the book with colour plates. He particularly likes the picture of the ship in its cradle under the trees, the ship that the family has built with tools salvaged from the wreck, to take them back home with all their animals, like Noah's Ark. It is a pleasure, like slipping into a warm bath, to leave Treasure Island behind and enter the world of the Swiss Family. In the Swiss Family there are no bad brothers, no murderous pirates; in their family everyone works happily together under the guidance of a wise, strong father (the pictures show him with a barrel chest and a long chestnut beard) who knows from the beginning what needs to be done to save them. The only thing that puzzles him is why, when they are so snug and happy on the island, they have to leave at all.

He owns a third book too, *Scott of the Antarctic*. Captain Scott is one of his unquestioned heroes: that is why the book was given to him. It has photographs, including one of Scott sitting and writing in the tent in which he later froze to death. He often looks at the photographs, but he does not get far with reading the book: it is boring, it is not a story. He only likes the bit about Titus Oates, the man with frostbite who, because he was holding up his companions, went out into the night, into the snow and ice, and perished quietly, without fuss. He hopes he can be like Titus Oates one day.

Once a year Boswell's Circus comes to Worcester. Everyone in his class goes; for a week beforehand talk is about the circus and nothing else. Even the Coloured children go, after a fashion: they hang around outside the tent for hours, listening to the band, peering in through gaps in the canvas.

They plan to go on the Saturday afternoon, when his father is playing cricket. His mother makes it into an outing for the three of them. But at the ticket booth she hears with a shock the high Saturday afternoon prices: 2/6 for children, 5/- for adults. She does not have enough money with her. She buys tickets for him and his brother. 'Go in, I'll wait here,' she says. He is unwilling, but she insists.

Inside, he is miserable, enjoys nothing; he suspects his brother feels the same way. When they emerge at the end of the show, she is still there. For days afterwards he cannot banish the thought: his mother waiting patiently in the blazing heat of December while he sits in the circus tent being entertained like a king. Her blinding, overwhelming, self-sacrificial love, for both him and his brother but for him in particular, disturbs him. He wishes she did not love him so much. She loves him absolutely, therefore he must love her absolutely: that is the logic she compels upon him. Never will he be able to pay back all the love she pours out upon him. The thought of a lifetime bowed under a debt of love baffles and infuriates him to the point where he will not kiss her, refuses to be touched by her. When she turns away in silent hurt, he deliberately hardens his heart against her, refusing to give in.

Sometimes, when she is feeling bitter, she makes long speeches to herself, contrasting her life on the barren housing estate with the life she lived before she was married, which she represents as a continual round of parties and picnics, of weekend visits to farms, of tennis and golf and walks with her dogs. She speaks in a low whispering voice in which only the sibilants stand out: he in his room, and his brother in his, strain their ears to hear, as she must know they will. That is another reason why his father calls her a witch: because she talks to herself, making up spells.

The idyll of life in Victoria West is substantiated by photographs from the albums: his mother, together with other women in long white dresses, standing with tennis racquets in what looks like the middle of the veld, his mother with her arm over the neck of a dog, an Alsatian.

'Was that your dog?' he asks.

'That is Kim. He was the best, the most faithful dog I ever had.'

'What happened to him?'

'He ate poisoned meat that the farmers had put down for jackals. He died in my arms.'

There are tears in her eyes.

After his father makes his appearance in the album, there are no more dogs. Instead he sees the couple at picnics with their friends from those days, or his father, with his dapper little moustache and his cocky look, posing against the bonnet of an old-fashioned black car. Then the pictures of himself begin, dozens of them, starting with the picture of a blank-faced, pudgy baby being held up to the camera by a dark, intense-looking woman.

In all these photographs, even the photographs with the baby, his mother strikes him as girlish. Her age is a mystery that intrigues him endlessly. She will not tell him, his father pretends not to know, even her brothers and sisters seem sworn to secrecy. While she is out of the house he searches through the papers in the bottom drawer of her dressing table, looking for a birth certificate, but without success. From a remark she has let slip he knows she is older than his father, who was born in 1912; but how much older? He decides she was born in 1910. That means she was thirty when he was born and is forty now. 'You're forty!' he tells her triumphantly one day, watching closely for signs that he is right. She gives a mysterious smile. 'I'm twenty-eight,' she says.

They have the same birthday. He was born to her on her birthday. This means, as she has told him, as she tells everyone, that he is a gift of God.

He calls her not Mother or Mom but Dinny. So do his father and his brother. Where does the name come from? No one seems to know; but her brothers and sisters call her Vera, so it cannot come from their childhood. He has to be careful not to call her Dinny in front of strangers, as he has to guard against calling his aunt and uncle plain Norman and Ellen instead of Uncle Norman and Aunt Ellen. But saying Uncle and Aunt like a good, obedient, normal child is as nothing beside the circumlocutions of Afrikaans. Afrikaners are afraid to say you to anyone older than themselves. He mocks his father's speech: 'Mammie moet 'n kombers oor Mammie se knieë trek anders word Mammie koud' – Mommy must put a blanket over Mommy's knees, otherwise Mommy will get cold. He is relieved he is not Afrikaans and is saved from having to talk like that, like a whipped slave.

His mother decides that she wants a dog. Alsatians are the best – the most intelligent, the most faithful – but they cannot find an Alsatian for sale. So they settle for a pup half Doberman, half something else. He insists on being the one to name it. He would like to call it Borzoi because he wants it to be a Russian dog, but since it is not in fact a borzoi he calls it Cossack. No one understands. People think the name is kos-sak, food-bag, which they find funny.

Cossack turns out to be a confused, undisciplined dog, roaming about the neighbourhood, trampling gardens, chasing chickens. One day the dog follows him all the way to school. Nothing he does will put him off: when he shouts and throws stones the dog drops his ears, puts his tail between his legs, slinks away; but as soon as he gets back on his bicycle the dog lopes after him again. In the end he has to drag him home by the collar, pushing his bicycle with the other hand. He gets home in a rage and refuses to go back to school, since he is late.

Cossack is not quite full grown when he eats the ground glass someone has put out for him. His mother administers enemas, trying to flush out the glass, but without success. On the third day, when the dog just lies still, panting, and will not even lick her hand, she sends him to the pharmacy to fetch a new medicine someone has recommended. He races there and races back, but he comes too late. His mother's face is drawn and remote, she will not even take the bottle from his hands.

He helps to bury Cossack, wrapped in a blanket, in the clay at the bottom of the garden. Over the grave he erects a cross with the name 'Cossack' painted on it. He does not want them to have another dog, not if this is how they must die.

His father plays cricket for Worcester. It ought to be yet another feather in his cap, another source of pride for him. His father is an attorney, which is almost as good as a doctor; he was a soldier in the war; he used to play rugby in the Cape Town league; he plays cricket. But in each case there is an embarrassing qualification. He is an attorney but no longer practises. He was a soldier but only a lance corporal. He played rugby, but only for Gardens second or perhaps even third team, and Gardens are a joke, they always come bottom of the Grand Challenge league. And now he plays cricket, but for the Worcester second team, which no one bothers to watch.

His father is a bowler, not a batsman. There is something wrong with his backlift that bedevils his batting; furthermore, he averts his eyes when he plays fast bowling. His idea of batting seems to be confined to pushing the bat forward and, if the ball slides off it, trotting a sedate single.

The reason why his father can't bat is of course that he grew up in the Karoo, where there was no proper cricket and no way of learning. Bowling is a different matter. It is a gift: bowlers are born, not made.

His father bowls slow off-spinners. Sometimes he is hit for six; sometimes, seeing the ball slowly floating towards him, the batsman loses his head, swings wildly, and is bowled. That seems to be his father's method: patience, cunning.

The coach for the Worcester teams is Johnny Wardle, who in the northern summer plays cricket for England. It is a great coup for Worcester that Johnny Wardle has chosen to come here. Wolf Heller is mentioned as an intercessor, Wolf Heller and his money.

He stands with his father behind the practice net watching Johnny Wardle bowl to the first-team batsmen. Wardle, a nondescript little man with sparse sandy hair, is supposed to be a slow bowler, but when he trots up and releases the ball he is surprised at how fast it travels. The batsman at the crease plays the ball easily enough, stroking it gently into the netting. Someone else bowls, then it is Wardle's turn again. Again the batsman strokes the ball gently away. The batsman is not winning, but neither is the bowler.

At the end of the afternoon he goes home disappointed. He had expected more of a gulf between the England bowler and the Worcester batsmen. He had expected to be witness to a more mysterious craft, to see the ball doing strange things in the air and off the pitch, floating and dipping and spinning, as great slow bowling is supposed to do according to the cricket books he reads. He was not expecting a talkative little man whose only mark of distinction is that he bowls spinners as fast as he himself can bowl at his fastest.

To cricket he looks for more than Johnny Wardle offers. Cricket must be like Horatius and the Etruscans, or Hector and Achilles. If Hector and Achilles were just two men hacking away at each other with swords, there would be no point to the story. But they are not just two men: they are mighty heroes, their names ring in legend. He is glad when, at the end of the season, Wardle is dropped from the England team.

Wardle bowls, of course, with a leather ball. He is unfamiliar with the leather ball: he and his friends play with what they call a cork ball, compacted out of some hard, grey material that is proof against the stones that tear the stitching of a leather ball to shreds. Standing behind the net watching Wardle, he hears for the first time the strange whistling of a leather ball as it approaches the batsman through the air.

His first chance comes to play on a proper cricket field. A match is organized for a Wednesday afternoon, between two teams from the junior school. Proper cricket means proper wickets, a proper pitch, no need to fight for a turn to bat.

His turn comes to bat. Wearing a pad on his left leg, carrying his father's bat that is much too heavy for him, he walks out to the middle. He is surprised at how big the field is. It is a great and lonely place: the spectators are so far away that they might as well not exist.

He takes his stand on the strip of rolled earth with a green coir mat spread over it and waits for the ball to come. This is cricket. It is called a game, but it feels to him more real than home, more real even than school. In this game there is no pretending, no mercy, no second chance. These other boys, whose names he does not know, are all against him. They are of one mind only: to cut short his pleasure. They will feel not one speck of remorse when he is out. In the middle of this huge arena he is on trial, one against eleven, with no one to protect him.

The fielders settle into position. He must concentrate, but there is something irritating he cannot put out of his mind: Zeno's paradox. Before the arrow can reach its target it must reach halfway; before it can reach halfway it must reach a quarter of the way; before it can reach a quarter of the way . . . Desperately he tries to stop thinking about it; but the very fact that he is trying not to think about it agitates him still further.

The bowler runs up. He hears particularly the thud of the last two steps. Then there is a space in which the only sound breaking the silence is the eerie rustling noise of the ball as it tumbles and dips towards him.

Is this what he is choosing when he chooses to play cricket: to be tested again and again and again, until he fails, by a ball that comes at him impersonally, indifferently, without mercy, seeking the chink in his defence, and faster than he expects, too fast for him to clear the confusion in his mind, compose his thoughts, decide properly what to do? And in the midst of this thinking, in the midst of this muddle, the ball arrives.

He scores two runs, batting in a state of disarray and, later, of gloom. He emerges from the game understanding less than ever the matter-of-fact way in which Johnny Wardle plays, chatting and joking all the while. Are all the fabled England players like that: Len Hutton, Alec Bedser, Denis Compton, Cyril Washbrook? He cannot believe it. To him, real cricket can only be played in silence, silence and apprehension, the heart thudding in the chest, the mouth dry.

Cricket is not a game. It is the truth of life. If it is, as the books say, a test of character, then it is a test he sees no way of passing yet does not know how to dodge. At the wicket the secret that he manages to cover up elsewhere is relentlessly probed and exposed. 'Let us see what you are made of,' says the ball as it whistles and tumbles through the air towards him. Blindly, confusedly, he pushes the bat forward, too soon or too late. Past the bat, past the pads, the ball finds its way. He is bowled, he has failed the test, he has been found out, there is nothing to do but hide his tears, cover his face, trudge back to the commiserating, politely schooled applause of the other boys.

Seven

On his bicycle is the British Small Arms emblem of two crossed rifles and the label 'Smiths – BSA'. He bought the bicycle for five pounds, second-hand, with the money for his eighth birthday. It is the most solid thing in his life. When other boys boast that they have Raleighs, he replies that he has a Smiths. 'Smiths? Never heard of Smiths,' they say.

There is nothing to match the elation of riding a bicycle, of leaning over and swooping through the curves. On his Smiths he rides to school every morning, the half-mile from Reunion Park to the railway crossing, then the mile on the quiet road alongside the railway line. Summer mornings are the best. Water murmurs in the roadside furrows, doves coo in the bluegum trees; now and then there is an eddy of warm air to warn of the wind that will blow later in the day, chasing gusts of fine red clay-dust before it.

In winter he has to set out for school while it is still dark. With his lamp casting a halo before him, he rides through the mist, breasting its velvety softness, breathing it in, breathing it out, hearing nothing but the soft swish of his tyres. Some mornings the metal of the handlebars is so cold that his bare hands stick to it.

He tries to get to school early. He loves to have the classroom to himself, to wander around the empty seats, to mount, surreptitiously, the teacher's podium. But he is never first at school: there are two brothers from De Doorns whose father works on the railways and who come in on the 6 a.m. train. They are poor, so poor that they own neither jerseys nor blazers nor shoes. There are other boys just as poor, particularly in the Afrikaans classes. Even on icy winter mornings they come to school in thin cotton shirts and serge short-pants so outgrown that their slim thighs can hardly move in them. Their tanned legs show chalk-white patches of cold; they blow on their hands and stamp their feet; snot is always running out of their noses.

Once there is an outbreak of ringworm, and the brothers from De Doorns have their heads shaved. On their bare skulls he can clearly see the whorls of the ringworm; his mother warns him to have no contact with them.

He prefers tight shorts to loose shorts. The clothes his mother buys for him are always too loose. He likes to gaze at slim, smooth brown legs in tight shorts. Best of all he loves the honeytan legs of boys with blond hair. The most beautiful boys, he is surprised to find, are in the Afrikaans classes, as are the ugliest, the ones with hairy legs and Adam's apples and pustules on their faces. Afrikaans children are almost like Coloured children, he finds, unspoiled and thoughtless, running wild, then suddenly, at a certain age, going bad, their beauty dying within them.

Beauty and desire: he is disturbed by the feelings that the legs of these boys, blank and perfect and inexpressive, create in him. What is there that can be done with legs beyond devouring them with one's eyes? What is desire for?

The naked sculptures in the Children's Encyclopaedia affect him in the same way: Daphne pursued by Apollo; Persephone ravished by Dis. It is a matter of shape, of perfection of shape. He has an idea of the perfect human body. When he sees that perfection manifested in white marble, something thrills inside him; a gulf opens up; he is on the edge of falling.

Of all the secrets that set him apart, this may in the end be the worst. Among all these boys he is the only one in whom this dark erotic current runs; among all this innocence and normality, he is the only one who desires.

Yet the language of the Afrikaans boys is filthy beyond belief. They command a range of obscenity far beyond his, to do with *fok* and *piel* and *poes*, words from whose monosyllabic heaviness he retreats in dismay. How are they written? Until he can write them he has no way of taming them in his mind. Is *fok* spelled with a *v*, which would make it more venerable, or with an *f*, which would make it a truly wild word, primeval, without ancestry? The dictionary says nothing, the words are not there, none of them.

Then there are *gat* and *poep-hol* and words like them, hurled back and forth in bouts of abuse whose force he does not understand. Why couple the back of the body with the front? What have the *gat*-words, so heavy and guttural and black, to do with sex, with its softly inviting *s* and its mysterious final *x*? He shuts his mind to the backside-words in distaste but continues to try to puzzle out the meaning of *effies* and FLs, things he has never seen but that belong, somehow, to the commerce of boys and girls in high school.

Yet he is not ignorant. He knows how babies are born. They come out of the mother's backside, neat and clean and white. So his mother told him years ago, when he was small. He believes her without question: it is a source of pride to him that she told him the truth about babies so early, when other children were still being fobbed off with lies. It is a mark of her enlightenment, of their family's enlightenment. His cousin Juan, who is a year younger than he, knows the truth too. His father, on the other hand, gets embarrassed and grumbles when there is talk of babies and where they come from; but that just proves once again the benightedness of his father's family.

His friends hold to a different story: that babies come out of the other hole.

He knows in the abstract of another hole, into which the penis goes and out of which the urine comes. But it makes no sense that the baby comes out of that hole. The baby is, after all, formed in the stomach. So it makes sense for the baby to come out of the backside.

Therefore he argues for the backside while his friends argue for the other hole, the *poes*. He is quietly convinced he is right. It is part of the trust between his mother and himself.

Eight

He and his mother are crossing a strip of public ground near the railway station. He is with her but separate from her, not holding her hand. He is, as ever, wearing grey: grey jersey, grey shorts, grey stockings. On his head is a navy-blue cap with the badge of Worcester Boys Primary School: a mountain peak surrounded by stars, and the legend PER ASPERA AD ASTRA.

He is just a boy walking beside his mother: from the outside he probably looks quite normal. But he thinks of himself as scuttling around her like a beetle, scuttling in fussy circles with his nose to the ground and his legs and arms pumping. In fact he can think of nothing about himself that is still. His mind in particular darts about here and there all the time, with an impatient will of its own.

This is the place where once a year the circus pitches its tent and parks cages in which lions drowse in their smelly straw. But today it is just a patch of red clay packed hard as rock, where grass will not grow.

There are other people too, other passers-by, on this bright, hot Saturday morning. One of them is a boy of his own age trotting across the square at an angle to them. And as soon as he sees him, he knows that this boy will be important to him, important beyond all measure, not because of who he is (he may never see him again) but because of the thoughts that are going on in his head, that burst out of him like a swarm of bees.

There is nothing unusual about the boy. He is Coloured, but there are Coloured people everywhere. He is wearing pants so short that they sit tightly across his neat buttocks and leave his slim clay-brown thighs almost naked. He wears no shoes; his soles are probably so hard that even if he trod on a *duwweltjie* thorn he would merely check his stride, reach down, brush it away.

There are hundreds of boys like him, thousands, thousands of girls too in short frocks that show off their slim legs. He wishes he had legs as beautiful as theirs. With legs like that he would float across the earth as this boy does, barely touching it.

The boy passes within a dozen paces of them. He is absorbed in himself, he does not glance at them. His body is perfect and unspoiled, as if it had emerged only yesterday from its shell. Why do children like this, boys and girls under no compulsion to go to school, free to roam far from the watching eyes of parents, whose bodies are their own to do with as they please – why do they not come together in a feast of sexual delight? Is the answer that they are too innocent to know what pleasures are available to them – that only dark and guilty souls know such secrets?

That is how the questioning always works. At first it may wander here and there; but in the end, unfailingly, it turns and gathers itself and points a finger at himself. Always it is he who sets the train of thinking in motion; always it is the thinking that slips out of his control and returns to accuse him. Beauty is innocence; innocence is ignorance; ignorance is ignorance of pleasure; pleasure is guilty; he is guilty. This boy, with his fresh, untouched body, is innocent, while he, ruled by his dark desires, is guilty. In fact, by this long path he has come within sight of the word *perversion*, with its dark, complex thrill, beginning with the enigmatic *p* that can mean anything, then swiftly tumbling via the ruthless *r* to the vengeful *v*. Not one accusation but two. The two accusations cross, and he is at their point of crossing, in the gunsight. For the one who brings the accusation to bear on him today is not only light as a deer and innocent while he is dark and heavy and guilty: he is also Coloured, which means that he has no money, lives in an obscure hovel, goes hungry; it means that if his mother were to call out 'Boy!' and wave, as she is quite capable of doing, this boy would have to stop in his tracks and come and do whatever she might tell him (carry her shopping basket, for instance), and at the end of it get a tickey in his cupped hands and be grateful for it. And if he were to be angry with his mother afterwards, she would simply smile and say, 'But they are used to it!'

So this boy who has unreflectingly kept all his life to the path of nature and innocence, who is poor and therefore good, as the poor always are in fairy tales, who is slim as an eel and quick as a hare and would defeat him with ease in any contest of swiftness of foot or skill of hand – this boy, who is a living reproof to him, is nevertheless subjected to him in ways that embarrass him so much that he squirms and wriggles his shoulders and does not want to look at him any longer, despite his beauty.

Yet one cannot dismiss him. One can dismiss the Natives, perhaps, but one cannot dismiss the Coloured people. The Natives can be argued away because they are latecomers, invaders from the north, and have no right to be here. The Natives one sees in Worcester are, for the most part, men dressed in old army coats, smoking hooked pipes, who live in tiny tent-shaped corrugated-iron kennels along the railway line, men whose strength and patience are legendary. They have been brought here because they do not drink, as Coloured men do, because they can do heavy labour under a blazing sun where lighter, more volatile Coloured men would collapse. They are men without women, without children, who arrive from nowhere and can be made to disappear into nowhere.

But against the Coloureds there is no such recourse. The Coloureds were fathered by the whites, by Jan van Riebeeck, upon the Hottentots: that much is plain, even in the veiled language of his school history book. In a bitter way it is even worse than that. For in the Boland the people called Coloured are not the great-great-grandchildren of Jan van Riebeeck or any other Dutchman. He is expert enough in physiognomy, has been expert enough as long as he can remember, to know that there is not a drop of white blood in them. They are Hottentots, pure and uncorrupted. Not only do they come with the land, the land comes with them, is theirs, has always been.

Nine

One of the conveniences of Worcester, one of the reasons, according to his father, why it is better living here than in Cape Town, is that shopping is so much easier. Milk is delivered every morning before dawn; one has only to pick up the telephone and, an hour or two later, the man from Schochat's will be at the door with one's meat and groceries. It is as simple as that.

The man from Schochat's, the delivery boy, is a Native who speaks only a few words of Afrikaans and no English. He wears a clean white shirt, a bow tie, two-tone shoes, and a Bobby Locke cap. His name is Josias. His parents disapprove of him as one of the feckless new generation of Natives who spend all their pay on fancy clothes and give no thought to the future.

When his mother is not at home, he and his brother receive the delivery from the hands of Josias, packing the groceries away on the kitchen shelf and the meat in the refrigerator. If there is condensed milk, they appropriate it as booty. They punch holes in the can and take turns sucking till it is dry. When their mother comes home they pretend that there was no condensed milk, or that Josias stole it.

Whether she believes their lie he is not sure. But this is not a deceit he feels particularly guilty about.

The neighbours on the east side are named Wynstra. They have three sons, an older one with knock knees named Gysbert and twins named Eben and Ezer too young to go to school. He and his brother ridicule Gysbert Wynstra for his funny name and for the soft, helpless way in which he runs. They decide he is an idiot, mentally deficient, and declare war on him. One afternoon they take the half-dozen eggs Schochat's boy has delivered, hurl them at the roof of the Wynstra house, and hide. The Wynstras do not emerge, but as the sun dries the smashed eggs they turn to ugly splashes of yellow.

The pleasure of throwing an egg, so much smaller and lighter than a cricket ball, of watching it fly through the air, end over end, of hearing the soft crunch of its impact, remains with him, long afterwards. Yet his pleasure is tinged with guilt. He cannot forget that it is food they are playing with. By what right does he use eggs as playthings? What would Schochat's boy say if he found they were throwing away the eggs he had brought all the way from town on his bicycle? He has a sense that Schochat's boy, who is in fact not a boy at all but a grown man, would not be so wrapped up in the image of himself in his Bobby Locke cap and bow-tie as to be indifferent. He has a sense that he would disapprove most strongly and would not hesitate to say so. 'How can you do that when children are hungry?' he would say in his bad Afrikaans; and there would be no answer. Perhaps elsewhere in the world one can throw eggs (in England, for instance, he knows they throw eggs at people in the stocks); but in this country there are judges who will judge by the standards of righteousness. In this country one cannot be thoughtless about food.

Josias is the fourth Native he has known in his life. The first, whom he remembers only dimly as wearing blue pyjamas all day long, was the boy who used to mop the stairs of the block of flats they lived in in Johannesburg. The second was Fiela in Plettenberg Bay, who took in their washing. Fiela was very black and very old and had no teeth and made long speeches about the past in beautiful, rolling English. She came from St Helena, she said, where she had been a slave. The third was also in Plettenberg Bay. There had been a great storm; a ship had sunk; the wind, which had blown for days and nights, was just beginning to die down. He and his mother and his brother were out on the beach inspecting the mounds of jetsam and seaweed that had been washed up, when an old man with a grey beard and a clerical collar, carrying an umbrella, came up to them and addressed them. 'Man builds great boats of iron,' said the old man, 'but the sea is stronger. The sea is stronger than anything man can build.'

When they were alone again, his mother had said: 'You must remember what he said. He was a wise old man.' It is the only time he can remember her using the word *wise*; in fact it is the only time he can remember anyone using the word outside of books. But it is not just the old-fashioned word that impresses him. It is possible to respect Natives – that is what she is saying. It is a great relief to hear that, to have it confirmed.

In the stories that have left the deepest mark on him, it is the third brother, the humblest and most derided, who, after the first and second brothers have disdainfully passed by, helps the old woman to carry her heavy load or draws the thorn from the lion's paw. The third brother is kind and honest and courageous while the first and second brothers are boastful, arrogant, uncharitable. At the end of the story the third brother is crowned prince, while the first and second brothers are disgraced and sent packing.

There are white people and Coloured people and Natives, of whom the Natives are the lowest and most derided. The parallel is inescapable: the Natives are the third brother.

At school they learn, over and over again, year after year, about Jan van Riebeeck and Simon van der Stel and Lord Charles Somerset and Piet Retief. After Piet Retief come the Kaffir Wars, when the Kaffirs poured over the borders of the Colony and had to be driven back; but the Kaffir Wars are so many and so confused and so hard to keep apart that they are not required to know them for examinations.

Although, in examinations, he gives the correct answers to the history questions, he does not know, in a way that satisfies his heart, why Jan van Riebeeck and Simon van der Stel were so good while Lord Charles Somerset was so bad. Nor does he like the leaders of the Great Trek as he is supposed to, except perhaps for Piet Retief, who was murdered after Dingaan tricked him into leaving his gun outside the kraal. Andries Pretorius and Gerrit Maritz and the others sound like the teachers in the high school or like Afrikaners on the radio: angry and obdurate and full of menaces and talk about God.

They do not cover the Boer War at school, at least not in English-medium classes. There are rumours that the Boer War is taught in the Afrikaans classes, under the name of the Tweede Vryheidsoorlog, the Second War of Liberation, but not for examination. Being a touchy subject, the Boer War is not officially on the syllabus. Even his parents will not say anything about the Boer War, about who was right and who was wrong. However, his mother does repeat a story about the Boer War that her own mother told her. When the Boers arrived on their farm, said her mother, they demanded food and money and expected to be waited on. When the British soldiers came, they slept in the stable, stole nothing, and before leaving courteously thanked their hosts.

The British, with their haughty, arrogant generals, are the villains of the Boer War. They are also stupid, for wearing red uniforms that make them easy targets for the Boer marksmen. In stories of the War one is supposed to side with the Boers, fighting for their freedom against the might of the British Empire. However, he prefers to dislike the Boers, not only for their long beards and ugly clothes, but for hiding behind rocks and shooting from ambush, and to like the British for marching to their death to the skirl of bagpipes.

In Worcester the English are a minority, in Reunion Park a tiny minority. Aside from himself and his brother, who are English only in a way, there are only two proper English boys: Rob Hart and a small, wiry boy named Billy Smith whose father works on the railways and who has a sickness that makes his skin flake off (his mother forbids him to touch any of the Smith children).

When he lets it slip that Rob Hart is being flogged by Miss Oosthuizen, his parents seem at once to know why. Miss Oosthuizen is one of the Oosthuizen clan, who are Nationalists; Rob Hart's father, who owns a hardware store, was a United Party town councillor until the elections of 1948.

His parents shake their heads over Miss Oosthuizen. They regard her as excitable, unstable; they disapprove of her hennaed hair. Under Smuts, his father says, something would have been done about a teacher who brought politics into school. His father is also United Party. In fact his father lost his job in Cape Town, the job with the title his mother was so proud of – Controller of Letting – when Malan beat Smuts in 1948. It was because of Malan that they had to leave the house in Rosebank that he looks back on with such longing, the house with the big overgrown garden and the observatory with the domed roof and the two cellars, had to leave Rosebank Junior School and his Rosebank friends, and come here to Worcester. In Cape Town his father used to set off to work in the mornings wearing a dapper double-breasted suit, carrying a leather attaché case. When other children asked what his father did, he could reply, 'He is Controller of Letting,' and they would fall respect-fully silent. In Worcester his father's work has no name. 'My father works for Standard Canners,' he has to say. 'But what does he do?' 'He is in the office, he keeps the books,' he has to say, lamely. He has no idea what 'keeping books' means.

Standard Canners produces canned Alberta peaches, canned Bartlett pears and canned apricots. Standard Canners cans more peaches than any other canner in the country: that is all it is famous for.

Despite the defeat of 1948 and the death of General Smuts, his father remains loyal to the United Party: loyal but gloomy. Advocate Strauss, the new leader of the United Party, is only a pale shadow of Smuts; under Strauss the UP has no hope of winning the next election. Furthermore, the Nats are assuring themselves of victory by redrawing the boundaries of constituencies to favour their supporters in the *platteland*, the countryside.

'Why don't they do something about it?' he asks his father.

'Who?' says his father. 'Who can stop them? They can do what they like, now that they are in power.'

He does not see the point of having elections if the party that wins can change the rules. It is like the batsman deciding who may and who may not bowl.

His father switches on the radio at news-time but really only to listen to the scores, cricket scores in the summer, rugby scores in the winter.

The news bulletin used once to come from England, before the Nats took over. First there would be 'God Save the King,' then there would be the six pips from Greenwich, then the announcer would say, 'This is London, here is the news,' and would read news from all over the world. Now all that is finished. 'This is the South African Broadcasting Corporation,' says the announcer, and plunges into a long recital of what Dr Malan said in Parliament.

What he hates most about Worcester, what most makes him want to escape, is the rage and resentment that he senses crackling through the Afrikaans boys. He fears and loathes the hulking, barefoot Afrikaans boys in their tight short trousers, particularly the older boys, who, given half a chance, will take you off to some quiet place in the veld and violate you in ways he has heard leeringly alluded to – *borsel* you, for instance, which as far as he can work out means pulling down your pants and brushing shoe polish into your balls (but why your balls? why shoe polish?) and sending you home through the streets half-naked and blubbering.

There is a lore that all Afrikaans boys seem to share, spread by the student teachers who visit the school, to do with initiation and what happens to you during initiation. The Afrikaans boys whisper about it in the same excited way that they talk of being caned. What he overhears repels him: walking around in a baby's nappy, for instance, or drinking urine. If that is what you have to go through before you can become a teacher, he refuses to become a teacher.

There are rumours that the Government is going to order all school-children with Afrikaans surnames to be transferred to Afrikaans classes. His parents talk about it in low voices; they are clearly worried. As for him, he is filled with panic at the thought of having to move to an Afrikaans class. He tells his parents he will not obey. He will refuse to go to school. They try to calm him. 'Nothing will happen,' they say. 'It is just talk. It will be years before they do anything.' He is not reassured.

It will be up to the school inspectors, he learns, to remove false English boys from the English classes. He lives in dread of the day when the inspector will come, run his finger down the register, call out his name, and tell him to pack his books. He has a plan for that day, carefully worked out. He will pack his books and leave the room without protest. But he will not go to the Afrikaans class. Instead, calmly, so as not to attract attention, he will walk over to the bicycle shed, take his bicycle, and ride home so fast that no one can catch him. Then he will close and lock the front door and tell his mother that he is not going back to school, that if she betrays him he will kill himself.

An image of Dr Malan is engraved in his mind. Dr Malan's round, bald face is without understanding or mercy. His gullet pulses like a frog's. His lips are pursed.

He has not forgotten Dr Malan's first act in 1948: to ban all Captain Marvel and Superman comics, allowing only comics with animal characters, comics intended to keep one a baby, to pass through the Customs.

He thinks of the Afrikaans songs they are made to sing at school. He has come to hate them so much that he wants to scream and shout and make farting noises during the singing, particularly during '*Kom ons gaan blomme pluk,*' with its children gambolling in the fields among chirping birds and jolly insects.

One Saturday morning he and two friends cycle out of Worcester along the De Doorns road. Within half an hour they are out of sight of human habitation. They leave their bicycles at the roadside and strike off into the hills. They find a cave, make a fire, and eat the sandwiches they have brought. Suddenly a huge, truculent Afrikaans boy in khaki shorts appears. '*Wie het julle toestemming gegee?*' – Who gave you permission?

They are struck dumb. A cave: do they need permission to be in a cave? They try to make up lies, but it is no use. '*Julle sal hier moet bly totdat my pa kom,*' the boy announces: You will have to wait here till my father comes. He mentions a *lat*, a *strop*: a cane, a strap; they are going to be taught a lesson.

He grows light-headed with fear. Here, out in the veld where there is no one to call to, they are going to be beaten. There is no appeal they can make. For the fact is they are guilty, he most of all. He was the one who assured the others, when they climbed through the fence, that it could not be a farm, it was just veld. He is the ringleader, it was his idea from the beginning, there is no one else on to whom the blame can be shifted.

The farmer arrives with his dog, a sly-looking, yellow-eyed Alsatian. Again the questions, this time in English, questions without answers. By what right are they here? Why did they not ask permission? Again the pathetic, stupid defence must be gone through: they did not know, they thought it was just veld. To himself he swears he will never make the same mistake again. Never again will he be so stupid as to climb through a fence and think he can get away with it. *Stupid!* he thinks to himself: *stupid, stupid, stupid!*

The farmer does not happen to have a *lat* or a strap or a whip with him. 'Your lucky day,' he says. They stand rooted to the spot, not understanding. 'Go.'

Stupidly they clamber down the hillside, careful not to run for fear the dog will come after them growling and slavering, to where their bicycles wait at the roadside. There is nothing they can say to redeem the experience. The Afrikaners have not even behaved badly. It is they who have lost.

Ten

In the early mornings there are Coloured children trotting along the National Road with pencil-cases and exercise books, some even with satchels on their backs, on their way to school. But they are young children, very young: by the time they have reached his age, ten or eleven, they will have left school behind and be out in the world earning their daily bread.

On his birthday, instead of a party, he is given ten shillings to take his friends for a treat. He invites his three best friends to the Globe Café; they sit at a marble-topped table and order banana splits or chocolate fudge sundaes. He feels princely, dispensing pleasure like this; the occasion would be a marvellous success, were it not spoiled by the ragged Coloured children standing at the window looking in at them.

On the faces of these children he sees none of the hatred which, he is prepared to acknowledge, he and his friends deserve for having so much money while they are penniless. On the contrary, they are like children at a circus, drinking in the sight, utterly absorbed, missing nothing.

If he were someone else, he would ask the Portuguese with the brilliantined hair who owns the Globe to chase them away. It is quite normal to chase beggar children away. You have only to contort your face into a scowl and wave your arms and shout, 'Voetsek, hotnot! Loop! Loop!' and then turn to whoever is watching, friend or stranger, and explain: 'Hulle soek net iets om te steel. Hull is almal skelms.' – They are just looking for something to steal. They are all thieves. But if he were to get up and go to the Portuguese, what would he say? 'They are spoiling my birthday, it is not fair, it hurts my heart to see them'? Whatever happens, whether they are chased away or not, it is too late, his heart is already hurt.

He thinks of Afrikaners as people in a rage all the time because their hearts are hurt. He thinks of the English as people who have not fallen into a rage because they live behind walls and guard their hearts well.

This is only one of his theories about the English and the Afrikaners. The fly in the ointment, unfortunately, is Trevelyan.

Trevelyan was one of the lodgers who boarded with them in the house in Liesbeeck Road, Rosebank, the house with the great oak tree in the front garden where he was happy. Trevelyan had the best room, the one with French windows opening on to the stoep. He was young, he was tall, he was friendly, he could not speak a word of Afrikaans, he was English through and through. In the mornings Trevelyan had breakfast in the kitchen before going off to work; in the evenings he came back and had supper with them. He kept his room, which was anyhow out of bounds, locked; but there was nothing interesting in it except an electric shaver made in America.

His father, though older than Trevelyan, became Trevelyan's friend. On Saturdays they listened to the radio together, to C K Friedlander broadcasting rugby matches from Newlands.

Then Eddie arrived. Eddie was a seven-year-old Coloured boy from Ida's Valley near Stellenbosch. He came to work for them: the arrangement was made between Eddie's mother and Aunt Winnie, who lived in Stellenbosch. In return for washing dishes and sweeping and polishing, Eddie would live with them in Rosebank and be given his meals, while on the first of every month his mother would be sent a postal order for two pounds ten shillings.

After two months of living and working in Rosebank, Eddie ran away. He disappeared during the night; his absence was discovered in the morning. The police were called in; Eddie was found not far away, hiding in the bushes along the Liesbeeck River. He was found not by the police but by Trevelyan, who dragged him back, crying and kicking shamelessly, and locked him up in the old observatory in the back garden.

Obviously Eddie would have to be sent back to Ida's Valley. Now that he had dropped the pretence of being content, he would run away at every opportunity. Apprenticeship had not worked.

But before Aunt Winnie in Stellenbosch could be telephoned there was the question of punishment for the trouble Eddie had caused: for the calling in of the police, for the ruined Saturday morning. It was Trevelyan who offered to carry out the punishment.

He peered into the observatory once while the punishment was going on. Trevelyan was holding Eddie by the two wrists and flogging him on the bare legs with a leather strap. His father was also there, standing to one side, watching. Eddie howled and danced; there were tears and snot everywhere. '*Asseblief, asseblief, my baas,*' he howled, '*ek sal nie weer nie!*' – I won't do it again! Then the two of them noticed him and waved him out.

The next day his aunt and uncle came from Stellenbosch in their black DKW to take Eddie back to his mother in Ida's Valley. There were no goodbyes.

So Trevelyan, who was English, was the one to beat Eddie. In fact, Trevelyan, who was ruddy of complexion and already a little fat, went even ruddier while he was applying the strap, and snorted with every blow, working himself into as much of a rage as any Afrikaner. How does Trevelyan, then, fit into his theory that the English are good?

There is a debt he still owes Eddie, which he has told no one about. After he had bought the Smiths bicycle with the money for his eighth birthday and then found he did not know how to ride, it was Eddie who pushed him on Rosebank Common, shouting commands, till all of a sudden he mastered the art of balancing.

He rode in a wide loop that first time, thrusting hard on the pedals to get through the sandy soil, till he came back to where Eddie was waiting. Eddie was excited, jumping up and down. '*Kan ek 'n kans kry?*' he clamoured – Can I have a turn? He passed the bicycle over to Eddie. Eddie didn't need to be pushed: he set off as fast as the wind, standing on the pedals, his old navy-blue blazer streaming behind him, riding a lot better than he did.

He remembers wrestling with Eddie on the lawn. Though Eddie was only seven months older than he, and no bigger, he had a wiry strength and a singleness of purpose that always made him the victor. The victor, but cautious in victory. Only for a moment, when he had his opponent pinned on his back, helpless, did Eddie allow himself a grin of triumph; then he rolled off and stood at a crouch, ready for the next round.

The smell of Eddie's body stays with him from those bouts, and the feel of his head, the high bullet-shaped skull and the close, coarse hair.

They have harder heads than white people, his father says. That is why they are so good at boxing. For the same reason, his father says, they will never be good at rugby. In rugby you have to think fast, you can't be a bonehead.

There is a moment as the two of them wrestle when his lips and nose are pressed against Eddie's hair. He breathes in the smell, the taste: the smell, the taste of smoke.

Every weekend Eddie gave himself a bath, standing in a footbath in the servant's lavatory and washing himself with a soapy rag. He and his brother hauled a dustbin below the tiny window and climbed up to peek. Eddie was naked but for his leather belt, which he still wore around his waist. Seeing the two faces at the window, he gave a big smile and shouted 'Hê!' and danced in the footbath, splashing the water, not covering himself.

Later he told his mother: 'Eddie didn't take off his belt in the bath.'

'Let him do what he wants,' said his mother.

He has never been to Ida's Valley, where Eddie comes from. He thinks of it as a cold, sodden place. In Eddie's mother's house there is no electric light. The roof leaks, everyone is always coughing. When you go outside you have to hop from stone to stone to avoid the puddles. What hope is there for Eddie now that he is back in Ida's Valley, in disgrace?

'What do you think Eddie is doing now?' he asks his mother.

'He is surely in a reformatory.'

'Why in a reformatory?'

'People like that always end up in a reformatory, and then in jail.'

He does not understand his mother's bitterness against Eddie. He does not understand these bitter moods of hers, when things almost at random come under the disparaging lash of her tongue: Coloured people, her own brothers and sisters, books, education, the Government. He does not really care what she believes about Eddie as long as she does not change her mind from day to day. When she lashes out like this he feels that the floor is crumbling beneath his feet and he is falling.

He thinks of Eddie in his old blazer, crouching to hide from the rain that is always falling in Ida's Valley, smoking stompies with the older Coloured boys. He is ten and Eddie, in Ida's Valley, is ten. For a while Eddie will be eleven while he is still ten; then he will be eleven too. Always he will be pulling level, staying with Eddie for a while, then getting left behind. How long will it go on? Will he ever escape from Eddie? If they passed each other in the street one day, would Eddie, despite all his drinking and dagga-smoking, despite all the jail and all the hardening, recognize him and stop and shout 'Jou moer!'

At this moment, in the leaky house in Ida's Valley, curled under a smelly blanket, still wearing his blazer, he knows that Eddie is thinking of him. In the dark Eddie's eyes are two yellow slits. One thing he knows for sure: Eddie will have no pity on him.

Eleven

Outside their circle of kinfolk they have few social contacts. On the occasions when strangers come to the house, he and his brother scuttle away like wild animals, then sneak back to lurk and eavesdrop. They have pierced spyholes in the ceiling, so that they can climb into the roof-space and peer into the living room from above. Their mother is embarrassed by the scuffling noises. 'Just the children playing,' she explains with a strained smile.

He flees polite talk because its formulas – 'How are you?' 'How are you enjoying school?' – baffle him. Not knowing the right answers, he mumbles and stammers like a fool. Yet finally he is not ashamed of his wildness, his impatience with the tame patter of genteel conversation.

'Can't you just be normal?' asks his mother.

'I hate normal people,' he replies hotly.

'I hate normal people,' his brother echoes. His brother is seven. He wears a continual tight, nervous smile; at school he sometimes throws up for no good reason and has to be fetched home.

Instead of friends they have family. His mother's family are the only people in the world who accept him more or less as he is. They accept him – rude, unsocialized, eccentric – not only because unless they accept him they cannot come visiting, but because they too were brought up wild and rude. His father's family, on the other hand, disapprove of him and of the upbringing he has had at the hands of his mother. In their company he feels constrained; as soon as he can escape he begins to mock the commonplaces of politeness ('En hoe gaan dit met jou mammie? En met jou broer? Dis goed, dis goed!' How is your mommy? Your brother?

Good!) Yet there is no evading them: without participating in their rituals there is no way of visiting the farm. So, squirming with embarrassment, despising himself for his cravenness, he submits. 'Dit *gaan goed*,' he says. 'Dit *gaan goed met ons almal*.' We're all fine.

He knows that his father sides with his family against him. This is one of his father's ways of getting back at his mother. He is chilled by the thought of the life he would face if his father ran the household, a life of dull, stupid formulas, of being like everyone else. His mother is the only one who stands between him and an existence he could not endure. So at the same time that he is irritated with her for her slowness and dullness, he clings to her as his only protector. He is her son, not his father's son. He denies and detests his father. He will not forget the day two years ago when his mother for the one and only time let his father loose on him, like a dog let loose from its chain ('I've reached the limit, I can't stand it any more!'), and his father's eyes glared blue and angry as he shook him and cuffed him.

He must go to the farm because there is no place on earth he loves more or can imagine loving more. Everything that is complicated in his love for his mother is uncomplicated in his love for the farm. Yet since as far back as he can remember this love has had an edge of pain. He may visit the farm but he will never live there. The farm is not his home; he will never be more than a guest, an uneasy guest. Even now, day by day, the farm and he are travelling different roads, separating, growing not closer but further apart. One day the farm will be wholly gone, wholly lost; already he is grieving over that loss.

The farm used to be his grandfather's, but his grandfather died and it passed to Uncle Son, his father's elder brother. Son was the only one with an aptitude for farming; the rest of the brothers and sisters all too eagerly fled to the towns and cities. Nevertheless, there is a sense in which the farm on which they grew up is still theirs. So at least once a year, and sometimes twice, his father goes back to the farm and takes him along.

The farm is called Voëlfontein, Bird fountain; he loves every stone of it, every bush, every blade of grass, loves the birds that give it its name, birds that as dusk falls gather in their thousands in the trees around the fountain, calling to each other, murmuring, ruffling their feathers, settling for the night. It is not conceivable that another person could love the farm as he does. But he cannot talk about his love, not only because normal people do not talk about such things but because confessing to it would be a betrayal of his mother. It would be a betrayal not only because she too comes from a farm, a rival farm in a far-off part of the world which she speaks of with a love and longing of her own but can never go back to because it was sold to strangers, but because she is not truly welcome on this farm, the real farm, Voëlfontein.

Why this is so she never explains – for which, in the end, he is grateful – but slowly he is able to piece the story together. For a long spell during the War, his mother lived with her two children in a single rented room in the town of Prince Albert, surviving on the six pounds a month his father remitted from his lance corporal's pay plus two pounds from the Governor-General's Distress Fund. During this time they were not once invited to the farm, though the farm was a mere two hours away by road. He knows this part of the story because even his father, when he came back from the War, was angry and ashamed of how they had been treated.

Of Prince Albert he remembers only the whine of mosquitoes in the long hot nights, and his mother walking to and fro in her petticoat, sweat standing out on her skin, her heavy, fleshy legs crisscrossed with varicose veins, trying to soothe his baby brother, forever crying; and days of terrible boredom spent behind closed shutters sheltering from the sun. That was how they lived, stuck, too poor to move, waiting for the invitation that did not come.

His mother's lips still grow tight when the farm is mentioned. Nevertheless, when they go to the farm for Christmas she comes along. The whole extended family congregates. Beds and mattresses and stretchers are set out in every room, and on the long stoep too: one Christmas he counts twenty-six of them. All day long his aunt and the two maids are busy in the steamy kitchen, cooking, baking, producing meal after meal, one round of tea or coffee and cake after another, while the men sit on the stoep, gazing lazily over the shimmering Karoo, swapping stories about the old days.

Greedily he drinks in the atmosphere, drinks in the happy, slapdash mixture of English and Afrikaans that is their common tongue when they get together. He likes this funny, dancing language, with its particles that slip here and there in the sentence. It is lighter, airier than the Afrikaans they study at school, which is weighed down with idioms that are supposed to come from the *volksmond*, the people's mouth, but seem to come only from the Great Trek, lumpish, nonsensical idioms about wagons and cattle and cattle-harness.

On his first visit to the farm, while his grandfather was still alive, all the barnyard animals of his story books were still there: horses, donkeys, cows with their calves, pigs, ducks, a colony of hens with a cock that crowed to greet the sun, nanny goats and bearded billy goats. Then, after his grandfather's death, the barnyard began to dwindle, till nothing was left but sheep. First the horses were sold, then the pigs were turned into pork (he watched his uncle shoot the last pig: the bullet took it behind the ear: it gave a grunt and a great fart and collapsed, first on its knees, then on its side, quivering). After that the cows went, and the ducks.

The reason was the wool price. The Japanese were paying a pound a pound for wool: it was easier to buy a tractor than keep horses, easier to drive to Fraserburg Road in the new Studebaker and buy frozen butter and powdered milk than milk a cow and churn the cream. Only sheep mattered, sheep with their golden fleece.

The burden of agriculture could be shed too. The only crop still grown on the farm is lucerne, in case the grazing runs out and the sheep have to be fed. Of the orchards, only a grove of orange trees remains, yielding year after year the sweetest of navels.

When, refreshed by an after-dinner nap, his aunts and uncles congregate on the stoep to drink tea and tell stories, their talk sometimes turns to old times on the farm. They reminisce about their father the 'gentleman farmer' who kept a carriage and pair, who grew corn on the lands below the dam which he threshed and ground himself. 'Yes, those were the days,' they say, and sigh.

They like to be nostalgic about the past, but none of them want to go back to it. He does. He wants everything to be as it was in the past.

In a corner of the stoep, in the shade of the bougainvillea, hangs a canvas water-bottle. The hotter the day, the cooler the water – a miracle, like the miracle of the meat that hangs in the dark of the storeroom and does not rot, like the miracle of the pumpkins that lie on the roof in the blazing sun and stay fresh. On the farm, it seems, there is no decay.

The water from the water-bottle is magically cool, but he pours no more than a mouthful at a time. He is proud of how little he drinks. It will stand him in good stead, he hopes, if he is ever lost in the veld. He wants to be a creature of the desert, this desert, like a lizard.

Just above the farmhouse is a stone-walled dam, twelve feet square, filled by a wind pump, which provides water for the house and garden. One hot day he and his brother launch a galvanized-iron bathtub into the dam, climb unsteadily in, and paddle it back and forth across the surface.

He fears water; he thinks of this adventure as a way of overcoming his fear. Their boat bobs about in the middle of the dam. Shafts of light flash from the dappled water; there is no sound but the trilling of cicadas. Between him and death there is only a thin sheet of metal. Nevertheless he feels quite secure, so secure that he can almost doze. This is the farm: no ill can happen here.

He has been in a boat only once before, when he was four. A man (who? – he tries to summon him up, but cannot) rowed them out on the lagoon at Plettenberg Bay. It was supposed to be a pleasure-trip, but all the while they rowed he sat frozen, fixing his eye on the far shore. Only once did he glance over the side. Fronds of water-grass rippled languidly deep below them. It was as he feared, and worse; his head spun. Only these fragile boards, which groaned with every oar stroke as if about to crack, kept him from plunging to his death. He gripped tighter and closed his eyes, beating down the panic inside him.

There are two Coloured families on Voëlfontein, each with a house of their own. There is also, near the dam wall, the house, now without a roof, in which Outa Jaap used to live. Outa Jaap was on the farm before his grandfather; he himself remembers Outa Jaap only as a very old man with milky-white, sightless eyeballs and toothless gums and knotted hands, sitting on a bench in the sun, to whom he was taken before he died, perhaps in order to be blessed, he is not sure. Though Outa Jaap is gone now, his name is still mentioned with deference. Yet when he asks what was special about Outa Jaap, the answers that come back are very ordinary. Outa Jaap came from the days before jackal-proof fences, he is told, when the shepherd who took his sheep to graze in one of the far-flung camps would be expected to live with them and guard them for weeks on end. Outa Jaap belonged to a vanished generation. That is all.

Nevertheless, he has a sense of what lies behind these words. Outa Jaap was part of the farm; though his grandfather may have been its purchaser and legal owner, Outa Jaap came with it, knew more about it, about sheep, veld, weather, than the newcomer would ever know. That was why Outa Jaap had to be deferred to; that is why there is no question of getting rid of Outa Jaap's son Ros, now in his middle years, though he is not a particularly good workman, unreliable and prone to get things wrong.

It is understood that Ros will live and die on the farm and be succeeded by one of his sons. Freek, the other hired man, is younger and more energetic than Ros, quicker on the uptake and more dependable. Nevertheless, he is not of the farm: it is understood that he will not necessarily stay.

Coming to the farm from Worcester, where Coloured people seem to have to beg for whatever they get (*Asseblief my nooi! Asseblief my basie!*), he is relieved at how correct and formal relations are between his uncle and the *volk*. Each morning his uncle confers with his two men about the day's tasks. He does not give them orders. Instead he proposes the tasks that need to be done, one by one, as if dealing cards on a table; his men deal their own cards too. In-between there are pauses, long, reflective silences in which nothing happens. Then all at once, mysteriously, the whole business seems to be settled: who will go where, who will do what. '*Nouja, dan sal ons maar loop, baas Sonnie!*' – We'll get going! And Ros and Freek don their hats and briskly set off.

It is the same in the kitchen. There are two women who work in the kitchen: Ros's wife Tryn, and Lientjie, his daughter from another marriage. They arrive at breakfast time and leave after the midday meal, the main meal of the day, the meal that is here called dinner. So shy is Lientjie of strangers that she hides her face and giggles when spoken to. But if he stands at the kitchen door he can hear, passing between his aunt and the two women, a low stream of talk that he loves to eavesdrop on: the soft, comforting gossip of women, stories passed from ear to ear to ear, till not only the farm but the village at Fraserburg Road and the location outside the village are covered by the stories, and all the other farms of the district too: a soft white web of gossip spun over past and present, a web being spun at the same moment in other kitchens too, the Van Rensburg kitchen, the Alberts kitchen, the Nigrini kitchen, the various Botes kitchens: who is getting married to whom, whose mother-in-law is going to have an operation for what, whose son is doing well at school, whose daughter is in trouble, who visited whom, who wore what when.

But it is Ros and Freek with whom he has more to do. He burns with curiosity about the lives they live. Do they wear vests and underpants like white people? Do they each have a bed? Do they sleep naked or in their work clothes or do they have pyjamas? Do they eat proper meals, sitting at table with knives and forks?

He has no way of answering these questions, for he is discouraged from visiting their houses. It would be rude, he is told – rude because Ros and Freek would find it embarrassing.

If it is not embarrassing to have Ros's wife and daughter work in the house, he wants to ask, cooking meals, washing clothes, making beds, why is it embarrassing to visit them in their house?

It sounds like a good argument, but there is a flaw in it, he knows. For the truth is that it is embarrassing to have Tryn and Lientjie in the house. He does not like it when he passes Lientjie in the passage and she has to pretend she is invisible and he has to pretend she is not there. He does not like to see Tryn on her knees at the washtub washing his clothes. He does not know how to answer her when she speaks to him in the third person, calling him 'die kleinbaas', the little master, as if he were not present. It is all deeply embarrassing.

It is easier with Ros and Freek. But even with them he has to speak tortuously constructed sentences to avoid calling them *jy* when they call him *kleinbaas*. He is not sure whether Freek counts as a man or a boy, whether he is making a fool of himself when he treats Freek as a man. With Coloured people in general, and with the people of the Karoo in particular, he simply does not know when they cease to be children and become men and women. It seems to happen so early and so suddenly: one day they are playing with toys, the next day they are out with the men, working, or in someone's kitchen, washing dishes.

Freek is gentle and soft-spoken. He has a bicycle with fat tyres and a guitar; in the evenings he sits outside his room and plays his guitar to himself, smiling his rather remote smile. On Saturday afternoons he cycles off to the Fraserburg Road location and stays there until Sunday evening, returning long after dark: from miles away they can see the tiny, wavering speck of light that is his bicycle lamp. It seems to him heroic to cycle that vast distance. He would hero-worship Freek if it were permitted.

Freek is a hired man, he is paid a wage, he can be given notice and sent packing. Nevertheless, seeing Freek sitting on his haunches, his pipe in his mouth, staring out over the veld, it seems to him that Freek belongs here more securely than the Coetzees do – if not to Voëlfontein, then to the Karoo. The Karoo is Freek's country, his home; the Coetzees, drinking tea and gossiping on the farmhouse stoep, are like swallows, seasonal, here today, gone tomorrow, or even like sparrows, chirping, light-footed, short-lived.

Best of all on the farm, best of everything, is the hunting. His uncle owns only one gun, a heavy Lee-Enfield .303 that fires a shell too large for any of the game (once his father shot a hare with it and nothing was left over but bloody scraps). So when he visits the farm they borrow from one of the neighbours an old .22. It takes a single cartridge, loaded straight into the breech; sometimes it misfires and he comes away with a singing in his ears that lasts for hours. He never manages to hit anything with this gun except frogs in the dam and muisvoëls in the orchard. Yet never does he live more intensely than in the early mornings when he and his father set off with their guns up the dry bed of the Boesmansrivier in search of game: steenbok, duiker, hares, and, on the bare slopes of the hills, korhaan.

December after December he and his father come to the farm to hunt. They catch the train – not the Trans-Karoo Express or the Orange Express, to say nothing of the Blue Train, all of which are too expensive and anyhow do not stop at Fraserburg Road – but the ordinary passenger train, the one that stops at all the stations, even the most obscure, and sometimes has to creep into sidings and wait until the more famous expresses have flashed past. He loves this slow train, loves sleeping snug and tight under the crisp white sheets and navy-blue blankets that the bedding attendant brings, loves waking in the night at some quiet station in the middle of nowhere, hearing the hiss of the engine at rest, the clang of the ganger's hammer as he tests the wheels. And then at dawn, when they arrive at Fraserburg Road, Uncle Son will be waiting for them, wearing his broad smile and his old, oil-stained felt hat, saying 'Jis-laaik, maar jy word darem groot, John!' – You're getting big! – and whistling through his teeth, and they can load their bags on the Studebaker and set off on the long drive.

He accepts without question the variety of hunting practised on Voëlfontein. He accepts that they have had a good hunt if they start a single hare or hear a pair of korhaan gargling in the distance. That is enough of a story to tell the rest of the family, who, by the time they return with the sun high in the sky, are sitting on the stoep drinking coffee. Most mornings they have nothing to report, nothing at all.

There is no point in going out to hunt in the heat of the day, when the animals they want to slay are dozing in the shade. But in the late afternoon they sometimes go touring the farm roads in the Studebaker, with Uncle Son driving and his father in the passenger seat holding the .303 and he and Ros in the dickey seat at the back.

Normally it would be Ros's job to jump out and open the camp gates for the car, wait for the car to go through, and then close the gates behind, one gate after another. But on these hunts it is his privilege to open the gates, while Ros watches and approves.

They are hunting the fabled paauw. However, since paauw are sighted only once or twice a year – so rare are they, indeed, that there is a fine of fifty pounds for shooting them, if you are caught – they settle for hunting korhaan. Ros is taken along on the hunt because, being a Bushman or nearly a Bushman, he must have preternaturally sharp vision.

And indeed it is Ros, with a slap on the roof of the car, who sees the korhaan first: grey-brown birds the size of pullets trotting among the bushes in groups of two or three. The Studebaker comes to a halt; his father rests the .303 on the window and takes aim; the clap of the shot echoes back and forth across the veld. Sometimes the birds, alarmed, take flight; more often they simply trot faster, making their characteristic gargling noise. Never does his father actually hit a korhaan, so never does he get to see one of these birds ('bush-bustard', says the Afrikaans-English dictionary) from close by.

His father was a gunner in the war: he manned a Bofors anti-aircraft gun shooting at German and Italian planes. He wonders whether he ever shot a plane down: he certainly never boasts of it. How did he come to be a gunner at all? He has no gift for it. Were soldiers just allotted things to do at random?

The only variety of hunting at which they do succeed is hunting by night, which, he soon discovers, is shameful and not to be boasted about. The method is simple. After supper they climb aboard the Studebaker and Uncle Son drives them in darkness across the lucerne fields. At a certain point he stops and switches on the headlights. Not thirty yards away a steenbok stands frozen, its ears cocked towards them, its dazzled eyes reflecting the lights. 'Skiet!' hisses his uncle. His father shoots and the buck falls.

They tell themselves it is acceptable to hunt in this way because the buck are a pest, eating lucerne that should go to the sheep. But when he sees how tiny the dead buck is, no larger than a poodle, he knows the argument is hollow. They hunt by night because they are not good enough to shoot anything by day.

On the other hand, the venison, steeped in vinegar and then roasted (he watches his aunt cut slits in the dark flesh and stuff it with cloves and garlic), is even more delicious than lamb, tangy and soft, so soft that it melts in the mouth. Everything in the Karoo is delicious, the peaches, the watermelons, the pumpkin, the mutton, as though whatever can find sustenance in this arid earth is thereby blessed.

They will never be famous hunters. Still, he loves the heft of the gun in his hand, the sound of their feet tramping the grey river-sand, the silence that descends heavy as a cloud when they stop, and always the landscape enclosing them, the beloved landscape of ochre and grey and fawn and olive-green.

On the last day of the visit, according to ritual, he may shoot up the remainder of his box of .22 cartridges at a tin can on a fence post. It is a difficult occasion. The borrowed gun is not a good one, he is not a good shot. With the family watching from the stoep, he fires off his shots hastily, missing more often than he hits.

One morning while he is out by himself in the riverbed, hunting muisvoëls, the .22 jams. He cannot find a way to release the cartridge-case stuck in the breech. He brings the gun back to the house, but Uncle Son and his father are away in the veld. 'Ask Ros or Freek,' his mother suggests. He seeks out Freek in the stable. Freek, however, does not want to touch the gun. It is the same with Ros, when he finds Ros. Though they will not explain themselves, they seem to have a holy terror of guns. So he has to wait for his uncle to come back and prise out the cartridge-case with his penknife. 'I asked Ros and Freek,' he complains, 'but they wouldn't help.' His uncle shakes his head. 'You mustn't ask them to touch guns,' he says. 'They know they mustn't.'

They mustn't. Why not? No one will tell him. But he broods on the word mustn't. He hears it more often on the farm than anywhere else, more often even than in Worcester. A strange word, easy to misspell because of the silent t hidden in the middle. 'You mustn't touch this.' 'You mustn't eat that.' Would that be the price, if he were to give up going to school and plead to live here on the farm: that he would have to stop asking questions, obey all the mustn'ts, just do as he was told? Would he be prepared to knuckle down and pay that price? Is there no way of living in the Karoo – the only place in the world where he wants to be – as he wants to live: without belonging to a family?

The farm is huge, so huge that when, on one of their hunts, he and his father come to a fence across the riverbed, and his father announces that they have reached the boundary between Voëlfontein and the next farm, he is taken aback. In his imagination Voëlfontein is a kingdom in its own right. There is not enough time in a single life to know all of Voëlfontein, know its every stone and bush. No time can be enough when one loves a place with such devouring love.

He knows Voëlfontein best in summer, when it lies flattened under an even, blinding light that pours down from the sky. Yet Voëlfontein has its mysteries too, mysteries that belong not to night and shadow but to hot afternoons when mirages dance on the horizon and the very air sings in his ears. Then, when everyone else is dozing, stunned by the heat, he can tiptoe out of the house and climb the hill to the labyrinth of stone-walled kraals that belong to the old days when the sheep in their thousands had to be brought in from the veld to be counted or shorn or dipped. The kraal walls are two feet thick and higher than his head; they are made of flat blue-grey stones, every one of them trundled here by donkey-cart. He tries to picture the herds of sheep, all of them dead and gone now, that must have sheltered from the sun in the lee of these walls. He tries to picture Voëlfontein as it must have been when the great house and its outbuildings and kraals were still in the process of being built: a site of patient, ant-like labour, year after year. Now the jackals that preyed on the sheep have been exterminated, shot or poisoned, and the kraals, without a use, are sliding into ruin.

The kraal walls ramble for miles up and down the hillside. Nothing grows here: the earth has been trampled flat and killed forever, he does not know how: it has a stained, unhealthy, yellow look. Once inside the walls, he is cut off from everything save the sky. He has been warned not to come here because of the danger of snakes, because no one will hear him if he shouts for help. Snakes, he is warned, revel in hot afternoons like these: they come out of their lairs – ringhals, puff-adder, skaapsteker – to bask in the sun, warming their cold blood.

He has yet to see a snake in the kraals; nevertheless, he watches his every step.

Freek comes across a skaapsteker behind the kitchen, where the women hang the laundry. He beats it to death with a stick and drapes the long yellow body over a bush. For weeks the women will not go there. Snakes marry for life, says Tryn; when you kill the male, the female comes in search of revenge.

Spring, September, is the best time to visit the Karoo, though the school vacation is only one week long. They are on the farm one September when the shearers arrive. They appear from nowhere, wild men who come on bicycles laden with bedrolls and pots and pans.

Shearers, he discovers, are special people. When they descend on the farm, it is good luck. To hold them there, a fat *hamel*, a wether, is picked out and slaughtered. They take possession of the old stable, which they turn into their barracks. A fire burns late into the night as they feast.

He listens to a long discussion between Uncle Son and their leader, a man so dark and fierce he could almost be a Native, with a pointed beard and trousers held up by rope. They talk about the weather, about the state of the grazing in the Prince Albert district, in the Beaufort district, in the Fraserburg district, about payment. The Afrikaans the shearers speak is so thick, so full of strange idioms, that he can barely understand it. Where do they come from? Is there a country deeper even than the country of Voëlfontein, a heartland even more secluded from the world?

The next morning, an hour before dawn, he is woken by the trampling of hooves as the first troops of sheep are driven past the house to be penned in the kraals beside the shearing-shed. The household begins to awake. There is a bustle in the kitchen, and the smell of coffee. By first light he is outside, dressed, too excited to eat.

He is given a task. He has charge of a tin mug full of dried beans. Each time a shearer finishes a sheep, and releases it with a slap on the hindquarters, and tosses the shorn pelt on to the sorting-table, and the sheep, pink and naked and bleeding where the shears have nipped it, trots nervously into the second pen – each time, the shearer may take a bean from the mug, which he does with a nod and a courteous 'My basie!'

When he is tired of holding the mug (the shearers can take the beans for themselves, they are country-bred and have never so much as heard of dishonesty), he and his brother help with the stuffing of the bales, jumping up and down on the mass of thick, hot, oily wool. His cousin Agnes is there too, visiting from Skipperskloof. She and her sister join in; the four of them tumble over each other, giggling and cavorting as if in a huge featherbed.

Agnes occupies a place in his life that he does not yet understand. He first set eyes on her when he was seven. Invited to Skipperskloof, they arrived late one afternoon after a long train journey. Clouds scudded across the sky, there was no warmth in the sun. Under the chill winter light the veld stretched out a deep reddish blue without trace of green. Even the farmhouse looked unwelcoming: an austere white rectangle with a steep zinc roof. It was not at all like Voëlfontein; he did not want to be there.

Agnes, a few months older than himself, was allotted to be his companion. She took him for a walk in the veld. She went barefoot; she did not even own shoes. Soon they were out of sight of the house, in the middle of nowhere. They began to talk. She had pigtails and a lisp, which he liked. He lost his reserve. As he spoke he forgot what language he was speaking: thoughts simply turned to words within him, transparent words.

What he said to Agnes that afternoon he can no longer remember. But he told her everything, everything he did, everything he knew, everything he hoped for. In silence she took it all in. Even as he spoke he knew the day was special because of her.

The sun began to sink, fiery crimson yet icy. The clouds darkened, the wind grew sharper, cutting through his clothes. Agnes was wearing nothing but a thin cotton dress; her feet were blue with cold.

'Where have you been? What have you been doing?' asked the grown-ups when they returned to the house. '*Niks nie,*' answered Agnes. Nothing.

Here on Voëlfontein Agnes is not allowed to go hunting, but she is free to wander with him in the veld or catch frogs with him in the big earth-dam. Being with her is different from being with his school friends. It has something to do with her softness, her readiness to listen, but also with her slim brown legs, her bare feet, the way she dances from stone to stone. He is clever, he is top of his class; she is reputed to be clever too; they roam around talking about things that the grown-ups would shake their heads over: whether the universe had a beginning; what lies beyond Pluto, the dark planet; where God is, if he exists.

Why is it that he can speak so easily to Agnes? Is it because she is a girl? To whatever comes from him she seems to answer without reserve, softly, readily. She is his first cousin, therefore they cannot fall in love and get married. In a way that is a relief: he is free to be friends with her, open his heart to her. But is he in love with her nevertheless? Is this love – this easy generosity, this sense of being understood at last, of not having to pretend?

All day and all of the next day the shearers work, barely stopping to eat, calling out challenges to each other to show who is fastest. By evening on the second day all the work is done, every sheep on the farm has been shorn. Uncle Son brings out a canvas bag full of notes and coins, and each shearer is paid according to his number of beans. Then there is another fire, another feast. The next morning they are gone and the farm can return to its old, slow ways.

The bales of wool are so many that they overflow the shed. Uncle Son goes from one to another with a stencil and ink-pad, painting on each his name, the name of the farm, the grade of wool. Days later a huge lorry arrives (how did it get across the sand-bed of the Boesmansrivier, where even cars stall?) and the bales are loaded and driven away.

Every year this happens. Every year the shearers come, every year there is this adventure and excitement. It will never end; there is no reason why it should ever end, as long as there are years.

The secret and sacred word that binds him to the farm is *belong*. Out in the veld by himself he can breathe the word aloud: I *belong on the farm*. What he really believes but does not utter, what he keeps to himself for fear that the spell will end, is a different form of the word: I *belong to the farm*.

He tells no one because the word is misunderstood so easily, turned so easily into its inverse: *The farm belongs to me*. The farm will never belong to him, he will never be more than a visitor: he accepts that. The thought of actually living on Voëlfontein, of calling the great old house his home, of no longer having to ask permission to do what he wants to do, turns him giddy; he thrusts it away. *I belong to the farm*: that is the furthest he is prepared to go, even in his most secret heart. But in his secret heart he knows what the farm in its way knows too: that Voëlfontein belongs to no one. The farm is greater than any of them. The farm exists from eternity to eternity. When they are all dead, when even the farmhouse has fallen into ruin like the kraals on the hillside, the farm will still be here.

Once, out in the veld far from the house, he bends down and rubs his palms in the dust as if washing them. It is ritual. He is making up a ritual. He does not know yet what the ritual means, but he is relieved there is no one to see and report him.

Belonging to the farm is his secret fate, a fate he was born into but embraces gladly. His other secret is that, fight though he may, he still belongs to his mother. It does not escape him that these two servitudes clash. Nor does it escape him that on the farm his mother's hold is at its weakest. Unable, as a woman, to hunt, unable even to walk about in the veld, she is here at a disadvantage.

He has two mothers. Twice-born: born from woman and born from the farm. Two mothers and no father.

Half a mile from the farmhouse the road breaks in two, the left fork going to Merweville, the right to Fraserburg. At the fork is the graveyard, a fenced plot with a gate of its own. Dominating the graveyard is his grandfather's marble headstone; clustered around it are a dozen other graves, lower and simpler, with headstones of slate, some with names and dates chipped into them, some with no words at all.

His grandfather is the only Coetzee there, the only one who has died since the farm passed into the family. This is where he ended, the man who began as a pedlar in Piketberg, then opened a shop in Laingsburg and became mayor of the town, then bought the hotel at Fraserburg Road. He lies buried, but the farm is still his. His children run like midgets on it, and his grandchildren, midgets of midgets.

On the other side of the road is a second graveyard, without a fence, where some of the grave-mounds are so weathered that they have been reabsorbed into the earth. Here lie the servants and hirelings of the farm, stretching back to Outa Jaap and far beyond. What few gravestones still stand are without names or dates. Yet here he feels more awe than among the generations of Botes clustering around his grandfather. It has nothing to do with spirits. No one in the Karoo believes in spirits. Whatever dies here dies firmly and finally: its flesh is picked off by the ants, its bones are bleached by the sun, and that is that. Yet among these graves he treads nervously. From the earth comes a deep silence, so deep that it could almost be a hum.

When he dies he wants to be buried on the farm. If they will not permit that, then he wants to be cremated and have his ashes scattered here.

The other place to which he does pilgrimage each year is Bloemhof, where the first farmhouse stood. Nothing remains now but the foundations, which are of no interest. In front of it there used to be a dam fed by an underground fountain; but the fountain long ago dried up. Of the garden and orchard that once grew here there is no trace. But beside the fountain, growing out of the bare earth, stands a huge, lonely palm tree. In the stem of this tree bees have made a nest, fierce little black bees. The trunk is blackened with the smoke of fires that people have lit over the years in order to rob the bees of their honey; yet the bees stay on, gathering nectar who knows where in this dry, grey landscape.

He would like the bees to recognize that he, when he visits, comes with clean hands, not to steal from them but to greet them, to pay his respects. But as he nears the palm tree they begin to buzz angrily; outriders swoop upon him, warning him away; once he has even to flee, running ignominiously across the veld with the swarm behind him, zigzagging and waving his arms, thankful there is no one to see him and laugh.

Every Friday a sheep is slaughtered for the people of the farm. He goes along with Ros and Uncle Son to pick out the one that is to die; then he stands by and watches as, in the slaughtering-place behind the shed, out of sight of the house, Freek holds down the legs while Ros, with his harmless-looking little pocketknife, cuts its throat, and then both men hold tight as the animal kicks and struggles and coughs while its lifeblood gushes out. He continues to watch as Ros flays the still-warm body and hangs the carcase from the seringa tree and splits it open and tugs the insides out into a basin: the great blue stomach full of grass, the intestines (from the bowel he squeezes out the last few droppings that the sheep did not have time to drop), the heart, the liver, the kidneys – all the things that a sheep has inside it and that he has inside him too.

Ros uses the same knife to castrate lambs. That event he watches too. The young lambs and their mothers are rounded up and penned. Then Ros moves among them, snatching lambs by the hind leg, one by one, pressing them to the ground while they bleat in terror, one despairing wail after another, and slitting open the scrotum. His head bobs down, he catches the testicles in his teeth and tugs them out. They look like two little jellyfish trailing blue and red blood-vessels.

Ros slices off the tail as well, while he is about it, and tosses it aside, leaving a bloody stump.

With his short legs, his baggy, castoff pants cut off below the knees, his homemade shoes and tattered felt hat, Ros shuffles around in the pen like a clown, picking out the lambs, doctoring them pitilessly. At the end of the operation the lambs stand sore and bleeding by their mothers' side, who have done nothing to protect them. Ros folds his pocketknife. The job is done; he wears a tight little smile.

There is no way of talking about what he has seen. 'Why do they have to cut off the lambs' tails?' he asks his mother. 'Because other-wise the blowflies would breed under their tails,' his mother replies. They are both pretending; both of them know what the question is really about.

Once Ros lets him hold his pocketknife, shows him how easily it cuts a hair. The hair does not bend, just springs in two at the merest touch of the blade. Ros sharpens the knife every day, spitting on the whet-stone, brushing the blade across it back and forth, lightly, easily. So much of the blade has been worn away with all the sharpening and all the cutting and all the sharpening again that there is only a sliver left. It is the same with Ros's spade: so long has he used it, so often sharpened it, that only an inch or two of steel remains; the wood of the grip is smooth and black with years of sweat.

'You shouldn't be watching that,' says his mother, after one of the Friday slaughterings.

'Why?'

'You just shouldn't.'

'I want to.'

And he goes off to watch Ros peg down the skin and sprinkle it with rock salt.

He likes watching Ros and Freek and his uncle at work. To take advantage of the high wool prices, Son wants to run more sheep on the farm. But after years of poor rain the veld is a desert, grass and bushes cropped to the ground. He therefore sets about re-fencing the entire farm, breaking it into smaller camps so that the sheep can be shifted from camp to camp and the veld given time to recover. He and Ros and Freek go out every day, driving fence posts into the rock-hard earth, spanning furlong after furlong of wire, drawing it taut as a bowstring, clamping it.

Uncle Son always treats him kindly, yet he knows he does not really like him. How does he know? By the uneasy look in Son's eyes when he is around, the forced tone in his voice. If Son really liked him, he would be as free and offhand with him as he is with Ros and Freek. Instead, Son is careful always to speak English to him, even though he speaks Afrikaans back. It has become a point of honour with both of them; they do not know how to get out of the trap.

He tells himself that the dislike is not personal, that it is only because he, the son of Son's younger brother, is older than Son's own son, who is still a baby. But he fears that the feeling runs deeper, that Son disapproves of him because he has given his allegiance to his mother, the interloper, rather than to his father; also because he is not straight, honest, truthful.

If he had a choice between Son and his own father as a father, he would choose Son, even though that would mean he would be irrecoverably Afrikaans and would have to spend years in the purgatory of an Afrikaans boarding school, as all farm-children do, before he would be allowed to come back to the farm.

Perhaps that is the deeper reason why Son dislikes him: he feels the obscure claim this strange child is making on him and rejects it, like a man shaking himself free of a clinging baby.

He watches Son all the time, admiring the skill with which he does everything from dosing a sick animal to repairing a wind pump. He is particularly fascinated by his knowledge of sheep. By looking at a sheep, Son can tell not only its age and its parentage, not only what kind of wool it will give, but what each part of its body will taste like. He can pick out a slaughter-sheep according to whether it has the right ribs for grilling or the right haunches for roasting.

He himself likes meat. He looks forward to the tinkle of the bell at midday and the huge repast it announces: dishes of roast potatoes, yellow rice with raisins, sweet potatoes with caramel sauce, pumpkin with brown sugar and soft bread-cubes, sweet-and-sour beans, beetroot salad, and, at the centre, in pride of place, a great platter of mutton with gravy to pour over it. Yet after seeing Ros slaughtering sheep he no longer likes to handle raw meat. Back in Worcester he prefers not to go into butchers' shops. He is repelled by the casual ease with which the butcher slaps down a cut of meat on the counter, slices it, rolls it up in brown paper, writes a price on it. When he hears the grating whine of the band saw cutting through bone, he wants to stop his ears. He does not mind looking at livers, about whose function in the body he is vague, but he turns his eyes away from the hearts in the display case, and particularly from the trays of offal. Even on the farm he refuses to eat offal, though it is considered a great delicacy.

He does not understand why sheep accept their fate, why they never rebel but instead go meekly to their death. If buck know that there is nothing worse on earth than falling into the hands of men, and to their last breath struggle to escape, why are sheep so stupid? They are animals, after all, they have the sharp senses of animals: why do they not hear the last bleatings of the victim behind the shed, smell its blood, and take heed?

Sometimes when he is among the sheep – when they have been rounded up to be dipped, and are penned tight and cannot get away – he wants to whisper to them, warn them of what lies in store. But then in their yellow eyes he catches a glimpse of something that silences him: a resignation, a foreknowledge not only of what happens to sheep at the hands of Ros behind the shed, but of what awaits them at the end of the long, thirsty ride to Cape Town on the transport lorry. They know it all, down to the finest detail, and yet they submit. They have calculated the price and are prepared to pay it – the price of being on earth, the price of being alive.

Twelve

In Worcester the wind is always blowing, thin and cold in the winter, hot and dry in summer. After an hour outdoors there is a fine red dust in one's hair, in one's ears, on one's tongue.

He is healthy, full of life and energy, yet seems always to have a cold. In the mornings he wakes up tight-throated, red-eyed, sneezing uncontrollably, his body temperature soaring and plunging. 'I'm sick,' he croaks to his mother. She rests the back of her hand against his forehead. 'Then you must surely stay in bed,' she sighs.

There is one more difficult moment to get through, the moment when his father says, 'Where's John?' and his mother says, 'He's sick,' and his father snorts and says, 'Pretending again.' Through this he lies as quiet as he can, till his father is gone and his brother is gone and he can at last settle down to a day of reading.

He reads at great speed and with total absorption. During his sick spells his mother has to visit the library twice a week to take out books for him: two on her cards, another two on his own. He avoids the library himself in case, when he brings his books to be stamped, the librarian should ask questions.

He knows that if he wants to be a great man he ought to be reading serious books. He ought to be like Abraham Lincoln or James Watt, studying by candlelight while everyone else is sleeping, teaching himself Latin and Greek and astronomy. He has not abandoned the idea of being a great man; he promises himself he will soon begin serious reading; but for the present all he wants to read are stories.

He reads all the Enid Blyton mystery stories, all the Hardy Boys stories, all the Biggles stories. But the books he likes best are the French Foreign Legion stories of P C Wren. 'Who is the greatest writer in the world?' he asks his father. His father says Shakespeare. 'Why not P C Wren?' he says. His father has not read P C Wren and, despite his soldiering background, does not seem interested in doing so. 'P C Wren wrote forty-six books. How many books did Shakespeare write?' he challenges, and starts reciting titles. His father says 'Aah!' in an irritated, dismissive way but has no reply.

If his father likes Shakespeare then Shakespeare must be bad, he decides. Nevertheless, he begins to read Shakespeare, in the yellowing edition with the tattered edges that his father inherited and that may be worth lots of money because it is old, trying to discover why people say Shakespeare is great. He reads *Titus Andronicus* because of its Roman name, then *Coriolanus*, skipping the long speeches as he skips the nature descriptions in his library books.

Besides Shakespeare, his father owns the poems of Wordsworth and the poems of Keats. His mother owns the poems of Rupert Brooke. These poetry books have pride of place on the mantelshelf in the living-room, along with Shakespeare, *The Story of San Michele* in a leather slip-case, and a book by A J Cronin about a doctor. Twice he tries to read *The Story of San Michele*, but gets bored. He can never work out who Axel Munthe is, whether the book is true or a story, whether it is about a girl or a place.

One day his father comes to his room with the Wordsworth book. 'You should read these,' he says, and points out poems he has ticked in pencil. A few days later he comes back, wanting to discuss the poems. 'The sounding cataract haunted me like a passion,' his father quotes. 'It's great poetry, isn't it?' He mumbles, refuses to meet his father's eye, refuses to play the game. It is not long before his father gives up.

He is not sorry about his churlishness. He cannot see how poetry fits into his father's life; he suspects it is just pretence. When his mother says that in order to escape the mockery of her sisters she had to take her book and creep away in the loft, he believes her. But he cannot imagine his father, as a boy, reading poetry, who nowadays reads nothing but the newspaper. All he can imagine his father doing at that age is joking and laughing and smoking cigarettes behind the bushes.

He watches his father reading the newspaper. He reads quickly, nervously, flipping through the pages as though looking for something that is not there, cracking and slapping the pages as he turns them. When he is done with reading he folds the paper into a narrow panel and sets to work on the crossword puzzle.

His mother too reveres Shakespeare. She thinks *Macbeth* is Shakespeare's greatest play. 'If but the something could trammel up the consequences then it were,' she gabbles, and comes to a stop; 'and bring with his surcease success,' she continues, nodding to keep the beat. 'All the perfumes of Arabia could not wash this little hand,' she adds. *Macbeth* was the play she studied in school; her teacher used to stand behind her, pinching her arm until she had recited the whole of the speech. '*Kom nou, Vera!*' he would say – 'Come on!' – pinching her, and she would bring out a few more words.

What he cannot understand about his mother is that, though she is so stupid that she cannot help him with his Standard Four homework, her English is faultless, particularly when she writes. She uses words in their right sense, her grammar is faultless. She is at home in the language, it is an area where she cannot be shaken. How did it happen? Her father was Piet Wehmeyer, a flat Afrikaans name. In the photograph album, in his collarless shirt and wide-brimmed hat, he looks like any ordinary farmer. In the Uniondale district where they lived there were no English; all the neighbours seem to have been named Zondagh. Her own mother was born Marie du Biel, of German parents with not a drop of English blood in their veins. Yet when she had children she gave them English names – Roland, Winifred, Ellen, Vera, Norman, Lancelot – and spoke English to them at home. Where could they have learned English, she and Piet?

His father's English is nearly as good, though his accent has more than a trace of Afrikaans in it and he says 'thutty' for 'thirty'. His father is always turning the pages of the Pocket Oxford English Dictionary for his crossword puzzles. He seems at least distantly familiar with every word in the dictionary, and every idiom too. He pronounces the more nonsensical idioms with relish, as though consolidating them in his memory: *pitch in, come a cropper.*

He himself does not read further than *Coriolanus* in the Shakespeare book. But for the sports page and the comic strips, the newspaper bores him. When he has nothing else to read, he reads the green books. 'Bring me a green book!' he calls to his mother from his sickbed. The green books are Arthur Mee's *Children's Encyclopaedia*, which have been travelling with them ever since he can remember. He has been through them scores of times; when he was still a baby he tore pages out of them, scrawled over them with crayons, broke their bindings, so that now they have to be handled gingerly.

He does not actually read the green books: the prose makes him too impatient, it is too gushing and childish, except for the second half of volume 10, the index, which is full of factual information. But he pores over the pictures, particularly the photographs of marble sculptures, naked men and women with wisps of cloth around their middles. Smooth, slim marble girls fill his erotic dreams.

The surprising thing about his colds is how quickly they clear up or seem to clear up. By eleven in the morning the sneezing has stopped, the stuffiness in his head has lifted, he feels fine. He has had enough of his sweaty, smelly pyjamas, of the stale blankets and sagging mattress, the soggy handkerchiefs all over the place. He gets out of bed but does not get dressed: that would be pushing his luck too far. Cautious not to show his face outdoors in case a neighbour or passer-by reports him, he plays with his Meccano set or sticks stamps in his album or threads buttons on strings or braids cords out of leftover skeins of wool. His drawer is full of cords he has braided, that have no use except as belts for the dressing gown he does not have. When his mother comes into his room he looks as hangdog as he can, bracing himself against her caustic remarks.

On every side he is suspected of being a cheat. He can never persuade his mother that he is really sick; when she gives in to his pleas, she does so ungraciously, and only because she does not know how to say no to him. His schoolfellows think he is a namby-pamby and a mother's darling.

Yet the truth is that many mornings he wakes struggling for breath; bouts of sneezing convulse him for minutes on end, till he is panting and weeping and wants to die. There is no feigning in these colds of his.

The rule is that when you have been absent from school, you have to bring a letter of excuse. He knows his mother's standard letter by heart: 'Please excuse John's absence yesterday. He was suffering from a bad cold, and I thought it advisable for him to stay in bed. Yours faithfully.' He hands in these letters, which his mother writes as lies and which are read as lies, with an apprehensive heart.

When at the end of the year he counts the days he has missed, they come to almost one in three. Yet he still comes first in class. The conclusion he draws is that what goes on in the classroom is of no importance. He can always catch up at home. If he had his way, he would stay away from school all year, making an appearance only to write the examinations.

Everything his teachers say comes out of the textbook. He does not look down on them for that, nor do the other boys. He does not like it when, as happens now and again, a teacher's ignorance is exposed. He would protect his teachers if he could. He listens with attention to their every word. But he listens less in order to learn than in case he is caught daydreaming ('What did I just say? Repeat what I just said'), in case he should be called out in front of the class and humiliated.

He is convinced that he is different, special. What he does not yet know is how he is special, why he is in the world. He suspects he will not be a King Arthur or an Alexander, revered in his lifetime. Not until after he is dead will it be understood what the world has lost.

He is waiting to be called. When the call comes, he will be ready. Unflinchingly he will answer, even if it means going to his death, like the men of the Light Brigade.

The standard he subjects himself to is the standard of the VC, the Victoria Cross. Only the English have the VC. The Americans do not have it, nor, to his disappointment, do the Russians. The South Africans certainly do not have it.

He does not fail to notice that VC are his mother's initials.

South Africa is a country without heroes. Wolraad Woltemade would perhaps count as a hero if he did not have such a funny name. Swimming out into the stormy sea time and time again to save hapless sailors is certainly courageous; but did the courage belong to the man or to the horse? The thought of Wolraad Woltemade's white horse steadfastly plunging back into the waves (he loves the redoubled, steady force of *steadfast*) brings a lump to his throat.

Vic Toweel fights against Manuel Ortiz for the bantamweight title of the world. The fight takes place on a Saturday night; he stays up late with his father to listen to the commentary on the radio. In the last round Toweel, bleeding and exhausted, hurls himself at his opponent. Ortiz reels; the crowd goes wild, the commentator's voice is hoarse with shouting. The judges announce their decision: South Africa's Viccie Toweel is the new champion of the world. He and his father shout with elation and embrace each other. He does not know how to express his joy. Impulsively he grips his father's hair, tugs with all his might. His father starts back, looks at him oddly.

For days the newspapers are full of pictures of the fight. Viccie Toweel is a national hero. As for him, his elation soon dwindles. He is still happy that Toweel has beaten Ortiz, but has begun to wonder why. Who is Toweel to him? Why should he not be free to choose between Toweel and Ortiz in boxing as he is free to choose between Hamiltons and Villagers in rugby? Is he bound to support Toweel, this ugly little man with hunched shoulders and a big nose and tiny blank, black eyes, because Toweel (despite his funny name) is a South African? Do South Africans have to support other South Africans even if they don't know them?

His father is no help. His father never says anything surprising. Unfailingly he predicts that South Africa is going to win or that Western Province is going to win, whether at rugby or cricket or anything else. 'Who do you think is going to win?' he challenges his father the day before Western Province plays Transvaal. 'Western Province, by a mile,' responds his father like clockwork. They listen to the match on the radio and Transvaal wins. His father is unshaken. 'Next year Western Province will win,' he says. 'Just watch.'

It seems to him stupid to believe that Western Province will win just because you come from Cape Town. Better to believe that Transvaal will win, and then get a pleasant surprise if they don't.

In his hand he retains the feel of his father's hair, coarse, sturdy. The violence of his action still puzzles and disturbs him. He has never been so free with his father's body before. He would prefer that it did not happen again.

Thirteen

It is late at night. Everyone else is asleep. He is lying in bed, thinking. Across his bed falls a strip of orange from the street lights that burn all night over Reunion Park.

He is remembering what happened that morning during assembly, while the Christians were singing their hymns and the Jews and Catholics were roaming free. Two older boys, Catholics, had penned him in a corner. 'When are you coming to catechism?' they had demanded. 'I can't come to catechism, I have to do errands for my mother on Friday afternoons,' he had lied. 'If you don't come to catechism you can't be a Catholic,' they had said. 'I am a Catholic,' he had insisted, lying again.

If the worst were to happen, he thinks now, facing the worst, if the Catholic priest were to visit his mother and ask why he never comes to catechism, or – the other nightmare – if the school principal were to announce that all boys with Afrikaans names were to be transferred to Afrikaans classes – if nightmare were to turn to reality and he were left with no recourse but to retreat into petulant shouting and storming and crying, into the baby behaviour that he knows is still inside him, coiled like a spring – if, after that tempest, he were as a last, desperate step to throw himself upon his mother's protection, refusing to go back to school, pleading with her to save him – if he were in this way to disgrace himself utterly and finally, revealing what only he in his way and his mother in her way and perhaps his father in his own scornful way know, namely that he is still a baby and will never grow up – if all the stories that have been built up around him, built by himself, built by years of normal behaviour, at least in public, were to collapse, and the ugly, black, crying, babyish core of him were to emerge for all to see and laugh at, would there be any way in which he could go on living? Would he not have become as bad as one of those deformed, stunted, mongol children with hoarse voices and slavering lips that might as well be given sleeping pills or strangled?

All the beds in the house are old and tired, their springs sag, they creak at the slightest movement. He lies as still as he can in the sliver of light from the window, conscious of his body drawn up on its side, of his fists clenched against his chest. In this silence he tries to imagine his death. He subtracts himself from everything: from the school, from the house, from his mother; he tries to imagine the days wheeling through their course without him. But he cannot. Always there is something left behind, something small and black, like a nut, like an acorn that has been in the fire, dry, ashy, hard, incapable of growth, but there. He can imagine himself dying but he cannot imagine himself disappearing. Try as he will, he cannot annihilate the last residue of himself.

What is it that keeps him in existence? Is it fear of his mother's grief, grief so great that he cannot bear to think of it for more than a flash? (He sees her in a bare room, standing silent, her hands covering her eyes; then he draws the blind on her, on the image.) Or is there something else in him that refuses to die?

He remembers the other time he was cornered, when the two Afrikaans boys pinned his hands behind his back and marched him behind the earth-wall at the far end of the rugby field. He remembers the bigger boy in particular, so fat that the fat flowed over his tight clothes – one of those idiots or near-idiots who can break your fingers or crush your windpipe as easily as they wring a bird's neck and smile placidly while they are doing it. He had been afraid, there was no doubt of that, his heart had been hammering. Yet how true was that fear? As he stumbled across the field with his captors, was there not something deeper inside him, something quite jaunty, that said, 'Never mind, nothing can touch you, this is just another adventure'?

Nothing can touch you, there is nothing you are not capable of. Those are the two things about him, two things that are really one thing, the thing that is right about him and the thing that is wrong about him at the same time. This thing that is two things means that he will not die, no matter what; but does it not also mean that he will not live?

He is a baby. His mother picks him up, face forward, gripping him under the arms. His legs hang, his head sags, he is naked; but his mother holds him up before her, advancing into the world. She has no need to see where she is going, she need only follow. Before him, as she advances, everything turns to stone and shatters. He is just a baby with a big belly and a lolling head, but he possesses this power.

Then he is asleep.

Fourteen

There is a telephone call from Cape Town. Aunt Annie has had a fall on the steps of her flat in Rosebank. She has been taken to hospital with a broken hip; someone must come and make arrangements for her.

It is July, mid-winter. Over the whole of the Western Cape there is a blanket of cold and rain. They catch the morning train to Cape Town, he and his mother and his brother, then a bus up Kloof Street to the Volkshospitaal. Aunt Annie, tiny as a baby in her flowered nightdress, is in the female ward. The ward is full: old women with cross, pinched faces shuffling about in their dressing gowns, hissing to themselves; fat, blowsy women with vacant faces sitting on the edges of their beds, their breasts carelessly spilling out. A loudspeaker in a corner plays Springbok Radio. Three o'clock, the afternoon request programme: 'When Irish Eyes are Smiling' with Nelson Riddle and his orchestra.

Aunt Annie takes his mother's arm in a wizened grip. 'I want to leave this place, Vera,' she says in her hoarse whisper. 'It is not the place for me.'

His mother pats her hand, tries to soothe her. On the bedside table, a glass of water for her teeth and a Bible.

The ward sister tells them that the broken hip has been set. Aunt Annie will have to spend another month in bed while the bone knits. 'She's not young any more, it takes time.' After that she will have to use a stick.

As an afterthought the sister adds that when Aunt Annie was brought in her toenails were as long and black as bird claws.

His brother, bored, has begun to whine, complaining he is thirsty.

His mother stops a nurse and persuades her to fetch a glass of water. Embarrassed, he looks away.

They are sent down the corridor to the social worker's office. 'Are you the relatives?' says the social worker. 'Can you offer her a home?'

His mother's lips tighten. She shakes her head.

'Why can't she go back to her flat?' he says to his mother afterwards.

'She can't climb the stairs. She can't get to the shops.'

'I don't want her to live with us.'

'She is not coming to live with us.'

The visiting hour is over, it is time to say goodbye. Tears well up in Aunt Annie's eyes. She clutches his mother's arm so tightly that her fingers have to be prised loose.

'Ek wil huistoe gaan, Vera,' she whispers – I want to go home.

'Just a few days more, Aunt Annie, till you can walk again,' says his mother in her most soothing voice.

He has never seen this side of her before: this treacherousness.

Then it is his turn. Aunt Annie reaches out a hand. Aunt Annie is both his great-aunt and his godmother. In the album there is a photograph of her with a baby in her arms said to be him. She is wearing a black dress down to her ankles and an old-fashioned black hat; in the background is a church. Because she is his godmother Aunt Annie believes she has a special relationship with him. She does not seem to be aware of the disgust he feels for her, wrinkled and ugly in her hospital bed, the disgust he feels for this whole ward full of ugly women. He tries to keep his disgust from showing; his heart burns with shame. He endures the hand on his arm, but he wants to be gone, to be out of this place and never to come back.

'You are so clever,' says Aunt Annie in the low, hoarse voice she has had ever since he can remember. 'You are a big man, your mother depends on you. You must love her and be a support for her and for your little brother too.'

A support for his mother? What nonsense. His mother is like a rock, like a stone column. It is not he who must be a support for her, it is she who must be a support for him! Why is Aunt Annie saying these things anyhow? She is pretending she is going to die when all she has is a broken hip.

He nods, tries to look serious and attentive and obedient while secretly he is only waiting for her to let go of him. She smiles the meaningful smile that is meant to be a sign of the special bond between her and Vera's firstborn, a bond he does not feel at all, does not acknowledge. Her eyes are flat, pale blue, washed out. She is eighty years old and nearly blind. Even with glasses she cannot read the Bible properly, only hold it on her lap and murmur the words to herself.

She relaxes her grip; he mumbles something and retreats.

His brother's turn. His brother submits to being kissed. 'Goodbye, dear Vera,' croaks Aunt Annie. '*Mag die Here jou seën, jou en die kinders*' — May the Lord bless you and the children.

It is five o'clock and beginning to get dark. In the unfamiliar bustle of the city rush-hour they catch a train to Rosebank. They are going to spend the night in Aunt Annie's flat: the prospect fills him with gloom.

Aunt Annie has no fridge. Her larder contains nothing but a few withered apples, a mouldy half-loaf of bread, a jar of fishpaste that his mother does not trust. She sends him out to the Indian shop; they have bread and jam and tea for supper.

The toilet bowl is brown with dirt. His stomach turns when he thinks of the old woman with the long black toenails squatting over it. He does not want to use it.

'Why have we got to stay here?' he asks. 'Why have we got to stay here?' echoes his brother. 'Because,' says his mother grimly.

Aunt Annie uses forty-watt bulbs to save electricity. In the dim yellow light of the bedroom his mother begins to pack Aunt Annie's clothes into cardboard boxes. He has never been into Aunt Annie's bedroom before. There are pictures on the walls, framed photographs of men and women with stiff, forbidding looks: Brechers, du Biels, his ancestors.

'Why can't she go and live with Uncle Albert?'

'Because Kitty can't look after two sick old people.'

'I don't want her to live with us.'

'She is not going to live with us.'

'Then where is she going to live?'

'We will find a home for her.'

'What do you mean, a home?'

'A home, a home, a home for old people.'

The only room in Aunt Annie's flat that he likes is the storeroom. The storeroom is piled to the ceiling with old newspapers and carton boxes. The shelves are full of books, all the same: a squat book in a red binding, printed on the thick, coarse paper used for Afrikaans books that looks like blotting-paper with flecks of chaff and fly-dirt trapped in it. The title on the spine is *Ewige Genesing*; on the front cover is the full title, *Deur 'n gevaarlike krankheid tot ewige genesing*, Through a Dangerous Illness to Eternal Healing. The book was written by his great-grandfather, Aunt Annie's father; to this book – he has heard the story many times – she has devoted most of her life, first translating the manuscript from German into Afrikaans, then spending her savings to pay a printer in Stellenbosch to print hundreds of copies, and a binder to bind them, then taking them from one bookshop in Cape Town to another. When the bookshops could not be persuaded to sell the book, she trudged from door to door herself, offering it for sale. The leftovers are on the shelves here in the storeroom; the boxes contain folded, unbound printed pages.

He has tried to read *Ewige Genesing*, but it is too boring. No sooner has Balthazar du Biel got under way with the story of his boyhood than he interrupts it with long reports of lights in the sky and voices speaking to him out of the heavens. The whole of the book seems to be like that: short bits about himself followed by long recountings of what the voices told him. He and his father have long-standing jokes about Aunt Annie and her father Balthazar du Biel. They intone the title of his book in the sententious, sing-song manner of a *predikant*, drawing out the vowels: *'Deur 'n gevaaaarlike krannnnkheid tot eeeewige geneeeeesing.'*

'Was Aunt Annie's father mad?' he asks his mother.

'Yes, I suppose he was mad.'

'Then why did she spend all her money printing his book?'

'She was surely afraid of him. He was a terrible old German, terribly cruel and autocratic. All his children were afraid of him.'

'But wasn't he already dead?'

'Yes, he was dead, but she surely had a sense of duty towards him.'

She does not want to criticize Aunt Annie and her sense of duty towards the mad old man.

The best thing in the storeroom is the book press. It is made of iron as heavy and solid as the wheel of a locomotive. He persuades his brother to lay his arms in the bed of the press; then he turns the great screw until his brother's arms are pinned and he cannot escape. After which they change places and his brother does the same to him.

One or two more turns, he thinks, and the bones will be crushed. What is it that makes them forbear, both of them?

During their first months in Worcester they were invited to one of the farms that supplied fruit to Standard Canners. While the grown-ups drank tea, he and his brother roamed around the farmyard. There they came upon a mealie-grinding machine. He persuaded his brother to put his hand down the funnel where the mealie-pits were thrown in; then he turned the handle. For an instant, before he stopped, he could actually feel the fine bones of his brother's fingers yield as the cogs crushed them. His brother stood with his hand trapped in the machine, ashen with pain, a puzzled, inquiring look on his face.

Their hosts rushed them to the hospital, where a doctor amputated the middle finger of his brother's left hand. For a while his brother walked around with his hand bandaged and his arm in a sling; then he wore a little black leather pouch over the finger-stump. He was six years old. Though no one pretended his finger would grow back, he did not complain.

He has never apologized to his brother, nor has he ever been reproached with what he did. Nevertheless, the memory lies like a weight upon him, the memory of the soft resistance of flesh and bone, and then the grinding.

'At least you can be proud to have someone in your family who did something with his life, who left something behind him,' says his mother.

'You said he was a horrible old man. You said he was cruel.'

'Yes, but he did something with his life.'

In the photograph in Aunt Annie's bedroom Balthazar du Biel has grim, staring eyes and a tight, harsh mouth. Beside him his wife looks tired and cross. Balthazar du Biel met her, the daughter of another missionary, when he came to South Africa to convert the heathen. Later, when he went to America to preach the gospel there, he took her and their three children along. On a paddle steamer on the Mississippi someone gave his daughter Annie an apple, which she brought to show him. He administered a thrashing to her for having spoken to a stranger. These are the few facts he knows about Balthazar, plus what is contained in the clumsy red book of which there are many more copies in the world than the world wants.

Balthazar's three children are Annie, Louisa – his mother's mother – and Albert, who figures in the photographs in Aunt Annie's bedroom as a frightened-looking boy in a sailor suit. Now Albert is Uncle Albert, a bent old man with pulpy white flesh like a mushroom who trembles all the time and has to be supported as he walks. Uncle Albert has never earned a proper salary in his life. He has spent his days writing books and stories; his wife has been the one to go out and work.

He asks his mother about Uncle Albert's books. She read one long ago, she says, but cannot remember it. 'They are very old-fashioned. People don't read books like that any more.'

He finds two books by Uncle Albert in the storeroom, printed on the same thick paper as *Ewige Genesing* but bound in brown, the same brown as benches on railways stations. One is called *Kain*, the other *Die Misdade van die vaders*, The Crimes of the Fathers. 'Can I take them?' he asks his mother. 'I'm sure you can,' she says. 'No one is going to miss them.'

He tries to read *Die Misdade van die vaders*, but does not get beyond page ten, it is too boring.

'You must love your mother and be a support for her.' He broods on Aunt Annie's instructions. *Love*: a word he mouths with distaste. Even his mother has learned not to say I love you to him, though now and then she slips in a soft *My love* when she says goodnight.

He sees no sense in love. When men and women kiss in films, and violins play low and lush in the background, he squirms in his seat. He vows he will never be like that: soft, soppy.

He does not allow himself to be kissed, except by his father's sisters, making an exception for them because that is their custom and they can understand nothing else. Kissing is part of the price he pays for going to the farm: a quick brush of his lips against theirs, which are fortunately always dry. His mother's family does not kiss. Nor has he seen his mother and father kiss properly. Sometimes, when there are other people present and for some reason they have to pretend, his father kisses his mother on the cheek. She presents her cheek to him reluctantly, angrily, as if she were being forced; his kiss is light, quick, nervous.

He has seen his father's penis only once. That was in 1945, when his father had just come back from the War and all the family was gathered on Voëlfontein. His father and two of his brothers went hunting, taking him along. It was a hot day; arriving at a dam, they decided to swim. When he saw that they were going to swim naked, he tried to withdraw, but they would not let him. They were gay and full of jokes; they wanted him to take off his clothes and swim too, but he would not. So he saw all three penises, his father's most vividly of all, pale and white. He remembers clearly how he resented having to look at it.

His parents sleep in separate beds. They have never had a double bed. The only double bed he has seen is on the farm, in the main bedroom, where his grandfather and grandmother used to sleep. He thinks of double beds as old-fashioned, belonging to the days when wives produced a baby a year, like ewes or sows. He is thankful his parents finished with that business before he understood it properly.

He is prepared to believe that, long ago, in Victoria West, before he was born, his parents were in love, since love seems to be a precondition for marriage. There are photographs in the album that seem to prove it: the two of them sitting close together at a picnic, for instance. But all of that must have stopped years ago, and to his mind they are all the better for it.

As for him, what does the fierce and angry emotion he feels for his mother have to do with the deliquescent swooning on the screen in the bioscope? His mother loves him, that he cannot deny; but that is precisely the problem, that is what is wrong, not what is right, in her attitude towards him. Her love emerges above all in her watchfulness, her readiness to pounce and save him should he ever be in danger. Should he choose (but he would never do so), he could relax into her care and for the rest of his life be borne by her. It is because he is so sure of her care that he is on his guard with her, never relaxing, never allowing her a chance.

He yearns to be rid of his mother's watchful attention. There may come a time when to achieve this he will have to assert himself, refuse her so brutally that with a shock she will have to step back and release him. Yet he has merely to think of that moment, imagine her surprised look, feel her hurt, and he is overtaken with a rush of guilt. Then he will do anything to soften the blow: console her, promise he is not going away.

Feeling her hurt, feeling it as intimately as if he were part of her, she part of him, he knows he is in a trap and cannot get out. Whose fault is it? He blames her, he is cross with her, but he is ashamed of his ingratitude too. *Love*: this is what love really is, this cage in which he rushes back and forth, back and forth, like a poor bewildered baboon. What can ignorant, innocent Aunt Annie know about love? He knows a thousand times more about the world than she does, slaving her life away over her father's crazy manuscript. His heart is old, it is dark and hard, a heart of stone. That is his contemptible secret.

Fifteen

His mother spent a year at university before she had to make way for brothers younger than her. His father is a qualified attorney; he works for Standard Canners only because to open a practice (so his mother tells him) would take more money than they have. Though he blames his parents because they have not brought him up as a normal child, he is proud of their education.

Because they speak English at home, because he always comes first in English at school, he thinks of himself as English. Though his surname is Afrikaans, though his father is more Afrikaans than English, though he himself speaks Afrikaans without an English accent, he could not pass for a moment as an Afrikaner. The range of Afrikaans he commands is thin and bodiless; there is a whole dense world of slang and allusion commanded by real Afrikaans boys – of which obscenity is only a part – to which he has no access.

There is a manner that Afrikaners have in common too – a surliness, an intransigence, and, not far behind it, a threat of physical force (he thinks of them as rhinoceroses, huge, lumbering, strong-sinewed, thudding against each other as they pass) – that he does not share and in fact shrinks from. The Afrikaners of Worcester wield their language like a club against their enemies. On the streets it is best to avoid groups of them; even singly they have a truculent, menacing air. Sometimes when the classes line up in the quadrangle in the mornings he scans the ranks of Afrikaans boys looking for someone who is different, who has a touch of softness; but there is no one. It is unthinkable that he should ever be cast among them: they would crush him, kill the spirit in him.

Yet he finds himself unwilling to yield up the Afrikaans language to them. He remembers his very first visit to Voëlfontein, when he was four or five and could not speak Afrikaans at all. His brother was still a baby, kept indoors out of the sun; there was no one to play with but the Coloured children. With them he made boats out of seed-pods and floated them down the irrigation furrows. But he was like a mute creature: everything had to be mimed; at times he felt he was going to burst with the things he could not say. Then suddenly one day he opened his mouth and found he could speak, speak easily and fluently and without stopping to think. He still remembers how he burst in on his mother, shouting 'Listen! I can speak Afrikaans!'

When he speaks Afrikaans all the complications of life seem suddenly to fall away. Afrikaans is like a ghostly envelope that accompanies him everywhere, that he is free to slip into, becoming at once another person, simpler, gayer, lighter in his tread.

One thing about the English that disappoints him, that he will not imitate, is their contempt for Afrikaans. When they lift their eyebrows and superciliously mispronounce Afrikaans words, as if *veld* spoken with a *v* were the sign of a gentleman, he draws back from them: they are wrong, and, worse than wrong, comical. For his part, he makes no concessions, even among the English: he brings out the Afrikaans words as they ought to be brought out, with all their hard consonants and difficult vowels.

In his class there are several boys besides himself with Afrikaans surnames. In the Afrikaans classes, on the other hand, there are no boys with English surnames. In the senior school he knows of one Afrikaans Smith who might as well be a Smit; that is all. It is a pity, but understandable: what Englishman would want to marry an Afrikaans woman and have an Afrikaans family when Afrikaans women are either huge and fat, with puffed-out breasts and bullfrog necks, or bony and misshapen?

He thanks God that his mother speaks English. Of his father he remains mistrustful, despite Shakespeare and Wordsworth and the crossword puzzles. He does not see why his father goes on making an effort to be English here in Worcester, where it would be so easy for him to slide back into being Afrikaans. The childhood in Prince Albert that he hears his father joking about with his brothers strikes him as no different from an Afrikaans life in Worcester. It centres just as much on being beaten and on nakedness, on body functions performed in front of other boys, on an animal indifference to privacy.

The thought of being turned into an Afrikaans boy, with shaven head and no shoes, makes him quail. It is like being sent to prison, to a life without privacy. He cannot live without privacy. If he were Afrikaans he would have to live every minute of every day and night in the company of others. It is a prospect he cannot bear.

He remembers the three days of the Scout camp, remembers his misery, his craving, continually thwarted, to sneak back to the tent and read a book by himself.

One Saturday his father sends him to buy cigarettes. He has a choice between cycling all the way to the town centre, where there are proper shops with display windows and cash registers, and going to the little Afrikaans shop near the railway crossing, which is just a room at the back of a house with a counter painted dark brown and almost nothing on the shelves. He chooses the nearer.

It is a hot afternoon. In the shop there are strips of biltong hanging from the ceiling, and flies everywhere. He is about to tell the boy behind the counter – an Afrikaans boy older than himself – that he wants twenty Springbok plain when a fly flies into his mouth. He spits it out in disgust. The fly lies on the counter before him, struggling in a pool of saliva.

'Sies!' says one of the other customers.

He wants to protest: 'What must I do? Must I not spit? Must I swallow the fly? I am just a child!' But explanations count for nothing among these merciless people. He wipes the spit off the counter with his hand and amid disapproving silence pays for the cigarettes.

Reminiscing about the old days on the farm, his father and his father's brothers come once again to the subject of their own father. ''n Ware ou jintlman!' they say, a real old gentleman, repeating their formula for him, and laugh: 'Dis wat hy op sy grafsteen sou gewens het: A farmer and a gentleman' – That's what he would have liked on his gravestone. They laugh most of all because their father continued to wear riding boots when everyone else on the farm wore *velskoen*.

His mother, listening to them, sniffs scornfully. 'Don't forget how frightened you were of him,' she says. 'You were afraid to light a cigarette in front of him, even when you were grown men.'

They are abashed, they have no reply: she has clearly touched a nerve.

His grandfather, the one with the gentlemanly pretensions, once owned not only the farm and a half-share in the hotel and general dealer's store at Fraserburg Road, but a house in Merweville with a flagpole in front of it on which he hoisted the Union Jack on the King's birthday.

''n Ware ou jintlman en 'n ware ou jingo!' add the brothers: a real old jingo! Again they laugh.

His mother is right about them. They sound like children saying naughty words behind a parent's back. Anyway, by what right do they make fun of their father? But for him they would not speak English at all: they would be like their neighbours the Botes and the Nigrinis, stupid and heavy, with no conversation except about sheep and the weather. At least when the family gets together there is a babble of jokes and laughter in a mishmash of tongues; whereas when the Nigrinis or the Botes come visiting the air at once turns sombre and heavy and dull. 'Ja-nee,' say the Botes, sighing. 'Ja-nee,' say the Coetzees, and pray that their guests will hurry up and leave.

What of himself? If the grandfather he reveres was a jingo, must he be a jingo too? Can a child be a jingo? He stands to attention when 'God Save the King' is played in the bioscope and the Union Jack waves on the screen. Bagpipe music sends a shiver down his spine, as do words like *stalwart*, *valorous*. Should he keep it a secret, this attachment of his to England?

He cannot understand why it is that so many people around him dislike England. England is Dunkirk and the Battle of Britain. England is doing one's duty and accepting one's fate in a quiet, unfussy way. England is the boy at the battle of Jutland, who stood by his guns while the deck was burning under his feet. England is Sir Lancelot of the Lake and Richard the Lionheart and Robin Hood with his longbow of yew and his suit of Lincoln green. What do the Afrikaners have to compare? Dirkie

Uys, who rode his horse till it died. Piet Retief, who was made a fool of by Dingaan. And then the Voortrekkers getting their revenge by shooting thousands of Zulus who didn't have guns, and being proud of it.

There is a Church of England church in Worcester, and a clergyman with grey hair and a pipe who doubles as Scoutmaster and whom some of the English boys in his class – the proper English boys, with English names and homes in the old, leafy part of Worcester – refer to familiarly as Padre. When the English talk like that he falls silent. There is the English language, which he commands with ease. There is England and everything that England stands for, to which he believes he is loyal. But more than that is required, clearly, before one will be accepted as truly English: tests to face, some of which he knows he will not pass.

Sixteen

Something has been arranged on the telephone, he does not know what, but it makes him uneasy. He does not like the pleased, secretive smile his mother wears, the smile that means she has been meddling in his affairs.

These are the last days before they leave Worcester. They are also the best days of the school year, with examinations over and nothing to do but help the teacher fill in his mark book.

Mr Gouws reads out lists of marks; the boys add them up, subject by subject, then work out the percentages, racing to be the first with his hand up. The game lies in guessing which marks belong to whom. Usually he can recognize his own marks as a sequence rising to nineties and hundreds for arithmetic and tailing off with seventies for history and geography.

He does not do well at history or geography because he hates memorizing. So much does he hate it that he postpones learning for history and geography examinations until the very last minute, until the night before the examination or even the morning of the examination. He hates the very sight of the history textbook, with its stiff chocolate-brown cover and its long, boring lists of the causes of things (the causes of the Napoleonic Wars, the causes of the Great Trek). Its authors are Taljaard and Schoeman. He imagines Taljaard as thin and dry, Schoeman as plump and balding and bespectacled; Taljaard and Schoeman on either side of a table in a room in Paarl, writing bad-tempered pages and passing them across to each other. He cannot imagine why they should have wanted to write their book in English except to mortify the *Engelse* children and teach them a lesson.

Geography is no better: lists of towns, lists of rivers, lists of products. When he is asked to name the products of a country he always ends his list with *hides and skins* and hopes he is right. He does not know the difference between a hide and a skin, but nor does anyone else.

As for the rest of the examinations, he does not look forward to them, yet, when the time comes, plunges into them willingly. He is good at examinations; if there were no examinations for him to be good at there would be little special about him. Examinations create in him a heady, trembling state of excitement during which he writes down the answers quickly and confidently. He does not like the state in itself but it is re-assuring to know it is there to be tapped.

Sometimes, striking two rocks against each other and inhaling, he can reinvoke this state, this smell, this taste: gunpowder, iron, heat, a steady thudding in the veins.

The secret behind the telephone call, and behind his mother's smile, is revealed at the mid-morning break, when Mr Gouws motions him to stay behind. There is a false air about Mr Gouws too, a friendliness he mistrusts.

Mr Gouws wants him to come to tea at his home. Dumbly he nods and memorizes the address.

This is not something he wants. Not that he dislikes Mr Gouws. If he does not trust him as much as he trusted Mrs Sanderson in Standard Four, that is only because Mr Gouws is a man, the first male teacher he has had, and he is wary of something that breathes from all men: a rest-lessness, a roughness barely curbed, a hint of pleasure in cruelty. He does not know how to behave towards Mr Gouws or towards men in general: whether to offer no resistance and court their approval, or to maintain a barrier of stiffness. Women are easier because they are kinder. But Mr Gouws – he cannot deny it – is as fair as a person can be. His command of English is good, and he seems to bear no grudge against the English or against boys from Afrikaans families who try to be English. During one of his many absences from school Mr Gouws taught the parsing of complements-of-the-predicate. He has trouble catching up with the class on complements-of-the-predicate. If complements-of-the-predicate made no sense, like idioms, then the other boys would also be having trouble with them. But the other boys, or most of them, seem to have attained an easy command of complements-of-the-predicate. The conclusion cannot be escaped: Mr Gouws knows something about English grammar that he does not.

Mr Gouws uses the cane as much as any other teacher. But the punishment he favours, when the class has been too noisy for too long, is to order them to put down their pens, shut their books, clasp their hands behind their heads, close their eyes, and sit absolutely still.

Save for Mr Gouws's footfalls as he patrols up and down the rows, there is absolute silence in the room. From the eucalyptus trees around the quadrangle comes the tranquil cooing of doves. This is a punishment he could endure forever, with equanimity: the doves, the soft breathing of the boys around him.

Disa Road, where Mr Gouws lives, is also in Reunion Park, in the new, northern extension of the township where he has never explored. Not only does Mr Gouws live in Reunion Park and cycle to school on a bicycle with fat tyres: he has a wife, a plain, dark woman, and, even more surprising, two small children. This he discovers in the living room of 11 Disa Road, where there are scones and a pot of tea waiting on the table, and where, as he had feared, he is at last left alone with Mr Gouws, having to make desperate, false conversation.

It gets even worse. Mr Gouws – who has put aside his tie and jacket for shorts and khaki socks – is trying to pretend to him that, now that the school year is over, now that he is about to leave Worcester, the two of them can be friends. In fact he is trying to suggest that they have been friends all year: the teacher and the cleverest boy, the class leader.

He grows flustered and stiff. Mr Gouws offers him a second scone, which he refuses. 'Come on!' says Mr Gouws, and smiles, and puts it on his plate anyway. He longs to be away.

He had wanted to leave Worcester with everything in order. He had been prepared to give Mr Gouws a place in his memory beside Mrs Sanderson: not quite with her, but close to her. Now Mr Gouws is spoiling it. He wishes he wouldn't.

The second scone sits on the plate uneaten. He will pretend no more: he grows mute and stubborn. 'Must you go?' says Mr Gouws. He nods.

Mr Gouws rises and accompanies him to the front gate, which is a copy of the gate at 12 Poplar Avenue, the hinges whining on exactly the same high note.

At least Mr Gouws has the sense not to make him shake hands or do something else stupid.

They are leaving Worcester. His father has decided that his future does not after all lie with Standard Canners, which, according to him, is on its way down. He is going to return to legal practice.

There is a farewell party for him at his office, from which he returns with a new watch. Shortly thereafter he sets off for Cape Town by himself, leaving his mother behind to supervise the moving. She hires a contractor named Retief, striking a bargain that for fifteen pounds he will convey not only the furniture but the three of them too, in the cab of his van.

Retief's men load the van; his mother and brother climb aboard. He makes a last dash around the empty house, saying goodbye. Behind the front door is the umbrella stand that usually holds two golf clubs and a walking stick but is now empty. 'They've left the umbrella stand!' he shouts. 'Come!' calls his mother – 'Forget that old umbrella stand!' 'No!' he shouts back, and will not leave until the men have loaded the umbrella stand. '*Dis net 'n ou stuk pyp,*' grumbles Retief – It's just an old piece of pipe.

So he learns that what he thought was an umbrella stand is nothing but a metre length of concrete sewer-pipe that his mother has painted green. This is what they are taking with them to Cape Town, along with the cushion covered in dog-hairs that Cossack used to sleep on, and the rolled-up netting-wire from the chicken-coop, and the machine that throws cricket balls, and the wooden stave with the Morse code. Labouring up Bain's Kloof Pass, Retief's van feels like Noah's Ark, bearing into the future the sticks and stones of their old life.

In Reunion Park they had paid twelve pounds a month for their house. The house his father has rented in Plumstead costs twenty-five pounds. It lies at the very limit of Plumstead, facing an expanse of sand and wattle bush where only a week after their arrival the police find a dead baby in a brown paper packet. A half-hour walk in the other direction lies Plumstead railway station. The house itself is newly built, like all the houses in Evremonde Road, with picture windows and parquet floors. The doors are warped, the locks do not lock, there is a pile of rubble in the backyard.

Next door live a couple newly arrived from England. The man is forever washing his car; the woman, wearing red shorts and sunglasses, spends her days in a deckchair sunning her long white legs.

The immediate task is to find schools for him and his brother. Cape Town is not like Worcester, where all the boys went to the boys' school and all the girls to the girls' school. In Cape Town there are schools to choose among, some of them good schools, some not. To get into a good school you need contacts, and they have few contacts.

Through the influence of his mother's brother Lance they get an interview at Rondebosch Boys' High. Dressed neatly in his shorts and shirt and tie and navy-blue blazer with the Worcester Boys' Primary badge on the breast pocket, he sits with his mother on a bench outside the headmaster's office. When their turn comes they are ushered into a wood-panelled room full of photographs of rugby and cricket teams. The headmaster's questions are all addressed to his mother: where they live, what his father does. Then comes the moment he has been waiting for. From her handbag she produces the report that proves he was first in class and that ought therefore to open all doors to him.

The headmaster puts on his reading-glasses. 'So you came first in your class,' he says. 'Good, good! But you won't find it so easy here.'

He had hoped to be tested: to be asked the date of the battle of Blood River, or, even better, to be given some mental arithmetic. But that is all, the interview is over. 'I can make no promises,' says the headmaster. 'His name will go down on the waiting list, then we must hope for a withdrawal.'

His name goes down on the waiting lists of three schools, with no success. Coming first in Worcester is evidently not good enough for Cape Town.

The last resort is the Catholic school, St Joseph's. St Joseph's has no waiting list: they will take anyone prepared to pay their fees, which for non-Catholics are twelve pounds a quarter.

What is being brought home to them, to him and his mother, is that in Cape Town different classes of people attend different schools. St Joseph's caters for, if not the lowest class, then the second lowest. Her failure to get him into a better school leaves his mother bitter but does not affect him. He is not sure what class they belong to, where they fit in. For the present he is content merely to get by. The threat of being sent to an Afrikaans school and consigned to an Afrikaans life has receded – that is all that matters. He can relax. He does not even have to go on pretending to be a Catholic.

The real English do not go to a school like St Joseph's. On the streets of Rondebosch, on their way to and from their own schools, he can see the real English every day, can admire their straight blond hair and golden skins, their clothes that are never too small or too large, their quiet confidence. They josh each other (a word he knows from the public-school stories he has read) in an easy way, without the raucousness and clumsiness he is used to. He has no aspiration to join them, but he watches closely and tries to learn.

The boys from Diocesan College, who are the most English of all and do not condescend even to play rugby or cricket against St Joseph's, live in select areas that, being far from the railway line, he hears of but never sees: Bishopscourt, Fernwood, Constantia. They have sisters who go to schools like Herschel and St Cyprian's, whom they genially watch over and protect. In Worcester he had rarely laid eyes on a girl: his friends seemed always to have brothers, not sisters. Now he glimpses for the first time the sisters of the English, so golden-blonde, so beautiful, that he cannot believe they are of this earth.

To be in time for school at 8.30 he needs to leave home by 7.30: a half-hour walk to the station, a fifteen-minute ride in the train, a five-minute walk from station to school, and a ten-minute cushion in case of delays. However, because he is nervous of being late, he leaves home at 7.00 and is at school by 8.00. There, in the classroom just unlocked by the janitor, he can sit at his desk with his head on his arms and wait.

He has nightmares of misreading his watch face, missing trains, taking wrong turns. In his nightmares he weeps in helpless despair.

The only boys who get to school before him are the De Freitas brothers, whose father, a greengrocer, drops them off at the crack of dawn from his battered blue truck, on his way to the Salt River produce market.

The teachers at St Joseph's belong to the Marist order. To him these Brothers, in their severe black cassocks and white starched stocks, are special people. Their air of mystery impresses him: the mystery of where they come from, the mystery of the names they have cast off. He does not like it when Brother Augustine, the cricket coach, comes to practice wearing a white shirt and black trousers and cricket boots like an ordinary person. He particularly does not like it when Brother Augustine, taking a turn to bat, slips a protector, a 'box,' under his trousers.

He does not know what the Brothers do when they are not teaching. The wing of the school building where they sleep and eat and live their private lives is off limits; he has no wish to penetrate it. He would like to think they live austere lives there, rising at four in the morning, spending hours in prayer, eating frugally, darning their own socks. When they behave badly, he does his best to excuse them. When Brother Alexis, for instance, who is fat and unshaven, breaks wind uncouthly and falls asleep in the Afrikaans class, he explains it to himself by saying that Brother Alexis is an intelligent man who finds teaching beneath him. When Brother Jean-Pierre is suddenly transferred from duty in the junior dormitory amid stories that he has been doing things to small boys, he simply puts the stories out of his mind. It is inconceivable to him that Brothers should have sexual desires and not withstand them.

Since few of the Brothers speak English as a first language, they have hired a Catholic layman to take the English classes. Mr Whelan is Irish: he hates the English and barely conceals his dislike of Protestants. He also makes no effort to pronounce Afrikaans names correctly, speaking them with lips distastefully pursed as though they were heathen gibberish.

Most of their time in English classes is spent on Shakespeare's *Julius Caesar*, where Mr Whelan's method is to assign the boys roles and have them read their parts aloud. They also do exercises out of the grammar textbook and, once a week, write an essay. They have thirty minutes to write the essay before handing it in; since he does not believe in taking work home, Mr Whelan uses the remaining ten minutes to mark the essays. His ten-minute marking sessions have become one of his *pièces de résistance*, watched by the boys with admiring smiles. Blue pencil poised, Mr Whelan skims swiftly through the pile of scripts, then shuffles them together and passes them to the class monitor. There is a subdued, ironic ripple of applause.

Mr Whelan's first name is Terence. He wears a brown leather motoring jacket and a hat. When it is cold he keeps his hat on indoors. He rubs his pale white hands together to warm them; he has the bloodless face of a corpse. What he is doing in South Africa, why he is not back in Ireland, is not clear. He seems to disapprove of the country and everything in it.

For Mr Whelan he writes essays on The Character of Mark Antony, on The Character of Brutus, on Road Safety, on Sport, on Nature. Most of his essays are dull, mechanical performances; but occasionally he feels a spurt of excitement as he writes, and the pen begins to fly over the page. In one of his essays a highwayman waits under cover at the roadside. His horse snorts softly, its breath turns to vapour in the cold night air. A ray of moonlight falls like a slash across his face; he holds his pistol under the flap of his coat to keep the powder dry.

The highwayman makes no impression on Mr Whelan. Mr Whelan's pale eyes flicker across the page, his pencil comes down: 6½. 6½ is the mark he almost always gets for his essays; never more than 7. Boys with English names get 7½ or 8. Despite his funny surname, a boy named Theo Stavropoulos gets 8, because he dresses well and takes elocution lessons. Theo is also always allotted the part of Mark Antony, which means that he gets to read out 'Friends, Romans, countrymen, lend me your ears,' the most famous speech in the play.

In Worcester he had gone to school in a state of apprehension but of excitement too. True, he might at any time be exposed as a liar, with terrible consequences. Yet school was fascinating: each day seemed to bring new revelations of the cruelty and pain and hatred raging beneath the everyday surface of things. What was going on was wrong, he knew, should not be allowed to happen; furthermore he was too young, too babyish and vulnerable, for what he was being exposed to. Nevertheless, the passion and fury of those Worcester days gripped him; he was shocked but he was greedy too to see more, to see all there was to see.

In Cape Town, by contrast, he feels he is wasting his time. School is no longer a place where great passions are aired. It is a shrunken little world, a more or less benign prison in which he might as well be weaving baskets as going through the classroom routine. Cape Town is not making him cleverer, it is making him stupider. The realization causes panic to well up in him. Whoever he truly is, whoever the true 'I' is that ought to be rising out of the ashes of his childhood, is not being allowed to be born, is being kept puny and stunted.

He has this feeling most despairingly in Mr Whelan's classes. There is a great deal more that he can write than Mr Whelan will ever allow. Writing for Mr Whelan is not like stretching one's wings; on the contrary, it is like huddling in a ball, making oneself as small and inoffensive as one can.

He has no wish to write about sport (*mens sana in corpore sano*) or road safety, which are so boring that he has to force out the words. He does not even want to write about highwaymen: he has a sense that the slivers of moonlight that fall across their faces and the white knuckles that grip their pistol-butts, whatever momentary impression they may make, do not come from him but from somewhere else, and arrive already wilted, stale. What he would write if he could, if it were not Mr Whelan who would read it, would be something darker, something that, once it began to flow from his pen, would spread across the page out of control, like spilt ink. Like spilt ink, like shadows racing across the face of still water, like lightning crackling across the sky.

To Mr Whelan is also allotted the task of keeping the non-Catholic boys of Standard Six busy while the Catholic boys are in catechism class. Mr Whelan is supposed to read the Gospel of St Luke with them, or the Acts of the Apostles. Instead they hear from him stories about Parnell and Roger Casement and the perfidy of the English, over and over again. On some days he comes to class bearing the day's *Cape Times*, boiling with rage at the newest outrages of the Russians in their satellite countries. 'In their schools they have created classes in atheism where children are forced to spit on Our Saviour,' he thunders. 'Can you believe it? And those poor children who remain true to their faith are sent off to the infamous prison camps of Siberia. That is the reality of Communism, which has the impudence to call itself the religion of Man.'

From Mr Whelan they hear news of Russia, from Brother Otto about the persecution of the faithful in China. Brother Otto is not like Mr Whelan: he is quiet, blushes easily, has to be coaxed into telling stories. But his stories have more authority because he has actually been in China. 'Yes, I have seen it with my own eyes,' he says in his stumbling English: 'people in a tiny cell, locked up, so many that they could not breathe any more, and died. I have seen it.'

Ching-Chong-Chinaman, the boys call Brother Otto behind his back. To them, what Brother Otto has to say about China or Mr Whelan about Russia is no more real than Jan van Riebeeck or the Great Trek. In fact, since Jan van Riebeeck and the Trek are on the Standard Six syllabus while Communism is not, what goes on in China and Russia may as well be ignored. China and Russia are just excuses to get Brother Otto or Mr Whelan talking.

As for him, he is confused. He knows that his teachers' stories must be lies – Communists are good, why would they behave so cruelly? – but he has no means of proving it. He is incensed at having to sit captive listening to them, but prudent enough not to protest or even demur. He has read the *Cape Times* himself, he knows what happens to Communist sympathizers. He has no wish to be denounced as a fellow-traveller and ostracized.

Though Mr Whelan is less than enthusiastic about teaching Scripture to the non-Catholics, he cannot entirely neglect the Gospels. 'Unto him that smiteth thee on the one cheek, offer also the other,' he reads from Luke. 'What does Jesus mean? Does he mean that we should refuse to stand up for ourselves? Does he mean that we should be namby-pambies? Of course not. But if a bully comes up to you spoiling for a fight, Jesus says: Don't be provoked. There are better ways of settling differences than by fisticuffs.

'Unto every one that hath shall be given; and from him that hath not, even that which he hath shall be taken away. What does Jesus mean? Does he mean that the only way to attain salvation is to give away all we have? No. If Jesus had meant us to walk around in rags, he would have said so. Jesus speaks in parables. He tells us that those of us who truly believe will be rewarded with heaven, while those who have no belief will suffer eternal punishment in hell.'

He wonders whether Mr Whelan checks with the Brothers – particularly with Brother Odilo, who is the bursar and collects the school fees – before preaching these doctrines to the non-Catholics. Mr Whelan, the lay teacher, clearly believes that non-Catholics are heathens, damned; whereas the Brothers themselves seem to be quite tolerant.

His resistance to Mr Whelan's Scripture lessons runs deep. He is sure that Mr Whelan has no idea of what Jesus' parables really mean. Though he himself is an atheist and has always been one, he feels he understands Jesus better than Mr Whelan does. He does not particularly like Jesus – Jesus flies into rages too easily – but he is prepared to put up with him. At least Jesus did not pretend to be God, and died before he could become a father. That is Jesus' strength; that is how Jesus keeps his power.

But there is one part in Luke's gospel that he does not like to hear read. When they come to it, he grows rigid, blocks his ears. The women arrive at the sepulchre to anoint the body of Jesus. Jesus is not there. Instead, they find two angels. 'Why seek ye the living among the dead?' say the angels: 'He is not here but is risen.' If he were to unblock his ears and let the words come through to him, he knows, he would have to stand on his seat, and shout and dance in triumph. He would have to make a fool of himself for ever.

He does not feel that Mr Whelan wishes him ill. Nevertheless, the highest mark he ever gets in English examinations is 70. With 70 he cannot come first in English: more favoured boys beat him comfortably. Nor does he do well in history or geography, which bore him more than ever. It is only the high marks he scores in mathematics and Latin that bring him tenuously to the head of the list, ahead of Oliver Matter, the Swiss boy who was cleverest in the class until he arrived.

Now that, in Oliver, he has come up against a worthy opponent, his old vow always to take home a first-place report becomes a matter of grim private honour. Though he says nothing about it to his mother, he is preparing for the day he cannot face, the day when he will have to tell her he has come second.

Oliver Matter is a gentle, smiling, moon-faced boy who does not seem to mind coming second. Every day he and Oliver vie with each other in the quick-answer contest that Brother Gabriel runs, lining the boys up, going up and down the line asking questions that have to be answered within five seconds, sending whoever misses an answer to the bottom of the line. By the end of the round it is always either he or Oliver who is at the top.

Then Oliver stops coming to school. After a month without explanation, Brother Gabriel makes an announcement. Oliver is in hospital, he has leukemia, everyone must pray for him. With bowed heads the boys pray. Since he does not believe in God, he does not pray, just moves his lips. He thinks: Everyone will think I want Oliver to die so that I can be first.

Oliver never comes back to school. He dies in hospital. The Catholic boys attend a special mass for the repose of his soul.

The threat has receded. He breathes more easily; but the old pleasure in coming first is spoiled.

Seventeen

Life in Cape Town is less varied than life in Worcester used to be. During weekends, in particular, there is nothing to do but read the *Reader's Digest* or listen to the radio or knock a cricket ball around. He no longer rides his bicycle: there is nowhere interesting to go in Plumstead, which is just miles of houses in every direction, and anyhow he has outgrown the Smiths, which is beginning to look like a child's bicycle.

Riding a bicycle around the streets has in fact begun to seem silly. Other things that used once to absorb him have lost their charm too: building Meccano models, collecting stamps. He can no longer understand why he wasted his time on them. He spends hours in the bathroom, examining himself in the mirror, not liking what he sees. He stops smiling, practises a scowl.

The only passion that has not abated is his passion for cricket. He knows no one who is as consumed by cricket as he is. He plays cricket at school, but that is never enough. The house in Plumstead has a slate-floored front stoep. Here he plays by himself, holding the bat in his left hand, throwing the ball against the wall with his right, striking it on the rebound, pretending he is on a cricket field. Hour after hour he drives the ball against the wall. The neighbours complain to his mother about the noise, but he pays no heed.

He has pored over coaching books, knows the various shots by heart, can execute them with the correct footwork. But the truth is, he has begun to prefer the solitary game on the stoep to real cricket. The prospect of batting on a real pitch thrills him but fills him with fear too. He is particularly afraid of fast bowlers: afraid of being struck, afraid of the pain. On the occasions when he plays real cricket he has to concentrate all his energies on not flinching, not showing he is a coward.

He hardly ever scores runs. If he is not bowled out at once he can sometimes bat for half an hour without scoring, irritating everyone, including his teammates. He seems to go into a trance of passivity in which it is enough, quite enough, to merely parry the ball. Looking back on these failures, he consoles himself with stories of test matches played on sticky wickets during which a solitary figure, usually a Yorkshireman, dogged, stoic, tight-lipped, bats through the innings, keeping his end up while all around him wickets are tumbling.

Opening the batting against Pinelands Under-13 one Friday afternoon, he finds himself facing a tall, gangly boy who, urged on by his team, bowls as fast and furiously as he can. The ball flies all over the place, missing the wickets, missing him, evading the wicketkeeper: he barely needs to use his bat.

During the third over a ball pitches on the clay outside the mat, rears up, and hits him on the temple. 'This is really too much!' he thinks to himself crossly: 'He has gone too far!' He is aware of the fielders looking at him oddly. He can still hear the impact of ball against bone: a dull crack, without echo. Then his mind goes blank and he falls.

He is lying at the side of the field. His face and hair are wet. He looks around for his bat but cannot see it.

'Lie and rest for a while,' says Brother Augustine. His voice is quite cheery. 'You took a knock.'

'I want to bat,' he mumbles, and sits up. It is the correct thing to say, he knows: it proves one isn't a coward. But he can't bat: he has lost his turn, someone else is already batting in his place.

He would have expected them to make more of it. He would have expected an outcry against dangerous bowling. But the game is going on, and his team is doing quite well. 'Are you OK? Is it sore?' asks one of his teammates, then barely listens to his reply. He sits on the boundary watching the rest of the innings. Later he fields. He would like to have a headache; he would like to lose his vision, or faint, or do something else dramatic. But he feels fine. He touches his temple. There is a tender spot. He hopes it swells up and turns blue before tomorrow, to prove he was really hit.

Like everyone at school, he has also to play rugby. Even a boy named Shepherd whose left arm is withered with polio has to play. They are given team positions quite arbitrarily. He is assigned to play prop for the Under-13Bs. They play on Saturday mornings. It is always raining on Saturdays: cold and wet and miserable, he trudges around the sodden turf from scrum to scrum, getting pushed around by bigger boys. Because he is a prop, no one passes the ball to him, for which he is grateful, since he is frightened of being tackled. Anyhow, the ball, which is coated in horse fat to protect the leather, is too slippery to hold on to.

He would pretend to be sick on Saturdays were it not for the fact that the team would then have only fourteen men. Not turning up for a rugby match is much worse than not coming to school.

The Under-13Bs lose all their matches. The Under-13As too lose most of the time. In fact, most of the St Joseph's teams lose most of the time. He does not understand why the school plays rugby at all. The Brothers, who are Austrian or Irish, are certainly not interested in rugby. On the few occasions when they come to watch, they seem bemused and don't understand what is going on.

In her bottom drawer his mother keeps a book with a black cover called *Ideal Marriage*. It is about sex; he has known about its existence for years. One day he spirits it out of the drawer and takes it to school. It causes a flurry among his friends; he appears to be the only one whose parents have such a book.

Though it is a disappointment to read – the drawings of the organs look like diagrams in science books, and even in the section on postures there is nothing exciting (inserting the male organ into the vagina sounds like an enema) – the other boys pore avidly over it, clamour to borrow it.

During the chemistry class he leaves the book behind in his desk. When they return Brother Gabriel, who is usually quite cheery, wears a frosty, disapproving look. He is convinced Brother Gabriel has opened his desk and seen the book; his heart pounds as he waits for the announcement and the shame that will follow. The announcement does not come; but in every passing remark of Brother Gabriel's he hears a veiled reference to the evil that he, a non-Catholic, has imported into the school. Everything is spoiled between Brother Gabriel and himself. Bitterly he regrets bringing the book; he takes it home, returns it to the drawer, never looks at it again.

For a while he and his friends continue to gather in a corner of the sports field during the break to talk about sex. To these discussions he contributes bits and pieces he has picked up from the book. But these are evidently not interesting enough: soon the older boys begin to separate off for conversations of their own in which there are sudden drops of tone, whisperings, outbursts of guffawing. At the centre of these conversations is Billy Owens, who is fourteen and has a sister of sixteen and knows girls and owns a leather jacket which he wears to dances and has possibly even had sexual intercourse.

He makes friends with Theo Stavropoulos. There are rumours that Theo is a *moffie*, a queer, but he is not prepared to believe them. He likes the look of Theo, likes his fine skin and his high colouring and his impeccable haircuts and the suave way he wears his clothes. Even the school blazer, with its silly vertical stripes, looks good on him.

Theo's father owns a factory. What exactly the factory makes no one quite knows, but it has something to do with fish. The family lives in a big house in the richest part of Rondebosch. They have so much money that the boys would undoubtedly go to Diocesan College were it not for the fact that they are Greek. Because they are Greek and have a foreign name they have to go to St Joseph's, which, he now sees, is a kind of basket to catch boys who fit nowhere else.

He glimpses Theo's father only once: a tall, elegantly dressed man with dark glasses. He sees his mother more often. She is small and slim and dark; she smokes cigarettes and drives a blue Buick which is reputed to be the only car in Cape Town – perhaps in South Africa – with automatic gears. There is also an older sister so beautiful, so expensively educated, so marriageable, that she is not allowed to be exposed to the gaze of Theo's friends.

The Stavropoulos boys are brought to school in the mornings in the blue Buick, driven sometimes by their mother but more often by a chauffeur in black uniform and peaked cap. The Buick sweeps grandly into the school quadrangle, Theo and his brother descend, the Buick sweeps off. He cannot understand why Theo allows this. If he were in Theo's place he would ask to be dropped off a block away. But Theo takes the jokes and jeers with equanimity.

One day after school Theo invites him to his house. When they get there he finds they are expected to have lunch. So at three in the afternoon they sit down at the dining table with silver cutlery and clean napkins and are served steak and chips by a steward in a white uniform who stands behind Theo's chair while they eat, waiting for orders.

He does his best to conceal his astonishment. He knows there are people who are waited on by servants; he did not realize that children could have servants too.

Then Theo's parents and sister go overseas – the sister, rumour has it, to be married off to an English baronet – and Theo and his brother become boarders. He expects Theo to be crushed by the experience: by the envy and malice of the other boarders, by the poor food, by the indignities of a life without privacy. He also expects Theo to have to submit to the same kind of haircut as everyone else. Yet somehow Theo manages to keep his hair elegantly styled; somehow, despite his name, despite being clumsy at sport, despite being thought to be a *moffie*, he maintains his suave smile, never complains, never allows himself to be humiliated.

Theo sits squashed against him in his desk beneath the picture of Jesus opening his chest to reveal a glowing ruby heart. They are supposed to be revising the history lesson; in fact they have a little grammar book in front of them from which Theo is teaching him Ancient Greek. Ancient Greek with Modern Greek pronunciation: he loves the eccentricity of it. *Aftós*, whispers Theo; *evdhemonía. Evdhemonía*, he whispers back.

Brother Gabriel pricks up his ears. 'What are you doing, Stavropoulos?' he demands.

'I'm teaching him Greek, Brother,' says Theo in his bland, confident way.

'Go and sit in your own desk.'

Theo smiles and strolls back to his own desk.

The Brothers do not like Theo. His arrogance annoys them; like the boys, they think he is spoiled, has too much money. The injustice of it angers him. He would like to do battle for Theo.

Eighteen

To tide them over until his father's new law practice begins to bring in money, his mother returns to teaching. To do the housework she hires a maid, a scrawny woman with hardly any teeth in her mouth named Celia. Sometimes Celia brings along her younger sister for company. Coming home one afternoon, he finds the two of them sitting in the kitchen drinking tea. The younger sister, who is more attractive than Celia, gives him a smile. There is something in her smile that confuses him; he does not know where to look and retires to his room. He can hear them laughing and knows they are laughing at him.

Something is changing. He seems to be embarrassed all the time. He does not know where to direct his eyes, what to do with his hands, how to hold his body, what expression to wear on his face. Everyone is staring at him, judging him, finding him wanting. He feels like a crab pulled out of its shell, pink and wounded and obscene.

Once upon a time he used to be full of ideas, ideas for places to go to, things to talk about, things to do. He was always a step ahead of everyone: he was the leader, the others followed. Now the energy that he used to feel streaming out of him is gone. At the age of thirteen he is becoming surly, scowling, dark. He does not like this new, ugly self, he wants to be drawn out of it, but that is something he cannot do by himself.

They visit his father's new office to see what it is like. The office is in Goodwood, which belongs to the string of Afrikaans suburbs Goodwood-Parow-Bellville. Its windows are painted dark green; over the green in gold lettering are the words PROKUREUR – Z COETZEE –

ATTORNEY. The interior is gloomy, with heavy furniture upholstered in horsehair and red leather. The law books that have travelled around South Africa with them since his father last practised in 1937 have emerged from their boxes and are on the shelf. Idly he looks up Rape. *Natives sometimes insert the male organ between the thighs of the woman without penetration*, says a footnote. *The practice falls under customary law. It does not constitute rape.*

Is this the kind of thing they do in law courts, he wonders: argue about where the penis went?

His father's practice appears to be flourishing. He employs not only a typist but an articled clerk named Eksteen. To Eksteen his father leaves the routine business of conveyancing and wills; his own efforts are devoted to the exciting court work of *getting people off*. Each day he comes home with new stories of people whom he has got off, and of how grateful they are to him.

His mother is less interested in the people he has got off than in the mounting list of monies owed. One name in particular keeps cropping up: Le Roux the car salesman. She badgers his father: he is a lawyer, surely he can get Le Roux to pay up. Le Roux will settle his debt for sure at the end of the month, replies his father, he has promised. But at the end of the month, once again, Le Roux does not settle.

Le Roux does not settle, nor does he make himself scarce. On the contrary, he invites his father for drinks, promises him more work, paints rosy pictures of the money to be made from repossessing cars.

The arguments at home become angrier but at the same time more guarded. He asks his mother what is going on. Bitterly she says, Jack has been lending Le Roux money.

He does not need to hear more. He knows his father, knows what is going on. His father craves approval, will do anything to be liked. In the circles in which his father moves there are two ways of getting to be liked: buying people drinks and lending them money.

Children are not supposed to go into bars. But in the bar of the Fraserburg Road hotel he and his brother used often to sit at a corner table, drinking orange squash, watching their father buy rounds of brandy and water for strangers, getting to know this other side of him. So he knows the mood of expansive bonhomie that brandy creates in him, the boasting, the large spendthrift gestures.

Avidly, gloomily, he listens to his mother's monologues of complaint. Though his father's wiles no longer take him in, he does not trust her to see through them: he has watched his father wheedle his way past her too often in the past. 'Don't listen to him,' he warns her. 'He lies to you all the time.'

The trouble with Le Roux deepens. There are long telephone calls. A new name starts cropping up: Bensusan. Bensusan is dependable, says his mother. Bensusan is a Jew, he doesn't drink. Bensusan is going to rescue Jack, put him back on the right track.

But there is not only Le Roux, it turns out. There are other men, other drinking companions, to whom his father has been lending money. He cannot believe it, cannot understand it. Where does all this money come from, when his father has only one suit and one pair of shoes and has to catch the train to work? Does one really make so much money so quickly getting people off?

He has never seen Le Roux but can picture him easily enough. Le Roux will be a ruddy Afrikaner with a blond moustache; he will wear a blue suit and a black tie; he will be slightly fat and sweat a lot and tell dirty jokes in a loud voice.

Le Roux sits with his father in the bar in Goodwood. When his father isn't looking Le Roux winks behind his back to the other men in the bar. Le Roux has picked out his father as a sucker. He burns with shame that his father should be so stupid.

The money his father has been lending, as it turns out, is not actually his to lend. That is why Bensusan has involved himself. Bensusan is acting for the Law Society. The matter is serious: the money has been taken from the trust account.

'What is a trust account?' he asks his mother.

'It's money he holds in trust.'

'Why do people give him their money in trust?' he says. 'They must be mad.'

His mother shakes her head. All attorneys have trust accounts, she says, God only knows why. 'Jack is like a child when it comes to money.'

Bensusan and the Law Society have entered the picture because there are people who want to save his father, people from the old days when he was Controller of Letting. They are well disposed towards him, they don't want him to go to jail. For old times' sake, and because he has a wife and children, they will close their eyes to certain things, make certain arrangements. He can make repayments over five years; once that is done, the book will be closed, the matter forgotten.

His mother takes legal advice herself. She would like her own possessions to be separated from her husband's before some new disaster strikes: the dining-room table, for instance; the chest of drawers with the mirror; the stinkwood coffee table that Aunt Annie gave her. She would like their marriage contract, which makes the two of them responsible for each other's debts, to be amended. But marriage contracts, it turns out, are immutable. If his father goes down, his mother goes down too, she and her children.

Eksteen and the typist are given notice, the practice in Goodwood is closed. He never gets to see what happens to the green window with the gold lettering. His mother continues to teach. His father starts looking for a job. Every morning, punctually at seven, he sets off for the city. But an hour or two later – this is his secret – when everyone else has left the house, he comes back. He puts on his pyjamas and gets back into bed with the *Cape Times* crossword and a quarter-litre of brandy. Then at about two in the afternoon, before his wife and children return, he dresses and goes to his club.

His club is called the Wynberg Club, but it is really just part of the Wynberg Hotel. There his father has supper and spends the evening drinking. Sometime after midnight – the noise wakes him, he does not sleep heavily – a car pulls up before the house, the front door opens, his father comes in and goes to the lavatory. Soon afterwards, from his parents' bedroom, comes a flurry of heated whispering. In the morning there are dark-yellow splashes on the lavatory floor and on the toilet seat, and a sickly sweet smell.

He writes a notice and puts it in the lavatory: PLEASE LIFT THE SEAT. The notice is ignored. Urinating on the toilet seat becomes his father's ultimate act of defiance against a wife and children who have turned their backs on him.

His father's secret life is revealed to him when one day he stays away from school, ill or pretending to be ill. From his bed he hears the scrape of the key in the front-door lock, hears his father settling down in the next room. Later, guilty, angry, they pass each other in the passage.

Before he leaves the house in the afternoons his father takes care to empty the mailbox and remove certain items, which he hides at the bottom of his wardrobe under the paper lining. When at last the flood-gates burst, it is the cache of letters in the wardrobe – bills from the Goodwood days, letters of demand, lawyers' letters – that his mother is most bitter about. 'If I had only known, I could have made a plan,' she says. 'Now our lives are ruined.'

The debts stretch everywhere. Callers come at all hours of the day and night, callers whom he does not get to see. Each time there is a knock at the front door his father shuts himself up in his bedroom. His mother greets the visitors in low tones, ushers them into the living room, closes the door. Afterwards he can hear her whispering angrily to herself in the kitchen.

There is talk of Alcoholics Anonymous, of how his father should go to Alcoholics Anonymous to prove his sincerity. His father promises to go but does not.

Two court officers arrive to take an inventory of the contents of the house. It is a sunny Saturday morning. He retreats to his bedroom and tries to read, but in vain: the men require access to his room, to every room. He goes into the backyard. Even there they follow him, peering around, making notes on a pad.

He seethes with rage all the time. *That man*, he calls his father when he speaks to his mother, too full of anger to give him a name: why do we have to have anything to do with *that man*? Why don't you let *that man* go to prison?

He has twenty-five pounds in his Post Office savings book. His mother swears to him that no one will take his twenty-five pounds away from him.

There is a visit from a Mr Golding. Though Mr Golding is Coloured, he is somehow in a position of power over his father. Careful preparations are made for the visit. Mr Golding will be received in the front room, like other callers. He will be served tea in the same tea service. In return for being treated so well, it is hoped that Mr Golding will not prosecute.

Mr Golding arrives. He wears a double-breasted suit, does not smile. He drinks the tea that his mother serves but will promise nothing. He wants his money.

After he has left there is a debate about what to do with the teacup. The custom, it appears, is that after a person of colour has drunk from a cup the cup must be smashed. He is surprised that his mother's family, which believes in nothing else, believes in this. However, in the end his mother simply washes the cup with bleach.

At the last minute Aunt Girlie from Williston comes to the rescue, for the honour of the family. In return for a loan she lays down certain conditions, one of them that Jack should never again practise as an attorney.

His father agrees to the conditions, agrees to sign the document. But when the time comes, it takes long cajoling to get him out of bed. At last he makes his appearance, in grey slacks and a pyjama top and bare feet. Wordlessly he signs; then he retires to his bed again.

Later that evening he gets dressed and goes out. Where he spends the night they do not know; he does not return until the next day.

'What's the point of making him sign?' he complains to his mother. 'He never pays his other debts, so why should he pay Girlie?'

'Never mind him, I'll pay her,' she replies.

'How?'

'I'll work for the money.'

There is something in his mother's behaviour that he can no longer close his eyes to, something extraordinary. With each new and bitter revelation she seems to grow stronger, more stubborn. It is as though she is inviting calamities upon herself for no other purpose than to show the world how much she can endure. 'I will pay all his debts,' she says. 'I will pay in instalments. I will work.'

Her ant-like determination angers him to the point that he wants to strike her. It is clear what lies behind it. She wants to sacrifice herself for her children. Sacrifice without end: he is all too familiar with that spirit. But once she has sacrificed herself entirely, once she has sold the clothes off her back, sold her very shoes, and is walking around on bloody feet, where will that leave him? It is a thought he cannot bear.

The December holidays arrive and still his father has no job. They are all four in the house now, with nowhere else to go, like rats in a cage. They avoid each other, hiding in separate rooms. His brother absorbs himself in comics: the *Eagle*, the *Beano*. His own favourite is the *Rover*, with its stories of Alf Tupper, the one-mile champion who works in a factory in Manchester and lives on fish and chips. He tries to lose himself in Alf Tupper, but he cannot help pricking his ears to every whisper and creak in the house.

One morning there is a strange silence. His mother is out, but from something in the air, a smell, an aura, a heaviness, he knows that *that man* is still here. Surely he cannot still be sleeping. Is it possible that, wonder of wonders, he has committed suicide? If so, if he has committed suicide, would it not be best to pretend not to notice, so that the sleeping pills or whatever he has taken can be given time to act? And how can he keep his brother from raising the alarm?

In the war he has waged on his father, he has never been entirely sure of his brother's support. As far back as he can remember, people have remarked that, whereas he takes after his mother, his brother has his father's looks. There are times when he suspects his brother may be soft on his father; he suspects his brother, with his pale, worried face and the tic on his eyelid, of being soft in general.

In any event, if his father has indeed committed suicide, it would be best to steer clear of his room, so that if there are questions afterwards, he will be able to say, 'I was talking to my brother,' or 'I was reading in my room.' Yet he cannot contain his curiosity. On tiptoe he approaches the door. He pushes it open, looks in.

It is a warm summer morning. The wind is still, so still that he can hear the chirruping of sparrows outside, the whirr of their wings. The shutters are closed, the curtains drawn shut. There is a smell of man's sweat. In the gloom he can make out his father lying on his bed. From the back of his throat comes a soft gargling as he breathes.

He steps closer. His eyes are growing accustomed to the dimness. His father is wearing pyjama pants and a cotton singlet. He has not shaved. There is a red V at his throat where sunburn gives way to the pallor of his chest. Beside the bed is a chamber pot in which cigarette stubs float in brownish urine. He has not seen an uglier spectacle in his life.

There is no sign of pills. The man is not dying, merely sleeping. So: He does not have the courage to take sleeping pills, just as he does not have the courage to go out and look for a job.

Since the day his father came back from war service they have battled each other in a second war which his father has stood no chance of winning because he could never have foreseen how pitiless, how tenacious his enemy would be. For seven years that war has ground on; today at last he has triumphed. He feels like the Russian soldier on the Brandenburg Gate, raising the red banner over the ruins of Berlin.

Yet at the same time he wishes he were not here, witnessing this shame. *Unfair!* he wants to cry: *I am just a child!* He wishes that someone, a woman, would take him in her arms, make the sore place better, soothe him, tell him it was just a bad dream. He thinks of his grandmother's cheek, soft and cool and dry as silk, offered to him to be kissed. He wishes his grandmother would come and put it all right.

A ball of phlegm catches in his father's throat. He coughs, turns on his side. His eyes open, the eyes of a man fully conscious, fully aware of where he is. The eyes take him in as he stands there, where he should not be, spying. The eyes are without judgment but without human kindness either.

Lazily the man's hand sweeps down and rearranges his pyjama pants.

He wants the man to say something, some ordinary word – 'What time is it?' – to make it easier for him. But the man says nothing. The eyes continue to regard him, peaceably, distantly. Then they close and he is asleep again.

He returns to his room, closes the door.

Sometimes, in the days that follow, the gloom lifts. The sky, that usually sits tight and closed over his head, not so near that it can be touched but not much further either, opens a slit, and for an interval he can see the world as it really is. He sees himself in his white shirt with rolled-up sleeves and the grey short trousers that he is on the point of outgrowing: not a child, not what a passer-by would call a child, too big for that now, too big to use that excuse, yet still as stupid and self-enclosed as a child: childish; dumb; ignorant; retarded. In a moment like this he can see his father and his mother too, from above, without anger: not as two grey and formless weights seating themselves on his shoulders, plotting his misery day and night, but as a man and a woman living dull and trouble-filled lives of their own. The sky opens, he sees the world as it is, then the sky closes and he is himself again, living the only story he will admit, the story of himself.

His mother stands at the sink, in the dimmest corner of the kitchen. She stands with her back to him, her arms flecked with soapsuds, scouring a pot, in no great hurry. As for him, he is roaming around, talking about something, he does not know what, talking with his usual vehemence, complaining.

His mother turns from her chore; her gaze flickers over him. It is a considered look, without any fondness. She is not seeing him for the first time. Rather, she is seeing him as he has always been and as she has always known him to be when she is not wrapped up in illusion. She sees him, sums him up, and is not pleased. She is even bored with him.

This is what he fears from her, from the person in all the world who knows him best, who has the huge, unfair advantage over him of knowing all about his first, most helpless, most intimate years, years of which, despite every effort, he himself can remember nothing; who probably knows as well, since she is inquisitive and has sources of her own, the paltry secrets of his school life. He fears his mother's judgment. He fears the cool thoughts that must be passing through her mind at moments like this, when there is no passion to colour them, no reason for her faculties to be anything but clear; above all he fears the moment, a moment that has not yet arrived, when she will pronounce her judgment. It will be like a stroke of lightning; he will not be able to withstand it. He does not want to hear it. So much does he not want to hear it that he can feel a hand go up inside his own head to block his ears, block his sight. He would rather be blind and deaf than know what his mother thinks of him. He would rather live like a tortoise inside its shell.

For it is not true that, as he likes to think, this woman was brought into the world for the sole purpose of loving him and protecting him and satisfying his wants. On the contrary, she had a life before he came into being, a life in which she gave him not the slightest thought. Then at a certain moment in history she gave birth to him. She bore him and she decided to love him; perhaps she chose to love him even before she bore him; nevertheless, she chose to love him, and therefore she can choose to stop loving him.

'Wait until you have children of your own,' she says to him in one of her bitter moods. 'Then you will know.' What will he know? It is a formula she uses, a formula that sounds as if it comes from the old days. Perhaps it is what each generation says to the next, as a warning, as a threat. But he does not want to hear it. *Wait until you have children.* What nonsense, what a contradiction! How can a child have children? Anyway, what he would know if he were a father, if he were his own father, is precisely what he does not want to know. He will not accept the vision of the world that she wants to force upon him: a sober, disappointed, disillusioned vision.

Nineteen

Aunt Annie is dead. Despite the promises of the doctors, she never walked after her fall, not even with a stick. From her bed in the Volkshospitaal she was transferred to a bed in an old-age home in Stikland, in the back of beyond, where no one had the time to visit her and where she died alone. Now she is to be buried in Woltemade cemetery no. 3.

At first he refuses to go. He has to listen to enough prayers at school, he says, he does not want to hear more. He is vocal in his scorn for the tears that are going to be shed. Giving Aunt Annie a proper funeral is just a way for her relatives to make themselves feel good. She should be buried in a hole in the garden of the old-age home. It would save money.

In his heart he does not mean it. But he is compelled to say things like this to his mother; he needs to watch her face tighten in hurt and outrage. How much more must he say before she will at last round on him and tell him to be quiet?

He does not like to think of death. He would prefer it if, when people got old and sick, they simply stopped existing and disappeared. He does not like ugly old bodies; the thought of old people taking off their clothes makes him shudder. He hopes that the bath in their house in Plumstead has never had an old person in it.

His own death is a different matter. He is always somehow present after his death, floating above the spectacle, enjoying the grief of those who caused it and who, now that it is too late, wish he were still alive.

In the end, however, he does go with his mother to Aunt Annie's funeral. He goes because she pleads with him, and he likes being pleaded with, likes the feeling of power it gives; also because he has never been to a funeral and wants to see how deep they dig the grave, how a coffin is lowered into it.

It is not a grand funeral at all. There are only five mourners, and a young Dutch Reformed *dominee* with pimples. The five are Uncle Albert and his wife and son, and then his mother and himself. He has not seen Uncle Albert for years. He is bent almost double over his stick; tears stream from his pale-blue eyes; the wings of his collar stick out as though his tie has been knotted by other hands.

The hearse arrives. The undertaker and his assistant are in formal black, far more smartly dressed than any of them (he is in his St Joseph's school uniform: he possesses no suit). The *dominee* says a prayer in Afrikaans for the departed sister; then the hearse is reversed to the graveside and the coffin is slid out, onto poles over the grave. To his disappointment, it is not lowered into the grave – that must wait, it appears, for the graveyard workers – but discreetly the undertaker gestures that they may toss clods of earth on to it.

A light rain begins to fall. The business is over; they are free to go, free to return to their own lives.

On the path back to the gate, through acres of graves old and new, he walks behind his mother and her cousin, Albert's son, who talk together in low voices. They have the same plodding gait, he notices, the same way of lifting their legs and setting them down heavily, left then right, like peasants in clogs. The du Biels of Pomerania: peasants from the countryside, too slow and heavy for the city; out of place.

He thinks of Aunt Annie, whom they have abandoned here in the rain, in godforsaken Woltemade, thinks of the long black talons that the nurse in the hospital cut for her, that no one will cut any more.

'You know so much,' Aunt Annie once said to him. It was not praise: though her lips were pursed in a smile, she was shaking her head at the same time. 'So young and yet you know so much. How are you ever going to keep it all in your head?' And she leaned over and tapped his skull with a bony finger.

The boy is special, Aunt Annie told his mother, and his mother in turn told him. But what kind of special? No one ever says.

They have reached the gate. It is raining harder. Even before they can catch their two trains, the train to Salt River and then the train to Plumstead, they will have to trudge through the rain to Woltemade station.

The hearse passes them. His mother holds out a hand to stop it, speaks to the undertaker. 'They will give us a lift in to town,' she says.

So he has to climb into the hearse and sit crammed between his mother and the undertaker, cruising sedately down Voortrekker Road, hating her for it, hoping that no one from his school will see him.

'The lady was a schoolteacher, I believe,' says the undertaker. He speaks with a Scots accent. An immigrant: what can he know of South Africa, of people like Aunt Annie?

He has never seen a hairier man. Black hair sprouts from his nose and his ears, sticks out in tufts from his starched cuffs.

'Yes,' says his mother. 'She taught for over forty years.'

'Then she left some good behind,' says the undertaker. 'A noble profession, teaching.'

'What has happened to Aunt Annie's books?' he asks his mother later, when they are alone again. He says books, but he means *Ewige Genesing* in its many copies.

His mother does not know or will not say. From the flat where she broke her hip to the hospital to the old-age home in Stikland to Woltemade no. 3, no one has given a thought to the books except perhaps Aunt Annie herself, the books that no one will ever read; and now Aunt Annie is lying in the rain waiting for someone to find the time to bury her. He alone is left to do the thinking. How will he keep them all in his head, all the books, all the people, all the stories? And if he does not remember them, who will?

Youth

Wer den Dichter will verstehen
muß in Dichters Lande gehen.
– Goethe

One

He lives in a one-room flat near Mowbray railway station, for which he pays eleven guineas a month. On the last working day of each month he catches the train in to the city, to Loop Street, where A. & B. Levy, property agents, have their brass plate and tiny office. To Mr B. Levy, younger of the Levy brothers, he hands the envelope with the rent. Mr Levy pours the money out onto his cluttered desk and counts it. Grunting and sweating, he writes a receipt. 'Voilà, young man!' he says, and passes it over with a flourish.

He is at pains not to be late with the rent because he is in the flat under false pretences. When he signed the lease and paid A. & B. Levy the deposit, he gave his occupation not as 'Student' but as 'Library Assistant', with the university library as his work address.

It is not a lie, not entirely. From Monday to Friday it is his job to man the reading room during evening hours. It is a job that the regular librarians, women for the most part, prefer not to do because the campus, up on the mountainside, is too bleak and lonely at night. Even he feels a chill down his spine as he unlocks the back door and gropes his way down a pitch-dark corridor to the mains switch. It would be all too easy for some malefactor to hide in the stacks when the staff go home at five o'clock, then rifle the empty offices and wait in the dark to waylay him, the night assistant, for his keys.

Few students make use of the evening opening; few are even aware of it. There is little for him to do. The ten shillings per evening he earns is easy money.

Sometimes he imagines a beautiful girl in a white dress wandering into the reading room and lingering distractedly after closing time; he imagines showing her over the mysteries of the bindery and cataloguing room, then emerging with her into the starry night. It never happens.

Working in the library is not his only employment. On Wednesday afternoons he assists with first-year tutorials in the Mathematics Department (three pounds a week); on Fridays he conducts the diploma students in drama through selected comedies of Shakespeare (two pounds ten); and in the late afternoons he is employed by a cram school in Rondebosch to coach dummies for their Matriculation exams (three shillings an hour). During vacations he works for the Municipality (Division of Public Housing) extracting statistical data from household surveys. All in all, when he adds up the monies, he is comfortably off – comfortably enough to pay his rent and university fees and keep body and soul together and even save a little. He may only be nineteen but he is on his own feet, dependent on no one.

The needs of the body he treats as a matter of simple common sense. Every Sunday he boils up marrowbones and beans and celery to make a big pot of soup, enough to last the week. On Fridays he visits Salt River market for a box of apples or guavas or whatever fruit is in season. Every morning the milkman leaves a pint of milk on his doorstep. When he has a surplus of milk he hangs it over the sink in an old nylon stocking and turns it into cheese. For the rest he buys bread at the corner shop. It is a diet Rousseau would approve of, or Plato. As for clothes, he has a good jacket and trousers to wear to lectures. Otherwise he makes old clothes last.

He is proving something: that each man is an island; that you don't need parents.

Some evenings, trudging along the Main Road in raincoat and shorts and sandals, his hair plastered flat by the rain, lit up by the headlights of passing cars, he has a sense of how odd he looks. Not eccentric (there is some distinction in looking eccentric), just odd. He grinds his teeth in chagrin and walks faster.

He is slim and loose limbed, yet at the same time flabby. He would like to be attractive but he knows he is not. There is something essential he lacks, some definition of feature. Something of the baby still lingers in him. How long before he will cease to be a baby? What will cure him of babyhood, make him into a man?

What will cure him, if it were to arrive, will be love. He may not believe in God but he does believe in love and the powers of love. The beloved, the destined one, will see at once through the odd and even dull exterior he presents, to the fire that burns within. Meanwhile, being dull and odd-looking are part of a purgatory he must pass through in order to emerge, one day, into the light: the light of love, the light of art. For he will be an artist, that has long been settled. If for the time being he must be obscure and ridiculous, that is because it is the lot of the artist to suffer obscurity and ridicule until the day when he is revealed in his true powers and the scoffers and mockers fall silent.

His sandals cost two shillings and sixpence a pair. They are of rubber, and are made somewhere in Africa, Nyasaland perhaps. When they get wet they do not grip the sole of the foot. In the Cape winter it rains for weeks on end. Walking along the Main Road in the rain, he sometimes has to stop to recapture a sandal that has slipped free. At such moments he can see the fat burghers of Cape Town chuckling as they pass in the comfort of their cars. Laugh! he thinks. Soon I will be gone!

He has a best friend, Paul, who like him is studying mathematics. Paul is tall and dark and in the midst of an affair with an older woman, a woman named Elinor Laurier, small and blonde and beautiful in a quick, birdlike way. Paul complains about Elinor's unpredictable moods, about the demands she makes on him. Nevertheless, he is envious of Paul. If he had a beautiful, worldly wise mistress who smoked with a cigarette-holder and spoke French, he would soon be transformed, even transfigured, he is sure.

Elinor and her twin sister were born in England; they were brought to South Africa at the age of fifteen, after the War. Their mother, according to Paul, according to Elinor, used to play the girls off against each other, giving love and approval first to the one, then to the other, confusing them, keeping them dependent on her. Elinor, the stronger of the two, retained her sanity, though she still cries in her sleep and keeps a teddy bear in a drawer. Her sister, however, was for a while crazy enough to be locked up. She is still under therapy, as she struggles with the ghost of the dead old woman.

Elinor teaches in a language school in the city. Since taking up with her, Paul has been absorbed into her set, a set of artists and intellectuals who live in the Gardens, wear black sweaters and jeans and rope sandals, drink rough red wine and smoke Gauloises, quote Camus and García Lorca, listen to progressive jazz. One of them plays the Spanish guitar and can be persuaded to do an imitation of *cante hondo*. Not having proper jobs, they stay up all night and sleep until noon. They detest the Nationalists but are not political. If they had the money, they say, they would leave benighted South Africa and move for good to Montmartre or the Balearic Islands.

Paul and Elinor take him along to one of their get-togethers, held in a bungalow on Clifton beach. Elinor's sister, the unstable one he has been told about, is among the company. According to Paul, she is having an affair with the owner of the bungalow, a florid-faced man who writes for the *Cape Times*.

The sister's name is Jacqueline. She is taller than Elinor, not as fine-featured but beautiful nonetheless. She is full of nervous energy, chain-smokes, gesticulates when she talks. He gets on with her. She is less caustic than Elinor, for which he is relieved. Caustic people make him uneasy. He suspects they pass witticisms about him when his back is turned.

Jacqueline suggests a walk on the beach. Hand in hand (how did that happen?) in the moonlight, they stroll the length of the beach. In a secluded space among the rocks she turns to him, pouts, offers her lips.

He responds, but uneasily. Where will this lead? He has not made love to an older woman before. What if he is not up to standard?

It leads, he discovers, all the way. Unresisting he follows, does his best, goes through with the act, even pretends at the last to be carried away.

In fact he is not carried away. Not only is there the matter of the sand, which gets into everything, there is also the nagging question of why this woman, whom he has never met before, is giving herself to him. Is it credible that in the course of a casual conversation she detected the secret flame burning in him, the flame that marks him as an artist? Or is she simply a nymphomaniac, and was that what Paul, in his delicate way, was warning him about when he said she was 'under therapy'?

In sex he is not utterly unschooled. If the man has not enjoyed the lovemaking, then the woman will not have enjoyed it either – that he knows, that is one of the rules of sex. But what happens afterwards, between a man and a woman who have failed at the game? Are they bound to recall their failure whenever they meet again, and feel embarrassed?

It is late, the night is getting cold. In silence they dress and make their way back to the bungalow, where the party has begun to break up. Jacqueline gathers her shoes and bag. 'Goodnight,' she says to their host, giving him a peck on the cheek.

'You're off?' he says.

'Yes, I'm giving John a ride home.'

Their host is not at all disconcerted. 'Have a good time then,' he says. 'Both of you.'

Jacqueline is a nurse. He has not been with a nurse before, but received opinion is that, from working among the sick and dying and attending to their bodily needs, nurses grow cynical about morality. Medical students look forward to the time when they will do night shifts at the hospital. Nurses are starved for sex, they say. They fuck anywhere, anytime.

Jacqueline, however, is no ordinary nurse. She is a Guy's nurse, she is quick to inform him, trained in midwifery at Guy's Hospital in London. On the breast of her tunic, with its red shoulder-tabs, she wears a little bronze badge, a casque and gauntlet with the motto PER ARDUA. She works not at Groote Schuur, the public hospital, but at a private nursing home, where the pay is better.

Two days after the event on Clifton beach he calls at the nurses' residence. Jacqueline is waiting for him in the entrance hall, dressed to go out, and they leave without delay. From an upstairs window faces crane down to stare; he is aware of other nurses glancing at him inquisitively. He is too young, clearly too young, for a woman of thirty; and, in his drab clothes, without a car, plainly not much of a catch either.

Within a week Jacqueline has quit the nurses' residence and moved in with him in his flat. Looking back, he cannot remember inviting her: he has merely failed to resist.

He has never lived with anyone before, certainly not with a woman, a mistress. Even as a child he had a room of his own with a door that locked. The Mowbray flat consists of a single long room, with an entryway off which lead a kitchen and a bathroom. How is he going to survive?

He tries to be welcoming to his sudden new companion, tries to make space for her. But within days he has begun to resent the clutter of boxes and suitcases, the clothes scattered everywhere, the mess in the bathroom. He dreads the rattle of the motor scooter that signals Jacqueline's return from the day shift. Though they still make love, there is more and more silence between them, he sitting at his desk pretending to be absorbed in his books, she mooning around, ignored, sighing, smoking one cigarette after another.

She sighs a great deal. That is the way her neurosis expresses itself, if that is what it is, neurosis: in sighing and feeling exhausted and sometimes crying soundlessly. The energy and laughter and boldness of their first meeting have dwindled to nothing. The gaiety of that night was a mere break in the cloud of gloom, it would seem, an effect of alcohol or perhaps even an act Jacqueline was putting on.

They sleep together in a bed built for one. In bed Jacqueline talks on and on about men who have used her, about therapists who have tried to take over her mind and turn her into their puppet. Is he one of those men, he wonders? Is he using her? And is there some other man to whom she complains about him? He falls asleep with her still talking, wakes up in the morning haggard.

Jacqueline is, by any standards, an attractive woman, more attractive, more sophisticated, more worldly wise than he deserves. The frank truth is that, were it not for the rivalry between the twin sisters, she would not be sharing his bed. He is a pawn in a game the two of them are playing, a game that long antedates his appearance on the scene – he has no illusions about that. Nevertheless, he is the one who has been favoured, he should not question his fortune. Here he is sharing a flat with a woman ten years older than he, a woman of experience who, during her stint at Guy's Hospital, slept (she says) with Englishmen, Frenchmen, Italians, even a Persian. If he cannot claim to be loved for himself, at least he has a chance to broaden his education in the realm of the erotic.

Such are his hopes. But after a twelve-hour shift at the nursing home followed by a supper of cauliflower in white sauce followed by an evening of moody silence, Jacqueline is not inclined to be generous with herself. If she embraces him she does so perfunctorily, since if it is not for the sake of sex that two strangers have penned themselves up together in such a cramped and comfortless living-space, then what reason have they for being there at all?

It all comes to a head when, while he is out of the flat, Jacqueline searches out his diary and reads what he has written about their life together. He returns to find her packing her belongings.

'What is going on?' he asks.

Tight-lipped, she points to the diary lying open on his desk.

He flares up in anger. 'You are not going to stop me from writing!' he vows. It is a non sequitur, and he knows it.

She is angry too, but in a colder, deeper way. 'If, as you say, you find me such an unspeakable burden,' she says, 'if I am destroying your peace and privacy and your ability to write, let me tell you from my side that I have hated living with you, hated every minute of it, and can't wait to be free.'

What he should have said was that one should not read other people's private papers. In fact, he should have hidden his diary away, not left it where it could be found. But it is too late now, the damage is done.

He watches while Jacqueline packs, helps her strap her bag on the pillion of her scooter. 'I'll keep the key, *with your permission*, until I have fetched the rest of my stuff,' she says. She snaps on her helmet. 'Goodbye. I'm really disappointed in you, John. You may be very clever — I wouldn't know about that — but you have a lot of growing up to do.' She kicks the starter pedal. The engine will not catch. Again she kicks it, and again. A smell of petrol rises in the air. The carburettor is flooded; there is nothing to do but wait for it to dry out. 'Come inside,' he suggests. Stony-faced, she refuses. 'I'm sorry,' he says. 'About everything.'

He goes indoors, leaving her in the alley. Five minutes later he hears the engine start and the scooter roar off.

Is he sorry? Certainly he is sorry Jacqueline read what she read. But the real question is, what was his motive for writing what he wrote? Did he perhaps write it in order that she should read it? Was leaving his true thoughts lying around where she was bound to find them his way of telling her what he was too cowardly to say to her face? What are his true thoughts anyway? Some days he feels happy, even privileged, to be living with a beautiful woman, or at least not to be living alone. On other days he feels differently. Is the truth the happiness, the unhappiness, or the average of the two?

The question of what should be permitted to go into his diary and what kept forever shrouded goes to the heart of all his writing. If he is to censor himself from expressing ignoble emotions – resentment at having his flat invaded, or shame at his own failures as a lover – how will those emotions ever be transfigured and turned into poetry? And if poetry is not to be the agency of his transfiguration from ignoble to noble, why bother with poetry at all? Besides, who is to say that the feelings he writes in his diary are his true feelings? Who is to say that at each moment while the pen moves he is truly himself? At one moment he might truly be himself, at another he might simply be making things up. How can he know for sure? Why should he even *want* to know for sure?

Things are rarely as they seem: that is what he should have said to Jacqueline. Yet what chance is there she would understand? How could she believe that what she read in his diary was not the truth, the ignoble truth, about what was going on in the mind of her companion during those heavy evenings of silence and sighings but on the contrary a fiction, one of many possible fictions, true only in the sense that a work of art is true – true to itself, true to its own immanent aims – when the ignoble reading conformed so closely to her own suspicion that her companion did not love her, did not even like her?

Jacqueline will not believe him, for the simple reason that he does not believe himself. He does not know what he believes. Sometimes he thinks he does not believe anything. But when all is said and done, the fact remains that his first try at living with a woman has ended in failure, in ignominy. He must return to living by himself; and there will be no little relief in that. Yet he cannot live alone for ever. Having mistresses is part of an artist's life: even if he steers clear of the trap of marriage, as he has vowed to do, he is going to have to find a way of living with women. Art cannot be fed on deprivation alone, on longing, loneliness. There must be intimacy, passion, love.

Picasso, who is a great artist, perhaps the greatest of all, is a living example. Picasso falls in love with women, one after another. One after another they move in with him, share his life, model for him. Out of the passion that flares up anew with each new mistress, the Doras and Pilars whom chance brings to his doorstep are reborn into everlasting art. That is how it is done. What of him? Can he promise that the women in his own life, not only Jacqueline but all the unimaginable women to come, will have a similar destiny? He would like to believe so, but he has his doubts. Whether he will turn out to be a great artist only time will tell, but one thing is sure, he is no Picasso. His whole sensibility is different from Picasso's. He is quieter, gloomier, more northern. Nor does he have Picasso's hypnotic black eyes. If ever he tries to transfigure a woman, he will not transfigure her as cruelly as Picasso does, bending and twisting her body like metal in a fiery furnace. Writers are not like painters anyway: they are more dogged, more subtle.

Is such the fate of all women who become mixed up with artists: to have their worst or their best extracted and worked into fiction? He thinks of Hélène in *War and Peace*. Did Hélène start off as one of Tolstoy's mistresses? Did she ever guess that, long after she was gone, men who had never laid eyes on her would lust after her beautiful bare shoulders?

Must it all be so cruel? Surely there is a form of cohabitation in which man and woman eat together, sleep together, live together, yet remain immersed in their respective inward explorations. Is that why the affair with Jacqueline was doomed to fail: because, not being an artist herself, Jacqueline could not appreciate the artist's need for inner solitude? If Jacqueline had been a sculptress, for instance, if one corner of the flat had been set aside for her to chip away at her marble while in another corner he wrestled with words and rhymes, would love have flourished between them? Is that the moral of the story of himself and Jacqueline: that it is best for artists to have affairs only with artists?

Two

The affair with Jacqueline is consigned to the past. After weeks of smothering intimacy he has a room of his own again. He piles Jacqueline's boxes and suitcases in a corner and waits for them to be fetched. It does not happen. Instead, one evening, Jacqueline herself reappears. She has come, she says, not to resume residence with him ('You are impossible to live with') but to patch up a peace ('I don't like bad blood, it depresses me'), a peace that entails first going to bed with him, then, in bed, haranguing him about what he said about her in his diary. On and on she goes: they do not get to sleep until two in the morning.

He wakes up late, too late for his eight o'clock lecture. It is not the first lecture he has missed since Jacqueline entered his life. He is falling behind in his studies and does not see how he will ever catch up. In his first two years at the university he had been one of the stars of the class. He found everything easy, was always a step ahead of the lecturer. But of late a fog seems to have descended on his mind. The mathematics they are studying has become more modern and abstract, and he has begun to flounder. Line by line he can still follow the exposition on the blackboard, but more often than not the larger argument eludes him. He has fits of panic in class which he does his best to hide.

Strangely, he seems to be the only one afflicted. Even the plodders among his fellow students have no more trouble than usual. While his marks fall month by month, theirs remain steady. As for the stars, the real stars, they have simply left him struggling in their wake.

Never in his life has he had to call on his utmost powers. Less than his best has always been good enough. Now he is in a fight for his life. Unless he throws himself wholly into his work, he is going to sink.

Yet whole days pass in a fog of grey exhaustion. He curses himself for letting himself be sucked back into an affair that costs him so much. If this is what having a mistress entails, how do Picasso and the others get by? He simply has not the energy to run from lecture to lecture, job to job, then when the day is done turn his attention to a woman who veers between euphoria and spells of the blackest gloom in which she thrashes around, brooding on a lifetime's grudges.

Although no longer formally living with him, Jacqueline feels free to arrive on his doorstep at all hours of the night and day. Sometimes she comes to denounce him for some word or other he let slip whose veiled meaning has only now become clear to her. Sometimes she is simply feeling low and wants to be cheered up. Worst are the days after therapy, when she rehearses over and over again what passed in her therapist's consulting room, picking over the implications of his tiniest gesture. She sighs and weeps, gulps down glass after glass of wine, goes dead in the middle of sex.

'You should have therapy yourself,' she tells him, blowing smoke.

'I'll think about it,' he replies. He knows enough, by now, not to disagree.

In fact he would not dream of going into therapy. The goal of therapy is to make one happy. What is the point of that? Happy people are not interesting. Better to accept the burden of unhappiness and try to turn it into something worthwhile, poetry or music or painting: that is what he believes.

Nevertheless, he listens to Jacqueline as patiently as he can. He is the man, she is the woman; he has had his pleasure of her, now he must pay the price: that seems to be the way affairs work.

Her story, spoken night after night in overlapping and conflicting versions into his sleep-befuddled ear, is that she has been robbed of her true self by a persecutor who is sometimes her tyrannical mother, sometimes her runaway father, sometimes one or other sadistic lover, sometimes a Mephistophelean therapist. What he holds in his arms, she says, is only

154

a shell of her true self; she will recover the power to love only when she has recovered her self.

He listens but does not believe. If she feels her therapist has designs on her, why not give up seeing him? If her sister disparages and belittles her, why not stop seeing her sister? As for himself, he suspects that if Jacqueline has come to treat him more as a confidant than as a lover, that is because he is not a good enough lover, not fiery or passionate enough. He suspects that if he were more of a lover Jacqueline would soon recover her missing self and her missing desire.

Why does he keep opening the door to her knock? Is it because this is what artists have to do — stay up all night, exhaust themselves, get their lives into a tangle — or is it because, despite all, he is bemused by this sleek, undeniably handsome woman who feels no shame in wandering around the flat naked under his gaze?

Why is she so free in his presence? Is it to taunt him (for she can feel his eyes upon her, he knows that), or do all nurses behave like this in private, dropping their clothes, scratching themselves, talking matter-of-factly about excretion, telling the same gross jokes that men tell in bars? Yet if she has indeed freed herself of all inhibitions, why is her lovemaking so distracted, so offhand, so disappointing?

It was not his idea to begin the affair nor his idea to continue it. But now that he is in the middle of it he has not the energy to escape. A fatalism has taken him over. If life with Jacqueline is a kind of sickness, let the sickness take its course.

He and Paul are gentlemen enough not to compare notes on their mistresses. Nevertheless he suspects that Jacqueline Laurier discusses him with her sister and her sister reports back to Paul. It embarrasses him that Paul should know what goes on in his intimate life. He is sure that, of the two of them, Paul handles women more capably.

One evening when Jacqueline is working the night shift at the nursing home, he drops by at Paul's flat. He finds Paul preparing to set off for his mother's house in St James, to spend the weekend. Why does he not come along, suggests Paul, for the Saturday at least?

They miss the last train, by a hair's breadth. If they still want to go to

St James, they will have to walk the whole twelve miles. It is a fine evening. Why not?

Paul carries his rucksack and his violin. He is bringing the violin along, he says, because it is easier to practise in St James where the neighbours are not so close.

Paul has studied the violin since childhood but has never got very far with it. He seems quite content to play the same little gigues and minuets as a decade ago. His own ambitions as a musician are far larger. In his flat he has the piano that his mother bought when at the age of fifteen he began to demand piano lessons. The lessons were not a success, he was too impatient with the slow, step-by-step methods of his teacher. Nevertheless, he is determined that one day he will play, however badly, Beethoven's opus 111, and, after that, the Busoni transcription of Bach's D minor Chaconne. He will arrive at these goals without making the usual detour through Czerny and Mozart. Instead he will practise these two pieces and them alone, unremittingly, first learning the notes by playing them very, very slowly, then pushing up the tempo day by day, for as long as is required. It is his own method of learning the piano, invented by himself. As long as he follows his schedule without wavering he can see no reason why it should not work.

What he is discovering, unfortunately, is that as he tries to progress from very, very slow to merely very slow, his wrists grow tense and lock, his finger-joints stiffen, and soon he cannot play at all. Then he flies into a rage, hammers his fists on the keys, and storms off in despair.

It is past midnight and he and Paul are no further than Wynberg. The traffic has died away, the Main Road is empty save for a street sweeper pushing his broom.

In Diep River they are passed by a milkman in his horse-drawn cart. They pause to watch as he reins in his horse, lopes up a garden path, sets down two full bottles, picks up the empties, shakes out the coins, lopes back to his cart.

'Can we buy a pint?' says Paul, and hands over fourpence. Smiling, the milkman watches while they drink. The milkman is young and hand-some and bursting with energy. Even the big white horse with the shaggy hooves does not seem to mind being up in the middle of the night.

He marvels. All the business he knew nothing about, being carried on while people sleep: streets being swept, milk being delivered on doorsteps! But one thing puzzles him. Why is the milk not stolen? Why are there not thieves who follow in the milkman's footsteps and filch each bottle he sets down? In a land where property is crime and anything and everything can be stolen, what renders milk exempt? The fact that stealing milk is too easy? Are there standards of conduct even among thieves? Or do thieves take pity on milkmen, who are for the most part young and black and powerless?

He would like to believe this last explanation. He would like to believe that, with regard to black people, there is enough pity around, enough of a longing to deal honourably with them, to make up for the cruelty of the laws and the misery of their lot. But he knows it is not so. Between black and white there is a gulf fixed. Deeper than pity, deeper than honourable dealings, deeper even than goodwill, lies an awareness on both sides that people like Paul and himself, with their pianos and violins, are here on this earth, the earth of South Africa, on the shakiest of pretexts. Even this young milkman, who a year ago must have been just a boy herding cattle in the deepest Transkei, must know it. In fact, from Africans in general, even from Coloured people, he feels a curious, amused tenderness emanating: a sense that he must be a simpleton, in need of protection, if he imagines he can get by on the basis of straight looks and honourable dealings when the ground beneath his feet is soaked with blood and the vast backward depth of history rings with shouts of anger. Why else would this young man, with the first stirrings of the day's wind fingering his horse's mane, smile so gently as he watches the two of them drink the milk he has given them?

They arrive at the house in St James as dawn is breaking. He falls asleep at once on a sofa, and sleeps until noon, when Paul's mother wakes them and serves breakfast on a sun porch with a view over the whole sweep of False Bay.

Between Paul and his mother there is a flow of conversation in which he is easily included. His mother is a photographer with a studio of her own. She is petite and well-dressed, with a smoker's husky voice and a restless air. After they have eaten she excuses herself: she has work to do, she says.

He and Paul walk down to the beach, swim, come back, play chess. Then he catches a train home. It is his first glimpse of Paul's home life, and he is full of envy. Why can he not have a nice, normal relationship with his own mother? He wishes his mother were like Paul's, wishes she had a life of her own outside their narrow family.

It was to escape the oppressiveness of family that he left home. Now he rarely sees his parents. Though they live only a short walk away, he does not visit. He has never brought Paul to see them, or any of his other friends, to say nothing of Jacqueline. Now that he has his own income, he uses his independence to exclude his parents from his life. His mother is distressed by his coldness, he knows, the coldness with which he has responded to her love all his life. All his life she has wanted to coddle him; all his life he has been resisting. Even though he insists, she cannot believe he has enough money to live on. Whenever she sees him she tries to slip money into his pocket, a pound note, two pounds. 'Just a little something,' she calls it. Given half a chance, she would sew curtains for his flat, take in his laundry. He must harden his heart against her. Now is not the time to let down his guard.

Three

He is reading *The Letters of Ezra Pound*. Ezra Pound was dismissed from his job at Wabash College, Indiana, for having a woman in his rooms. Infuriated by such provincial smallmindedness, Pound quit America. In London he met and married the beautiful Dorothy Shakespear, and went to live in Italy. After World War II he was accused of aiding and abetting the Fascists. To escape the death sentence he pleaded insanity and was locked up in a mental asylum.

Now, in 1959, having been set free, Pound is back in Italy, still working on his life's project, the *Cantos*. All of the *Cantos* that have been published thus far are in the University of Cape Town library, in Faber editions in which the procession of lines in elegant dark typeface is interrupted now and again, like strokes of a gong, by huge Chinese characters. He is engrossed by the *Cantos*; he reads and rereads them (guiltily skipping the dull sections on Van Buren and the Malatestas), using Hugh Kenner's book on Pound as a guide. T. S. Eliot magnanimously called Pound *il miglior fabbro*, the better craftsman. Much as he admires Eliot's own work, he thinks Eliot is right.

Ezra Pound has suffered persecution most of his life: driven into exile, then imprisoned, then expelled from his homeland a second time. Yet despite being labelled a madman Pound has proved he is a great poet, perhaps as great as Walt Whitman. Obeying his daimon, Pound has sacrificed his life to his art. So has Eliot, though Eliot's suffering has been of a more private nature. Eliot and Pound have lived lives of sorrow and sometimes of ignominy. There is a lesson for him in that, driven home on every page of their poetry – of Eliot's, with which he had his first overwhelming encounter while he was still at school, and now of Pound's. Like Pound and Eliot, he must be prepared to endure all that life has stored up for him, even if that means exile, obscure labour, and obloquy. And if he fails the highest test of art, if it turns out that after all he does not have the blessed gift, then he must be prepared to endure that too: the incontestable verdict of history, the fate of being, despite all his present and future sufferings, minor. Many are called, few are chosen. For every major poet a cloud of minor poets, like gnats buzzing around a lion.

His passion for Pound is shared by only one of his friends, Norbert. Norbert was born in Czechoslovakia, came to South Africa after the War, and speaks English with a faint German lisp. He is studying to be an engineer, like his father. He dresses with elegant European formality and is conducting a highly respectable courtship of a beautiful girl of good family with whom he goes walking once a week. He and Norbert have meetings in a tea room on the slopes of the mountain at which they comment on each other's latest poems and read aloud to each other favourite passages from Pound.

It strikes him as interesting that Norbert, an engineer to be, and he, a mathematician to be, should be disciples of Ezra Pound, while the other student poets he knows, those studying literature and running the university's literary magazine, follow Gerard Manley Hopkins. He himself went through a brief Hopkins phase at school, during which he crammed lots of stressed monosyllables into his verses and avoided words of Romance origin. But in time he lost his taste for Hopkins, just as he is in the process of losing his taste for Shakespeare. Hopkins's lines are packed too tight with consonants, Shakespeare's too tight with metaphors. Hopkins and Shakespeare also set too much store on uncommon words, particularly Old English words: *maw*, *reck*, *pelf*. He does not see why verse has always to be rising to a declamatory pitch, why it cannot be content to follow the flexions of the ordinary speaking voice – in fact, why it has to be so different from prose.

He has begun to prefer Pope to Shakespeare, and Swift to Pope. Despite the cruel precision of his phrasing, of which he approves, Pope strikes him as still too much at home among petticoats and periwigs, whereas Swift remains a wild man, a solitary.

He likes Chaucer too. The Middle Ages are boring, obsessed with chastity, overrun with clerics; medieval poets are for the most part timid, for ever scuttling to the Latin fathers for guidance. But Chaucer keeps a nice ironic distance from his authorities. And, unlike Shakespeare, he does not get into a froth about things and start ranting.

As for the other English poets, Pound has taught him to smell out the easy sentiment in which the Romantics and Victorians wallow, to say nothing of their slack versifying. Pound and Eliot are trying to revitalize Anglo-American poetry by bringing back to it the astringency of the French. He is fully in accord. How he could once have been so infatuated with Keats as to write Keatsian sonnets he cannot comprehend. Keats is like watermelon, soft and sweet and crimson, whereas poetry should be hard and clear like a flame. Reading half a dozen pages of Keats is like yielding to seduction.

He would be more secure in his discipleship to Pound if he could actually read French. But all his efforts to teach himself lead nowhere. He has no feel for the language, with its words that start out boldly only to tail off in a murmur. So he must take it on trust from Pound and Eliot that Baudelaire and Nerval, Corbière and Laforgue, point the way he must follow.

His plan, when he entered the university, was to qualify as a mathematician, then go abroad and devote himself to art. That is as far as the plan went, as far as it needed to go, and he has not thus far deviated from it. While perfecting his poetic skills abroad he will earn a living doing something obscure and respectable. Since great artists are fated to go unrecognized for a while, he imagines he will serve out his probationary years as a clerk humbly adding up columns of figures in a back room. He will certainly not be a Bohemian, that is to say, a drunk and a sponger and a layabout.

What draws him to mathematics, besides the arcane symbols it uses, is its purity. If there were a department of Pure Thought at the university he would probably enrol in Pure Thought too; but pure mathematics appears to be the closest approach the academy affords to the realm of the forms.

There is, unfortunately, an obstacle to his plan of study: regulations do not permit one to study pure mathematics to the exclusion of everything else. Most of the students in his class do a mix of pure mathematics, applied mathematics, and physics. This is not a direction he finds himself able to follow. Though as a child he had a desultory interest in rocketry and nuclear fission, he has no feel for what is called the real world, fails to understand why things in physics are as they are. Why, for instance, does a bouncing ball eventually stop bouncing? His fellow students have no difficulty with the question: because its coefficient of elasticity is less than one, they say. But why does it have to be so, he asks? Why can the coefficient not be exactly one, or more than one? They shrug their shoulders. We live in the real world, they say: in the real world the coefficient of elasticity is always less than one. It does not sound to him like an answer.

Since he would appear to have no sympathy with the real world, he avoids the sciences, filling in the empty slots in his curriculum with courses in English, philosophy, classical studies. He would like to be thought of as a mathematics student who happens to take a few arts courses; but among the science students he is, to his chagrin, viewed as an outsider, a dilettante who turns up for mathematics lectures and then disappears, God knows where.

Since he is going to be a mathematician, he ought to spend most of his time on mathematics. But mathematics is easy, whereas Latin is not. Latin is his weakest subject. Years of drilling at his Catholic school have embedded in him the logic of Latin syntax; he can write correct if plodding Ciceronian prose; but Virgil and Horace, with their haphazard word order and rebarbative word-stock, continue to baffle him.

He is assigned to a Latin tutorial group in which most of the other students take Greek as well. Knowing Greek makes Latin easy for them; he has to struggle to keep up, not to make a fool of himself. He wishes he had gone to a school that taught Greek.

One of the attractions of mathematics is that it uses the Greek alphabet. Though he knows no Greek words beyond *hubris* and *areté* and *eleutheria*, he spends hours perfecting his Greek script, pressing harder on the downstrokes to give the effect of a Bodoni typeface.

Greek and pure mathematics are in his eyes the noblest subjects one can study at a university. From afar he reveres the lecturers in Greek, whose courses he cannot take: Anton Paap, papyrologist; Maurice Pope, translator of Sophocles; Maurits Heemstra, commentator on Heraclitus. Together with Douglas Sears, Professor of Pure Mathematics, they inhabit an exalted realm.

Despite his best efforts, his marks for Latin are never high. It is Roman history that brings him down every time. The lecturer assigned to teach Roman history is a pale, unhappy young Englishman whose real interest is *Digenis Akritas*. The law students, taking Latin under compulsion, sense his weakness and torment him. They come in late and leave early; they throw paper aeroplanes; they whisper loudly while he is talking; when he produces one of his limp witticisms they laugh raucously and drum with their feet and will not stop.

The truth is, he is as bored as the law students, and perhaps their lecturer too, by fluctuations in the price of wheat during the reign of Commodus. Without facts there is no history, and he has never had a head for facts: when examinations come around and he is invited to offer his thoughts on what caused what in the late Empire, he stares at the blank page in misery.

They read Tacitus in translation: dry recitals of the crimes and excesses of the emperors in which only the puzzling hurry of sentence after sentence hints at irony. If he is going to be a poet he ought to be taking lessons from Catullus, poet of love, whom they are translating in tutorials; but it is Tacitus the historian, whose Latin is so difficult that he cannot follow it in the original, who truly grips him.

Following Pound's recommendation he has read Flaubert, first *Madame Bovary*, then *Salammbô*, Flaubert's novel of ancient Carthage. Sternly he has refrained from reading Victor Hugo. Hugo is a windbag, says Pound, whereas Flaubert brings to the writing of prose the hard, jeweller's craft of poetry. Out of Flaubert come first Henry James, then Conrad and Ford Madox Ford.

He likes Flaubert. Emma Bovary in particular, with her dark eyes, her restless sensuality, her readiness to give herself, has him in her thrall. He would like to go to bed with Emma, hear the famous belt whistle like a snake as she undresses. But would Pound approve? He is not sure that itching to meet Emma is a good enough reason for admiring Flaubert. In his sensibility there is still, he suspects, something rotten, something Keatsian.

Of course Emma Bovary is a fictional creation, he will never run into her in the street. But Emma was not created out of nothing: she had her origin in the flesh and blood experiences of her author, experiences that were then subjected to the transfiguring fire of art. If Emma had an original, or several originals, then it follows that women like Emma and Emma's original should exist in the real world. And even if this is not so, even if no woman in the real world is quite like Emma, there must be many women so deeply affected by their reading of *Madame Bovary* that they fall under Emma's spell and are transformed into versions of her. They may not be the real Emma but in a sense they have become her living embodiment.

His ambition is to read everything worth reading before he goes overseas, so that he will not arrive in Europe a provincial bumpkin. As guides to reading he relies upon Eliot and Pound. On their authority he dismisses without a glance shelf after shelf of Scott, Dickens, Thackeray, Trollope, Meredith. Nor is anything that comes out of nineteenth-century Germany or Italy or Spain or Scandinavia worthy of attention. Russia may have produced some interesting monsters, but as artists the Russians have nothing to teach us. Civilization since the eighteenth century has been an Anglo-French affair.

On the other hand, there are pockets of high civilization in remoter times that one cannot afford to neglect: not only Athens and Rome but also the Germany of Walther von der Vogelweide, the Provence of Arnaut Daniel, the Florence of Dante and Guido Cavalcanti, to say nothing of Tang China and Moghul India and Almoravid Spain. So unless he learns Chinese and Persian and Arabic, or at least enough of the languages to read their classics with a crib, he might as well be a barbarian. Where will he find the time?

*

In his English courses he did not at first fare well. His tutor in literature was a young Welshman named Mr Jones. Mr Jones was new to South Africa; this was his first proper job. The law students, enrolled only because English, like Latin, was a required subject, had sniffed out his uncertainty at once: they yawned in his face, played stupid, parodied his speech, until sometimes he grew visibly desperate.

Their first tutorial assignment was to write a critical analysis of a poem by Andrew Marvell. Though not sure what exactly was meant by critical analysis, he did his best. Mr Jones gave him a gamma. Gamma was not the lowest mark on the scale – there was still gamma-minus, to say nothing of the varieties of delta – but it was not good. Numbers of students, including law students, were awarded betas; there was even a solitary alpha-minus. Indifferent to poetry though they might be, there was something these classmates of his knew that he did not. But what was it? How did one get to be good at English?

Mr Jones, Mr Bryant, Miss Wilkinson: all his teachers were young and, it seemed to him, helpless, suffering the persecutions of the law students in helpless silence, hoping against hope that they would grow tired and relent. For his part, he felt little sympathy for their plight. What he wanted from his teachers was authority, not revelations of vulnerability.

In the three years since Mr Jones, his marks for English have slowly crept up. But he has never been at the top of the class, has always, in a certain sense, been struggling, unsure of what the study of literature ought to be. Compared with literary criticism, the philological side of English studies has been a relief. At least, with Old English verb conjugations or sound changes in Middle English, one knows where one is.

Now, in his fourth year, he has enrolled for a course in early English prose writers taught by Professor Guy Howarth. He is the only student. Howarth has a reputation for being dry, pedantic, but he does not mind that. He has nothing against pedants. He prefers them to showmen.

They meet once a week in Howarth's office. Howarth reads his lecture aloud while he takes notes. After a few meetings Howarth simply lends him the text of the lecture to take home and read.

The lectures, which are typed in faint ribbon on crisp, yellowing paper, come out of a cabinet in which there seems to be a file on every

English-language author from Austen to Yeats. Is that what one has to do to become a professor of English: read the canonical authors and write a lecture on each? How many years of one's life will that eat up? And what will it do to one's spirit?

Howarth, who is an Australian, seems to have taken a liking to him, he cannot see why. For his part, though he cannot say he likes Howarth, he does feel protective of him for his gaucherie, for his delusion that South African students care in the least what his opinion is of Gascoigne or Lyly or for that matter Shakespeare.

On the last day of term, after their final session together, Howarth issues an invitation. 'Come by the house tomorrow evening for a drink.'

He obeys, but with a sinking heart. Beyond their exchanges on the Elizabethan prosaists, he has nothing to say to Howarth. In addition, he does not like drinking. Even wine, after the first sip, tastes sour to him, sour and heavy and unpleasant. He cannot see why people pretend to enjoy it.

They sit in the dim, high-ceilinged living room of the Howarths' home in the Gardens. He appears to be the only one invited. Howarth talks about Australian poetry, about Kenneth Slessor and A. D. Hope. Mrs Howarth breezes in, breezes out. He senses that she does not like him, finds him a prig, lacking in *joie de vivre*, lacking in repartee. Lilian Howarth is Howarth's second wife. No doubt she was a beauty in her day, but now she is simply a squat little woman with spindly legs and too much powder on her face. She is also, according to report, a lush, given to embarrassing scenes when drunk.

It emerges that he has been invited for a purpose. The Howarths are going abroad for six months. Would he be prepared to stay in their house and look after it? There will be no rent to pay, no bills, few responsibilities.

He accepts on the spot. He is flattered to be asked, even if it is only because he seems dull and dependable. Also, if he gives up his flat in Mowbray, he can save more quickly towards a boat ticket to England. And the house – a huge, rambling pile on the lower slopes of the mountain with dark passages and musty, unused rooms – has an allure of its own.

There is one catch. For the first month he will have to share the house with guests of the Howarths, a woman from New Zealand and her three-year-old daughter.

The woman from New Zealand turns out to be another drinker. Shortly after he has moved in, she wanders into his room in the middle of the night and into his bed. She embraces him, presses against him, gives him wet kisses. He does not know what to do. He does not like her, does not desire her, is repelled by her slack lips seeking out his mouth. First a cold shiver runs through him, then panic. 'No!' he cries out. 'Go away!' And he curls himself up in a ball.

Unsteadily she clambers out of his bed. 'Bastard!' she hisses, and is gone.

They continue to share the big house until the end of the month, avoiding each other, listening for the creak of a floorboard, averting their gaze when their paths happen to cross. They have made fools of themselves, but at least she was a reckless fool, which is forgivable, while he was a prude and a dummy.

He has never been drunk in his life. He abhors drunkenness. He leaves parties early to escape the stumbling, inane talk of people who have drunk too much. In his opinion, drunken drivers ought to have their sentences doubled instead of halved. But in South Africa every excess committed under the influence of liquor is looked on indulgently. Farmers can flog their labourers to death as long as they are drunk when they do so. Ugly men can force themselves on women, ugly women make overtures to men; if one resists, one is not playing the game.

He has read Henry Miller. If a drunken woman had slipped into bed with Henry Miller, the fucking and no doubt the drinking would have gone on all night. Were Henry Miller merely a satyr, a monster of indiscriminate appetite, he could be ignored. But Henry Miller is an artist, and his stories, outrageous though they may be and probably full of lies, are stories of an artist's life. Henry Miller writes about the Paris of the 1930s, a city of artists and women who loved artists. If women threw themselves at Henry Miller, then, *mutatis mutandis*, they must have thrown themselves at Ezra Pound and Ford Madox Ford and Ernest Hemingway and all the other great artists who lived in Paris in those years, to say nothing of Pablo Picasso. What is *he* going to do once he is in Paris or London? Is he going to persist in not playing the game?

Besides his horror of drunkenness he has a horror of physical ugliness. When he reads Villon's *Testament*, he can think only of how ugly the *belle heaumière* sounds, wrinkled and unwashed and foulmouthed. If one is to be an artist, must one love women indiscriminately? Does an artist's life entail sleeping with anyone and everyone, in the name of life? If one is finicky about sex, is one rejecting life?

Another question: What made Marie, from New Zealand, decide he was worth getting into bed with? Was it simply because he was there, or had she heard from Howarth that he was a poet, a poet to be? Women love artists because they burn with an inner flame, a flame that consumes yet paradoxically renews all that it touches. When she slipped into his bed, Marie might perhaps have thought she would be licked by the flame of art, and experience an ecstasy beyond words. Instead she found herself being pushed away by a panic-stricken boy. Surely, one way or another, she will have her revenge. Surely, in the next letter from her, her friends the Howarths will get a version of events in which he will come out looking like a nincompoop.

He knows that to condemn a woman for being ugly is morally despicable. But fortunately, artists do not have to be morally admirable people. All that matters is that they create great art. If his own art is to come out of the more contemptible side of himself, so be it. Flowers grow best on dungheaps, as Shakespeare never tires of saying. Even Henry Miller, who presents himself as such a straightforward fellow, ready to make love to any woman no matter her shape or size, probably has a dark side which he is prudent enough to conceal.

Normal people find it hard to be bad. Normal people, when they feel badness flare up within them, drink, swear, commit violence. Badness is to them like a fever: they want it out of their system, they want to go back to being normal. But artists have to live with their fever, whatever its nature, good or bad. The fever is what makes them into artists; the fever must be kept alive. That is why artists can never be wholly present to the world: one eye has always to be turned inward. As for women who flock after artists, they cannot wholly be trusted. For just as the spirit of the artist is both flame and fever, so the woman who yearns to be licked by tongues of flame will at the same time do her best to quench the fever and bring down the artist to common ground. Therefore women have to be resisted even when they are loved. They cannot be allowed close enough to the flame to nip it out.

Four

In a perfect world he would sleep only with perfect women, women of perfect femininity yet with a certain darkness at their core that will respond to his own darker self. But he knows no such women. Jacqueline – any darkness at whose core he has failed to detect – has without warning ceased visiting him, and he has had the good sense not to try to find out why. So he has to make do with other women – in fact with girls who are not yet women and may have no authentic core at all, or none to speak of: girls who sleep with a man only reluctantly, because they have been talked into it or because their friends are doing it and they don't want to be left behind or because it is sometimes the only way to hold on to a boyfriend.

He gets one of them pregnant. When she telephones to break the news, he is astonished, floored. How could he have got someone pregnant? In a certain sense he knows exactly how. An accident: haste, confusion, a mess of the kind that never finds its way into the novels he reads. Yet at the same time he cannot believe it. In his heart he does not feel himself to be more than eight years old, ten at the most. How can a child be a father?

Perhaps it is not true, he tells himself. Perhaps it is like one of those exams you are sure you have failed, yet when the results come out you have not done badly after all.

But it does not work like that. Another telephone call. In matter-of-fact tones the girl reports that she has seen a doctor. There is the tiniest pause, long enough for him to accept the opening and speak. 'I will stand by you,' he could say. 'Leave it all to me,' he could say. But how can he say he will stand by her when what *standing by her* will mean in reality fills him with foreboding, when his whole impulse is to drop the telephone and run away?

The pause comes to an end. She has the name, she continues, of someone who will take care of the problem. She has accordingly made an appointment for the next day. Is he prepared to drive her to the place of appointment and bring her back afterwards, since she has been advised that after the event she will be in no state to drive?

Her name is Sarah. Her friends call her Sally, a name he does not like. It reminds him of the line 'Come down to the sally gardens'. What on earth are sally gardens? She comes from Johannesburg, from one of those suburbs where people spend their Sundays cantering around the estate on horseback calling out 'Jolly good!' to each other while black menservants wearing white gloves bring them drinks. A childhood of cantering around on horses and falling off and hurting herself but not crying has turned Sarah into a brick. 'Sal is a real brick,' he can hear her Johannesburg set saying. She is not beautiful – too solid-boned, too fresh-faced for that – but she is healthy through and through. And she does not pretend. Now that disaster has struck, she does not hide away in her room pretending nothing is wrong. On the contrary, she has found out what needs to be found out – how to get an abortion in Cape Town – and has made the necessary arrangements. In fact, she has put him to shame.

In her little car they drive to Woodstock and stop before a row of identical little semi-detached houses. She gets out and knocks at the door of one of them. He does not see who opens it, but it can be no one but the abortionist herself. He imagines abortionists as blowsy women with dyed hair and caked makeup and none too clean fingernails. They give the girl a glass of neat gin, make her lie back, then carry out some unspeakable manipulation inside her with a piece of wire, something that involves hooking and dragging. Sitting in the car, he shudders. Who would guess that in an ordinary house like this, with hydrangeas in the garden and a plaster gnome, such horrors go on!

Half an hour passes. He grows more and more nervous. Is he going to be able to do what will be required of him?

Then Sarah emerges, and the door closes behind her. Slowly, with an air of concentration, she walks towards the car. When she gets closer he sees she is pale and sweating. She does not speak.

He drives her to the Howarths' big house and instals her in the bedroom overlooking Table Bay and the harbour. He offers her tea, offers her soup, but she wants nothing. She has brought a suitcase; she has brought her own towels, her own sheets. She has thought of everything. He has merely to be around, to be ready if something goes wrong. It is not much to expect.

She asks for a warm towel. He puts a towel in the electric oven. It comes out smelling of burn. By the time he has brought it upstairs it can barely be called warm. But she lays it on her belly and closes her eyes and seems to be soothed by it.

Every few hours she takes one of the pills the woman has given her, followed by water, glass after glass. For the rest she lies with her eyes closed, enduring the pain. Sensing his squeamishness, she has hidden from his sight the evidence of what is going on inside her body: the bloody pads and whatever else there is.

'How are you?' he asks.

'Fine,' she murmurs.

What he will do if she ceases to be fine, he has no idea. Abortion is illegal, but how illegal? If he called in a doctor, would the doctor report them to the police?

He sleeps on a mattress at the bedside. As a nurse he is useless, worse than useless. What he is doing cannot in fact be called nursing. It is merely a penance, a stupid and ineffectual penance.

On the morning of the third day she appears at the door of the study downstairs, pale and swaying on her feet but fully dressed. She is ready to go home, she says.

He drives her to her lodgings, with her suitcase and the laundry bag that presumably contains the bloody towels and sheets. 'Would you like me to stay a while?' he asks. She shakes her head. 'I'll be all right,' she says. He kisses her on the cheek and walks home.

She has issued no reproofs, made no demands; she has even paid the abortionist herself. In fact, she has taught him a lesson in how to behave.

As for him, he has emerged ignominiously, he cannot deny it. What help he has given her has been fainthearted and, worse, incompetent. He prays she will never tell the story to anyone.

His thoughts keep going to what was destroyed inside her – that pod of flesh, that rubbery manikin. He sees the little creature flushed down the toilet at the Woodstock house, tumbled through the maze of sewers, tossed out at last into the shallows, blinking in the sudden sun, struggling against the waves that will carry it out into the bay. He did not want it to live and now he does not want it to die. Yet even if he were to run down to the beach, find it, save it from the sea, what would he do with it? Bring it home, keep it warm in cotton wool, try to get it to grow? How can he who is still a child bring up a child?

He is out of his depth. He has barely emerged into the world himself and already he has a death chalked up against him. How many of the other men he sees in the streets carry dead children with them like baby shoes slung around their necks?

He would rather not see Sarah again. If he could be by himself he might be able to recover, return to being as he used to be. But to desert her now would be too shameful. So each day he drops by at her room and sits holding her hand for a decent period. If he has nothing to say, it is because he has not the courage to ask what is happening to her, in her. Is it like a sickness, he wonders to himself, from which she is now in the process of recuperating, or is it like an amputation, from which one never recovers? What is the difference between an abortion and a miscarriage and what in books is called *losing a child*? In books a woman who loses a child shuts herself off from the world and goes into mourning. Is Sarah still due to enter a time of mourning? And what of him? Is he too going to mourn? How long does one mourn, if one mourns? Does the mourning come to an end, and is one the same after the mourning as before; or does one mourn forever for the little thing that bobs in the waves off Woodstock, like the little cabin boy who fell overboard and was not missed? *Weep, weep!* cries the cabin boy, who will not sink and will not be stilled.

To bring in more money, he takes on a second afternoon of tutoring in the Mathematics Department. The first-year students who attend his tutorial are free to bring in questions on applied mathematics as well as pure mathematics. With only a single year of applied mathematics to his credit, he is barely ahead of the students he is supposed to be assisting: each week he has to spend hours on preparation.

Wrapped up though he is in his private worries, he cannot fail to see that the country around him is in turmoil. The pass laws to which Africans and Africans alone are subjected are being tightened even further, and protests are breaking out everywhere. In the Transvaal the police fire shots into a crowd, then, in their mad way, go on firing into the backs of fleeing men, women and children. From beginning to end the business sickens him: the laws themselves; the bully-boy police; the government, stridently defending the murderers and denouncing the dead; and the press, too frightened to come out and say what anyone with eyes in his head can see.

After the carnage of Sharpeville nothing is as it was before. Even in the pacific Cape there are strikes and marches. Wherever a march takes place there are policemen with guns hovering around the edges, waiting for an excuse to shoot.

It all comes to a head one afternoon while he is on tutorial duty. The tutorial room is quiet; he is patrolling from desk to desk, checking how students are getting on with the assigned exercises, trying to help those in difficulty. Suddenly the door swings open. One of the senior lecturers strides in and raps on the table. 'May I have your attention!' he calls out. There is a nervous crack in his voice; his face is flushed. 'Please put down your pens and give me your attention! There is at this moment a workers' march taking place along De Waal Drive. For reasons of safety, I am asked to announce that no one is being allowed to leave the campus, until further notice. I repeat: no one is being allowed to leave. This is an order issued by the police. Are there any questions?'

There is one question at least, but this is not the right time to voice it: What is the country coming to when one cannot run a mathematics tutorial in peace? As for the police order, he does not believe for a moment that the police are sealing off the campus for the sake of the students. They are sealing it off so that students from this notorious hotbed of leftism will not join the march, that is all.

There is no hope of continuing with the mathematics tutorial. Around the room there is a buzz of conversation; students are already packing their bags and exiting, eager to see what is up.

He follows the crowd to the embankment above De Waal Drive. All traffic has been halted. The marchers are coming up Woolsack Road in a thick snake, ten, twenty abreast, then turning north on to the motorway. They are men, most of them, in drab clothing – overalls, army surplus coats, woollen caps – some carrying sticks, all walking swiftly, silently. There is no end to the column in sight. If he were the police, he would be frightened.

'It's PAC,' says a Coloured student nearby. His eyes glisten, he has an intent look. Is he right? How does he know? Are there signs one ought to be able to recognize? The PAC is not like the ANC. It is more ominous. *Africa for the Africans!* says the PAC. *Drive the whites into the sea!*

Thousands upon thousands, the column of men winds its way up the hill. It does not look like an army, but that is what it is, an army called into being of a sudden out of the wastelands of the Cape Flats. Once they reach the city, what will they do? Whatever it is, there are not enough policemen in the land to stop them, not enough bullets to kill them.

When he was twelve he was herded into a bus full of schoolchildren and driven to Adderley Street, where they were given paper orange-white-and-blue flags and told to wave them as the parade of floats passed by (Jan van Riebeeck and his wife in sober burgher dress; Voortrekkers with muskets; portly Paul Kruger). Three hundred years of history, three hundred years of Christian civilization at the tip of Africa, said the politicians in their speeches: to the Lord let us give thanks. Now, before his eyes, the Lord is withdrawing his protective hand. In the shadow of the mountain he is watching history being unmade.

In the hush around him, among these neat, well-dressed products of Rondebosch Boys High School and the Diocesan College, these youths who half an hour ago were busy calculating angles of vector and dreaming of careers as civil engineers, he can feel the same shock of dismay. They were expecting to enjoy a show, to snicker at a procession of garden boys, not to behold this grim host. The afternoon is ruined for them; all they want now is to go home, have a Coke and sandwich, forget what has passed.

And he? He is no different. *Will the ships still be sailing tomorrow? – that* is his one thought. *I must get out before it is too late!*

The next day, when it is all over and the marchers have gone home, the newspapers find ways of talking about it. *Giving vent to pent-up anger,* they call it. *One of many protest marches country-wide in the wake of Sharpeville. Defused,* they say, *by the good sense (for once) of the police and the co-operation of march leaders. The government,* they say, *would be well advised to sit up and take note.* So they tame the event, making it less than what it was. He is not deceived. The merest whistle, and from the shacks and barracks of the Cape Flats the same army of men will spring up, stronger than before, more numerous. Armed too, with guns from China. What hope is there of standing against them when you do not believe in what you are standing for?

There is the matter of the Defence Force. When he left school they were conscripting only one white boy in three for military training. He was lucky enough not to be balloted. Now all that is changing. There are new rules. At any time he can find a call-up notice in his letterbox: *You are required to present yourself at the Castle at 9 a.m. on such-and-such a date. Bring only toilet items.* Voortrekkerhoogte, somewhere in the Transvaal, is the training camp he has heard the most about. It is where they send conscripts from the Cape, far from home, to break them. In a week he could find himself behind barbed wire in Voortrekkerhoogte, sharing a tent with thuggish Afrikaners, eating bully-beef out of cans, listening to Johnnie Ray on Springbok Radio. He would not be able to endure it; he would slash his wrists. There is only one course open: to flee. But how can he flee without taking his degree? It would be like departing on a long journey, a life's journey, with no clothes, no money, no (the comparison comes more reluctantly) weapon.

Five

It is late, past midnight. In the faded blue sleeping bag he has brought from South Africa, he is lying on the sofa in his friend Paul's bedsitter in Belsize Park. On the other side of the room, in the proper bed, Paul has begun to snore. Through a gap in the curtain glares a night sky of sodium-orange tinged with violet. Though he has covered his feet with a cushion, they remain icy. No matter: he is in London.

There are two, perhaps three places in the world where life can be lived at its fullest intensity: London, Paris, perhaps Vienna. Paris comes first: city of love, city of art. But to live in Paris one must have gone to the kind of upper-class school that teaches French. As for Vienna, Vienna is for Jews coming back to reclaim their birthright: logical positivism, twelve-tone music, psychoanalysis. That leaves London, where South Africans do not need to carry papers and where people speak English. London may be stony, labyrinthine, and cold, but behind its forbidding walls men and women are at work writing books, painting paintings, composing music. One passes them every day in the street without guessing their secret, because of the famous and admirable British reserve.

For a half-share of the bedsitter, which consists of a single room and an annex with a gas stove and cold-water sink (the bathroom and toilet upstairs serve the whole house), he pays Paul two pounds a week. His entire savings, which he has brought with him from South Africa, amount to eighty-four pounds. He must find a job at once.

He visits the offices of the London County Council and enters his name on a list of relief teachers, teachers ready to fill vacancies at short notice. He is sent for an interview to a secondary modern school in Barnet at the far end of the Northern Line. His degree is in mathematics and English. The headmaster wants him to teach social studies; in addition, to supervise swimming two afternoons a week.

'But I can't swim,' he objects.

'Then you'll have to learn, won't you?' says the headmaster.

He leaves the school premises with a copy of the social studies textbook under his arm. He has the weekend to prepare for his first class. By the time he gets to the station he is cursing himself for accepting the job. But he is too much of a coward to go back and say he has changed his mind. From the post office in Belsize Park he mails the book back, with a note: 'Unforeseen eventualities make it impossible for me to take up my duties. Please accept my sincerest apologies.'

An advertisement in the *Guardian* takes him on a trip to Rothamsted, the agricultural station outside London where Halsted and MacIntyre, authors of *The Design of Statistical Experiments*, one of his university textbooks, used once to work. The interview, preceded by a tour of the station's gardens and greenhouses, goes well. The post he has applied for is that of Junior Experimental Officer. The duties of a JEO, he learns, consist in laying out grids for test plantings, recording yields under different regimens, then analyzing the data on the station's computer, all under the direction of one of the Senior Officers. The actual agricultural work is done by gardeners supervised by Agricultural Officers; he will not be expected to get his hands dirty.

A few days later a letter arrives confirming that he is being offered the job, at a salary of six hundred pounds a year. He cannot contain his joy. What a coup! To work at Rothamsted! People in South Africa will not believe it!

There is one catch. The letter ends: 'Accommodation can be arranged in the village or on the council housing estate.' He writes back: he accepts the offer, he says, but would prefer to go on living in London. He will commute to Rothamsted.

In reply he receives a telephone call from the personnel office. Commuting will not be practicable, he is told. What he is being offered is not a desk job with regular hours. On some mornings he will have to start work very early; at other times he will have to work late, or over weekends. Like all officers, he will therefore have to reside within reach of the station. Will he reconsider his position and communicate a final decision?

His triumph is dashed. What is the point of coming all the way from Cape Town to London if he is to be quartered on a housing estate miles outside the city, getting up at the crack of dawn to measure the height of bean plants? He wants to join Rothamsted, wants to find a use for the mathematics he has laboured over for years, but he also wants to go to poetry readings, meet writers and painters, have love affairs. How can he ever make the people at Rothamsted – men in tweed jackets smoking pipes, women with stringy hair and owlish glasses – understand that? How can he bring out words like *love, poetry* before them?

Yet how can he turn the offer down? He is within inches of having a real job, and in England too. He need only say one word – *Yes* – and he will be able to write to his mother giving her the news she is waiting to hear, namely that her son is earning a good salary doing something respectable. Then she in turn will be able to telephone his father's sisters and announce, 'John is working as a scientist in England.' *That* will finally put an end to their carping and sneering. A scientist: what could be more solid than that?

Solidity is what he has always lacked. Solidity is his Achilles' heel. Of cleverness he has enough (though not as much as his mother thinks, and as he himself once used to think); solid he has never been. Rothamsted would give him, if not solidity, not at once, then at least a title, an office, a shell. Junior Experimental Officer, then one day Experimental Officer, then Senior Experimental Officer: surely behind so eminently respectable a shield, in private, in secrecy, he will be able to go on with the work of transmuting experience into art, the work for which he was brought into the world.

That is the argument for the agricultural station. The argument against the agricultural station is that it is not in London, city of romance.

He writes to Rothamsted. On mature reflection, he says, taking into consideration all circumstances, he thinks it best to decline.

The newspapers are full of advertisements for computer programmers.

A degree in science is recommended but not required. He has heard of computer programming but has no clear idea of what it is. He has never laid eyes on a computer, except in cartoons, where computers appear as box-like objects spitting out scrolls of paper. There are no computers in South Africa that he knows of.

He responds to the advertisement by IBM, IBM being the biggest and best, and goes for an interview wearing the black suit he bought before he left Cape Town. The IBM interviewer, a man in his thirties, wears a black suit of his own, but of smarter, leaner cut.

The first thing the interviewer wants to know is whether he has left South Africa for good.

He has, he replies.

Why, asks the interviewer?

'Because the country is heading for revolution,' he replies.

There is a silence. Revolution: not the right word, perhaps, for the halls of IBM.

'And when would you say,' says the interviewer, 'that this revolution will take place?'

He has his answer ready. 'Five years.' That is what everyone has said since Sharpeville. Sharpeville signalled the beginning of the end for the white régime, the *increasingly desperate* white régime.

After the interview he is given an IQ test. He has always enjoyed IQ tests, always done well at them. Generally he is better at tests, quizzes, examinations than at real life.

Within days IBM offers him a position as a trainee programmer. If he does well in his training course, and then passes his probationary period, he will become first a Programmer proper, then one day a Senior Programmer. He will commence his career at IBM's data-processing bureau in Newman Street, off Oxford Street in the heart of the West End. The hours will be nine to five. His initial salary will be seven hundred pounds a year.

He accepts the terms without hesitation.

The same day he passes a placard in the London Underground, a job advertisement. Applications are invited for the position of trainee station foreman, at a salary of seven hundred pounds a year. Minimum educational requirement: a school certificate. Minimum age: twenty-one.

Are all jobs in England paid equally, he wonders? If so, what is the point of having a degree?

In his programming course he finds himself in the company of two other trainees – a rather attractive girl from New Zealand and a young Londoner with a spotty face – together with a dozen or so IBM clients, businessmen. By rights he ought to be the best of the lot, he and perhaps the girl from New Zealand, who also has a mathematics degree; but in fact he struggles to understand what is going on and does badly in the written exercises. At the end of the first week they write a test, which he barely scrapes through. The instructor is not pleased with him and does not hesitate to express his displeasure. He is in the world of business, and in the world of business, he discovers, one does not need to be polite.

There is something about programming that flummoxes him, yet that even the businessmen in the class have no trouble with. In his naïveté he had imagined that computer programming would be about ways of translating symbolic logic and set theory into digital codes. Instead the talk is all about inventories and outflows, about Customer A and Customer B. What are inventories and outflows, and what have they to do with mathematics? He might as well be a clerk sorting cards into batches; he might as well be a trainee station foreman.

At the end of the third week he writes his final test, passes in undistinguished fashion, and graduates to Newman Street, where he is allocated a desk in a room with nine other young programmers. All the office furniture is grey. In the desk drawer he finds paper, a ruler, pencils, a pencil sharpener, and a little appointments book with a black plastic cover. On the cover, in solid capitals, is the word THINK. On the supervisor's desk, in his cubicle off the main office, is a sign reading THINK. THINK is the motto of IBM. What is special about IBM, he is given to understand, is that it is unrelentingly committed to thinking. It is up to employees to think at all times, and thus to live up to the ideal of IBM's founder Thomas J. Watson. Employees who do not think do not belong in IBM, which is the aristocrat of the business machine world. At its headquarters in White Plains, New York, IBM has laboratories in which more cutting-edge research in computer science is performed than in all the universities of the world together. Scientists in White Plains are paid better than university professors, and provided with everything they can conceivably need. All they are required to do in return is think.

Though the hours at the Newman Street bureau are nine to five, he soon discovers that it is frowned upon for male employees to leave the premises promptly at five. Female employees with families to take care of may leave at five without reproach; men are expected to work until at least six. When there is a rush job they may have to work all night, with a break to go to a pub for a bite. Since he dislikes pubs, he simply works straight through. He rarely gets home before ten o'clock.

He is in England, in London; he has a job, a proper job, better than mere teaching, for which he is being paid a salary. He has escaped South Africa. Everything is going well, he has attained his first goal, he ought to be happy. In fact, as the weeks pass, he finds himself more and more miserable. He has attacks of panic, which he beats off with difficulty. In the office there is nothing to rest the eye on but flat metallic surfaces. Under the shadowless glare of the neon lighting, he feels his very soul to be under attack. The building, a featureless block of concrete and glass, seems to give off a gas, odourless, colourless, that finds its way into his blood and numbs him. IBM, he can swear, is killing him, turning him into a zombie.

Yet he cannot give up. Barnet Hill Secondary Modern, Rothamsted, IBM: he dare not fail for a third time. Failing would be too much like his father. Through the grey, heartless agency of IBM the real world is testing him. He must steel himself to endure.

Six

His refuge from IBM is the cinema. At the Everyman in Hampstead his eyes are opened to films from all over the world, made by directors whose names are quite new to him. He goes to the whole of an Antonioni season. In a film called *L'Eclisse* a woman wanders through the streets of a sunstruck, deserted city. She is disturbed, anguished. What she is anguished about he cannot quite define; her face reveals nothing.

The woman is Monica Vitti. With her perfect legs and sensual lips and abstracted look, Monica Vitti haunts him; he falls in love with her. He has dreams in which he, of all men in the world, is singled out to be her comfort and solace. There is a tap at his door. Monica Vitti stands before him, a finger raised to her lips to signal silence. He steps forward, enfolds her in his arms. Time ceases; he and Monica Vitti are one.

But is he truly the lover Monica Vitti seeks? Will he be any better than the men in her films at stilling her anguish? He is not sure. Even if he were to find a room for the two of them, a secret retreat in some quiet, fogbound quarter of London, he suspects she would still, at three in the morning, slip out of bed and sit at the table under the glare of a single lamp, brooding, prey to anguish.

The anguish with which Monica Vitti and other of Antonioni's characters are burdened is of a kind he is quite unfamiliar with. In fact it is not anguish at all but something more profound: Angst. He would like to have a taste of Angst, if only to know what it is like. But, try though he may, he cannot find anything in his heart that he can recognize as Angst. Angst seems to be a European, a properly European, thing; it has yet to find its way to England, to say nothing of England's colonies.

In an article in the *Observer*, the Angst of the European cinema is explained as stemming from a fear of nuclear annihilation; also from uncertainty following the death of God. He is not convinced. He cannot believe that what sends Monica Vitti out into the streets of Palermo under the angry red ball of the sun, when she could just as well stay behind in the cool of a hotel room and be made love to by a man, is the hydrogen bomb or a failure on God's part to speak to her. Whatever the true explanation, it must be more complicated than that.

Angst gnaws at Ingmar Bergman's people too. It is the cause of their irremediable solitariness. Regarding Bergman's Angst, however, the *Observer* recommends that it not be taken too seriously. It smells of pretentiousness, says the *Observer*; it is an affectation not unconnected with long Nordic winters, with nights of excessive drinking and hangovers.

Even newspapers that are supposed to be liberal – the *Guardian*, the *Observer* – are hostile, he is beginning to find, to the life of the mind. Faced with something deep and serious, they are quick to sneer, to brush it off with a witticism. Only in tiny enclaves like the Third Programme is new art – American poetry, electronic music, abstract expressionism – taken seriously. Modern England is turning out to be a disturbingly philistine country, little different from the England of W. E. Henley and the *Pomp and Circumstance* marches that Ezra Pound was fulminating against in 1912.

What then is he doing in England? Was it a huge mistake to have come here? Is it too late to move? Would Paris, city of artists, be more congenial, if somehow he could master French? And what of Stockholm? Spiritually he would feel at home in Stockholm, he suspects. But what about Swedish? And what would he do for a living?

At IBM he has to keep his fantasies of Monica Vitti to himself, and the rest of his arty pretensions too. For reasons that are not clear to him, he has been adopted as a chum by a fellow programmer named Bill Briggs. Bill Briggs is short and pimply; he has a girlfriend named Cynthia whom he is going to marry; he is looking forward to making the down payment on a terrace house in Wimbledon. Whereas the other programmers speak with unplaceable grammar-school accents and start the day by flipping to the financial pages of the *Telegraph* to check the share prices, Bill Briggs has a marked London accent and stores his money in a building society account.

Despite his social origins, there is no reason why Bill Briggs should not succeed in IBM. IBM is an American company, impatient of Britain's class hierarchy. That is the strength of IBM: men of all kinds can get to the top because all that matters to IBM is loyalty and hard, concentrated work. Bill Briggs is hardworking, and unquestioningly loyal to IBM. Furthermore, Bill Briggs seems to have a grasp of the larger goals of IBM and of its Newman Street data-processing centre, which is more than can be said of him.

IBM employees are provided with booklets of luncheon vouchers. For a three-and-sixpenny voucher one can get a quite decent meal. His own inclination is towards the Lyons brasserie on Tottenham Court Road, where one can visit the salad bar as often as one likes. But Schmidt's in Charlotte Street is the preferred haunt of the IBM programmers. So with Bill Briggs he goes to Schmidt's and eats Wiener Schnitzel or jugged hare. For variety they sometimes go to the Athena on Goodge Street for moussaka. After lunch, if it is not raining, they take a brief stroll around the streets before returning to their desks.

The range of subjects that he and Bill Briggs have tacitly agreed not to broach in their conversations is so wide that he is surprised there is anything left. They do not discuss their desires or larger aspirations. They are silent on their personal lives, on their families and their upbringing, on politics and religion and the arts. Football would be acceptable were it not for the fact that he knows nothing about the English clubs. So they are left with the weather, train strikes, house prices, and IBM: IBM's plans for the future, IBM's customers and those customers' plans, who said what at IBM.

It makes for dreary conversation, but there is an obverse to it. A bare two months ago he was an ignorant provincial stepping ashore into the drizzle of Southampton docks. Now here he is in the heart of London town, indistinguishable in his black uniform from any other London office-worker, exchanging opinions on everyday subjects with a full-blooded

Londoner, successfully negotiating all the conversational proprieties. Soon, if his progress continues and he is careful with his vowels, no one will be sparing him a second glance. In a crowd he will pass as a Londoner, perhaps even, in due course, as an Englishman.

Now that he has an income, he is able to rent a room of his own in a house off Archway Road in north London. The room is on the second floor, with a view over a water reservoir. It has a gas heater and a little alcove with a gas cooker and shelves for food and crockery. In a corner is the meter: you put in a shilling and get a shilling's supply of gas.

His diet is unvarying: apples, oats porridge, bread and cheese, and spiced sausages called chipolatas, which he fries over the cooker. He prefers chipolatas to real sausages because they do not need to be refrigerated. Nor do they ooze grease when they fry. He suspects there is lots of potato flour mixed in with the ground meat. But potato flour is not bad for one.

Since he leaves early in the mornings and comes home late, he rarely lays eyes on the other lodgers. A routine soon sets in. He spends Saturdays in bookshops, galleries, museums, cinemas. On Sundays he reads the *Observer* in his room, then goes to a film or for a walk on the Heath.

Saturday and Sunday evenings are the worst. Then the loneliness that he usually manages to keep at bay sweeps over him, loneliness indistinguishable from the low, grey, wet weather of London or from the iron-hard cold of the pavements. He can feel his face turning stiff and stupid with muteness; even IBM and its formulaic exchanges are better than this silence.

His hope is that from the featureless crowds amidst which he moves there will emerge a woman who will respond to his glance, glide wordlessly to his side, return with him (still wordless – what could their first word be? – it is unimaginable) to his bedsitter, make love to him, vanish into the darkness, reappear the next night (he will be sitting over his books, there will be a tap at the door), again embrace him, again, on the stroke of midnight, vanish, and so forth, thereby transforming his life and releasing a torrent of pent-up verse on the pattern of Rilke's *Sonnets to Orpheus*.

A letter arrives from the University of Cape Town. On the strength of his Honours examinations, it says, he has been awarded a bursary of two hundred pounds for postgraduate study.

The amount is too small, far too small, to allow him to enrol at a British university. Anyhow, now that he has found a job he cannot think of giving it up. Short of refusing the bursary, there is only one option left: to register with the University of Cape Town as a Master's student in *absentia*. He completes the registration form. Under 'Area of Concentration' he writes, after due thought, 'Literature'. It would be nice to write 'Mathematics', but the truth is that he is not clever enough to go on with mathematics. Literature may not be as noble as mathematics, but at least there is nothing about literature that intimidates him. As for the topic of his research, he toys with the idea of proposing the *Cantos* of Ezra Pound, but in the end goes for the novels of Ford Madox Ford. To read Ford one does at least not need to know Chinese.

Ford, born Hueffer, grandson of the painter Ford Madox Brown, published his first book in 1891 at the age of eighteen. From then on, until his death in 1939, he earned his bread solely by literary pursuits. Pound called him the greatest prose stylist of his day and excoriated the English public for ignoring him. He himself has thus far read five of Ford's novels – *The Good Soldier* and the four books constituting *Parade's End* – and is convinced that Pound is right. He is dazzled by the complicated, staggered chronology of Ford's plots, by the cunning with which a note, casually struck and artlessly repeated, will stand revealed, chapters later, as a major motif. He is moved too by the love between Christopher Tietjens and the much younger Valentine Wannop, a love which Tietjens abstains from consummating, despite Valentine's readiness, because (says Tietjens) a fellow doesn't go about deflowering virgins. Tietjens's ethos of laconic common decency seems to him wholly admirable, the quintessence of Englishness.

If Ford could write five such masterpieces, he tells himself, surely there must be further masterworks, as yet unrecognized, among the sprawling and only just catalogued corpus of his writings, masterworks that he can help bring to light. He embarks at once on a reading of the Ford oeuvre, spending entire Saturdays in the Reading Room of the

British Museum, as well as the two evenings a week when the Reading Room stays open late. Though the early works turn out to be disappointing, he presses on, excusing Ford because he must still have been learning his craft.

One Saturday he falls into conversation with the reader at the next desk, and they have tea together in the Museum tea room. Her name is Anna; she is Polish by origin and still has a faint accent. She works as a researcher, she tells him; visits to the Reading Room are part of her job. She is at present exploring materials for a life of John Speke, discoverer of the source of the Nile. For his part, he tells her about Ford and Ford's collaboration with Joseph Conrad. They talk about Conrad's time in Africa, about his early life in Poland and his later aspiration to become an English squire.

As they speak he wonders: Is it an omen that in the Reading Room of the British Museum he, a student of F. M. Ford, should meet a countrywoman of Conrad's? Is Anna his Destined One? She is no beauty, certainly: she is older than he; her face is bony, even gaunt; she wears sensible flat shoes and a shapeless grey skirt. But who is to say that he deserves better?

He is on the point of asking her out, perhaps to a film; but then his courage fails him. What if, even when he has declared himself, there is no spark? How would he extricate himself without ignominy?

There are other habitués of the Reading Room as lonely, he suspects, as he. An Indian with a pitted face, for instance, who gives off a smell of boils and old bandages. Every time he goes to the toilet the Indian seems to follow him, to be on the point of speaking, but then unable to.

At last, one day, as they stand side by side at the washbasin, the man speaks. Is he from King's College? the man asks stiffly. No, he replies, from the University of Cape Town. Would he like to have tea, asks the man?

They sit down together in the tea room; the man launches into a long account of his research, which is into the social makeup of audiences at the Globe Theatre. Though he is not particularly interested, he does his best to pay attention.

The life of the mind, he thinks to himself: is that what we have dedicated ourselves to, I and these other lonely wanderers in the bowels of the British Museum? Will there be a reward for us one day? Will our solitariness lift, or is the life of the mind its own reward?

Seven

It is three o'clock on a Saturday afternoon. He has been in the Reading Room since opening time, reading Ford's *Mr Humpty Dumpty*, a novel so tedious that he has to fight to stay awake.

In a short while the Reading Room will close for the day, the whole great Museum will close. On Sundays the Reading Room does not open; between now and next Saturday, reading will be a matter of an hour snatched here and there of an evening. Should he soldier on until closing time, though he is racked with yawns? What is the point of this enter-prise anyway? What is the good to a computer programmer, if computer programming is to be his life, to have an MA in English literature? And where are the unrecognized masterpieces that he was going to uncover? *Mr Humpty Dumpty* is certainly not one of them. He shuts the book, packs up.

Outside the daylight is already waning. Along Great Russell Street he trudges to Tottenham Court Road, then south towards Charing Cross. Of the throng on the sidewalks, most are young people. Strictly speaking he is their contemporary, but he does not feel like that. He feels middle-aged, prematurely middle-aged: one of those bloodless, high-domed, exhausted scholars whose skin flakes at the merest touch. Deeper than that he is still a child, ignorant of his place in the world, frightened, indecisive. What is he doing in this huge, cold city where merely to stay alive means holding tight all the time, trying not to fall?

The bookshops on Charing Cross Road stay open until six. Until six he has somewhere to go. After that he will be adrift amid the Saturday-night fun-seekers. For a while he can follow the flow, pretending he too is seeking fun, pretending he has somewhere to go, someone to meet; but in the end he will have to give up and catch the train back to Archway station and the solitude of his room.

Foyles, the bookshop whose name is known as far away as Cape Town, has proved a disappointment. The boast that Foyles stocks every book in print is clearly a lie, and anyway the assistants, most of them younger than himself, don't know where to find things. He prefers Dillons, haphazard though the shelving at Dillons may be. He tries to call in there once a week to see what is new.

Among the magazines he comes across in Dillons is *The African Communist*. He has heard about *The African Communist* but not actually seen it hitherto, since it is banned in South Africa. Of the contributors, some, to his surprise, turn out to be contemporaries of his from Cape Town – fellow students of the kind who slept all day and went to parties in the evenings, got drunk, sponged on their parents, failed examinations, took five years over three-year degrees. Yet here they are writing authoritative-sounding articles about the economics of migratory labour or uprisings in rural Transkei. Where, amid all the dancing and drinking and debauchery, did they find the time to learn about such things?

What he really comes to Dillons for, however, are the poetry magazines. There is a careless stack of them on the floor behind the front door: *Ambit* and *Agenda* and *Pawn*; cyclostyled leaflets from out-of-the-way places like Keele; odd numbers, long out of date, of reviews from America. He buys one of each and takes the pile back to his room, where he pores over them, trying to work out who is writing what, where he would fit in if he too were to try to publish.

The British magazines are dominated by dismayingly modest little poems about everyday thoughts and experiences, poems that would not have raised an eyebrow half a century ago. What has happened to the ambitions of poets here in Britain? Have they not digested the news that Edward Thomas and his world are gone for ever? Have they not learned the lesson of Pound and Eliot, to say nothing of Baudelaire and Rimbaud, the Greek epigrammatists, the Chinese?

But perhaps he is judging the British too hastily. Perhaps he is reading the wrong magazines; perhaps there are other, more adventurous publications that do not find their way to Dillons. Or perhaps there is a circle of creative spirits so pessimistic about the prevailing climate that they do not bother to send to bookshops like Dillons the magazines in which they publish. *Botthege Oscure*, for instance: where does one buy *Botthege Oscure*? If such enlightened circles exist, how will he ever find out about them, how will he ever break into them?

As for his own writing, he would hope to leave behind, were he to die tomorrow, a handful of poems that, edited by some selfless scholar and privately printed in a neat little duodecimo pamphlet, would make people shake their heads and murmur beneath their breath, 'Such promise! Such a waste!' That is his hope. The truth, however, is that the poems he writes are becoming not only shorter and shorter but – he cannot help feeling – less substantial too. He no longer seems to have it in him to produce poetry of the kind he wrote at the age of seventeen or eighteen, pieces sometimes pages long, rambling, clumsy in parts, but daring nevertheless, full of novelties. Those poems, or most of them, came out of a state of anguished being-in-love, as well as out of the torrents of reading he was doing. Now, four years later, he is still anguished, but his anguish has become habitual, even chronic, like a headache that will not go away. The poems he writes are wry little pieces, minor in every sense. Whatever their nominal subject, it is he himself – trapped, lonely, miserable – who is at their centre; yet – he cannot fail to see it – these new poems lack the energy or even the desire to explore his impasse of spirit seriously.

In fact he is exhausted all the time. At his grey-topped desk in the big IBM office he is overcome with gales of yawning that he struggles to conceal; at the British Museum the words swim before his eyes. All he wants to do is sink his head on his arms and sleep.

Yet he cannot accept that the life he is leading here in London is without plan or meaning. A century ago poets deranged themselves with opium or alcohol so that from the brink of madness they could issue reports on their visionary experiences. By such means they turned themselves into seers, prophets of the future. Opium and alcohol are not his way, he is too frightened of what they might do to his health. But are exhaustion and misery not capable of performing the same work? Is living on the brink of psychic collapse not as good as living on the brink of madness? Why is it a greater sacrifice, a greater extinction of personality, to hide out in a garret room on the Left Bank for which you have not paid the rent, or wander from café to café, bearded, unwashed, smelly, bumming drinks from friends, than to dress in a black suit and do soul-destroying office work and submit to either loneliness unto death or sex without desire? Surely absinthe and tattered clothes are old-fashioned by now. And what is heroic, anyway, about cheating a landlord out of his rent?

T. S. Eliot worked for a bank. Wallace Stevens and Franz Kafka worked for insurance companies. In their unique ways Eliot and Stevens and Kafka suffered no less than Poe or Rimbaud. There is no dishonour in electing to follow Eliot and Stevens and Kafka. His choice is to wear a black suit as they did, wear it like a burning shirt, exploiting no one, cheating no one, paying his way. In the Romantic era artists went mad on an extravagant scale. Madness poured out of them in reams of delirious verse or great gouts of paint. That era is over: his own madness, if it is to be his lot to suffer madness, will be otherwise – quiet, discreet. He will sit in a corner, tight and hunched, like the robed man in Dürer's etching, waiting patiently for his season in hell to pass. And when it has passed he will be all the stronger for having endured.

That is the story he tells himself on his better days. On other days, bad days, he wonders whether emotions as monotonous as his will ever fuel great poetry. The musical impulse within him, once so strong, has already waned. Is he now in the process of losing the poetic impulse? Will he be driven from poetry to prose? Is that what prose secretly is: the second-best choice, the resort of failing creative spirits?

The only poem he has written in the past year that he likes is a mere five lines long.

The wives of the rock-lobster fishermen
have grown accustomed to waking alone,

their husbands having for centuries fished at dawn;
nor is their sleep as troubled as mine.
If you have gone, go then to the Portuguese rock-lobster fishermen.

The Portuguese rock-lobster fishermen: he is quietly pleased to have sneaked so mundane a phrase into a poem, even if the poem itself, looked at closely, makes less and less sense. He has lists of words and phrases he has stored up, mundane or recondite, waiting to find homes for them. *Perfervid*, for instance: one day he will lodge *perfervid* in an epigram whose occult history will be that it will have been created as a setting for a single word, as a brooch can be a setting for a single jewel. The poem will seem to be about love or despair, yet it will all have blossomed out of one lovely sounding word of whose meaning he is as yet not entirely sure.

Will epigrams be enough to build a career in poetry on? As a form there is nothing wrong with the epigram. A world of feeling can be compressed into a single line, as the Greeks proved again and again. But his epigrams do not always achieve a Greek compression. Too often they lack feeling; too often they are merely bookish.

'Poetry is not a turning loose of emotion but an escape from emotion,' says Eliot in words he has copied into his diary. 'Poetry is not an expression of personality but an escape from personality.' Then as a bitter afterthought Eliot adds: 'But only those who have personality and emotions know what it means to want to escape from these things.'

He has a horror of spilling mere emotion on to the page. Once it has begun to spill out he would not know how to stop it. It would be like severing an artery and watching one's lifeblood gush out. Prose, fortunately, does not demand emotion: there is that to be said for it. Prose is like a flat, tranquil sheet of water on which one can tack about at one's leisure, making patterns on the surface.

He sets aside a weekend for his first experiment with prose. The story that emerges from the experiment, if that is what it is, a story, has no real plot. Everything of importance happens in the mind of the narrator, a nameless young man all too like himself who takes a nameless girl to a lonely beach and watches while she swims. From some small action of hers, some unconscious gesture, he is suddenly convinced she has been unfaithful to him; furthermore, he realizes that she has seen he knows, and does not care. That is all. That is how the piece ends. That is the sum of it.

Having written this story, he does not know what to do with it. He has no urge to show it to anyone except perhaps to the original of the nameless girl. But he has lost touch with her, and she would not recognize herself anyway, not without being prompted.

The story is set in South Africa. It disquiets him to see that he is still writing about South Africa. He would prefer to leave his South African self behind as he has left South Africa itself behind. South Africa was a bad start, a handicap. An undistinguished, rural family, bad schooling, the Afrikaans language: from each of these component handicaps he has, more or less, escaped. He is in the great world earning his own living and not doing too badly, or at least not failing, not obviously. He does not need to be reminded of South Africa. If a tidal wave were to sweep in from the Atlantic tomorrow and wash away the southern tip of the African continent, he will not shed a tear. He will be among the saved.

Though the story he has written is minor (no doubt about that), it is not bad. Nevertheless, he sees no point in trying to publish it. The English will not understand it. For the beach in the story they will summon up an English idea of a beach, a few pebbles lapped by wavelets. They will not see a dazzling space of sand at the foot of rocky cliffs pounded by breakers, with gulls and cormorants screaming overhead as they battle the wind.

There are other ways too, it appears, in which prose is not like poetry. In poetry the action can take place everywhere and nowhere: it does not matter whether the lonely wives of the fishermen live in Kalk Bay or Portugal or Maine. Prose, on the other hand, seems naggingly to demand a specific setting.

He does not as yet know England well enough to do England in prose. He is not even sure he can do the parts of London he is familiar with, the London of crowds trudging to work, of cold and rain, of bedsitters with curtainless windows and forty-watt bulbs. If he were to try, what would come out would be no different, he suspects, from the London of any other bachelor clerk. He may have his own vision of London, but there is nothing unique to that vision. If it has a certain intensity, that is only because it is narrow, and it is narrow because it is ignorant of everything outside itself. He has not mastered London. If there is any mastering going on, it is London mastering him.

Eight

Does his first venture into prose herald a change of direction in his life? Is he about to renounce poetry? He is not sure. But if he is going to write prose then he may have to go the whole hog and become a Jamesian. Henry James shows one how to rise above mere nationality. In fact, it is not always clear where a piece by James is set, in London or Paris or New York, so supremely above the mechanics of daily life is James. People in James do not have to pay the rent; they certainly do not have to hold down jobs; all they are required to do is to have supersubtle conversations whose effect is to bring about tiny shifts of power, shifts so minute as to be invisible to all but a practised eye. When enough such shifts have taken place, the balance of power between the personages of the story is (Voilà!) revealed to have suddenly and irreversibly changed. And that is that: the story has fulfilled its charge and can be brought to an end.

He sets himself exercises in the style of James. But the Jamesian manner proves less easy to master than he had thought. Getting the characters he dreams up to have supersubtle conversations is like trying to make mammals fly. For a moment or two, flapping their arms, they support themselves in thin air. Then they plunge.

Henry James's sensibility is finer than his, there can be no doubt about that. But that does not explain the whole of his failure. James wants one to believe that conversations, exchanges of words, are all that matters. Though it is a credo he is ready to accept, he cannot actually follow it, he finds, not in London, the city on whose grim cogs he is being broken, the city from which he must learn to write, otherwise why is he here at all?

Once upon a time, when he was still an innocent child, he believed that cleverness was the only yardstick that mattered, that as long as he was clever enough he would attain everything he desired. Going to university put him in his place. The university showed him he was not the cleverest, not by a long chalk. And now he is faced with real life, where there are not even examinations to fall back on. In real life all that he can do well, it appears, is be miserable. In misery he is still top of the class. There seems to be no limit to the misery he can attract to himself and endure. Even as he plods around the cold streets of this alien city, heading nowhere, just walking to tire himself out, so that when he gets back to his room he will at least be able to sleep, he does not sense within himself the slightest disposition to crack under the weight of misery. Misery is his element. He is at home in misery like a fish in water. If misery were to be abolished, he would not know what to do with himself.

Happiness, he tells himself, teaches one nothing. Misery, on the other hand, steels one for the future. Misery is a school for the soul. From the waters of misery one emerges on the far bank purified, strong, ready to take up again the challenges of a life of art.

Yet misery does not feel like a purifying bath. On the contrary, it feels like a pool of dirty water. From each new bout of misery he emerges not brighter and stronger but duller and flabbier. How does it actually work, the cleansing action that misery is reputed to have? Has he not swum deep enough? Will he have to swim beyond mere misery into melancholia and madness? He has never yet met anyone who could be called properly mad, but he has not forgotten Jacqueline, who was, as she herself put it, 'in therapy', and with whom he spent six months, on and off, sharing a one-room flat. At no time did Jacqueline blaze with the divine and exhilarating fire of creativity. On the contrary, she was self-obsessed, unpredictable, fatiguing to be with. Is that the kind of person he must descend to being before he can be an artist? And anyway, whether mad or miserable, how can one write when tiredness is like a gloved hand gripping one's brain and squeezing? Or is what he likes to call tiredness in fact a test, a disguised test, a test he is moreover failing? After tiredness, are there further tests to come, as many as there are circles in Dante's Hell? Is tiredness simply the first of the tests that the great masters had to pass, Hölderlin and Blake, Pound and Eliot?

He wishes it could be granted to him to come alive and just for a minute, just for a second, know what it is to burn with the sacred fire of art.

Suffering, madness, sex: three ways of calling down the sacred fire upon oneself. He has visited the lower reaches of suffering, he has been in touch with madness; what does he know of sex? Sex and creativity go together, everyone says so, and he does not doubt it. Because they are creators, artists possess the secret of love. The fire that burns in the artist is visible to women, by means of an instinctive faculty. Women themselves do not have the sacred fire (there are exceptions: Sappho, Emily Brontë). It is in quest of the fire they lack, the fire of love, that women pursue artists and give themselves to them. In their lovemaking artists and their mistresses experience briefly, tantalizingly, the life of gods. From such lovemaking the artist returns to his work enriched and strengthened, the woman to her life transfigured.

What of him then? If no woman has yet detected, behind his woodenness, his clenched grimness, any flicker of the sacred fire; if no woman seems to give herself to him without the severest qualms; if the lovemaking he is familiar with, the woman's as well as his own, is either anxious or bored or both anxious and bored – does it mean that he is not a real artist, or does it mean that he has not suffered enough yet, not spent enough time in a purgatory that includes by prescription bouts of passionless sex?

With his lofty unconcern for mere living, Henry James exerts a strong pull on him. Yet, try though he may, he cannot feel the ghostly hand of James extended to touch his brow in blessing. James belongs to the past: by the time he himself was born, James had been dead for twenty years. James Joyce was still alive, though only by a whisker. He admires Joyce, he can even recite passages from Ulysses by heart. But Joyce is too bound up with Ireland and Irish affairs to be in his pantheon. Ezra Pound and T. S. Eliot, tottering though they may be, and myth-shrouded, are still alive, the one in Rapallo, the other here in London. But if he is going to abandon poetry (or poetry is going to abandon him), what example can Pound or Eliot any longer offer?

Of the great figures of the present age, that leaves only one: D. H. Lawrence. Lawrence too died before he was born, but that can be discounted as an accident, since Lawrence died young. He first read Lawrence as a schoolboy, when *Lady Chatterley's Lover* was the most notorious of all forbidden books. By his third year at university he had consumed the whole of Lawrence, save for the apprentice work. Lawrence was being absorbed by his fellow students too. From Lawrence they were learning to smash the brittle shell of civilized convention and let the secret core of their being emerge. Girls wore flowing dresses and danced in the rain and gave themselves to men who promised to take them to their dark core. Men who failed to take them there they impatiently discarded.

He himself had been wary of becoming a cultist, a Lawrentian. The women in Lawrence's books made him uneasy; he imagined them as remorseless female insects, spiders or mantises. Under the gaze of the pale, black-clad, intent-eyed priestesses of the cult at the university he felt like a nervous, scurrying little bachelor insect. With some of them he would have liked to go to bed, that he could not deny – only by bringing a woman to her own dark core, after all, could a man reach his own dark core – but he was too scared. Their ecstasies would be volcanic; he would be too puny to survive them.

Besides, women who followed Lawrence had a code of chastity of their own. They fell into long periods of iciness during which they wished only to be by themselves or with their sisters, periods during which the thought of offering up their bodies was like a violation. From their icy sleep they could be awoken only by the imperious call of the dark male self. He himself was neither dark nor imperious, or at least his essential darkness and imperiousness had yet to emerge. So he made do with other girls, girls who had not yet become women and might never become women, since they had no dark core or none to speak of, girls who in their hearts didn't want to do it, just as in his heart of hearts he could not have been said to want to do it either.

In his last weeks in Cape Town he had begun an affair with a girl named Caroline, a drama student with stage ambitions. They had gone to the theatre together, they had stayed up all night arguing the merits of Anouilh as against Sartre, Ionesco as against Beckett; they had slept together. Beckett was his favourite but not Caroline's: Beckett was too gloomy, she said. Her real reason, he suspected, was that Beckett did not write parts for women. At her prodding he had even embarked on a play himself, a verse drama about Don Quixote. But he soon found himself at a dead end – the mind of the old Spaniard was too remote, he could not think his way into it – and gave up.

Now, months later, Caroline turns up in London and gets in touch with him. They meet in Hyde Park. She still has a southern-hemisphere tan, she is full of vitality, elated to be in London, elated too to see him. They stroll through the park. Spring has arrived, the evenings are growing longer, there are leaves on the trees. They catch a bus back to Kensington, where she lives.

He is impressed by her, by her energy and enterprise. A few weeks in London and she has already found her feet. She has a job; her CV has gone out to all the theatrical agents; and she has a flat in a fashionable quarter, which she shares with three English girls. How did she meet her flatmates, he asks? Friends of friends, she replies.

They resume their affair, but it is difficult from the start. The job she has found is as a waitress in a nightclub in the West End; the hours are unpredictable. She prefers that he meet her at her flat, not fetch her at the club. Since the other girls object to strangers having keys, he has to wait outside in the street. So at the end of his own working day he catches a train back to Archway Road, has a supper of bread and sausages in his room, reads for an hour or two or listens to the radio, then catches the last bus to Kensington and begins his wait. Sometimes Caroline comes back from the club as early as midnight, sometimes as late as 4 a.m. They have their time together, fall asleep. At seven o'clock the alarm clock rings: he must be out of the flat before her friends wake up. He catches the bus back to Highgate, has breakfast, dons his black uniform, and sets off for the office.

It soon becomes a routine, a routine which, when he is able to stand back for a moment and reflect, astonishes him. He is having an affair in which the rules are being set by the woman and by the woman alone. Is this what passion does to a man: robs him of his pride? Is he passionate about Caroline? He would not have imagined so. In the time they were apart he barely gave her a thought. Why then this docility on his part, this abjectness? Does he want to be made unhappy? Is that what unhappiness has become for him: a drug he cannot do without?

Worst are the nights when she does not come home at all. He paces the sidewalk hour after hour, or, when it rains, huddles in the doorway. Is she really working late, he wonders despairingly, or is the club in Bayswater a huge lie and is she at this very moment in bed with someone else?

When he taxes her directly, he gets only vague excuses. It was a hectic night at the club, we stayed open till dawn, she says. Or she didn't have cash for a taxi. Or she had to go for a drink with a client. In the acting world, she reminds him tartly, contacts are all-important. Without contacts her career will never take off.

They still make love, but it is not as it was before. Caroline's mind is elsewhere. Worse than that: with his glooms and his sulks he is fast becoming a burden to her, he can feel that. If he had any sense he would break off the affair right now, clear out. But he does not. Caroline may not be the mysterious, dark-eyed beloved he came to Europe for, she may be nothing but a girl from Cape Town from a background as humdrum as his own, but she is, for the present, all he has.

Nine

In England girls pay no attention to him, perhaps because there still lingers about his person an air of colonial gaucherie, perhaps simply because his clothes are not right. When he is not dressed up in one of his IBM suits, he has only the grey flannels and green sports jacket he brought with him from Cape Town. The young men he sees in the trains and the streets, in contrast, wear narrow black trousers, pointed shoes, tight, box-like jackets with many buttons. They also wear their hair long, hanging over their foreheads and ears, while he still has the short back and sides and the neat parting impressed on him in his childhood by country-town barbers and approved of by IBM. In the trains the eyes of girls slide over him or glaze with disdain.

There is something not quite fair in his plight: he would protest if he only knew where and to whom. What kind of jobs do his rivals have that allow them to dress as they please? And why should he be compelled to follow fashion anyway? Do inner qualities count for nothing?

The sensible thing would be to buy himself an outfit like theirs and wear it at weekends. But when he imagines dressing up in such clothes, clothes that seem to him not only alien to his character but Latin rather than English, he feels his resistance stiffening. He cannot do it: it would be like giving himself up to a charade, an act.

London is full of beautiful girls. They come from all over the world: as au pairs, as language students, simply as tourists. They wear their hair in wings over their cheekbones; their eyes are dark-shadowed; they have an air of suave mystery. The most beautiful are the tall, honey-skinned Swedes; but the Italians, almond-eyed and petite, have their own allure. Italian lovemaking, he imagines, will be sharp and hot, quite different from Swedish, which will be smiling and languorous. But will he ever get a chance to find out for himself? If he could ever pluck up the courage to speak to one of these beautiful foreigners, what would he say? Would it be a lie if he introduced himself as a mathematician rather than just a computer programmer? Would the attentions of a mathematician impress a girl from Europe, or would it be better to tell her that, despite his dull exterior, he is a poet?

He carries a book of poetry around with him in his pocket, sometimes Hölderlin, sometimes Rilke, sometimes Vallejo. In the trains he ostentatiously brings forth his book and absorbs himself in it. It is a test. Only an exceptional girl will appreciate what he is reading and recognize in him an exceptional spirit too. But none of the girls on the trains pay him any attention. That seems to be one of the first things girls learn when they arrive in England: to pay no attention to signals from men.

What we call beauty is simply a first intimation of terror, Rilke tells him. We prostrate ourselves before beauty to thank it for disdaining to destroy us. Would they destroy him if he ventured too close, these beautiful creatures from other worlds, these angels, or would they find him too negligible for that?

In a poetry magazine – *Ambit* perhaps, or *Agenda* – he finds an announcement for a weekly workshop run by the Poetry Society for the benefit of young, unpublished writers. He turns up at the advertised time and place wearing his black suit. The woman at the door inspects him suspiciously, demands his age. 'Twenty-one,' he says. It is a lie: he is twenty-two.

Sitting around in leather armchairs, his fellow poets eye him, nod distantly. They seem to know one another; he is the only newcomer. They are younger than he, teenagers in fact, except for a middle-aged man with a limp who is something in the Poetry Society. They take turns to read out their latest poems. The poem he himself reads ends with the words 'the furious waves of my incontinence.' The man with the limp deems his word choice unfortunate. To anyone who has worked in a hospital, he says, incontinence means urinary incontinence or worse.

He turns up again the next week, and after the session has coffee with a girl who has read out a poem about the death of a friend in a car accident, a good poem in its way, quiet, unpretentious. When she is not writing poetry, the girl informs him, she is a student at King's College, London; she dresses with appropriate severity in dark skirt and black stockings. They arrange to meet again.

They meet at Leicester Square on a Saturday afternoon. They had half agreed to go to a film; but as poets they have a duty to life at its fullest, so they repair to her room off Gower Street instead, where she allows him to undress her. He marvels at the shapeliness of her naked body, the ivory whiteness of her skin. Are all Englishwomen as beautiful when their clothes are off, he wonders?

Naked they lie in each other's arms, but there is no warmth between them; and warmth, it becomes clear, will not grow. At last the girl withdraws, folds her arms across her breasts, pushes his hands away, shakes her head mutely.

He could try to persuade her, induce her, seduce her; he might even succeed; but he lacks the spirit for it. She is not only a woman, after all, with a woman's intuitions, but an artist too. What he is trying to draw her into is not the real thing – she must know that.

In silence they get dressed. 'I'm sorry,' she says. He shrugs. He is not cross. He does not blame her. He is not without intuitions of his own. The verdict she has delivered on him would be his verdict too.

After this episode he stops going to the Poetry Society. He has never felt welcome there anyway.

He has no further luck with English girls. There are English girls enough at IBM, secretaries and punch operators, and opportunities to chat to them. But from them he feels a certain resistance, as if they are not sure who he is, what his motives might be, what he is doing in their country. He watches them with other men. Other men flirt with them in a jolly, coaxing English way. They respond to being flirted with, he can see that: they open like flowers. But flirting is not something he has learned to do. He is not even sure he approves of it. And anyhow, he cannot let it become known among the IBM girls that he is a poet. They would giggle among themselves, they would spread the story all over the building.

His highest aspiration, higher than for an English girlfriend, higher even than for a Swede or an Italian, is to have a French girl. If he had a passionate affair with a French girl he would be touched and improved, he is sure, by the grace of the French language, the subtlety of French thought. But why should a French girl, any more than an English girl, deign to speak to him? And anyway, he has not so much as laid eyes on a French girl in London. The French have France, after all, the most beautiful country in the world. Why should they come to chilly England to look after the natives' babies?

The French are the most civilized people in the world. All the writers he respects are steeped in French culture; most regard France as their spiritual home – France and, to an extent, Italy, though Italy seems to have fallen on hard times. Since the age of fifteen, when he sent off a postal order for five pounds ten shillings to the Pelman Institute and received in return a grammar book and a set of exercise sheets to be completed and returned to the Institute for marking, he has been trying to learn French. In his trunk, brought all the way from Cape Town, he has the five hundred cards on which he has written out a basic French vocabulary, one word per card, to carry around and memorize; through his mind runs a patter of French locutions – *je viens de*, I have just; *il me faut*, I must.

But his efforts have got him nowhere. He has no feel for French. Listening to French language records he cannot, most of the time, tell where one word ends and the next begins. Though he can read simple prose texts, he cannot in his inner ear hear what they sound like. The language resists him, excludes him; he cannot find a way in.

In theory he ought to find French easy. He knows Latin; for the pleasure of it he sometimes reads passages of Latin aloud – not the Latin of the Golden or the Silver Age but the Latin of the Vulgate, with its brash disregard for classical word order. He picks up Spanish without difficulty. He reads Cesar Vallejo in a dual-language text, reads Nicolas Guillén, reads Pablo Neruda. Spanish is full of barbaric-sounding words whose meaning he cannot even guess at, but that does not matter. At least every letter is pronounced, down to the double r.

The language for which he discovers a real feeling, however, is

German. He tunes in to broadcasts from Cologne and, when they are not too tedious, from East Berlin as well, and for the most part understands them; he reads German poetry and follows it well enough. He approves of the way in which every syllable in German is given its due weight. With the ghost of Afrikaans still in his ears, he is at home in the syntax. In fact, he takes pleasure in the length of German sentences, in the complex pile-up of verbs at the end. There are times, reading German, when he forgets he is in a foreign language.

He reads Ingeborg Bachmann over and over; he reads Bertolt Brecht, Hans Magnus Enzensberger. There is a sardonic undercurrent in German that attracts him though he is not sure he quite grasps why it is there – indeed wonders whether he is not just imagining it. He could ask, but he knows no one else who reads German poetry, just as he knows no one who speaks French.

Yet in this huge city there must be thousands of people steeped in German literature, thousands more who read poetry in Russian, Hungarian, Greek, Italian – read it, translate it, even write it: poets in exile, men with long hair and horn-rimmed glasses, women with sharp foreign faces and full, passionate lips. In the magazines he buys at Dillons he finds evidence enough of their existence: translations that must be their handiwork. But how will he ever meet them? What do they do, these special beings, when they are not reading and writing and translating? Does he, unbeknown to himself, sit amongst them in the audience at the Everyman, walk amongst them on Hampstead Heath?

On an impulse he strolls behind a likely looking couple on the Heath. The man is tall and bearded, the woman has long blonde hair swept casually back. He is sure they are Russian. But when he gets close enough to eavesdrop they turn out to be English; they are talking about the price of furniture at Heal's.

There remains Holland. At least he has an insider's knowledge of Dutch, at least he has that advantage. Among all the circles in London, is there a circle of Dutch poets too? If there is, will his acquaintance with the language give him an entrée to it?

Dutch poetry has always struck him as rather boring, but the name Simon Vinkenoog keeps cropping up in poetry magazines. Vinkenoog is the one Dutch poet who seems to have broken on to the international stage. He reads everything there is by Vinkenoog in the British Museum, and is not encouraged. Vinkenoog's writings are raucous, crass, lacking any dimension of mystery. If Vinkenoog is all that Holland can offer, then his worst suspicion is confirmed: that of all nations the Dutch are the dullest, the most antipoetic. So much for his Netherlandic heritage. He might as well be monolingual.

Every now and again Caroline phones him at work and arranges to meet him. Once they are together, however, she does not conceal her impatience with him. How can he come all the way to London, she says, and then spend his days adding up numbers on a machine? Look around, she says: London is a gallery of novelties and pleasures and amusements. Why does he not come out of himself, have some fun?

'Some of us are not built for fun,' he replies. She takes it as one of his little jokes, does not try to understand.

Caroline has never yet explained where she gets the money for the flat in Kensington and the new outfits she keeps appearing in. Her stepfather in South Africa is in the motor business. Is the motor business lucrative enough to fund a life of pleasure for a stepdaughter in London? What does Caroline actually do at the club where she spends the night hours? Hang coats in the cloakroom and collect tips? Carry trays of drinks? Or is working in a club a euphemism for something else?

Among the contacts she has made at the club, she informs him, is Laurence Olivier. Laurence Olivier is taking an interest in her acting career. He has promised her a part in an as yet unspecified play; he has also invited her to his house in the country.

What must he make of this information? The part in a play sounds like a lie; but is Laurence Olivier lying to Caroline or is Caroline lying to him? Laurence Olivier must by now be an old man with false teeth. Can Caroline take care of herself against Laurence Olivier, if the man who has invited her to his house in the country is indeed Olivier? What do men of that age do with girls for pleasure? Is it appropriate to be jealous of a man who can probably no longer manage an erection? Is jealousy anyhow an out-of-date emotion, here in London in 1962?

Most likely Laurence Olivier, if that is who it is, will give her the full country-house treatment, including a chauffeur to meet her at the station and a butler to wait on them at the dinner table. Then when she is befuddled with claret he will conduct her to his bed and fiddle with her, and she will let it happen, out of politeness, to thank him for the evening, and for the sake of her career too. In their tête-à-têtes will she bother to mention that there is a rival in the background, a clerk who works for an adding machine company and lives in a room off the Archway Road where he sometimes writes verses?

He does not understand why Caroline does not break off with him, the clerk boyfriend. Creeping home in the early morning dark after a night with her, he can only pray she will not get in touch with him again. And indeed, a week will sometimes pass with no word from her. Then, just as he is beginning to feel the affair is past history, she will telephone and the cycle will recommence.

He believes in passionate love and its transfiguring power. His experience, however, is that amatory relations devour his time, exhaust him, and cripple his work. Is it possible that he was not made to love women, that in truth he is a homosexual? If he were homosexual, that would explain his woes from beginning to end. Yet ever since he turned sixteen he has been fascinated by the beauty of women, by their air of mysterious unattainability. As a student he was in a continual fever of lovesickness, now for one girl, now for another, sometimes for two at the same time. Reading the poets only heightened his fever. Through the blinding ecstasy of sex, said the poets, one is transported into brightness beyond compare, into the heart of silence; one becomes at one with the elemental forces of the universe. Though brightness beyond compare has eluded him thus far, he does not doubt for a moment that the poets are correct.

One evening he allows himself to be picked up in the street, by a man. The man is older than he – in fact, of another generation. They go by taxi to Sloane Square, where the man lives – it would seem alone – in a flat full of tasselled cushions and dim table lamps.

They barely talk. He allows the man to touch him through his clothes; he offers nothing in return. If the man has an orgasm, he manages it discreetly. Afterwards he lets himself out and goes home.

Is that homosexuality? Is that the sum of it? Even if there is more to it than that, it seems a puny activity compared with sex with a woman: quick, absent-minded, devoid of dread but also devoid of allure. There seems to be nothing at stake: nothing to lose but nothing to win either. A game for people afraid of the big league; a game for losers.

Ten

The plan at the back of his mind when he came to England, insofar as he had a plan, had been to find a job and save money. When he had enough money he would give up the job and devote himself to writing. When his savings ran out he would find a new job, and so forth.

He soon discovers how naïve that plan is. His salary at IBM, before deductions, is sixty pounds a month, of which he can save at most ten. A year of labour will earn him two months of freedom; much of that free time will be eaten up in searching for the next job. The scholarship money from South Africa will barely pay his academic fees.

Furthermore, he learns, he is not at liberty to change employers at will. New regulations governing aliens in England specify that each change of employment be approved by the Home Office. It is forbidden to be footloose: if he resigns from IBM he must promptly find other work or else leave the country.

He has been with IBM long enough by now to be habituated to the routine. Yet still he finds the work day hard to get through. Though he and his fellow programmers are continually urged, at meetings, in memos, to remember they are the cutting edge of the data-processing profession, he feels like a bored clerk in Dickens sitting on a stool, copying musty documents.

The sole interruptions to the tedium of the day come at eleven and three-thirty, when the tea lady arrives with her trolley to slap down a cup of strong English tea before each of them ('There you go, love'). Only when the five o'clock flurry is past – the secretaries and punch opera-tors leave on the dot, no question of overtime with them – and the evening deepens is he free to leave his desk, wander around, relax. The machine room downstairs, dominated by the huge memory cabinets of the 7090, is more often than not empty; he can run programs on the little 1401 computer, even, surreptitiously, play games on it.

At such times he finds his job not just bearable but pleasing. He would not mind spending all night in the bureau, running programs of his own devising until he grows dozy, then brushing his teeth in the toilet and spreading a sleeping bag under his desk. It would be better than catching the last train and trudging up Archway Road to his lonely room. But such irregular behaviour would be frowned on by IBM.

He makes friends with one of the punch operators. Her name is Rhoda; she is somewhat thick-legged but has an attractively silky olive complexion. She takes her work seriously; sometimes he stands in the doorway watching her, hunched over her keyboard. She is aware of him watching but does not seem to mind.

He never gets to talk to Rhoda about anything beyond work. Her English, with its triphthongs and glottal stops, is not easy to follow. She is a native in a way that his fellow programmers, with their grammar-school backgrounds, are not; the life she leads outside work hours is a closed book to him.

He had prepared himself, when he arrived in the country, for the famous British coldness of temperament. But the girls at IBM, he finds, are not like that at all. They have a cosy sensuality of their own, the sensuality of animals brought up together in the same steamy den, familiar with each other's body habits. Though they cannot compete in glamour with the Swedes and Italians, he is attracted to these English girls, to their equability and humorousness. He would like to get to know Rhoda better. But how? She belongs to a foreign tribe. The barriers he would have to work his way past, to say nothing of the conventions of tribal courtship, baffle and dishearten him.

The efficiency of the Newman Street operation is measured by the use it makes of the 7090. The 7090 is the heart of the bureau, the reason for its existence. When the 7090 is not running its time is called idle time. Idle time is inefficient, and inefficiency is a sin. The ultimate goal of the bureau is to keep the 7090 running all day and all night; the most valued clients are those who occupy the 7090 for hours on end. Such clients are the fief of the senior programmers; he has nothing to do with them.

One day, however, one of the serious clients runs into difficulties with his data cards, and he is assigned to help him. The client is a Mr Pomfret, a little man in a rumpled suit and glasses. He comes to London each Thursday from somewhere in the north of England, bringing boxes and boxes of punched cards; he has a regular six-hour booking on the 7090, starting at midnight. From gossip in the office he learns that the cards contain wind-tunnel data for a new British bomber, the TSR-2, being developed for the RAF.

Mr Pomfret's problem, and the problem of Mr Pomfret's colleagues back north, is that the results of the last two weeks' runs are anomalous. They make no sense. Either the test data are faulty or there is something wrong with the design of the plane. His assignment is to reread Mr Pomfret's cards on the auxiliary machine, the 1401, carrying out checks to determine whether any have been mispunched.

He works past midnight. Batch by batch he passes Mr Pomfret's cards through the card-reader. In the end he is able to report there is nothing wrong with the punching. The results were indeed anomalous; the problem is real.

The problem is real. In the most incidental, the most minor way, he has joined the TSR-2 project, become part of the British defence effort; he has furthered British plans to bomb Moscow. Is this what he came to England for: to participate in evil, an evil in which there is no reward, not even the most imaginary? Where is the romance in staying up all night so that Mr Pomfret the aeronautical engineer, with his soft and rather helpless air and his suitcase full of cards, can catch the first train north so as to get back to the lab in time for his Friday morning meeting?

He mentions in a letter to his mother that he has been working on wind-tunnel data for the TSR-2, but his mother has not the faintest idea what the TSR-2 is.

The wind-tunnel tests come to an end. Mr Pomfret's visits to London cease. He watches the newspapers for further news of the TSR-2, but there is nothing. The TSR-2 seems to have gone into limbo.

Now that it is too late, he wonders what would have happened if, while the TSR-2 cards were in his hands, he had surreptitiously doctored the data on them. Would the whole bomber project have been thrown into confusion, or would the engineers in the north have detected his meddling? On the one hand, he would like to do his bit to save Russia from being bombed. On the other, has he a moral right to enjoy British hospitality while sabotaging their air force? And anyhow, how would the Russians ever get to know that an obscure sympathizer in an IBM office in London had won them a few days' breathing-space in the Cold War?

He does not see what the British have against the Russians. Britain and Russia have been on the same side in all the wars he knows of since 1854. The Russians have never threatened to invade Britain. Why then are the British siding with the Americans, who behave like bullies in Europe as all over the world? It is not as though the British actually like the Americans. Newspaper cartoonists are always taking digs at American tourists, with their cigars and pot bellies and flowered Hawaiian shirts and the fistfuls of dollars they brandish. In his opinion, the British ought to take their lead from the French and get out of NATO, leaving the Americans and their new chums the West Germans to pursue their grudge against Russia.

The newspapers are full of CND, the Campaign for Nuclear Disarmament. The pictures they print of weedy men and plain girls with ratty hair waving placards and shouting slogans do not predispose him to like CND. On the other hand, Khrushchev has just carried out a tactical masterstroke: he has built Russian missile-pods in Cuba to counteract the American missiles that ring Russia. Now Kennedy is threatening to bombard Russia unless the Russian missiles are removed from Cuba. This is what CND is agitating against: a nuclear strike in which American bases in Britain would participate. He cannot but approve of its stand.

American spy-planes take pictures of Russian freighters crossing the Atlantic on their way to Cuba. The freighters are carrying more missiles, say the Americans. In the pictures the missiles – vague shapes under tarpaulins – are circled in white. In his view, the shapes could just as well be lifeboats. He is surprised that the papers don't question the American story.

Wake up! clamours CND: *we are on the brink of nuclear annihilation!* Might it be true, he wonders? Is everyone going to perish, himself included?

He goes to a big CND rally in Trafalgar Square, taking care to stay on the fringes as a way of signalling that he is only an onlooker. It is the first mass meeting he has ever been to: fist-shaking and slogan-chanting, the whipping up of passion in general, repel him. Only love and art are, in his opinion, worthy of giving oneself to without reserve.

The rally is the culmination of a fifty-mile march by CND stalwarts that started a week ago outside Aldermaston, the British atomic weapons station. For days the *Guardian* has been carrying pictures of sodden marchers on the road. Now, on Trafalgar Square, the mood is dark. As he listens to the speeches it becomes clear that these people, or some of them, do indeed believe what they say. They believe that London is going to be bombed; they believe they are all going to die.

Are they right? If they are, it seems vastly unfair: unfair to the Russians, unfair to the people of London, but unfair most of all to him, having to be incinerated as a consequence of American bellicosity.

He thinks of young Nikolai Rostov on the battlefield of Austerlitz, watching like a hypnotized rabbit as the French grenadiers come charging at him with their grim bayonets. *How can they want to kill me,* he protests to himself – *me, whom everyone is so fond of?*

From the frying pan into the fire! What an irony! Having escaped the Afrikaners who want to press-gang him into their army and the blacks who want to drive him into the sea, to find himself on an island that is shortly to be turned to cinders! What kind of world is this? Where can one go to be free of the fury of politics? Only Sweden seems to be above the fray. Should he throw up everything and catch the next boat to Stockholm? Does one have to speak Swedish to get into Sweden? Does Sweden need computer programmers? Does Sweden even have computers?

The rally ends. He goes back to his room. He ought to be reading *The Golden Bowl* or working on his poems, but what would be the point, what is the point of anything?

Then a few days later the crisis is suddenly over. In the face of Kennedy's threats, Khrushchev capitulates. The freighters are ordered to turn back.

The missiles already in Cuba are disarmed. The Russians produce a form of words to explain their action, but they have clearly been humiliated. From this episode in history only the Cubans emerge with credit. Undaunted, the Cubans vow that, missiles or not, they will defend their revolution to the last drop of blood. He approves of the Cubans, and of Fidel Castro. At least Fidel is not a coward.

At the Tate Gallery he falls into conversation with a girl he takes to be a tourist. She is plain, bespectacled, solidly planted on her feet, the kind of girl he is not interested in but probably belongs with. Her name is Astrid, she tells him. She is from Austria – from Klagenfurt, not Vienna.

Astrid is not a tourist, it turns out, but an au pair. The next day he takes her to a film. Their tastes are quite dissimilar, he sees that at once. Nevertheless, when she invites him back to the house where she works, he does not say no. He gets a brief glimpse of her room: a garret with blue gingham curtains and matching coverlet and a teddy bear propped against the pillow.

Downstairs he has tea with her and her employer, an Englishwoman whose cool eyes take his measure and find him wanting. This is a European house, her eyes say: we don't need a graceless colonial here, and a Boer to boot.

It is not a good time to be a South African in England. With great show of self-righteousness, South Africa has declared itself a republic and promptly been expelled from the British Commonwealth. The message contained in that expulsion has been unmistakable. The British have had enough of the Boers and of Boer-led South Africa, a colony that has always been more trouble than it has been worth. They would be content if South Africa would quietly vanish over the horizon. They certainly do not want forlorn South African whites cluttering their doorstep like orphans in search of parents. He has no doubt that Astrid will be obliquely informed by this suave Englishwoman that he is not a desirable.

Out of loneliness, out of pity too, perhaps, for this unhappy, graceless foreigner with her poor English, he invites Astrid out again. Afterwards, for no good reason, he persuades her to come back with him to his room. She is not yet eighteen, still has baby fat on her; he has never been with someone so young – a child, really. Her skin, when he undresses her, feels cold and clammy. He has made a mistake, already he knows it. He feels no desire; as for Astrid, though women and their needs are usually a mystery to him, he is sure she feels none either. But they have come too far, the two of them, to pull back, so they go through with it.

In the weeks that follow they spend several more evenings together. But time is always a problem. Astrid can come out only after her employers' children have been put to bed; they have at most a hurried hour together before the last train back to Kensington. Once she is brave enough to stay the whole night. He pretends to like having her there, but the truth is he does not. He sleeps better by himself. With someone sharing his bed he lies tense and stiff all night, wakes up exhausted.

Eleven

Years ago, when he was still a child in a family trying its best to be normal, his parents used to go to Saturday night dances. He would watch while they made their preparations; if he stayed up late enough, he could interrogate his mother afterwards. But what actually went on in the ball-room of the Masonic Hotel in the town of Worcester he never got to see: what kind of dances his parents danced, whether they pretended to gaze into each other's eyes while they did it, whether they danced only with each other or whether, as in American films, a stranger was allowed to put a hand on the woman's shoulder and take her away from her partner, so that the partner would have to find another partner for himself or else stand in a corner smoking a cigarette and sulking.

Why people who were already married should go to the trouble of dressing up and going to a hotel to dance when they could have done it just as well in the living room, to music on the radio, he found hard to understand. But to his mother Saturday nights at the Masonic Hotel were apparently important, as important as being free to ride a horse or, when no horse was to be had, a bicycle. Dancing and horse riding stood for the life that had been hers before she married, before, in her version of her life-story, she became a prisoner ('I will not be a prisoner in this house!').

Her adamancy got her nowhere. Whoever it was from his father's office who had given them lifts to the Saturday night dances moved house or stopped going. The shiny blue dress with its silver pin, the white gloves, the funny little hat that sat on the side of the head, vanished into closets and drawers, and that was that.

As for himself, he was glad the dancing had come to an end, though he did not say so. He did not like his mother to go out, did not like the abstracted air that came over her the next day. In dancing itself he saw no sense anyway. Films that promised to have dancing in them he avoided, repelled by the goofy, sentimental look that people got on their faces.

'Dancing is good exercise,' insisted his mother. 'It teaches you rhythm and balance.' He was not persuaded. If people needed exercise, they could do calisthenics or swing barbells or run around the block.

In the years that have passed since he left Worcester behind he has not changed his mind about dancing. When as a university student he found it too much of an embarrassment to go to parties and not know how to dance, he enrolled for a package of lessons at a dance school, paying for them out of his own pocket: quickstep, waltz, twist, cha-cha. It did not work: within months he had forgotten everything, in an act of willed forgetting. Why that happened he knows perfectly well. Never for a moment, even during the lessons, was he really giving himself to the dance. Though his feet followed the patterns, inwardly he remained rigid with resistance. And so it still is: at the deepest level he can see no reason why people need to dance.

Dancing makes sense only when it is interpreted as something else, something that people prefer not to admit. That *something else* is the real thing: the dance is merely a cover. Inviting a girl to dance stands for inviting her to have intercourse; accepting the invitation stands for agreeing to have intercourse; and dancing is a miming and fore-shadowing of intercourse. So obvious are the correspondences that he wonders why people bother with dancing at all. Why the dressing up, why the ritual motions; why the huge sham?

Old-fashioned dance music with its clodhopping rhythms, the music of the Masonic Hotel, has always bored him. As for the crude music from America to which people of his own age dance, he feels only a fastidious distaste for it.

Back in South Africa the songs on the radio all came from America. In the newspapers the antics of American film stars were obsessively followed, American crazes like the hula hoop slavishly imitated. Why? Why look to America in everything? Disowned by the Dutch and now by the British, had South Africans made up their minds to become fake Americans, even though most had never in their lives clapped eyes on a real American?

In Britain he had expected to get away from America – from American music, American fads. But to his dismay the British are no less eager to ape America. The popular newspapers carry pictures of girls screaming their heads off at concerts. Men with hair down to their shoulders shout and whine in fake American accents and then smash their guitars to pieces. It is all beyond him.

Britain's saving grace is the Third Programme. If there is one thing he looks forward to after a day at IBM, it is coming home to the quiet of his room and switching on the radio and being visited with music he has never heard before, or cool, intelligent talk. Evening after evening, without fail and at no cost, the portals open at his touch.

The Third Programme broadcasts only on long wave. If the Third Programme were on short wave he might have picked it up in Cape Town. In that case, what need would there have been to come to London?

There is a talk in the 'Poets and Poetry' series about a Russian named Joseph Brodsky. Accused of being a social parasite, Joseph Brodsky has been sentenced to five years of hard labour in a camp on the Archangel peninsula in the frozen north. The sentence is still running. Even as he sits in his warm room in London, sipping his coffee, nibbling his dessert of raisins and nuts, there is a man of his own age, a poet like himself, sawing logs all day, nursing frostbitten fingers, patching his boots with rags, living on fish heads and cabbage soup.

'As dark as the inside of a needle,' writes Brodsky in one of his poems. He cannot get the line out of his mind. If he concentrated, truly concentrated, night after night, if he compelled, by sheer attention, the blessing of inspiration to descend upon him, he might be able to come up with something to match it. For he has it in him, he knows, his imagination is of the same colour as Brodsky's. But how to get word through to Archangel afterwards?

On the basis of the poems he has heard on the radio and nothing else, he knows Brodsky, knows him through and through. That is what poetry is capable of. Poetry is truth. But of him in London Brodsky can know nothing. How to tell the frozen man he is with him, by his side, day by day?

Joseph Brodsky, Ingeborg Bachmann, Zbigniew Herbert: from lone rafts tossed on the dark seas of Europe they release their words into the air, and along the airwaves the words speed to his room, the words of the poets of his time, telling him of what poetry can be and therefore of what he can be, filling him with joy that he inhabits the same earth as they. 'Signal heard in London – please continue to transmit': that is the message he would send them if he could.

In South Africa he had heard one or two pieces by Schoenberg and Berg – Verklärte Nacht, the violin concerto. Now for the first time he hears the music of Anton von Webern. He has been warned against Webern. Webern goes too far, he has read: what Webern writes is no longer music, just random sounds. Crouched over the radio, he listens. First one note, then another, then another, cold as ice crystals, strung out like stars in the sky. A minute or two of this raptness, then it is over.

Webern was shot in 1945 by an American soldier. A misunderstanding, it was called, an accident of war. The brain that mapped those sounds, those silences, that sound-and-silence, extinguished for ever.

He goes to an exhibition of the abstract expressionists at the Tate Gallery. For a quarter of an hour he stands before a Jackson Pollock, giving it a chance to penetrate him, trying to look judicious in case some suave Londoner is keeping an amused eye on this provincial ignoramus. It does not help. The painting means nothing to him. There is something about it he does not get.

In the next room, high up on a wall, sits a huge painting consisting of no more than an elongated black blob on a white field. Elegy for the Spanish Republic 24 by Robert Motherwell, says the label. He is transfixed. Menacing and mysterious, the black shape takes him over. A sound like the stroke of a gong goes out from it, leaving him shaken and weak-kneed.

Where does its power come from, this amorphous shape that bears no resemblance to Spain or anything else, yet stirs up a well of dark feeling within him? It is not beautiful, yet it speaks like beauty, imperiously. Why does Motherwell have this power and not Pollock, or Van

Gogh, or Rembrandt? Is it the same power that makes his heart leap at the sight of one woman and not another? Does *Elegy for the Spanish Republic* correspond to some indwelling shape in his soul? What of the woman who is to be his fate? Is her shadow already stored in his inner darkness? How much longer before she reveals herself? When she does, will he be prepared?

What the answer is he cannot say. But if he can meet her as an equal, her, the Destined One, then their lovemaking will be unexampled, that he is sure of, an ecstasy bordering on death; and when he returns to life afterwards it will be as a new being, transformed. A flash of extinction like the touching of opposite poles, like the mating of twins; then the slow rebirth. He must be ready for it. Readiness is all.

At the Everyman Cinema there is a season of Satyajit Ray. He watches the Apu trilogy on successive nights in a state of rapt absorption. In Apu's bitter, trapped mother, his engaging, feckless father, he recognizes, with a pang of guilt, his own parents. But it is the music above all that grips him, dizzyingly complex interplays between drums and stringed instruments, long arias on the flute whose scale or mode – he does not know enough about music theory to be sure which – catches at his heart, sending him into a mood of sensual melancholy that lasts long after the film has ended.

Hitherto he has found in Western music, in Bach above all, everything he needs. Now he encounters something that is not in Bach, though there are intimations of it: a joyous yielding of the reasoning, comprehending mind to the dance of the fingers.

He hunts through record shops, and in one of them finds an LP of a sitar player named Ustad Vilayat Khan, with his brother – a younger brother, to judge from the picture – on the veena, and an unnamed tabla player. He does not have a gramophone of his own, but he is able to listen to the first ten minutes in the shop. It is all there: the hovering exploration of tone-sequences, the quivering emotion, the ecstatic rushes. He cannot believe his good fortune. A new continent, and all for a mere nine shillings! He takes the record back to his room, packs it away between sleeves of cardboard till the day when he will be able to listen to it again.

There is an Indian couple living in the room below him. They have a baby that sometimes, faintly, cries. He exchanges nods with the man when they pass on the stairs. The woman rarely emerges.

One evening there is a knock at his door. It is the Indian. Would he like to have a meal with them?

He accepts, but with misgivings. He is not used to strong spices. Will he be able to eat without spluttering and making a fool of himself? But he is at once put at his ease. The family is from South India; they are vegetarians. Hot spices are not an essential part of Indian cuisine, explains his host: they were introduced only to hide the taste of rotting meat. South Indian food is quite gentle on the palate. And indeed, so it proves to be. What is set before him – coconut soup spiced with cardamom and cloves, an omelette – is positively milky.

His host is an engineer. He and his wife have been in England for several years. They are happy here, he says. Their present accommodation is the best they have had thus far. The room is spacious, the house quiet and orderly. Of course they are not fond of the English climate. But – he shrugs his shoulders – one must take the rough with the smooth.

His wife barely enters the conversation. She serves them without herself eating, then retires to the corner where the baby lies in his cot. Her English is not good, her husband says.

His engineer neighbour admires Western science and technology, complains that India is backward. Though paeans to machines usually bore him, he says nothing to contradict the man. These are the first people in England to invite him into their home. More than that: they are people of colour, they are aware he is South African, yet they have extended a hand to him. He is grateful.

The question is, what should he do with his gratitude? It is inconceivable that he should invite them, husband and wife and no doubt crying baby, to his room on the top floor to eat packet soup followed by, if not chipolatas, then macaroni in cheese sauce. But how else does one return hospitality?

A week passes and he does nothing, then a second week. He feels more and more embarrassed. He begins listening at his door in the mornings, waiting for the engineer to leave for work before he steps out on to the landing.

There must be some gesture to make, some simple act of reciprocation, but he cannot find it, or else will not, and it is fast becoming too late anyway. What is wrong with him? Why does he make the most ordinary things so hard for himself? If the answer is that it is his nature, what is the good of having a nature like that? Why not change his nature?

But is it his nature? He doubts that. It does not feel like nature, it feels like a sickness, a moral sickness: meanness, poverty of spirit, no different in its essence from his coldness with women. Can one make art out of a sickness like that? And if one can, what does that say about art?

On a noticeboard outside a Hampstead newsagent's he reads an advertisement: 'Fourth required for flat in Swiss Cottage. Own room, share kitchen.'

He does not like sharing. He prefers living on his own. But as long as he lives on his own he will never break out of his isolation. He telephones, makes an appointment.

The man who shows him the flat is a few years older than he. He is bearded, wears a blue Nehru jacket with gold buttons down the front. His name is Miklos, and he is from Hungary. The flat itself is clean and airy; the room that will be his is larger than the room he rents at present, more modern too. 'I'll take it,' he tells Miklos without hesitation. 'Shall I give you a deposit?'

But it is not as simple as that. 'Leave your name and number and I'll put you on the list,' says Miklos.

For three days he waits. On the fourth day he telephones. Miklos is not in, says the girl who answers. The room? Oh, the room is gone, it went days ago.

Her voice has a faint foreign huskiness to it; no doubt she is beautiful, intelligent, sophisticated. He does not ask whether she is Hungarian too. But if he had got the room, he would now be sharing a flat with her. Who is she? What is her name? Was she his destined love, and has his destiny now escaped him? Who is the fortunate one who has been granted the room and the future that should have been his?

He had the impression, when he called at the flat, that Miklos was showing him around rather perfunctorily. He can only think that Miklos was looking for someone who would bring more to the economy of the household than just a quarter of the rent, someone who would offer gaiety or style or romance as well. Summing him up in a glance, Miklos found him lacking in gaiety, style and romance, and rejected him.

He should have taken the initiative. 'I am not what I may seem to be,' he should have said. 'I may look like a clerk, but in reality I am a poet, or a poet to be. Furthermore, I will pay my share of the rent punctiliously, which is more than most poets will do.' But he had not spoken up, had not pleaded, however abjectly, for himself and his vocation; and now it is too late.

How does a Hungarian come to dispose over a flat in fashionable Swiss Cottage, to dress in the latest mode, to wake up in the lazy late morning with the no doubt beautiful girl with the husky voice beside him in bed, while he has to slave the day away for IBM and live in a dreary room off the Archway Road? How have the keys that unlock the pleasures of London come into the possession of Miklos? Where do such people find the money to support their life of ease?

He has never liked people who disobey the rules. If the rules are ignored, life ceases to make sense: one might as well, like Ivan Karamazov, hand back one's ticket and retire. Yet London seems to be full of people who ignore the rules and get away with it. He seems to be the only one stupid enough to play by the rules, he and the other dark-suited, bespectacled, harried clerks he sees in the trains. What, then, should he do? Should he follow Ivan? Should he follow Miklos? Whichever he follows, it seems to him, he loses. For he has no talent for lying or deception or rule-bending, just as he has no talent for pleasure or fancy clothes. His sole talent is for misery, dull, honest misery. If this city offers no reward for misery, what is he doing here?

Twelve

Each week a letter arrives from his mother, a pale-blue aerogramme addressed in neat block capitals. It is with exasperation that he receives these evidences of her unvarying love for him. Will his mother not understand that when he departed Cape Town he cut all bonds with the past? How can he make her accept that the process of turning himself into a different person that began when he was fifteen will be carried through remorselessly until all memory of the family and the country he left behind is extinguished? When will she see that he has grown so far away from her that he might as well be a stranger?

In her letters his mother tells him family news, tells him of her latest work assignments (she moves from school to school substituting for teachers away on sick leave). She ends her letters hoping that his health is good, that he is taking care to wear warm clothes, that he has not succumbed to the influenza she has heard to be sweeping across Europe. As for South African affairs, she does not write about those because he has made it plain he is not interested.

He mentions that he has mislaid his gloves on a train. A mistake. Promptly a package arrives by air mail: a pair of sheepskin mittens. The stamps cost more than the mittens.

She writes her letters on Sunday evenings and posts them in time for the Monday morning collection. He can imagine the scene all too easily, in the flat into which she and his father and his brother moved when they had to sell the house in Rondebosch. Supper is over. She clears the table, dons her glasses, draws the lamp nearer. 'What are you doing now?' asks his father, who dreads Sunday evenings, when the *Argus* has been read from end to end and there is nothing left to do. 'I must write to John,' she replies, pursing her lips, shutting him out. *Dearest John*, she begins.

What does she hope to achieve by her letters, this obstinate, graceless woman? Can she not recognize that proofs of her fidelity, no matter how dogged, will never make him relent and come back? Can she not accept that he is not normal? She should concentrate her love on his brother and forget him. His brother is a simpler and more innocent being. His brother has a soft heart. Let his brother take on the burden of loving her; let his brother be told that from now on he is her first-born, her best beloved. Then he, the new-forgotten one, will be free to make his own life.

She writes every week but he does not write every week in return. That would be too much like reciprocation. Only now and then does he reply, and his letters are brief, saying little except that, by the fact of their having been written, he must still be in the land of the living.

That is the worst of it. That is the trap she has built, a trap he has not yet found a way out of. If he were to cut all ties, if he were not to write at all, she would draw the worst conclusion, the worst possible; and the very thought of the grief that would pierce her at that moment makes him want to block his ears and eyes. As long as she is alive he dare not die. As long as she is alive, therefore, his life is not his own. He may not be reckless with it. Though he does not particularly love himself, he must, for her sake, take care of himself, to the point even of dressing warmly, eating the right food, taking vitamin C. As for suicide, of that there can be no question.

What news he gets about South Africa comes from the BBC and the *Manchester Guardian*. He reads the Guardian reports with dread. A farmer ties one of his workers to a tree and flogs him to death. Police fire at random into a crowd. A prisoner is found dead in his cell, hanging from a strip of blanket, his face bruised and bloody. Horror upon horror, atrocity upon atrocity, without relief.

He knows his mother's opinions. She thinks South Africa is misunderstood by the world. Blacks in South Africa are better off than anywhere else in Africa. The strikes and protests are fomented by communist agitators. As for the farm labourers who are paid their wages in the form of mealie-meal and have to dress their children in jute bags against the winter cold, his mother concedes that that is a disgrace. But such things happen only in the Transvaal. It is the Afrikaners of the Transvaal, with their sullen hatreds and their hard hearts, who give the country such a bad name.

His own opinion, which he does not hesitate to communicate to her, is that, instead of making speech after speech at the United Nations, the Russians ought to invade South Africa without delay. They should land paratroops in Pretoria, take Verwoerd and his cronies captive, line them up against a wall, and shoot them.

What the Russians should do next, after shooting Verwoerd, he does not say, not having thought it out. Justice must be done, that is all that matters; the rest is politics, and he is not interested in politics. As far back as he can remember, Afrikaners have trampled on people because, they claim, they were once trampled upon. Well, let the wheel turn, let force be replied to with greater force. He is glad to be out of it.

South Africa is like an albatross around his neck. He wants it removed, he does not care how, so that he can begin to breathe.

He does not have to buy the *Manchester Guardian*. There are other, easier newspapers: *The Times*, for instance, or the *Daily Telegraph*. But the *Manchester Guardian* can be relied on not to miss anything from South Africa that will make the soul cringe within him. Reading the *Manchester Guardian*, he can at least be sure he knows the worst.

He has not contacted Astrid for weeks. Now she telephones. Her time in England is up, she is going home to Austria. 'I guess I won't see you again,' she says, 'so I called to say goodbye.'

She is trying to be matter-of-fact, but he can hear the tearfulness in her voice. Guiltily he proposes a meeting. They have coffee together; she comes back to his room and spends the night ('our last night,' she calls it), clinging to him, crying softly. Early the next morning (it is a Sunday) he hears her creep out of bed and tiptoe to the bathroom on the landing to get dressed. When she comes back he pretends to be asleep. He has only to give the slightest signal, he knows, and she will stay. If there are things he would prefer to do first, before paying attention to her, like reading the newspaper, she will sit quietly in a corner and wait. That seems to be how girls are taught to behave in Klagenfurt: to demand nothing, to wait until the man is ready, and then to serve him.

He would like to be nicer to Astrid, so young, so alone in the big city. He would like to dry her tears, make her smile; he would like to prove to her that his heart is not as hard as it seems, that he is capable of responding to her willingness with a willingness of his own, a willingness to cuddle her as she wants to be cuddled and give ear to her stories about her mother and brothers back home. But he must be careful. Too much warmth and she might cancel her ticket, stay in London, move in with him. Two of the defeated sheltering in each other's arms, consoling each other: the prospect is too humiliating. They might as well get married, he and Astrid, then spend the rest of their lives looking after each other like invalids. So he gives no signal, but lies with his eyelids clenched till he hears the creak of the stairs and the click of the front door.

It is December, and the weather has turned bitter. Snow falls, the snow turns to slush, the slush freezes: on the sidewalks one has to pick one's way from foothold to foothold like a mountaineer. A blanket of fog enfolds the city, fog thick with coal dust and sulphur. The electricity fails; trains stop running; old people freeze to death in their homes. The worst winter of the century, say the newspapers.

He tramps up Archway Road, slipping and sliding on the ice, holding a scarf over his face, trying not to breathe. His clothes smell of sulphur, there is a foul taste in his mouth, when he coughs he coughs up black phlegm. In South Africa it is summer. If he were there he could be on Strandfontein beach, running over mile after mile of white sand under a great blue sky.

During the night a pipe bursts in his room. The floor is flooded. He wakes up surrounded by a sheet of ice.

It is like the blitz all over again, say the newspapers. They print stories of soup kitchens for the homeless run by women's auxiliaries, of repair crews toiling through the night. The crisis is bringing out the best in

Londoners, they say, who confront adversity with quiet strength and a ready quip.

As for him, he may dress like a Londoner, tramp to work like a Londoner, suffer the cold like a Londoner, but he has no ready quips. Not in a month of Sundays would Londoners take him for the real thing. On the contrary, Londoners recognize him at once as another of those foreigners who for daft reasons of their own choose to live where they don't belong.

How long will he have to live in England before it is allowed that he has become the real thing, become English? Will getting a British passport be enough, or does an odd-sounding foreign name mean he will be shut out for ever? And 'becoming English' – what does that mean anyhow? England is the home of two nations: he will have to choose between them, choose whether to be middle-class English or working-class English. Already he seems to have chosen. He wears the uniform of the middle class, reads a middle-class newspaper, imitates middle-class speech. But mere externals such as those are not going to be enough to get him admission, not by a long chalk. Admission to the middle class – full admission, not a temporary ticket valid for certain times of the day on certain days of the year – was decided, as far as he can tell, years ago, even generations ago, according to rules that will forever be dark to him.

As for the working class, he does not share its recreations, can barely understand its speech, has never felt the slightest motion of welcome from it. The girls at IBM have their own working-class boyfriends, are wrapped up in thoughts of marriage and babies and council houses, respond frostily to overtures. He may be living in England, but it is certainly not by invitation of the English working class.

There are other South Africans in London, thousands of them, if he is to believe report. There are Canadians too, Australians, New Zealanders, even Americans. But these people are not immigrants, are not here to settle, to become English. They have come to have fun or to study or to earn some money before going on a tour of Europe. When they have had enough of the Old World they will go home and take up their real lives.

There are Europeans in London as well, not only language students but refugees from the Eastern Bloc and, further back, from Nazi Germany. But their situation is different from his. He is not a refugee; or rather, a claim on his part to be a refugee will get him nowhere with the Home Office. Who is oppressing you, the Home Office will say? From what are you fleeing? From boredom, he will reply. From philistinism. From atrophy of the moral life. From shame. Where will such a plea get him?

Then there is Paddington. He walks along Maida Vale or Kilburn High Road at six o'clock in the evening and sees, under the ghostly sodium lights, throngs of West Indians trudging back to their lodgings, muffled against the cold. Their shoulders are bowed, their hands are thrust deep in their pockets, their skins have a greyish, powdery hue. What draws them from Jamaica and Trinidad to this heartless city where the cold seeps up from the very stones of the streets, where the hours of daylight are spent in drudgery and the evenings huddled over a gas fire in a hired room with peeling walls and sagging furniture? Surely they are not all here to find fame as poets.

The people he works with are too polite to express their opinion of foreigner visitors. Nevertheless, from certain of their silences he knows he is not wanted in their country, not positively wanted. On the subject of West Indians they are silent too. But he can read the signs. NIGGER GO HOME say slogans painted on walls. NO COLOURED say notices in the windows of lodging houses. Month by month the government tightens its immigration laws. West Indians are halted at the dockside in Liverpool, detained until they grow desperate, then shipped back to where they came from. If he is not made to feel as nakedly unwelcome as they are, it can only be because of his protective coloration: his Moss Brothers suit, his pale skin.

Thirteen

'After careful consideration I have reached the conclusion . . .' 'After much soul-searching I have come to the conclusion . . .'

He has been in the service of IBM for over a year: winter, spring, summer, autumn, another winter, and now the beginning of another spring. Even inside the Newman Street bureau, a box-like building with sealed windows, he can feel the suave change in the air. He cannot go on like this. He cannot sacrifice any more of his life to the principle that human beings should have to labour in misery for their bread, a principle he seems to adhere to though he has no idea where he picked it up. He cannot forever be demonstrating to his mother in Cape Town that he has made a solid life for himself and therefore that she can stop worrying about him. Usually he does not know his own mind, does not care to know his own mind. To know one's own mind too well spells, in his view, the death of the creative spark. But in this case he cannot afford to drift on in his usual haze of indecision. He must leave IBM. He must get out, no matter how much it will cost in humiliation.

Over the past year his handwriting has, beyond his control, been growing smaller, smaller and more secretive. Now, sitting at his desk, writing what will be the announcement of his resignation, he tries consciously to make the letters larger, the loops fatter and more confident-seeming.

'After lengthy reflection,' he writes at last, 'I have reached the conclusion that my future does not lie with IBM. In terms of my contract I therefore wish to tender one month's notice.'

He signs the letter, seals it, addresses it to Dr B. L. McIver, Manager,

Programming Division, and drops it discreetly in the tray marked INTERNAL. No one in the office gives him a glance. He takes his seat again.

Until three o'clock, when the mail is next collected, there is time for second thoughts, time to slip the letter out of the tray and tear it up. Once the letter is delivered, however, the die will be cast. By tomorrow the news will have spread through the building: one of McIver's people, one of the programmers on the second floor, the South African, has resigned. No one will want to be seen speaking to him. He will be sent to Coventry. That is how it is at IBM. No false sentiment. He will be marked as a quitter, a loser, unclean.

At three o'clock the woman comes around for the mail. He bends over his papers, his heart thumping.

Half an hour later he is summoned to McIver's office. McIver is in a cold fury. 'What is this?' he says, indicating the letter that lies open on his desk.

'I have decided to resign.'

'Why?'

He had guessed McIver would take it badly. McIver is the one who interviewed him for the job, who accepted and approved him, who swallowed the story that he was just an ordinary bloke from the colonies planning a career in computers. McIver has his own bosses, to whom he will have to explain his mistake.

McIver is a tall man. He dresses sleekly, speaks with an Oxford accent. He has no interest in programming as a science or skill or craft or whatever it is. He is simply a manager. That is what he is good at: allotting tasks to people, managing their time, driving them, getting his money's worth out of them.

'Why?' says McIver again, impatiently.

'I don't find working for IBM very satisfying at a human level. I don't find it fulfilling.'

'Go on.'

'I was hoping for something more.'

'And what may that be?'

'I was hoping for friendships.'

'You find the atmosphere unfriendly?'

'No, not unfriendly, not at all. People have been very kind. But being friendly is not the same thing as friendship.'

He had hoped the letter would be allowed to be his last word. But that hope was naïve. He should have realized they would receive it as nothing but the first shot in a war.

'What else? If there is something else on your mind, this is your chance to bring it out.'

'Nothing else.'

'Nothing else. I see. You are missing friendships. You haven't found friends.'

'Yes, that's right. I'm not blaming anyone. The fault is probably my own.'

'And for that you want to resign.'

'Yes.'

Now that the words are out they sound stupid, and they are stupid. He is being manoeuvred into saying stupid things. But he should have expected that. That is how they will make him pay for rejecting them and the job they have given him, a job with IBM, the market leader. Like a beginner in chess, pushed into corners and mated in ten moves, in eight moves, in seven moves. A lesson in domination. Well, let them do it. Let them play their moves, and let him play his stupid, easily foreseen, easily countered return moves, until they are bored with the game and let him go.

With a brusque gesture McIver terminates the interview. That, for the moment, is that. He is free to return to his desk. For once there is not even the obligation to work late. He can leave the building at five, win the evening for himself.

The next morning, through McIver's secretary – McIver himself sweeps past him, not returning his greeting – he is instructed to report without delay to IBM Head Office in the City, to the Personnel Department.

The man in Personnel who hears his case has clearly had recounted to him his complaint about the friendships IBM has failed to supply. A folder lies open on the desk before him; as the interrogation proceeds, he ticks off points. How long has he been unhappy in his work? Did he at any stage discuss his unhappiness with his superior? If not, why not?

Have his colleagues at Newman Street been positively unfriendly? No? Then would he expand on his complaint?

The more often the words *friend, friendship, friendly* are spoken, the odder they sound. If you are looking for friends, he can imagine the man saying, join a club, play skittles, fly model planes, collect stamps. Why expect your employer, IBM, International Business Machines, manufacturer of electronic calculators and computers, to provide them for you?

And of course the man is right. What right has he to complain, in this country above all, where everyone is so cool to everyone else? Is that not what he admires the English for: their emotional restraint? Is that not why he is writing, in his spare time, a thesis on the works of Ford Madox Ford, half-German celebrator of English laconism?

Confused and stumbling, he expands on his complaint. His expansion is as obscure to the Personnel man as is the complaint itself. *Misapprehension*: that is the word the man is hunting for. *Employee was under a misapprehension*: that would be an appropriate formulation. But he does not feel like being helpful. Let them find their own way of pigeonholing him.

What the man is particularly keen to find out is what he will do next. Is his talk about lack of friendship merely a cover for a move from IBM to one of IBM's competitors in the field of business machines? Have promises been made to him, have inducements been offered?

He could not be more earnest in his denials. He does not have another job lined up, with a rival or anyone else. He has not been interviewed. He is leaving IBM simply to get out of IBM. He wants to be free, that is all.

The more he talks, the sillier he sounds, the more out of place in the world of business. But at least he is not saying, 'I am leaving IBM in order to become a poet.' That secret, at least, is still his own.

Out of the blue, in the midst of all this, comes a phone call from Caroline. She is on vacation on the south coast, in Bognor Regis, and at a loose end. Why does he not catch a train and spend Saturday with her?

She meets him at the station. From a shop on the Main Street they hire bicycles; soon they are cycling along empty country lanes amid fields of young wheat. It is unseasonably warm. Sweat pours from him. His clothes are wrong for the occasion: grey flannels, a jacket. Caroline wears a brief tomato-coloured tunic and sandals. Her blonde hair flashes, her long legs gleam as she turns the pedals; she looks like a goddess.

What is she doing in Bognor Regis, he asks? Staying with an aunt, she replies, a long-lost English aunt. He does not inquire further.

They stop at the roadside, cross a fence. Caroline has brought sand-wiches; they find a spot in the shade of a chestnut tree and have their picnic. Afterwards, he senses she would not mind if he made love to her. But he is nervous, out here in the open where at any moment a farmer or even a constable might descend on them and demand to know what they think they are up to.

'I've resigned from IBM,' he says.

'That's good. What will you do next?'

'I don't know. I'll just drift for a while, I think.'

She waits to hear more, waits to hear his plans. But he has no more to offer, no plans, no ideas. What a dullard he is! Why does a girl like Caroline bother to keep him in tow, a girl who has acclimatized to England, made a success of her life, left him behind in every way? Only one explanation occurs to him: that she still sees him as he was in Cape Town, when he could still present himself as a poet to be, when he was not yet what he has become, what IBM has made of him: a eunuch, a drone, a worried boy hurrying to catch the 8.17 to the office.

Elsewhere in Britain, employees who resign are given a send-off – if not a gold watch then at least a get-together during the tea break, a speech, a round of applause and good wishes, whether sincere or insincere. He has been in the country long enough to know that. But not at IBM. IBM is not Britain. IBM is the new wave, the new way. That is why IBM is going to cut a swathe through the British opposition. The opposition is still caught up in old, slack, inefficient British ways. IBM, on the contrary, is lean and hard and merciless. So there is no send-off for him on his last day at work. He clears his desk in silence, says his goodbyes to his programmer colleagues. 'What will you be doing?' asks one of them cautiously. All have clearly heard the friendship story; it makes them stiff and uncomfortable. 'Oh, I'll see what comes up,' he replies.

It is an interesting feeling, waking up the next morning with nowhere in particular to go. A sunny day: he catches a train to Leicester Square, does a tour of the bookshops on Charing Cross Road. He has a day's growth of stubble; he has decided to wear a beard. With a beard he will perhaps not look so out of place among the elegant young men and beautiful girls who pour out of the language schools and ride the Underground. Then let chance take its course.

From now on, he has decided, he will put himself in chance's way at every turn. Novels are full of chance meetings that lead to romance – romance or tragedy. He is ready for romance, ready even for tragedy, ready for anything, in fact, so long as he will be consumed by it and remade. That is why he is in London, after all: to be rid of his old self and revealed in his new, true, passionate self; and now there is no impediment to his quest.

The days pass and he simply does as he wishes. Technically speaking, his position is illegal. Clipped to his passport is the work permit that allows him to reside in Britain. Now that he has no work, the permit has lost its power. But if he lies low, perhaps they – the authorities, the police, whoever is responsible – will overlook him.

Ahead on the horizon looms the problem of money. His savings will not last indefinitely. He has nothing worth selling. Prudently he gives up buying books; he walks, when the weather is good, rather than catching trains; he lives on bread and cheese and apples.

Chance does not bestow any of her blessings on him. But chance is unpredictable, one must give chance time. For the day when chance will at last smile on him he can only wait in readiness.

Fourteen

With freedom to do as he pleases, he has soon read to the end of the sprawling corpus of Ford's writings. The time is nigh for him to deliver his judgment. What will he say? In the sciences one is permitted to report negative results, failures to confirm hypotheses. How about the arts? If he has nothing new to say about Ford, would the correct, the honourable action be to confess he has made a mistake, resign his studentship, return his bursary; or, in place of a thesis, would it be permissible to turn in a report on what a let-down his subject has been, how disappointed he is in his hero?

Briefcase in hand, he strolls out of the British Museum and joins the crowd passing down Great Russell Street: thousands of souls, not one of whom cares a fig what he thinks of Ford Madox Ford or anything else. When he first arrived in London he used to stare boldly into the faces of these passers-by, searching out the unique essence of each. *Look, I am looking at you!* he was saying. But bold stares got him nowhere in a city where, he soon discovered, neither men nor women met his gaze but, on the contrary, coolly evaded it.

Each refusal of his gaze felt like a tiny knife-prick. Again and again he was being noted, found wanting, turned down. Soon he began to lose his nerve, to flinch even before the refusal came. With women he found it easier to look covertly, steal looks. That, it would seem, was how looking was done in London. But in stolen looks there was – he could not rid himself of the feeling – something shifty, unclean. Preferable not to look at all. Preferable to be incurious about one's neighbours, indifferent.

In the time he has been here he has changed a great deal; he is not sure it is for the better. During the winter just past there were times when he thought he would die of cold and misery and loneliness. But he has pulled through, after a fashion. By the time the next winter arrives, cold and misery will have less purchase on him. Then he will be on his way to becoming a proper Londoner, hard as stone. Turning to stone was not one of his aims, but it may be what he will have to settle for.

All in all, London is proving to be a great chastener. Already his ambitions are more modest than they used to be, much more modest. Londoners disappointed him, at first, with the poverty of their ambitions. Now he is on his way to joining them. Each day the city chastens him, chastises him; like a beaten dog, he is learning.

Not knowing what, if anything, he wants to say about Ford, he lies abed later and later in the mornings. When finally he sits down at his desk he is unable to concentrate. Summertime contributes to his confusion. The London he knows is a city of winter where one plods through each day with nothing to look forward to but nightfall and bedtime and oblivion. Through these balmy summer days, which seem made for ease and pleasure, the testing continues: what part is being tested he is no longer sure. Sometimes it seems he is being tested simply for testing's sake, to see whether he will endure the test.

About quitting IBM he has no regrets. But now he has no one at all to speak to, not even Bill Briggs. Day after day goes by when not a word passes his lips. He begins to mark them off with an S in his diary: days of silence.

Outside the Underground station he bumps by mistake against a little old man selling newspapers. 'Sorry!' he says. 'Watch where you're going!' snarls the man. 'Sorry!' he repeats.

Sorry: the word comes heavily out of his mouth, like a stone. Does a single word of indeterminate grammatical class count as speech? Has what has occurred between himself and the old man been an instance of human contact, or is it better described as mere social interaction, like the touching of antennae between ants? To the old man, certainly, it was nothing. All day long the old man stands there with his stack of papers, muttering angrily to himself; he is always waiting for a chance to abuse some passer-by. Whereas in his own case the memory of that single word will persist for weeks, perhaps for the rest of his life. Bumping into people, saying 'Sorry!', getting abused: a ruse, a cheap way of forcing a conversation. How to trick loneliness.

He is in the vale of testing and not doing very well. Yet he cannot be the only one to be tested. There must be people who have passed through the vale and come out on the other side; there must be people who have dodged the testing entirely. He too could dodge the test if he preferred. He could run away to Cape Town, for instance, and never come back. But is that what he wants to do? Surely not, not yet.

Yet what if he stays on and fails the test, fails disgracefully? What if, alone in his room, he begins to cry and cannot cease? What if one morning he finds that he lacks the courage to get up, finds it easier to spend the day in bed – that day and the next, and the next, in sheets that get grubbier and grubbier? What happens to people like that, people who cannot stand up to the testing, and crack?

He knows the answer. They are shipped off somewhere to be taken care of – to some hospital, home, institution. In his case he will simply be shipped back to South Africa. The English have enough of their own to take care of, enough people who fail the testing. Why should they take care of foreigners too?

He hovers before a doorway in Greek Street, Soho. *Jackie – Model*, says the card above the bell. He is in need of human intercourse: what could be more human than sexual intercourse? Artists have frequented prostitutes since time immemorial and are none the worse for it, that he knows from his reading. In fact, artists and prostitutes are on the same side of the social battle-lines. But *Jackie – Model*: is a model in this country always a prostitute, or in the business of selling oneself are there gradations, gradations no one has told him about? Might model in Greek Street stand for something quite specialized, for specialized tastes: a woman posing naked under a light, for instance, with men in raincoats standing around in the shadows, gazing shiftily at her, leering? Once he has rung the bell, will there be a way of inquiring, finding out what is what, before he is entirely sucked in? What if Jackie herself turns out to be old or fat or ugly? And what of the etiquette? Is this how one visits someone like Jackie – unannounced – or is one expected to telephone beforehand and make an appointment? How much does one pay? Is there a scale that every man in London knows, every man except him? What if he is identified at once as a hick, a dummy, and overcharged?

He falters, retreats.

In the street a man in a dark suit passes by who seems to recognize him, seems about to stop and speak. It is one of the senior programmers from his IBM days, someone he did not have much contact with, but always thought well disposed towards him. He hesitates, then with an embarrassed nod hurries past.

'So what are you doing with yourself these days – leading a life of pleasure?' – that is what the man would say, smiling genially. What could he say in return? That we cannot always be working, that life is short, we must taste its pleasures while we can? What a joke, and what a scandal too! For the stubborn, mean lives that his ancestors lived, sweating in their dark clothes in the heat and dust of the Karoo, to eventuate in this: a young man sauntering around a foreign city, eating up his savings, whoring, pretending to be an artist! How can he so casually betray them and then hope to escape their avenging ghosts? It was not in the nature of those men and women to be gay and have pleasure, and it is not in his. He is their child, foredoomed from birth to be gloomy and suffer. How else does poetry come anyway, except out of suffering, like blood squeezed from a stone?

South Africa is a wound within him. How much longer before the wound stops bleeding? How much longer will he have to grit his teeth and endure before he is able to say, 'Once upon a time I used to live in South Africa but now I live in England'?

Now and again, for an instant, it is given to him to see himself from the outside: a whispering, worried boy-man, so dull and ordinary that one would not spare him a second glance. These flashes of illumination disturb him; rather than holding on to them, he tries to bury them in darkness, forget them. Is the self he sees at such moments merely what he appears to be, or is it what he really is? What if Oscar Wilde is right, and there is no deeper truth than appearance? Is it possible to be dull and ordinary not only on the surface but to one's deepest depths, and yet be an artist? Might T. S. Eliot, for instance, be secretly dull to his depths, and might Eliot's claim that the artist's personality is irrelevant to his work be nothing but a stratagem to conceal his own dullness?

Perhaps; but he does not believe it. If it comes down to a choice between believing Wilde and believing Eliot, he chooses to believe Eliot. If Eliot chooses to seem dull, chooses to wear a suit and work in a bank and call himself J. Alfred Prufrock, it must be as a disguise, as part of the necessary cunning of the artist in the modern age.

Sometimes, as a relief from walking the city streets, he retreats to Hampstead Heath. There the air is gently warm, the paths full of young mothers pushing prams or chatting to each other as their children gambol. Such peace and contentment! He used to be impatient of poems about budding flowers and zephyrous breezes. Now, in the land where those poems were written, he begins to understand how deep gladness can run at the return of the sun.

Tired out, one Sunday afternoon, he folds his jacket into a pillow, stretches out on the greensward, and sinks into a sleep or half-sleep in which consciousness does not vanish but continues to hover. It is a state he has not known before: in his very blood he seems to feel the steady wheeling of the earth. The faraway cries of children, the birdsong, the whirr of insects gather force and come together in a paean of joy. His heart swells. At last! he thinks. At last it has come, the moment of ecstatic unity with the All! Fearful that the moment will slip away, he tries to put a halt to the clatter of thought, tries simply to be a conduit for the great universal force that has no name.

It lasts no more than seconds in clock time, this signal event. But when he gets up and dusts off his jacket, he is refreshed, renewed. He journeyed to the great dark city to be tested and transformed, and here, on this patch of green under the mild spring sun, word of progress has, surprisingly, come. If he has not utterly been transfigured, then at least he has been blessed with a hint that he belongs on this earth.

Fifteen

He must find ways to save money. Lodging is his single biggest expense. He advertises in the classified section of the Hampstead local paper: 'House-sitter available, responsible professional man, long or short term.' To the two callers who respond he gives IBM as his work address and hopes they will not check up. The impression he tries to create is of rigid propriety. The act works well enough for him to be engaged to look after a flat in Swiss Cottage for the month of June.

He will not, alas, have the flat to himself. The flat belongs to a divorced woman with a small daughter. While she is away in Greece, the child and the child's nanny will be in his care. His duties will be simple: to attend to the mail, pay the bills, be at hand in case of emergencies. He will have one room as his own, and access to the kitchen.

There is also an ex-husband in the picture. The ex-husband will appear on Sundays to take his daughter out. He is, as his employer or patroness puts it, 'a bit hot-tempered', and should not be allowed to 'get away with anything'. What exactly might the husband want to get away with, he inquires? Keeping the child overnight, he is told. Sniffing through the flat. Taking things. On no account, no matter what story he spins – she gives him a meaningful look – should he be allowed to take things.

So he begins to understand why he is needed. The nanny, who comes from Malawi, no great distance from South Africa, is perfectly capable of cleaning the flat, doing the shopping, feeding the child, walking her to and from kindergarten. She is perhaps even capable of paying the bills. What she is not capable of is standing up to the man who until recently was her employer and whom she still refers to as *the master*.

The job he has let himself in for is in fact that of a guard, guarding the flat and its contents from the man who until recently used to live here.

On the first day of June he hires a taxi and moves, with his trunk and suitcase, from the seedy surroundings of Archway Road to the discreet elegance of Hampstead.

The flat is large and airy; sunlight streams in through the windows; there are soft white carpets, bookcases full of promising-looking books. It is quite unlike what he has seen thus far in London. He cannot believe his luck.

While he unpacks, the little girl, his new charge, stands at the door of his room watching his every movement. He has never had to look after a child before. Does he, because he is in a sense young, have a natural bond with children? Slowly, gently, wearing his most reassuring smile, he closes the door on her. After a moment she pushes it open and gravely continues to inspect him. *My house*, she seems to be saying. *What are you doing in my house?*

Her name is Fiona. She is five years old. Later in the day he makes an effort to befriend her. In the living room, where she is playing, he gets down on his knees and strokes the cat, a huge, sluggish, neutered male. The cat tolerates the stroking as, it would appear, it tolerates all attentions.

'Does the kitty want his milk?' he asks. 'Shall we get the kitty some milk?'

The child does not stir, does not appear to hear him.

He goes to the fridge, pours milk into the cat's bowl, brings the bowl back, and sets it before the cat. The cat sniffs at the cold milk but does not drink.

The child is winding cord around her dolls, stuffing them into a laundry bag, pulling them out again. If it is a game, it is a game whose meaning he cannot fathom.

'What are your dolls' names?' he asks.

She does not reply.

'What is the golliwog's name? Is it Golly?'

'He's not a golliwog,' says the child.

He gives up. 'I have work to do now,' he says, and retires.

He has been told to call the nanny Theodora. Theodora has yet to reveal her name for him: certainly not *the master*. She occupies a room at the end of the corridor, next to the child's. It is understood that these two rooms and the laundry room are her province. The living room is neutral territory.

Theodora is, he would guess, in her forties. She has been in the Merringtons' service since their last spell in Malawi. The hot-tempered ex-husband is an anthropologist; the Merringtons were in Theodora's country on a field trip, making recordings of tribal music and collecting instruments. Theodora soon became, in Mrs Merrington's words, 'not just a house-help but a friend'. She was brought back to London because of the bond she had forged with the child. Each month she sends home the wages that keep her own children fed and clothed and in school.

And now, all of a sudden, a stranger half this treasure's age has been put in charge of her domain. By her bearing, by her silences, Theodora gives him to understand that she resents his presence.

He does not blame her. The question is, is there more underlying her resentment than just hurt pride? She must know he is not an Englishman. Does she resent him in his person as a South African, a white, an Afrikaner? She must know what Afrikaners are. There are Afrikaners – big-bellied, red-nosed men in short pants and hats, rolypoly women in shapeless dresses – all over Africa: in Rhodesia, in Angola, in Kenya, certainly in Malawi. Is there anything he can do to make her understand that he is not one of them, that he has quit South Africa, is resolved to put South Africa behind him for ever? *Africa belongs to you, it is yours to do with as you wish*: if he were to say that to her, out of the blue, across the kitchen table, would she change her mind about him?

Africa is yours. What had seemed perfectly natural while he still called that continent his home seems more and more preposterous from the perspective of Europe: that a handful of Hollanders should have waded ashore on Woodstock beach and claimed ownership of foreign territory they had never laid eyes on before; that their descendants should now regard that territory as theirs by birthright. Doubly absurd, given that the first landing-party misunderstood its orders, or chose to misunderstand them. Its orders were to dig a garden and grow spinach and onions for the East India fleet. Two acres, three acres, five acres at most: that was all that was needed. It was never intended that they should steal the best part of Africa. If they had only obeyed their orders, he would not be here, nor would Theodora. Theodora would happily be pounding millet under Malawian skies and he would be – what? He would be sitting at a desk in an office in rainy Rotterdam, adding up figures in a ledger.

Theodora is a fat woman, fat in every detail, from her chubby cheeks to her swelling ankles. Walking, she rocks from side to side, wheezing from the exertion. Indoors she wears slippers; when she takes the child to school in the mornings she squeezes her feet into tennis shoes, puts on a long black coat and knitted hat. She works six days of the week. On Sundays she goes to church, but otherwise spends her day of rest at home. She never uses the telephone; she appears to have no social circle. What she does when she is by herself he cannot guess. He does not venture into her room or the child's, even when they are out of the flat: in return, he hopes, they will not poke around in his room.

Among the Merringtons' books is a folio of pornographic pictures from imperial China. Men in oddly shaped hats part their robes and aim grossly distended penises at the genitals of tiny women who obligingly part and raise their legs. The women are pale and soft, like bee-grubs; their puny legs seem merely glued to their abdomens. Do Chinese women still look like that, he wonders, with their clothes off, or has re-education and labour in the fields given them proper bodies, proper legs? What chance is there he will ever find out?

Since he got free lodging by masquerading as a dependable professional man, he has to keep up the pretence of having a job. He gets up early, earlier than he is used to, in order to have breakfast before Theodora and the child begin to stir. Then he shuts himself up in his room. When Theodora returns from taking the child to school, he leaves the flat, ostensibly to go to work. At first he even dons his black suit, but soon relaxes that part of the deception. He comes home at five, sometimes at four.

It is lucky that it is summer, that he is not restricted to the British Museum and the bookshops and cinemas, but can stroll around the public parks. This must have been more or less how his father lived

246

during the long spells when he was out of work: roaming the city in his office clothes or sitting in bars watching the hands of the clock, waiting for a decent hour to go home. Is he after all going to turn out to be his father's son? How deep does it run in him, the strain of fecklessness? Will he turn out to be a drunkard too? Does one need a certain temperament to become a drunkard?

His father's drink was brandy. He tried brandy once, but can recollect nothing save an unpleasant, metallic aftertaste. In England people drink beer, whose sourness he dislikes. If he doesn't like liquor, is he safe, inoculated against becoming a drunkard? Are there other, as yet unguessed-at ways in which his father is going to manifest himself in his life?

The ex-husband does not take long to make an appearance. It is Sunday morning, he is dozing in the big, comfortable bed, when suddenly there is a ring at the doorbell and the scrape of a key. He springs out of bed cursing himself. 'Hello, Fiona, Theodora!' comes a voice. There is a scuffling sound, running feet. Then without so much as a knock the door of his room swings open and they are surveying him, the man with the child in his arms. He barely has his trousers on. 'Hello!' says the man, 'what have we here?'

It is one of those expressions the English use – an English policeman, for instance, catching one in a guilty act. Fiona, who could explain what we have here, chooses not to. Instead, from her perch in her father's arms, she looks upon him with undisguised coldness. Her father's daughter: same cool eyes, same brow.

'I'm looking after the flat in Mrs Merrington's absence,' he says.

'Ah yes,' says the man, 'the South African. I had forgotten. Let me introduce myself. Richard Merrington. I used to be lord of the manor here. How are you finding things? Settling in well?'

'Yes, I'm fine.'

'Good.'

Theodora appears with the child's coat and boots. The man lets his daughter slide from his arms. 'And do a wee-wee too,' he tells her, 'before we get in the car.'

Theodora and the child go off. They are left together, he and this handsome, well-dressed man in whose bed he has been sleeping.

'And how long do you plan to be here?' says the man.

'Just till the end of the month.'

'No, I mean how long in this country?'

'Oh, indefinitely. I've left South Africa.'

'Things pretty bad there, are they?'

'Yes.'

'Even for whites?'

How does one respond to a question like that? *One leaves in order not to perish of shame? One leaves in order to escape the impending cataclysm?* Why do big words sound so out of place in this country?

'Yes,' he says. 'At least I think so.'

'That reminds me,' says the man. He crosses the room to the rack of gramophone records, flips through them, extracting one, two, three.

This is exactly what he was warned against, exactly what he must not allow to happen. 'Excuse me,' he says, 'Mrs Merrington asked me specifically . . .'

The man rises to his full height and faces him. 'Diana asked you what specifically?'

'Not to allow anything to leave the flat.'

'Nonsense. These are my records, she has no use for them.' Coolly he resumes his search, removing more records. 'If you don't believe me, give her a call.'

The child clumps into the room in her heavy boots. 'Ready to go, are we, darling?' says the man. 'Goodbye. I hope all goes well. Goodbye, Theodora. Don't worry, we'll be back before bath time.' And, bearing his daughter and the records, he is gone.

Sixteen

A letter arrives from his mother. His brother has bought a car, she writes, an MG that has been in a crash. Instead of studying, his brother is now spending all his time fixing the car, trying to get it to run. He has found new friends too, whom he does not introduce to her. One of them looks Chinese. They all sit around in the garage, smoking; she suspects the friends bring liquor. She is worried. His brother is on the downward path; how is she to save him?

For his part, he is intrigued. So his brother is at last beginning to free himself from their mother's embrace! Yet what an odd way to choose: automotive mechanics! Does his brother really know how to fix cars? Where did he learn? He had always thought that, of the two, he was better with his hands, more blessed with mechanical sense. Was he wrong about that all the time? What else does his brother have up his sleeve?

There is further news in the letter. His cousin Ilse and a friend will shortly be arriving in England en route to a camping trip in Switzerland. Will he show them around London? She gives the address of the hostel in Earls Court where they will be staying.

He is astonished that, after all he has said to her, his mother can think that he wants contact with South Africans, and with his father's family in particular. He has not laid eyes on Ilse since they were children. What can he possibly have in common with her, a girl who went to school in the back of nowhere and can think of nothing better to do with a holiday in Europe – a holiday no doubt paid for by her parents – than to tramp around *gemütliche* Switzerland, a country that in all its history has not given birth to one great artist?

Yet now that her name has been mentioned, he cannot put Ilse out of his mind. He remembers her as a rangy, swift-footed child with long blonde hair tied in a pigtail. By now she must be at least eighteen. What will she have turned into? What if all that outdoor living has made of her, for however brief a spell, a beauty? For he has seen the phenomenon many times among farm children: a springtime of physical perfection before the coarsening and thickening commences that will turn them into copies of their parents. Ought he really to turn down the chance of walking the streets of London with a tall Aryan huntress at his side?

In his fantasy he recognizes the erotic tingle. What is it about his girl cousins, even the idea of them, that sparks desire in him? Is it simply that they are forbidden? Is that how taboo operates: creating desire by forbidding it? Or is the genesis of his desire less abstract: memories of tussles, girl against boy, body to body, stored since childhood and released now in a rush of sexual feeling? That, perhaps, and the promise of ease, of easiness: two people with a history in common, a country, a family, a blood intimacy from before the first word was spoken. No introductions needed, no fumbling around.

He leaves a message at the Earls Court address. Some days later there is a call: not from Ilse but from the friend, the companion, speaking English clumsily, getting *is* and *are* wrong. She has bad news: Ilse is ill, with flu that has turned into pneumonia. She is in a nursing home in Bayswater. Their travel plans are held up until she gets better.

He visits Ilse in the nursing home. All his hopes are dashed. She is not a beauty, not even tall, just an ordinary moon-faced girl with mousy hair who wheezes when she talks. He greets her without kissing her, for fear of infection.

The friend is in the room too. Her name is Marianne; she is small and plump; she wears corduroy trousers and boots and exudes good health. For a while they all speak English, then he relents and switches to the language of the family, to Afrikaans. Though it is years since he spoke Afrikaans, he can feel himself relax at once as though sliding into a warm bath.

He had expected to be able to show off his knowledge of London. But the London Ilse and Marianne want to see is not a London he knows. He can tell them nothing about Madame Tussaud's, the Tower, St Paul's, none of which he has visited. He has no idea how one gets to Stratford-on-Avon. What he is able to tell them – which cinemas show foreign films, which bookshops are best for what – they do not care to know.

Ilse is on antibiotics; it will be days before she is herself again. In the meantime Marianne is at a loose end. He suggests a walk along the Thames embankment. In her hiking boots, with her no-nonsense haircut, Marianne from Ficksburg is out of place among the fashionable London girls, but she does not seem to care. Nor does she care if people hear her speaking Afrikaans. As for him, he would prefer it if she lowered her voice. Speaking Afrikaans in this country, he wants to tell her, is like speaking Nazi, if there were such a language.

He has made a mistake about their ages. They are not children at all: Ilse is twenty, Marianne twenty-one. They are in their final year at the University of the Orange Free State, both studying social work. He does not voice an opinion, but to his mind social work – helping old women with their shopping – is not a subject a proper university would teach.

Marianne has never heard of computer programming and is incurious about it. But she does ask when he will be coming, as she puts it, home, *tuis*.

He does not know, he replies. Perhaps never. Is she not concerned about the direction in which South Africa is heading?

She gives a fling of the head. South Africa is not as bad as the English newspapers make out, she says. Blacks and whites would get along fine if they were just left alone. Anyway, she is not interested in politics.

He invites her to a film at the Everyman. It is Godard's *Bande à part*, which he has seen before but could see many times more, since it stars Anna Karina, with whom he is as much in love now as he was with Monica Vitti a year ago. Since it is not a highbrow film, or not obviously so, just a story about a gang of incompetent, amateurish criminals, he sees no reason why Marianne should not enjoy it.

Marianne is not a complainer, but throughout the film he can sense her fidgeting beside him. When he steals a glance, she is picking her finger-nails, not watching the screen. Didn't you like it, he asks afterwards? I couldn't work out what it was about, she replies. It turns out she has never seen a film with subtitles.

He takes her back to his flat, or the flat that is his for the time being, for a cup of coffee. It is nearly eleven; Theodora has gone to bed. They sit cross-legged on the thick pile carpet in the living room, with the door shut, talking in low tones. She is not his cousin, but she is his cousin's friend, she is from home, and an air of illegitimacy hangs excitingly around her. He kisses her; she does not seem to mind being kissed. Face to face they stretch out on the carpet; he begins to unbutton, unlace, unzip her. The last train south is at 11.30. She will certainly miss it.

Marianne is a virgin. He finds this out when at last he has her naked in the big double bed. He has never slept with a virgin before, has never given a thought to virginity as a physical state. Now he learns his lesson. Marianne bleeds while they are making love and goes on bleeding afterwards. At the risk of waking the maid, she has to creep off to the bathroom to wash herself. While she is gone he switches on the light. There is blood on the sheets, blood all over his body. They have been – the vision comes to him distastefully – wallowing in blood like pigs.

She returns with a bath towel wrapped around her. 'I must leave,' she says. 'The last train has gone,' he replies. 'Why don't you stay the night?'

The bleeding does not stop. Marianne falls asleep with the towel, growing more and more soggy, stuffed between her legs. He lies awake beside her fretting. Should he be calling an ambulance? Can he do so without waking Theodora? Marianne does not seem to be worried, but what if that is only pretence, for his sake? What if she is too innocent or too trustful to assess what is going on?

He is convinced he will not sleep, but he does. He is woken by voices and the sound of running water. It is five o'clock; already the birds are singing in the trees. Groggily he gets up and listens at the door: Theodora's voice, then Marianne's. What they are saying he cannot hear, but it cannot reflect well on him.

He strips off the bedclothes. The blood has soaked through to the mattress, leaving a huge, uneven stain. Guiltily, angrily, he heaves the mattress over. Only a matter of time before the stain is discovered. He must be gone by then, he will have to make sure of that.

Marianne returns from the bathroom wearing a robe that is not hers. She is taken aback by his silence, his cross looks. 'You never told me not to,' she says. 'Why shouldn't I talk to her? She's a nice old woman. A nice old *aia*.'

He telephones for a taxi, then waits pointedly at the front door while she dresses. When the taxi arrives he evades her embrace, puts a pound note in her hand. She regards it with puzzlement. 'I've got my own money,' she says. He shrugs, opens the door of the taxi for her.

For the remaining days of his tenancy he avoids Theodora. He leaves early in the mornings, comes home late. If there are messages for him, he ignores them. When he took on the flat, he engaged to guard it from the husband and generally *be at hand*. He has failed in his undertaking once and is failing again, but he does not care. The unsettling love-making, the whispering women, the bloody sheets, the stained mattress: he would like to put the whole shameful business behind him, close the door on it.

Muffling his voice, he calls the hostel in Earls Court and asks to speak to his cousin. She has left, they say, she and her friend. He puts the telephone down and relaxes. They are safely away, he need not face them again.

There remains the question of what to make of the episode, how to fit it into the story of his life that he tells himself. He has behaved dishonourably, no doubt about that, behaved like a cad. The word may be old-fashioned but it is exact. He deserves to be slapped in the face, even to be spat on. In the absence of anyone to administer the slap, he has no doubt that he will gnaw away at himself. *Agenbyte of inwit.* Let that be his contract then, with the gods: he will punish himself, and in return will hope the story of his caddish behaviour will not get out.

Yet what does it matter, finally, if the story does get out? He belongs to two worlds tightly sealed from each other. In the world of South Africa he is no more than a ghost, a wisp of smoke fast dwindling away, soon to have vanished for good. As for London, he is as good as unknown here. Already he has begun his search for new lodgings. When he has found a room he will break off contact with Theodora and the Merrington household and vanish into a sea of anonymity.

There is more to the sorry business, however, than just the shame of it. He has come to London to do what is impossible in South Africa: to explore the depths. Without descending into the depths one cannot be an artist. But what exactly are the depths? He had thought that trudging down icy streets, his heart numb with loneliness, was the depths. But perhaps the real depths are different, and come in unexpected form: in a flare-up of nastiness against a girl in the early hours of the morning, for instance. Perhaps the depths that he has wanted to plumb have been within him all the time, closed up in his chest: depths of coldness, callousness, caddishness. Does giving rein to one's penchants, one's vices, and then afterwards gnawing at oneself, as he is doing now, help to qualify one to be an artist? He cannot, at this moment, see how.

At least the episode is closed, closed off, consigned to the past, sealed away in memory. But that is not true, not quite. A letter arrives postmarked Lucerne. Without second thought he opens it and begins to read. It is in Afrikaans. 'Dear John, I thought I should let you know that I am OK. Marianne is OK too. At first she did not understand why you did not phone, but after a while she cheered up, and we have been having a good time. She doesn't want to write, but I thought I would write anyway, to say I hope you don't treat all your girls like that, even in London. Marianne is a special person, she doesn't deserve that kind of treatment. You should think twice about the life you lead. Your cousin, Ilse.'

Even in London. What does she mean? That even by the standards of London he has behaved disgracefully? What do Ilse and her friend, fresh from the wastes of the Orange Free State, know about London and its standards? London gets worse, he wants to say. If you would stay on for a while, instead of running away to the cowbells and the meadows, you might find that out for yourself. But he does not really believe the fault is London's. He has read Henry James. He knows how easy it is to be bad, how one has only to relax for the badness to emerge.

The most hurtful moments in the letter are at the beginning and the end. Beste John is not how one addresses a family member, it is the way one addresses a stranger. And Your cousin, Ilse: who would have thought a farm girl capable of such a telling thrust!

For days and weeks, even after he has crumpled it up and thrown it away, his cousin's letter haunts him – not the actual words on the page, which he soon manages to blank out, but the memory of the moment when, despite having noticed the Swiss stamp and the childishly rounded handwriting, he slit open the envelope and read. What a fool! What was he expecting: a paean of thanks?

He does not like bad news. Particularly he does not like bad news about himself. *I am hard enough on myself*, he tells himself; *I do not need the help of others.* It is a sophistical trick that he falls back on time and again when he wants to block his ears to criticism. He learned its useful-ness when Jacqueline, from the perspective of a woman of thirty, gave him her opinion of him as a lover. Now, as soon as an affair begins to run out of steam, he withdraws. He abominates scenes, angry outbursts, home truths ('Do you want to know the truth about yourself?'), and does all in his power to evade them. What is truth anyway? If he is a mystery to himself, how can he be anything but a mystery to others? There is a pact he is ready to offer the women in his life: if they will treat him as a mystery, he will treat them as a closed book. On that basis and that alone will commerce be possible.

He is not a fool. As a lover his record is undistinguished, and he knows it. Never has he provoked in the heart of a woman what he would call a grand passion. In fact, looking back, he cannot recall having been the object of a passion, a true passion, of any degree. That must say some-thing about him. As for sex itself, narrowly understood, what he provides is, he suspects, rather meagre; and what he gets in return is meagre too. If the fault is anyone's, it is his own. For as long as he lacks heart and holds himself back, why should the woman not hold herself back too?

Is sex the measure of all things? If he fails in sex, does he fail the whole test of life? Things would be easier if that were not true. But when he looks around, he can see no one who does not stand in awe of the god of sex, except perhaps for a few dinosaurs, holdovers from Victorian times. Even Henry James, on the surface so proper, so Victorian, has pages where he darkly hints that everything, finally, is sex.

Of all the writers he follows, he trusts Pound the most. There is passion aplenty in Pound – the ache of longing, the fire of consummation – but it is passion untroubled, without a darker side. What is the key to Pound's equanimity? Is it that, as a worshipper of the Greek gods rather than the Hebrew god, he is immune to guilt? Or is Pound so steeped in great poetry that his physical being is in harmony with his emotions, a harmony that communicates itself immediately to women and opens their hearts to him? Or, on the contrary, is Pound's secret simply a certain briskness in the conduct of life, a briskness to be attributed to an American upbringing rather than to the gods or poetry, welcomed by women as a sign that the man knows what he wants and in a firm yet friendly way will take charge of where she and he are going? Is that what women want: to be taken charge of, to be led? Is that why dancers follow the code they do, the man leading, the woman following?

His own explanation for his failures in love, hoary by now and less and less to be trusted, is that he has yet to meet the right woman. The right woman will see through the opaque surface he presents to the world, to the depths inside; the right woman will unlock the hidden intensities of passion in him. Until that woman arrives, until that day of destiny, he is merely passing the time. That is why Marianne can be ignored.

One question still nags at him, and will not go away. Will the woman who unlocks the store of passion within him, if she exists, also release the blocked flow of poetry; or on the contrary is it up to him to turn himself into a poet and thus prove himself worthy of her love? It would be nice if the first were true, but he suspects it is not. Just as he has fallen in love at a distance with Ingeborg Bachmann in one way and with Anna Karina in another, so, he suspects, the intended one will have to know him by his works, to fall in love with his art before she will be so foolish as to fall in love with him.

Seventeen

From Professor Guy Howarth, his thesis supervisor back in Cape Town, he receives a letter requesting him to do some academic chores. Howarth is at work on a biography of the seventeenth-century playwright John Webster: he wants him to make copies of certain poems in the British Museum's manuscript collection that might have been written by Webster as a young man, and, while he is about it, of any manuscript poem he comes across signed 'I. W.' that sounds as if it might have been written by Webster.

Though the poems he finds himself reading are of no particular merit, he is flattered by the commission, with its implication that he will be able to recognize the author of *The Duchess of Malfi* by his style alone. From Eliot he has learned that the test of the critic is his ability to make fine discriminations. From Pound he has learned that the critic must be able to pick out the voice of the authentic master amid the babble of mere fashion. If he cannot play the piano, he can at least, when he switches on the radio, tell the difference between Bach and Telemann, Haydn and Mozart, Beethoven and Spohr, Bruckner and Mahler; if he cannot write, he at least possesses an ear that Eliot and Pound would approve of.

The question is, is Ford Madox Ford, on whom he is lavishing so much time, an authentic master? Pound promoted Ford as the sole heir in England of Henry James and Flaubert. But would Pound have been so sure of himself had he read the whole Ford oeuvre? If Ford was such a fine writer, why, mixed in with his five good novels, is there so much rubbish?

Though he is supposed to be writing about Ford's fiction, he finds Ford's minor novels less interesting than his books about France. To Ford there can be no greater happiness than to pass one's days by the side of a good woman in a sunlit house in the south of France, with an olive tree at the back door and a good *vin de pays* in the cellar. Provence, says Ford, is the cradle of all that is gracious and lyrical and humane in European civilization; as for the women of Provence, with their fiery temperament and their aquiline good looks they put the women of the north to shame.

Is Ford to be believed? Will he himself ever see Provence? Will the fiery Provençal women pay any attention to him, with his notable lack of fire?

Ford says that the civilization of Provence owes its lightness and grace to a diet of fish and olive oil and garlic. In his new lodgings in Highgate, out of deference to Ford, he buys fish fingers instead of sausages, fries them in olive oil instead of butter, sprinkles garlic salt over them.

The thesis he is writing will have nothing new to say about Ford, that has become clear. Yet he does not want to abandon it. Giving up undertakings is his father's way. He is not going to be like his father. So he commences the task of reducing his hundreds of pages of notes in tiny handwriting to a web of connected prose.

On days when, sitting in the great, domed Reading Room and finding himself too exhausted or bored to write any more, he allows himself the luxury of dipping into books about the South Africa of the old days, books to be found only in great libraries, memoirs of visitors to the Cape like Dapper and Kolbe and Sparrman and Barrow and Burchell, published in Holland or Germany or England two centuries ago.

It gives him an eerie feeling to sit in London reading about streets – Waalstraat, Buitengracht, Buitencingel – along which he alone, of all the people around him with their heads buried in their books, has walked. But even more than by accounts of old Cape Town is he captivated by stories of ventures into the interior, reconnaissances by ox-wagon into the desert of the Great Karoo, where a traveller could trek for days on end without clapping eyes on a living soul. Zwartberg, Leeuwrivier, Dwyka: it is his country, the country of his heart, that he is reading about.

Patriotism: is that what is beginning to afflict him? Is he proving himself unable to live without a country? Having shaken the dust of the ugly new South Africa from his feet, is he yearning for the South Africa of the old days, when Eden was still possible? Do these Englishmen around him feel the same tug at the heartstrings when there is mention of Rydal Mount or Baker Street in a book? He doubts it. This country, this city, are by now wrapped in centuries of words. Englishmen do not find it at all strange to be walking in the footsteps of Chaucer or Tom Jones.

South Africa is different. Were it not for this handful of books, he could not be sure he had not dreamed up the Karoo yesterday. That is why he pores over Burchell in particular, in his two heavy volumes. Burchell may not be a master like Flaubert or James, but what Burchell writes really happened. Real oxen hauled him and his cases of botanical specimens from stopping-place to stopping-place in the Great Karoo; real stars glimmered above his head, and his men's, while they slept. It dizzies him even to think about it. Burchell and his men may be dead, and their wagons turned to dust, but they really lived, their travels were real travels. The proof is the book he holds in his hands, the book called for short Burchell's Travels, and in specific the copy lodged in the British Museum.

If Burchell's travels are proved real by Burchell's Travels, why should other books not make other travels real, travels that are as yet only hypothetical? The logic is of course false. Nevertheless, he would like to do it: write a book as convincing as Burchell's and lodge it in this library that defines all libraries. If, to make his book convincing, there needs to be a grease-pot swinging under the bed of the wagon as it bumps across the stones of the Karoo, he will do the grease-pot. If there have to be cicadas trilling in the tree under which they stop at noon, he will do the cicadas. The creak of the grease-pot, the trilling of the cicadas – those he is confident he can bring off. The difficult part will be to give to the whole the aura that will get it onto the shelves and thus into the history of the world: the aura of truth.

It is not forgery he is contemplating. People have tried that route before: pretended to find, in a chest in an attic in a country house, a journal, yellow with age, stained with damp, describing an expedition across the deserts of Tartary or into the territories of the Great Moghul. Deceptions of that kind do not interest him. The challenge he faces is a purely literary one: to write a book whose horizon of knowledge will be that of Burchell's time, the 1820s, yet whose response to the world around it will be alive in a way that Burchell, despite his energy and intelligence and curiosity and sangfroid, could not be because he was an Englishman in a foreign country, his mind half occupied with Pembrokeshire and the sisters he had left behind.

He will have to school himself to write from within the 1820s. Before he can bring that off he will need to know less than he knows now; he will need to forget things. Yet before he can forget he will have to know what to forget; before he can know less he will have to know more. Where will he find what he needs to know? He has no training as an historian, and anyway what he is after will not be in history books, since it belongs to the mundane, a mundane as common as the air one breathes. Where will he find the common knowledge of a bygone world, a knowledge too humble to know it is knowledge?

Eighteen

What happens next happens swiftly. In the mail on the table in the hallway there appears a buff envelope marked OHMS, addressed to him. He takes it to his room and with a sinking heart opens it. He has twenty-one days, the letter tells him, in which to renew his work permit, failing which permission to reside in the United Kingdom will be withdrawn. He may renew the permit by presenting himself, his passport, and a copy of Form I-48, completed by his employer, at the Home Office premises on Holloway Road on any weekday between the hours of 9.00 and 12.30, and 1.30 and 4.00.

So IBM has betrayed him. IBM has told the Home Office he has left their employ.

What must he do? He has enough money for a one-way ticket back to South Africa. But it is inconceivable that he should reappear in Cape Town like a dog with its tail between its legs, defeated. What is there for him to do in Cape Town anyway? Resume his tutoring at the University? How long can that go on? He is too old by now for scholarships, he would be competing against younger students with better records. The fact is, if he goes back to South Africa he will never escape again. He will become like the people who gather on Clifton beach in the evenings to drink wine and tell each other about the old days on Ibiza.

If he wants to stay on in England, there are two avenues he can see open to him. He can grit his teeth and try schoolmastering again; or he can go back to computer programming.

There is a third option, hypothetical. He can quit his present address and melt into the masses. He can go hop-picking in Kent (one does not need papers for that), work on building sites. He can sleep in youth hostels, in barns. But he knows he will do none of this. He is too incompetent to lead a life outside the law, too prim, too afraid of getting caught.

The job listings in the newspapers are full of appeals for computer programmers. England cannot, it would seem, find enough of them. Most are for openings in payroll departments. These he ignores, responding only to the computer companies themselves, the rivals, great and small, of IBM. Within days he has had an interview with International Computers, and, without hesitation, accepted their offer. He is exultant. He is employed again, he is safe, he is not going to be ordered out of the country.

There is one catch. Though International Computers has its head office in London, the work for which they want him is out in the country, in Berkshire. It takes a trip to Waterloo, followed by a one-hour train journey, followed by a bus ride, to get there. It will not be possible to live in London. It is the Rothamsted story all over again.

International Computers is prepared to lend new employees the down payment on an appropriately modest home. In other words, with a stroke of a pen he can become a house owner (he! a house owner!) and by the same act commit himself to mortgage repayments that would bind him to his job for the next ten or fifteen years. In fifteen years he will be an old man. A single rushed decision and he will have signed away his life, signed away all chance of becoming an artist. With a little house of his own in a row of redbrick houses, he will be absorbed without trace into the British middle class. All that will be needed to complete the picture will be a little wife and car.

He finds an excuse not to sign up for the house loan. Instead he signs a lease on a flat on the top floor of a house on the fringes of the town. The landlord is an ex-Army officer, now a stockbroker, who likes to be addressed as Major Arkwright. To Major Arkwright he explains what computers are, what computer programming is, what a solid career it affords ('There is bound to be huge expansion in the industry'). Major Arkwright jocularly calls him a boffin ('We've never had a boffin in the upstairs flat before'), a designation he accepts without murmur.

Working for International Computers is quite unlike working for IBM. To begin with, he can pack his black suit away. He has an office of his own, a cubicle in a Quonset hut in the back garden of the house that International Computers has outfitted as its computing laboratory. 'The Manor House': that is what they call it, a rambling old building at the end of a leaf-strewn driveway two miles outside Bracknell. Presumably it has a history, though no one knows what that history is.

Despite the designation 'Computing Laboratory', there is no actual computer on the premises. To test the programs he is being hired to write, he will have to travel to Cambridge University, which owns one of the three Atlas computers, the only three in existence, each slightly different from the others. The Atlas computer – so he reads in the brief placed before him on his first morning – is Britain's reply to IBM. Once the engineers and programmers of International Computers have got these prototypes running, Atlas will be the biggest computer in the world, or at least the biggest that can be bought on the open market (the American military have computers of their own, of unrevealed power, and presumably the Russian military too). Atlas will strike a blow for the British computer industry from which IBM will take years to recover. That is what is at stake. That is why International Computers has assembled a team of bright young programmers, of whom he has now become one, in this rural retreat.

What is special about Atlas, what makes it unique among the world's computers, is that it has self-consciousness of a kind. At regular intervals – every ten seconds, or even every second – it interrogates itself, asking itself what tasks it is performing and whether it is performing them with optimal efficiency. If it is not performing efficiently, it will rearrange its tasks and carry them out in a different, better order, thus saving time, which is money.

It will be his task to write the routine for the machine to follow at the end of each swing of the magnetic tape. Should it read another swing of tape, it must ask itself? Or should it, on the contrary, break off and read a punched card or a strip of paper tape? Should it write some of the output that has accumulated onto another magnetic tape, or should it do a burst of computing? These questions are to be answered according to the overriding principle of efficiency. He will have as much time as he needs (but preferably only six months, since International Computers is in a race against time) to reduce questions and answers to machine-readable code and test that they are optimally formulated. Each of his fellow programmers has a comparable task and a similar schedule. Meanwhile, engineers at the University of Manchester will be working day and night to perfect the electronic hardware. If all goes according to plan, Atlas will go into production in 1965.

A race against time. A race against the Americans. That is something he can understand, something he can commit himself to more whole-heartedly than he could commit himself to IBM's goal of making more and more money. And the programming itself is interesting. It requires mental ingenuity; it requires, if it is to be well done, a virtuoso command of Atlas's two-level internal language. He arrives for work in the mornings looking forward to the tasks that await him. To stay alert he drinks cup after cup of coffee; his heart hammers, his brain seethes; he loses track of time, has to be called to lunch. In the evenings he takes his papers back to his rooms at Major Arkwright's and works into the night.

So this is what, unbeknown to myself, I was preparing for, he thinks! So this is where mathematics leads one!

Autumn turns to winter; he is barely aware of it. He is no longer reading poetry. Instead he reads books on chess, follows grandmaster games, does the chess problems in the *Observer*. He sleeps badly; sometimes he dreams about programming. It is a development within himself that he watches with detached interest. Will he become like those scientists whose brains solve problems while they sleep?

There is another thing he notices. He has stopped yearning. The quest for the mysterious, beautiful stranger who will set free the passion within him no longer preoccupies him. In part, no doubt, that is because Bracknell offers nothing to match the parade of girls in London. But he cannot help seeing a connection between the end of yearning and the end of poetry. Does it mean he is growing up? Is that what growing up amounts to: growing out of yearning, of passion, of all intensities of the soul?

The people among whom he works – men, without exception – are

more interesting than the people at IBM: more lively, and perhaps cleverer too, in a way he can understand, a way that is much like being clever
at school. They have lunch together in the canteen of the Manor House.
There is no nonsense about the food they are served: fish and chips,
bangers and mash, toad in the hole, bubble and squeak, rhubarb tart
with ice cream. He likes the food, has two helpings if he can, makes it
the main meal of the day. In the evenings, at home (if that is what they
are now, his rooms at the Arkwrights'), he does not bother to cook,
simply eats bread and cheese over the chessboard.

Among his co-workers is an Indian named Ganapathy. Ganapathy
often arrives late to work; on some days he does not come at all. When
he does come, he does not appear to be working very hard: he sits in
his cubicle with his feet on the desk, apparently dreaming. For his
absences he has only the most cursory of excuses ('I was not well').
Nevertheless, he is not chided. Ganapathy, it emerges, is a particularly
valuable acquisition for International Computers. He has studied in
America, holds an American degree in computer science.

He and Ganapathy are the two foreigners in the group. Together, when
the weather allows, they go for after-lunch strolls in the manor grounds.
Ganapathy is disparaging about International Computers and the whole
Atlas project. Coming back to England was a mistake on his part, he
says. The English do not know how to think big. He should have stayed
in America. What is life like in South Africa? Would there be prospects
for him in South Africa?

He dissuades Ganapathy from trying South Africa. South Africa is very
backward, he tells him, there are no computers there. He does not tell
him that outsiders are not welcome unless they are white.

A bad spell sets in, day after day of rain and blustery wind. Ganapathy
does not come to work at all. Since no one else asks why, he takes it
upon himself to investigate. Like him, Ganapathy has evaded the home-
ownership option. He lives in a flat on the third floor of a council block.
For a long while there is no answer to his knocking. Then Ganapathy
opens the door. He is wearing a dressing gown over pyjamas and sandals;
from the interior comes a gush of steamy warmth and a smell of rotten-
ness. 'Come in, come in!' says Ganapathy. 'Come out of the cold!'

There is no furniture in the living room except for a television set with an armchair before it, and two blazing electric heaters. Behind the door is a pile of black rubbish bags. It is from them that the bad smell comes. With the door closed the smell is quite nauseating. 'Why don't you take the bags out?' he asks. Ganapathy is evasive. Nor will he say why he has not been to work. In fact, he does not appear to want to talk at all.

He wonders whether Ganapathy has a girl in the bedroom, a local girl, one of the pert little typists or shop assistants from the housing estate whom he sees on the bus. Or perhaps, indeed, an Indian girl. Perhaps that is the explanation for all of Ganapathy's absences: there is a beautiful Indian girl living with him, and he prefers making love to her, practising Tantra, deferring orgasm for hours on end, to writing machine code for Atlas.

When he makes a move to leave, however, Ganapathy shakes his head. 'Would you like some water?' he offers.

Ganapathy offers him tap water because he has run out of tea and coffee. He has also run out of food. He does not buy food, except for bananas, because, it emerges, he does not cook – does not like cooking, does not know how to cook. The rubbish bags contain, for the most part, banana peels. That is what he lives on: bananas, chocolates, and, when he has it, tea. It is not the way he would like to live. In India he lived at home, and his mother and sisters took care of him. In America, in Columbus, Ohio, he lived in what he calls a dormitory, where food appeared on the table at regular intervals. If you were hungry between meals you went out and bought a hamburger. There was a hamburger place open twenty-four hours a day on the street outside the dormitory. In America things were always open, not like in England. He should never have come back to England, a country without a future where even the heating does not work.

He asks Ganapathy whether he is ill. Ganapathy brushes aside his concern: he wears the dressing gown for warmth, that is all. But he is not convinced. Now that he knows about the bananas, he sees Ganapathy with new eyes. Ganapathy is as tiny as a sparrow, with not a spare ounce of flesh. His face is gaunt. If he is not ill, he is at least starving. Behold:

in Bracknell, in the heart of the Home Counties, a man is starving because he is too incompetent to feed himself.

He invites Ganapathy to lunch the next day, giving him precise instructions for how to get to Major Arkwright's. Then he goes out, searches for a shop that is open on a Saturday afternoon, and buys what it has to offer: bread in a plastic wrapper, cold meats, frozen green peas. At noon the next day he lays out the repast and waits. Ganapathy does not arrive. Since Ganapathy does not have a telephone, there is nothing he can do about it short of conveying the meal to Ganapathy's flat.

Absurd, but perhaps that is what Ganapathy wants: to have his food brought to him. Like himself, Ganapathy is a spoiled, clever boy. Like himself, Ganapathy has run away from his mother and the smothering ease she offers. But in Ganapathy's case, running away seems to have used up all his energy. Now he is waiting to be rescued. He wants his mother, or someone like her, to come and save him. Otherwise he will simply waste away and die, in his flat full of garbage.

International Computers ought to hear about this. Ganapathy has been entrusted with a key task, the logic of the job-scheduling routines. If Ganapathy falls out, the whole Atlas project will be delayed. But how can International Computers be made to understand what ails Ganapathy? How can anyone in England understand what brings people from the far corners of the earth to die on a wet, miserable island which they detest and to which they have no ties?

The next day Ganapathy is at his desk as usual. For the missed appointment he offers no word of explanation. At lunchtime, in the canteen, he is in good spirits, even excited. He has entered a raffle for a Morris Mini, he says. He has bought a hundred tickets – what else should he do with the big salary International Computers pays him? If he wins, they can drive to Cambridge together to do their program testing, instead of catching trains. Or they can drive to London for the day.

Is there something about the whole business that he has failed to understand, something Indian? Does Ganapathy belong to a caste to which it is taboo to eat at the table of a Westerner? If so, what is he doing with a plate of cod and chips in the Manor House canteen? Should the invitation to lunch have been made more formally and confirmed in writing? By not arriving, was Ganapathy graciously saving him the embarrassment of finding a guest at his front door whom he had invited on an impulse but did not really want? Did he somehow give the impression, when he invited Ganapathy, that it was not a real, substantial invitation he was extending, merely a gesture towards an invitation, and that true politeness on Ganapathy's part would consist in acknowledging the gesture without putting his host to the trouble of providing a repast? Does the notional meal (cold meats and boiled frozen peas with butter) that they would have eaten together have the same value, in the transaction between himself and Ganapathy, as cold meats and boiled frozen peas actually offered and consumed? Is everything between himself and Ganapathy as before, or better than before, or worse?

Ganapathy has heard about Satyajit Ray but does not think he has seen any of his films. Only a tiny sector of the Indian public, he says, would be interested in such films. In general, he says, Indians prefer to watch American films. Indian films are still very primitive.

Ganapathy is the first Indian he has known more than casually, if this can be called knowing – chess games and conversations comparing England unfavourably with America, plus the one surprise visit to Ganapathy's flat. Conversation would no doubt improve if Ganapathy were an intellectual instead of being just clever. It continues to astound him that people can be as clever as people are in the computer industry, yet have no outside interests beyond cars and house prices. He had thought it was just the notorious philistinism of the English middle class manifesting itself, but Ganapathy is no better.

Is this indifference to the world a consequence of too much intercourse with machines that give the appearance of thinking? How would he fare if one day he were to quit the computer industry and rejoin civilized society? After spending his best energies for so long on games with machines, would he be able to hold his own in conversation? Is there anything he would have gained from years with computers? Would he not at least have learned to think logically? Would logic not by then have become his second nature?

He would like to believe so, but he cannot. Finally he has no respect for any version of thinking that can be embodied in a computer's circuitry.

The more he has to do with computing, the more it seems to him like chess: a tight little world defined by made-up rules, one that sucks in boys of a certain susceptible temperament and turns them half-crazy, as he is half-crazy, so that all the time they deludedly think they are playing the game, the game is in fact playing them.

It is a world he can escape – it is not too late for that. Alternatively he can make his peace with it, as he sees the young men around him do, one by one: settle for marriage and a house and car, settle for what life realistically has to offer, sink their energies in their work. He is chagrined to see how well the reality principle operates, how, under the prod of loneliness, the boy with spots settles for the girl with the dull hair and the heavy legs, how everyone, no matter how unlikely, finds, in the end, a partner. Is that his problem, and is it as simple as that: that all the time he has been overestimating his worth on the market, fooling himself into believing he belongs with sculptresses and actresses when he really belongs with the kindergarten teacher on the housing estate or the apprentice manageress of the shoe store?

Marriage: who would have imagined he would be feeling the tug, however faint, of marriage! He is not going to give in, not yet. But it is an option he plays with on the long winter evenings, eating his bread and sausages in front of Major Arkwright's gas fire, listening to the radio, while the rain patters in the background against the window.

Nineteen

It is raining. He and Ganapathy are alone in the canteen, playing lightning chess on Ganapathy's pocket set. Ganapathy is beating him, as usual.

'You should go to America,' says Ganapathy. 'You are wasting your time here. We are all wasting our time.'

He shakes his head. 'That's not realistic,' he replies.

He has thought more than once of trying for a job in America, and decided against it. A prudent decision, but a correct one. As a programmer he has no particular gifts. His colleagues on the Atlas team may not have advanced degrees, but their minds are clearer than his, their grasp of computational problems is quicker and keener than his will ever be. In discussion he can barely hold his own; he is always having to pretend to understand when he does not really understand, and then work things out for himself afterwards. Why should businesses in America want someone like him? America is not England. America is hard and merciless: if by some miracle he bluffed his way into a job there, he would soon be found out. Besides, he has read Allen Ginsberg, read William Burroughs. He knows what America does to artists: sends them mad, locks them up, drives them out.

'You could get a fellowship at a university,' says Ganapathy. 'I got one, you would have no trouble.'

He stares hard. Is Ganapathy really such an innocent? There is a Cold War on the go. America and Russia are competing for the hearts and minds of Indians, Iraquis, Nigerians; scholarships to universities are among the inducements they offer. The hearts and minds of whites are of no interest to them, certainly not the hearts and minds of a few out-of-place whites in Africa.

'I'll think about it,' he says, and changes the subject. He has no intention of thinking about it.

In a photograph on the front page of the *Guardian* a Vietnamese soldier in American-style uniform stares helplessly into a sea of flames. 'RAIDERS WREAK HAVOC AT U.S. BASE,' reads the headline. A band of Viet Cong sappers have cut their way through the barbed wire around the American air base at Pleiku, blown up twenty-four aircraft, and set fire to the fuel storage tanks. They have given up their lives in the action.

Ganapathy, who shows him the newspaper, is exultant; he himself feels a surge of vindication. Ever since he arrived in England the British newspapers and BBC have carried stories of American feats of arms in which Viet Cong are killed by the thousand while the Americans get away unscathed. If there is ever a word of criticism of America, it is of the most muted kind. He can barely bring himself to read the war reports, so much do they sicken him. Now the Viet Cong have given their undeniable, heroic reply.

He and Ganapathy have never discussed Vietnam. Because Ganapathy studied in America, he has assumed that Ganapathy either supports the Americans or is as indifferent to the war as everyone else at International Computers. Now, suddenly, in his smile, the glint in his eye, he is seeing Ganapathy's secret face. Despite his admiration for American efficiency and his longing for American hamburgers, Ganapathy is on the side of the Vietnamese because they are his Asian brothers.

That is all. That is the end of it. There is no further mention of the war between them. But he wonders more than ever what Ganapathy is doing in England, in the Home Counties, working on a project he has no respect for. Would he not be better off in Asia, fighting the Americans? Should he have a chat to him, tell him so?

And what of himself? If Ganapathy's destiny lies in Asia, where does his lie? Would the Viet Cong ignore his origins and accept his services, if not as a soldier or suicide bomber then as a humble porter? If not, what of the friends and allies of the Viet Cong, the Chinese?

He writes to the Chinese Embassy in London. Since he suspects the Chinese have no use for computers, he says nothing about computer programming. He is prepared to come and teach English in China, he says, as a contribution to the world struggle. What he is paid is of no importance to him.

He mails the letter and waits for a reply. Meanwhile he buys *Teach Yourself Chinese* and begins to practise the strange clenched-teeth sounds of Mandarin.

Day after day passes; from the Chinese there is no word. Have the British secret services intercepted his letter and destroyed it? Do they intercept and destroy all letters to the Embassy? If so, what is the point in letting the Chinese have an embassy in London? Or, having intercepted his letter, have the secret services forwarded it to the Home Office with a note to say that the South African working for International Computers in Bracknell has betrayed communist leanings? Is he going to lose his job and be expelled from England on account of politics? If it happens, he will not contest it. Fate will have spoken; he is prepared to accept the word of fate.

On his trips to London he still goes to the cinema, but his pleasure is more and more spoiled by the deterioration of his eyesight. He has to sit in the front row to be able to read the subtitles, and even then he must screw up his eyes and strain.

He visits an optician and comes away with a pair of black horn-rimmed spectacles. In the mirror he resembles even more closely Major Arkwright's comic boffin. On the other hand, looking out through the window he is amazed to discover he can make out individual leaves on the trees. Trees have been a blur of green ever since he can remember. Should he have been wearing glasses all his life? Does this explain why he was so bad at cricket, why the ball always seemed to be coming at him out of nowhere?

We end up looking like our ideal selves, says Baudelaire. The face we are born with is slowly overwhelmed by the desired face, the face of our secret dreams. Is the face in the mirror the face of his dreams, this long, lugubrious face with the soft, vulnerable mouth and now the blank eyes shielded behind glass?

The first film he sees with his new glasses is Pasolini's *Gospel According to St Matthew*. It is an unsettling experience. After five years of Catholic schooling he had thought he was forever beyond the appeal of the Christian message. But he is not. The pale, bony Jesus of the film, shrinking back from the touch of others, striding about barefoot issuing prophecies and fulminations, is real in a way that Jesus of the bleeding heart never was. He winces when nails are hammered through the hands of Jesus; when his tomb is revealed to be empty and the angel announces to the mourning women, 'Look not here, for he is risen,' and the *Missa Luba* bursts out and the common folk of the land, the halt and the maimed, the despised and rejected, come running or hobbling, their faces alight with joy, to share in the good news, his own heart wants to burst; tears of an exultation he does not understand stream down his cheeks, tears that he has surreptitiously to wipe away before he can emerge into the world again.

In the window of a second-hand bookseller off Charing Cross Road, on another of his expeditions to the city, he spots a chunky little book with a violet cover: *Watt*, by Samuel Beckett, published by Olympia Press. Olympia Press is notorious: from a safe haven in Paris it publishes pornography in English for subscribers in England and America. But as a sideline it also publishes the more daring writings of the avant-garde – Vladimir Nabokov's *Lolita*, for instance. It is hardly likely that Samuel Beckett, author of *Waiting for Godot* and *Endgame*, writes pornography. What kind of book, then, is *Watt*?

He pages through it. It is printed in the same full-bodied serif type as Pound's *Selected Poems*, a type that evokes for him intimacy, solidity. He buys the book and takes it back to Major Arkwright's. From the first page he knows he has hit on something. Propped up in bed with light pouring through the window, he reads and reads.

Watt is quite unlike Beckett's plays. There is no clash, no conflict, just the flow of a voice telling a story, a flow continually checked by doubts and scruples, its pace fitted exactly to the pace of his own mind. *Watt* is also funny, so funny that he rolls about laughing. When he comes to the end he starts again at the beginning.

Why did people not tell him Beckett wrote novels? How could he have imagined he wanted to write in the manner of Ford when Beckett was around all the time? In Ford there has always been an element of the stuffed shirt that he has disliked but has been hesitant to acknowledge, something to do with the value Ford places on knowing where in the West End to buy the best motoring gloves or how to tell a Médoc from a Beaune; whereas Beckett is classless, or outside class, as he himself would prefer to be.

The testing of the programs they write has to be done on the Atlas machine in Cambridge, during the night hours when the mathematicians who enjoy first claim on it are sleeping. So every second or third week he catches the train to Cambridge, carrying a satchel with his papers and his rolls of punched tape and his pyjamas and his toothbrush. While in Cambridge he resides at the Royal Hotel, at International Computers' expense. From six in the evening until six in the morning he works on Atlas. In the early morning he returns to the hotel, has breakfast, and retires to bed. In the afternoon he is free to wander around the town, perhaps going to a film. Then it is time to return to the Mathematical Laboratory, the huge, hangar-like building that houses Atlas, for the night's stint.

It is a routine that suits him down to the ground. He likes train trips, likes the anonymity of hotel rooms, likes huge English breakfasts of bacon and sausages and eggs and toast and marmalade and coffee. Since he does not have to wear a suit, he can mix easily with students on the street, even seem to be one of them. And being with the huge Atlas machine all night, alone save for the duty engineer, watching the roll of computer code that he has written speed through the tape reader, watching the magnetic tape disks begin to spin and the lights on the console begin to flash at his command, gives him a sense of power that he knows is childish but that, with no one watching, he can safely revel in.

Sometimes he has to stay on at the Mathematical Laboratory into the morning to confer with members of the Mathematics Department. For everything that is truly novel about the Atlas software comes not from International Computers but from a handful of mathematicians at Cambridge. From a certain point of view, he is merely one of a team of professional programmers from the computer industry that the Cambridge Mathematics Department has hired to implement its ideas, just as from the same point of view International Computers is a firm of engineers hired by Manchester University to build a computer according to its design. From that point of view, he himself is merely a skilled workman in the pay of the university, not a collaborator entitled to speak on an equal footing with these brilliant young scientists.

For brilliant they are indeed. Sometimes he shakes his head in disbelief at what is happening. Here he is, an undistinguished graduate from a second-class university in the colonies, being permitted to address by first name men with doctorates in mathematics, men who, once they get talking, leave him dizzied in their wake. Problems over which he has dully wrestled for weeks are solved by them in a flash. More often than not, behind what he had thought were problems they see what are the *real* problems, which they pretend for his sake he has seen too.

Are these men truly so lost in the higher reaches of computational logic that they do not see how stupid he is; or – for reasons that are dark to him, since he must count as nothing to them – are they graciously seeing to it that he does not lose face in their company? Is that what civilization is: an unwhispered agreement that no one, no matter how insignificant, should be allowed to lose face? He can believe it of Japan; does it hold for England too? Whatever the case, how truly admirable!

He is in Cambridge, on the premises of an ancient university, hobnobbing with the great. He has even been given a key to the Mathematical Laboratory, a key to the side door, to let himself in and out. What more could he hope for? But he must be wary of getting carried away, of getting inflated ideas. He is here by luck and nothing else. He could never have studied at Cambridge, was never good enough to win a scholarship. He must continue to think of himself as a hired hand: if not, he will become an impostor in the same way that Jude Fawley amid the dreaming spires of Oxford was an impostor. One of these days, quite soon, his tasks will be done, he will have to give back his key, the visits to Cambridge will cease. But let him at least enjoy them while he can.

Twenty

He is into his third summer in England. After lunch, on the lawn behind the Manor House, he and the other programmers have taken to playing cricket with a tennis ball and an old bat found in a broom closet. He has not played cricket since he left school, when he decided to renounce it on the grounds that team sports were incompatible with the life of a poet and an intellectual. Now he finds to his surprise how much he still enjoys the game. Not only does he enjoy it, he is good at it. All the strokes he strove as a child so ineffectually to master come back unbidden, with an ease and fluency that are new because his arms are stronger and because there is no reason to be frightened of the soft ball. He is better, much better, as a batsman and as a bowler too, than his fellow players. How, he asks himself, did these young Englishmen spend their school days? Must he, a colonial, teach them to play their own game?

His obsession with chess is waning, he is beginning to read again. Though the Bracknell library in itself is tiny and inadequate, the librarians are ready to order him any book he wants from the county network. He is reading in the history of logic, pursuing an intuition that logic is a human invention, not part of the fabric of being, and therefore (there are many intermediate steps, but he can fill them in later) that computers are simply toys invented by boys (led by Charles Babbage) for the amusement of other boys. There are many alternative logics, he is convinced (but how many?), each just as good as the logic of *either-or*. The threat of the toy by which he earns his living, the threat that makes it more than just a toy, is that it will burn *either-or* paths in the brains of its users and thus lock them irreversibly into its binary logic.

He pores over Aristotle, over Peter Ramus, over Rudolf Carnap. Most of what he reads he does not understand, but he is used to not understanding. All he is searching for at present is the moment in history when *either-or* is chosen and *and/or* discarded.

He has his books and his projects (the Ford thesis, now nearing completion, the dismantling of logic) for the empty evenings, cricket at midday, and, every second week, a spell at the Royal Hotel with the luxury of nights alone with Atlas, the most redoubtable computer in the world. Could a bachelor's life, if it has to be a bachelor's life, be any better?

There is only one shadow. A year has passed since he last wrote a line of poetry. What has happened to him? Is it true that art comes only out of misery? Must he become miserable again in order to write? Does there not also exist a poetry of ecstasy, even a poetry of lunchtime cricket as a form of ecstasy? Does it matter where poetry finds its impetus as long as it is poetry?

Although Atlas is not a machine built to handle textual materials, he uses the dead hours of the night to get it to print out thousands of lines in the style of Pablo Neruda, using as a lexicon a list of the most powerful words in *The Heights of Macchu Picchu*, in Nathaniel Tarn's translation. He brings the thick wad of paper back to the Royal Hotel and pores over it. 'The nostalgia of teapots.' 'The ardour of shutters.' 'Furious horsemen.' If he cannot, for the present, write poetry that comes from the heart, if his heart is not in the right state to generate poetry of its own, can he at least string together pseudo-poems made up of phrases generated by a machine, and thus, by going through the motions of writing, learn again to write? Is it fair to be using mechanical aids to writing – fair to other poets, fair to the dead masters? The Surrealists wrote words on slips of paper and shook them up in a hat and drew words at random to make up lines. William Burroughs cuts up pages and shuffles them and puts the bits together. Is he not doing the same kind of thing? Or do his huge resources – what other poet in England, in the world, has a machine of this size at his command – turn quantity into quality? Yet might it not be argued that the invention of computers has changed the nature of art, by making the author and the condition of the author's heart irrelevant? On the Third Programme he has heard music from the studios of Radio Cologne, music spliced together from electronic whoops and crackles and street noise and snippets of old recordings and fragments of speech. Is it not time for poetry to catch up with music?

He sends a selection of his Neruda poems to a friend in Cape Town, who publishes them in a magazine he edits. A local newspaper reprints one of the computer poems with a derisive commentary. For a day or two, back in Cape Town, he is notorious as the barbarian who wants to replace Shakespeare with a machine.

Besides the Atlas computers in Cambridge and Manchester, there is a third Atlas. It is housed at the Ministry of Defence's atomic weapons research station outside Aldermaston, not far from Bracknell. Once the software that runs Atlas has been tested in Cambridge and found good, it is to be installed on the Aldermaston machine. Assigned to instal it are the programmers who wrote it. But first these programmers have to pass a security check. Each is given a long questionnaire to fill in about his family, his personal history, his work experience; each is visited at home by men who introduce themselves as from the police but are more likely from Military Intelligence.

All the British programmers are cleared and given cards to wear around their necks during visits, with their photographs on them. Once they have presented themselves at the entrance to Aldermaston and been escorted to the computer building, they are left more or less free to move around as they please.

For Ganapathy and himself, however, there is no question of clearance, since they are foreigners, or, as Ganapathy qualifies it, non-American foreigners. At the entrance gate the two of them therefore have guards assigned to them individually, who conduct them from place to place, stand watch over them at all times, and refuse to be engaged in conversation. When they go to the toilet, their guard stands at the cubicle door; when they eat, their guard stands behind them. They are allowed to speak to other International Computers personnel but to no one else.

His involvement with Mr Pomfret in the IBM days, and his part in furthering the development of the TSR-2 bomber, seem in retrospect so trivial, even comic, that his conscience is easily set at rest. Aldermaston is a different kettle of fish. He spends a total of ten days there, over a period of weeks. By the time he is finished, the tape-scheduling routines are working as well as they work at Cambridge. His task is done. Doubtless there are other people who could have installed the routines, but not as well as he, who wrote them and knows them inside out. Other people could have done the job, but other people did not. Though he could have made a case for being excused (he could, for instance, have pointed to the unnatural circumstance of being observed in all his actions by a poker-faced guard, and the effect of that on his state of mind), he did not make such a case. Mr Pomfret may have been a joke, but he cannot pretend Aldermaston is a joke.

He has never known a place like Aldermaston. In atmosphere it is quite unlike Cambridge. The cubicle where he works, as with every other cubicle and everything inside them, is cheap, functional, and ugly. The whole base, made up of low, scattered brick buildings, is ugly with the ugliness of a place that knows no one will look at it or care to look at it; perhaps with the ugliness of a place that knows, when war comes, it will be blown off the face of the earth.

No doubt there are clever people here, as clever as the Cambridge mathematicians, or nearly so. No doubt some of the people he glimpses in the corridors, Operations Supervisors, Research Officers, Technical Officers Grades I, II and III, Senior Technical Officers, people he is not allowed to speak to, are themselves graduates of Cambridge. He has written the routines he is installing, but the planning behind them was done by Cambridge people, people who could not have been unaware that the machine in the Mathematical Laboratory had a sinister sister at Aldermaston. The hands of the people at Cambridge are not a great deal cleaner than his own hands. Nevertheless, by passing through these gates, by breathing the air here, he has aided the arms race, become an accomplice in the Cold War, and on the wrong side too.

Tests no longer seem to come with fair warning these days, as they did when he was a schoolboy, or even to announce themselves as tests. But in this case it is hard to plead unpreparedness as an excuse. From the moment the word *Aldermaston* was first uttered he knew Aldermaston would be a test and knew he was not going to pass, was going to lack what it took to pass. By working at Aldermaston he has lent himself to evil, and, from a certain point of view, lent himself more culpably than his English colleagues, who if they had refused to participate would have risked their careers far more seriously than he, a transient and an outsider to this quarrel between Britain and America on the one hand and Russia on the other.

Experience. That is the word he would like to fall back on to justify himself to himself. The artist must taste all experience, from the noblest to the most degraded. Just as it is the artist's destiny to experience supreme creative joy, so he must be prepared to take upon himself all in life that is miserable, squalid, ignominious. It was in the name of experience that he underwent London – the dead days of IBM, the icy winter of 1962, one humiliating affair after another: stages in the poet's life, all of them, in the testing of his soul. Similarly Aldermaston – the wretched cubicle in which he works, with its plastic furniture and its view on to the back of a furnace, the armed man at his back – can be regarded simply as experience, as a further stage in his journey into the depths.

It is a justification that does not for a moment convince him. It is sophistry, that is all, contemptible sophistry. And if he is further going to claim that, just as sleeping with Astrid and her teddy bear was getting to know moral squalor, so telling self-justifying lies to oneself is getting to know intellectual squalor at first hand, then the sophistry will only become more contemptible. There is nothing to be said for it; nor, to be ruthlessly honest, is there anything to be said for its having nothing to be said for it. As for ruthless honesty, ruthless honesty is not a hard trick to learn. On the contrary, it is the easiest thing in the world. As a poisonous toad is not poison to itself, so one soon develops a hard skin against one's own honesty. Death to reason, death to talk! All that matters is doing the right thing, whether for the right reason or the wrong reason or no reason at all.

Working out the right thing to do is not difficult. He does not need to think overlong to know what the right thing is. He could, if he chose, do the right thing with near infallible accuracy. What gives him pause is the question of whether he can go on being a poet while doing the right thing. When he tries to imagine what sort of poetry would flow from doing the right thing time after time after time, he sees only blank emptiness. The right thing is boring. So he is at an impasse: he would rather be bad than boring, has no respect for a person who would rather be bad than boring, and no respect either for the cleverness of being able to put his dilemma neatly into words.

Despite cricket and books, despite the ever-cheerful birds greeting the sunrise with chirrups from the apple tree beneath his window, weekends remain hard to get through, particularly Sundays. He dreads waking up on Sunday mornings. There are rituals to help one through Sunday, principally going out and buying the newspaper and reading it on the sofa and clipping out the chess problems. But the newspaper will not take one much beyond eleven in the morning; and anyhow, reading the Sunday supplements is too transparently a way of killing time.

He is killing time, he is trying to kill Sunday so that Monday will come sooner, and with Monday the relief of work. But in a larger sense work is a way of killing time too. Everything he has done since he stepped ashore at Southampton has been a killing of time while he waits for his destiny to arrive. Destiny would not come to him in South Africa, he told himself; she would come (come like a bride!) only in London or Paris or perhaps Vienna, because only in the great cities of Europe does destiny reside. For nearly two years he waited and suffered in London, and destiny stayed away. Now, having not been strong enough to bear London, he has beaten a retreat into the countryside, a strategic retreat. Whether destiny pays visits to the countryside is not certain, even if it is the English countryside, and even if it is barely an hour by train from Waterloo.

Of course in his heart he knows destiny will not visit him unless he makes her do so. He has to sit down and write, that is the only way. But he cannot begin writing until the moment is right, and no matter how scrupulously he prepares himself, wiping the table clean, positioning the lamp, ruling a margin down the side of the blank page, sitting with his eyes shut, emptying his mind in readiness – in spite of all this, the words will not come to him. Or rather, many words will come, but not the right words, the sentence he will recognize at once, from its weight, from its poise and balance, as the destined one.

He hates these confrontations with the blank page, hates them to the extent of beginning to avoid them. He cannot bear the weight of despair that descends at the end of each fruitless session, the realization that again he has failed. Better not to wound oneself in this way, over and over. One might cease to be able to respond to the call when it comes, might become too weak, too abject.

He is well aware that his failure as a writer and his failure as a lover are so closely parallel that they might as well be the same thing. He is the man, the poet, the maker, the active principle, and the man is not supposed to wait for the woman's approach. On the contrary, it is the woman who is supposed to wait for the man. The woman is the one who sleeps until aroused by the prince's kiss; the woman is the bud that unfolds under the caress of the sun's rays. Unless he wills himself to act, nothing will happen, in love or in art. But he does not trust the will. Just as he cannot will himself to write but must wait for the aid of some force from outside, a force that used to be called the Muse, so he cannot simply will himself to approach a woman without some intimation (from where? – from her? from within him? from above?) that she is his destiny. If he approaches a woman in any other spirit, the result is an entanglement like the wretched one with Astrid, an entanglement he was trying to escape from almost before it began.

There is another and more brutal way of saying the same thing. In fact there are hundreds of ways: he could spend the rest of his life listing them. But the most brutal way is to say that he is afraid: afraid of writing, afraid of women. He may pull faces at the poems he reads in *Ambit* and *Agenda*, but at least they are there, in print, in the world. How is he to know that the men who wrote them did not spend years squirming as fastidiously as he in front of the blank page? They squirmed, but then finally they pulled themselves together and wrote as best they could what had to be written, and mailed it out, and suffered the humiliation of rejection or the equal humiliation of seeing their effusions in cold print, in all their poverty. In the same way these men would have found an excuse, however lame, for speaking to some or other beautiful girl in the Underground, and if she turned her head away or passed a scornful remark in Italian to a friend, well, they would have found a way of suffering the rebuff in silence and the next day would have tried again with another girl. That is how it is done, that is how the world works. And one day they, these men, these poets, these lovers, would be lucky: the girl, no matter how exaltedly beautiful, would speak back, and one thing would lead to another and their lives would be transformed, both their lives, and that would be that. What more is required than a kind of stupid, insensitive doggedness, as lover, as writer, together with a readiness to fail and fail again?

What is wrong with him is that he is not prepared to fail. He wants an A or an alpha or one hundred per cent for his every attempt, and a big *Excellent!* in the margin. Ludicrous! Childish! He does not have to be told so: he can see it for himself. Nevertheless. Nevertheless he cannot do it. Not today. Perhaps tomorrow. Perhaps tomorrow he will be in the mood, have the courage.

If he were a warmer person he would no doubt find it all easier: life, love, poetry. But warmth is not in his nature. Poetry is not written out of warmth anyway. Rimbaud was not warm. Baudelaire was not warm. Hot, indeed, yes, when it was needed – hot in life, hot in love – but not warm. He too is capable of being hot, he has not ceased to believe that. But for the present, the present indefinite, he is cold: cold, frozen.

And what is the upshot of this lack of heat, this lack of heart? The upshot is that he is sitting alone on a Sunday afternoon in an upstairs room in a house in the depths of the Berkshire countryside, with crows cawing in the fields and a grey mist hanging overhead, playing chess with himself, growing old, waiting for evening to fall so that he can with a good conscience fry his sausages and bread for supper. At eighteen he might have been a poet. Now he is not a poet, not a writer, not an artist. He is a computer programmer, a twenty-four-year-old computer programmer in a world in which there are no thirty-year-old computer programmers. At thirty one is too old to be a programmer: one turns oneself into something else – some kind of businessman – or one shoots oneself. It is only because he is young, because the neurons in his brain are still firing more or less infallibly, that he has a toehold in the British computer industry, in British society, in Britain itself. He and Ganapathy are two sides of the same coin: Ganapathy starving not because he is cut off from Mother India but because he doesn't eat properly, because despite his M.Sc. in computer science he doesn't know about vitamins and minerals and amino acids; and he locked into an attenuating endgame, playing himself, with each move, further into a corner and into defeat. One of these days the ambulance men will call at Ganapathy's flat and bring him out on a stretcher with a sheet over his face. When they have fetched Ganapathy they might as well come and fetch him too.

Summertime

Notebooks 1972-75

22 August 1972

IN YESTERDAY'S *Sunday Times*, a report from Francistown in Botswana. Sometime last week, in the middle of the night, a car, a white American model, drove up to a house in a residential area. Men wearing balaclavas jumped out, kicked down the front door, and began shooting. When they had done with shooting they set fire to the house and drove off. From the embers the neighbours dragged seven charred bodies: two men, three women, two children.

The killers appeared to be black, but one of the neighbours heard them speaking Afrikaans among themselves and was convinced they were whites in blackface. The dead were South Africans, refugees who had moved into the house mere weeks ago.

Approached for comment, the South African Minister of Foreign Affairs, through a spokesman, calls the report 'unverified'. Inquiries will be undertaken, he says, to determine whether the deceased were indeed South African citizens. As for the military, an unnamed source denies that the SA Defence Force had anything to do with the matter. The killings are probably an internal ANC matter, he suggests, reflecting 'ongoing tensions' between factions.

So they come out, week after week, these tales from the borderlands, murders followed by bland denials. He reads the reports and feels soiled. So this is what he has come back to! Yet where in the world can one hide where one will not feel soiled? Would he feel any cleaner in the snows of Sweden, reading at a distance about his people and their latest pranks?

How to escape the filth: not a new question. An old rat-question that will not let go, that leaves its nasty, suppurating wound.

'I see the Defence Force is up to its old tricks again,' he remarks to his father. 'In Botswana this time.' But his father is too wary to rise to the bait. When his father picks up the newspaper, he takes care to skip straight to the sports pages, missing out the politics – the politics and the killings.

His father has nothing but disdain for the continent to the north of them. *Buffoons* is the word he uses to dismiss the leaders of African states: petty tyrants who can barely spell their own names, chauffeured from one banquet to another in their Rolls-Royces, wearing Ruritanian uniforms festooned with medals they have awarded themselves. Africa: a place of starving masses with homicidal buffoons lording it over them.

'They broke into a house in Francistown and killed everyone,' he presses on nonetheless. 'Executed them. Including the children. Look. Read the report. It's on the front page.'

His father shrugs. His father can find no form of words spacious enough to cover his distaste for, on the one hand, thugs who slaughter defenceless women and children and, on the other, terrorists who wage war from havens across the border. He resolves the problem by immersing himself in the cricket scores. As a response to a moral dilemma it is feeble; yet is his own response – fits of rage and despair – any better?

Once upon a time he used to think that the men who dreamed up the South African version of public order, who brought into being the vast system of labour reserves and internal passports and satellite townships, had based their vision on a tragic misreading of history. They had misread history because, born on farms or in small towns in the hinterland, and isolated within a language spoken nowhere else in the world, they had no appreciation of the scale of the forces that had since 1945 been sweeping away the old colonial world. Yet to say they had misread history was in itself misleading. For they read no history at all. On the contrary, they turned their backs on it, dismissing it as a mass of slanders put together by foreigners who held Afrikaners in contempt and would turn a blind eye if they were massacred by the blacks, down to the last woman and child. Alone and friendless at the remote tip of a hostile continent, they erected their fortress state and retreated behind its walls: there they would keep the flame of Western Christian civilization burning until finally the world came to its senses.

That was the way they spoke, more or less, the men who ran the National Party and the security state, and for a long time he thought they spoke from the heart. But not any more. Their talk of saving civilization, he now tends to think, has never been anything but a bluff. Behind a smokescreen of patriotism they are at this very moment sitting and calculating how long they can keep the show running (the mines, the factories) before they will need to pack their bags, shred any incriminating documents, and fly off to Zürich or Monaco or San Diego, where under the cover of holding companies with names like Algro Trading or Handfast Securities they years ago bought themselves villas and apartments as insurance against the day of reckoning (dies irae, dies illa).

According to his new, revised way of thinking, the men who ordered the killer squad into Francistown have no mistaken vision of history, much less a tragic one. Indeed, they most likely laugh up their sleeves at folk so silly as to have visions of any kind. As for the fate of Christian civilization in Africa, they have never given two hoots about it. And these – these! – are the men under whose dirty thumb he lives!

To be expanded on: his father's response to the times as compared to his own; their differences, their (overriding) similarities.

1 September 1972

The house that he shares with his father dates from the 1920s. The walls, built in part of baked brick but in the main of mud and straw, are by now so rotten with damp creeping up from the earth that they have begun to crumble. To insulate them from the damp is an impossible task; the best that can be done is to lay an impermeable concrete apron around the periphery of the house and hope that slowly they will dry out.

From a home improvement guide he learns that for each metre of concrete he will require three bags of sand, five bags of stone, and one bag of cement. If he makes the apron around the house ten centimetres deep, he calculates, he will need thirty bags of sand, fifty bags of stone, and ten bags of cement, which will entail six trips to the builders' yard, six full loads in a one-ton truck.

Halfway through the first day of work it dawns on him that he has made a mistake of a calamitous order. Either he misread the guide or in his calculations he confused cubic metres with square metres. It is going to take many more than ten bags of cement, plus sand and stone, to lay ninety-six square metres of concrete. It is going to take many more than six trips to the builders' yard; he is going to have to give up more than just a few weekends of his life.

Week after week, using a shovel and a wheelbarrow, he mixes sand, stone, cement and water; block after block he pours liquid concrete and levels it. His back hurts, his arms and wrists are so stiff that he can barely hold a pen. Above all the labour bores him. Yet he is not unhappy. What he finds himself doing is what people like him should have been doing ever since 1652, namely, his own dirty work. In fact, once he forgets about the time he is spending, the work begins to take on its own pleasure. There is such a thing as a well-laid slab whose well-laidness is plain for all to see. The slabs he is laying will outlast his tenancy of the house, may even outlast his spell on earth; in which case he will in a certain sense have cheated death. One might spend the rest of one's life laying slabs, and fall each night into the profoundest sleep, tired with the ache of honest toil.

How many of the ragged workingmen who pass him in the street are secret authors of works that will outlast them: roads, walls, pylons? Immortality of a kind, a limited immortality, is not so hard to achieve after all. Why then does he persist in making marks on paper, in the faint hope that people not yet born will take the trouble to decipher them?

To be expanded on: his readiness to throw himself into half-baked projects; the alacrity with which he retreats from creative work into mindless industry.

16 April 1973

The same *Sunday Times* which, in among exposés of torrid love affairs between teachers and schoolgirls in country towns, in among pictures of pouting starlets in exiguous bikinis, comes out with revelations of atrocities committed by the security forces, reports that the Minister of the Interior has granted a visa allowing Breyten Breytenbach to come back to the land of his birth to visit his ailing parents. A compassionate visa, it is called; it covers both Breytenbach and his wife.

Breytenbach left the country years ago to live in Paris, and soon thereafter queered his pitch by marrying a Vietnamese woman, that is to say, a non-white, an Asiatic. He not only married her but, if one is to believe the poems in which she figures, is passionately in love with her. Despite which, says the *Sunday Times*, the Minister in his compassion will permit the couple a thirty-day visit during which the so-called Mrs Breytenbach will be treated as a white person, a temporary white, an honorary white.

From the moment they arrive in South Africa Breyten and Yolande, he swarthily handsome, she delicately beautiful, are dogged by the press. Zoom lenses capture every intimate moment as they picnic with friends or paddle in a mountain stream.

The Breytenbachs make a public appearance at a literary conference in Cape Town. The hall is packed to the rafters with people come to gape. In his speech Breyten calls Afrikaners a bastard people. It is because they are bastards and ashamed of their bastardy, he says, that they have concocted their cloud-cuckoo scheme of forced separation of the races.

His speech is greeted with huge applause. Soon thereafter he and Yolande fly home to Paris, and the Sunday newspapers return to their menu of naughty nymphets, errant spouses, and state murders.

To be explored: the envy felt by white South Africans (men) for Breytenbach, for his freedom to roam the world and for his unlimited access to a beautiful, exotic sex-companion.

2 September 1973

At the Empire Cinema in Muizenberg last night, an early film of Kurosawa's, *To Live*. A stodgy bureaucrat learns that he has cancer and has only months to live. He is stunned, does not know what to do with himself, where to turn.

He takes his secretary, a bubbly but mindless young woman, out to tea. When she tries to leave he holds her back, gripping her arm. 'I want to be like you!' he says. 'But I don't know how!' She is repelled by the nakedness of his appeal.

Question: How would he react if his father were to grip his arm like that?

13 September 1973

From an employment bureau where he has left his particulars he receives a call. A client seeks expert advice on language matters, will pay by the hour – is he interested? Language matters of what nature, he inquires? The bureau is unable to say.

He calls the number provided, makes an appointment to come to an address in Sea Point. His client is a woman in her sixties, a widow whose husband has departed this world leaving the bulk of his considerable estate in a trust controlled by his brother. Outraged, the widow has resolved to challenge the will. But all the lawyers she has consulted have counselled her against trying. The will is, they say, watertight. Nevertheless she refuses to give up. The lawyers, she is convinced, have misread the wording of the will. She is therefore giving up on lawyers and instead soliciting expert linguistic advice.

With a cup of tea at his elbow he peruses the last testament of the deceased. Its meaning is perfectly plain. To the widow goes the flat in Sea Point and a sum of money. The remainder of the estate goes into a trust for the benefit of his children by a former marriage.

'I fear I cannot help you,' he says. 'The wording is unambiguous. There is only one way in which it can be read.'

'What about here?' she says. She leans over his shoulder and stabs a finger at the text. Her hand is tiny, her skin mottled; on the third finger is a diamond in an extravagant setting. 'Where it says *Notwithstanding the aforesaid.*'

'It says that if you can demonstrate financial distress you are entitled to apply to the trust for support.'

'What about *notwithstanding*?'

'It means that what is stated in this clause is an exception to what has been stated before and takes precedence over it.'

'But it also means that the trust cannot withstand my claim. What does *withstand* mean if it doesn't mean that?'

'It is not a question of what *withstand* means. It is a question of what *Notwithstanding the aforesaid* means. You must take the phrase as a whole.'

She gives an impatient snort. 'I am paying for your services as an expert on English, not as a lawyer,' she says. 'The will is written in English, in English words. What do the words mean? What does *notwithstanding* mean?'

A madwoman, he thinks. *How am I going to get out of this?* But of course she is not mad. She is simply in the grip of rage and greed: rage against the husband who has slipped her grasp, greed for his money.

'The way I understand the clause,' she says, 'if I make a claim then no one, including my brother-in-law, can withstand it. Because that is what *not withstand* means: he can't withstand me. Otherwise what is the point of using the word? Do you see what I mean?'

'I see what you mean,' he says.

He leaves the house with a cheque for ten rands in his pocket. Once he has delivered his report, his expert report, to which he will have attached a copy, attested by a Commissioner of Oaths, of the degree certificate that makes him an expert commentator on the meaning of English words, including the word *notwithstanding*, he will receive the remaining thirty rands of his fee.

He delivers no report. He forgoes the money that is owed him. When the widow telephones to ask what is up, he quietly puts down the receiver.

Features of his character that emerge from the story: (a) integrity (he declines to read the will as his employer wants him to); (b) naïveté (he misses an opportunity to make some badly needed money).

31 May 1975

South Africa is not formally in a state of war, but it might as well be. As resistance has grown, the rule of law has step by step been suspended. The police and the people who run the police (as hunters run packs of dogs) are by now more or less unconstrained. In the guise of news, radio and television relay the official lies. Yet over the whole sorry, murderous show there hangs an air of staleness. The old rallying cries – *Uphold white Christian civilization! Honour the sacrifices of the forefathers!* – have lost all force. The chess players have moved into the endgame, and everyone knows it.

Yet as the game slowly winds down, human lives are still being consumed – consumed and shat out. As it is the fate of some generations to be destroyed by war, so it seems the fate of the present one to be ground down by politics.

If Jesus had stooped to play politics he might have become a key man in Roman Judaea, a big operator. It was because he was indifferent to politics, and made his indifference clear, that he was liquidated. How to live one's life outside politics, and one's death too: that was the example he set for his followers.

Odd to find himself considering Jesus as a guide. But where should he search for a better one?

Caution: Avoid pushing his interest in Jesus too far and turning this into a narrative about finding the true way.

2 June 1975

The house across the street has new owners, a couple of more or less his own age with young children and a BMW. He pays no attention to them until one day there is a knock at the door. 'Hello, I'm David Truscott, your new neighbour. I've locked myself out. Could I use your telephone?' And then, as an afterthought: 'Don't I know you?'

Recognition dawns. They do indeed know each other. In 1952 David

Truscott and he were in the same class, Standard Six, at St Joseph's College. He and David Truscott might have progressed side by side through the rest of high school but for the fact that David failed Standard Six and had to be kept behind. It was not hard to see why he failed. In Standard Six came algebra, and about algebra David could not grasp the first thing, the first thing being that x, y and z were there to liberate one from the tedium of arithmetic. In Latin too, David never quite got the hang of things – of the subjunctive, for example. Even at so early an age it seemed to him clear that David would be better off out of school, away from Latin and algebra, in the real world, counting out banknotes in a bank or selling shoes.

But despite being regularly flogged for not grasping things – floggings that he accepted philosophically, though now and again his glasses would cloud with tears – David Truscott persisted in his schooling, pushed no doubt from behind by his parents. Somehow or other he struggled through Standard Six and then Standard Seven and so on to Standard Ten; and now here he is, twenty years later, neat and bright and prosperous and, it emerges, so preoccupied with matters of business that when he set off for the office in the morning he forgot his house key and – since his wife has taken the children to a party – can't get into the family home.

'And what is your line of business?' he inquires of David, more than curious.

'Marketing. I'm with the Woolworths Group. How about you?'

'Oh, I'm in-between. I used to teach at a university in the United States, now I'm looking for a position here.'

'Well, we must get together. You must come over for a drink, exchange notes. Do you have children?'

'I am a child. I mean, I live with my father. My father is getting on in years. He needs looking after. But come in. The telephone is over there.'

So David Truscott, who did not understand x and y, is a flourishing marketer or marketeer, while he, who had no trouble understanding x and y and much else besides, is an unemployed intellectual. What does that suggest about the workings of the world? What it seems most obviously to suggest is that the path that leads through Latin and algebra is not the path to material success. But it may suggest more besides: that understanding things is a waste of time; that if you want to succeed in the world and have a happy family and a nice home and a BMW you should not try to understand things but just add up the numbers or press the buttons or do whatever else it is that marketers are so richly rewarded for doing.

In the event, David Truscott and he do not get together to have the promised drink and exchange the promised notes. If of an evening it happens that he is in the front garden raking leaves at the time when David Truscott returns from work, the two of them give a neighbourly wave or nod across the street, but no more than that. He sees somewhat more of Mrs Truscott, a pale little creature forever chivvying children into or out of the second car; but he is not introduced to her and has no occasion to speak to her. Tokai Road is a busy thoroughfare, dangerous for children. There is no good reason for the Truscotts to cross to his side, or for him to cross to theirs.

3 June 1975

From where he and the Truscotts live one has only to stroll a kilometre or so in a southerly direction to come face to face with Pollsmoor. Pollsmoor – no one bothers to call it Pollsmoor Prison – is a place of incarceration ringed around with high walls and barbed wire and watch towers. Once upon a time it stood all alone in a waste of sandy scrubland. But over the years, first hesitantly, then more confidently, the suburban developments have crept closer, until now, hemmed in by neat rows of homes from which upright citizens emerge each morning to play their part in the national economy, it is Pollsmoor that has become the anomaly in the landscape.

It is of course an irony that the South African *gulag* should protrude so obscenely into white suburbia, that the same air that he and the Truscotts breathe should have passed through the lungs of miscreants and criminals. But to the barbarians, as Zbigniew Herbert has pointed out, irony is like salt: you crunch it between your teeth, you enjoy a momentary savour, but when the savour is gone the brute facts are still before you. So: What does one do with the brute fact of Pollsmoor once the irony is used up?

Continuation: the Prisons Service vans that pass along Tokai Road on their way from the courts; flashes of faces, fingers gripping the grated windows; what stories the Truscotts tell their children to explain those hands and faces, some defiant, some forlorn.

Julia

DR FRANKL, YOU HAVE had a chance to read the pages I sent you from John Coetzee's notebooks for the years 1972-75, the years, more or less, when you were friendly with him. As a way of getting into your story, I wonder whether you have any thoughts about those entries. Do you recognize in them the man you knew? Do you recognize the country and the times he describes?

Yes, I remember South Africa. I remember Tokai Road, I remember the vans crammed with prisoners on their way to Pollsmoor. I remember it all quite clearly.

Nelson Mandela was of course imprisoned at Pollsmoor. Are you surprised that Coetzee doesn't mention Mandela as a near neighbour?

Mandela wasn't moved to Pollsmoor until later. In 1975 he was still on Robben Island.

Of course, I had forgotten that. And what of Coetzee's relations with his father? He and his father lived together for some while after his mother's death. Did you ever meet his father?

Several times.

Did you see the father in the son?

Do you mean, was John like his father? Physically, no. His father was

298

smaller and slighter: a neat little man, handsome in his way, though plainly not well. He drank on the sly, and smoked, and generally did not look after himself, whereas John was a quite ferocious abstainer.

And in other respects? Were they alike in other respects?

They were both loners. Socially inept. Repressed, in the wider sense of the word.

And how did you come to meet John Coetzee?

I'll tell you in a moment. But first, there was something I didn't understand about the pages you sent me from his diaries. Those italicized passages – *To be expanded on* and so forth – who wrote them? Did you?

No, Coetzee wrote them himself. They are memos addressed to himself. He wrote them in 1999 or 2000, when he was thinking of reworking his diaries as a book. He later dropped the idea.

I see. How I met John. I first bumped into him in a supermarket. This was in the summer of 1972, not long after we had moved to the Cape. I seemed to be spending a lot of time in supermarkets in those days, even though our needs – I mean my needs and my child's – were quite simple. I shopped because I was bored, because I needed to get away from the house, but mainly because the supermarket gave me peace and gave me pleasure: the airiness, the whiteness, the cleanness, the muzak, the quiet hiss of trolley wheels. And then there were all the choices – this spaghetti sauce against that spaghetti sauce, this toothpaste against that toothpaste, and so forth, on and on. I found it calming. It was good for my soul. Other women I knew played tennis or did yoga. I shopped.

This was the heyday of apartheid, the 1970s, so you didn't see many people of colour in a supermarket, except of course the staff. Didn't see many men either. That was part of the pleasure. I didn't have to put on a performance. I could be myself.

You didn't see many men, but in the Tokai branch of Pick n Pay there was one I noticed now and again. I noticed him but he didn't notice me, he was too absorbed in his shopping. I approved of that. In appearance he was not what most people would call attractive. He was scrawny, he had a beard, he wore horn-rimmed glasses and sandals. He looked out of place, like a bird, one of those flightless birds; or like an abstracted scientist who had wandered by mistake out of his laboratory. There was an air of seediness about him too, an air of failure. I suspected there was no woman in his life, and it turned out I was right. What he plainly needed was someone to take charge of him, some veteran hippie with beads and hairy armpits and no makeup who would do the shopping and the cooking and cleaning and maybe supply him with dope too. I didn't get close enough to check out his feet, but I was ready to bet his toenails weren't trimmed.

I was always conscious, in those days, of when a man was looking at me. I could feel a pressure on my limbs, on my breasts, the pressure of the male gaze, sometimes subtle, sometimes not so subtle. You won't understand what I am talking about, but any woman will. With this man there was no pressure detectable. None.

Then one day that changed. I was standing in front of the stationery rack. Christmas was around the corner, and I was selecting wrapping paper – you know, paper with jolly Christmas motifs, candles, fir trees, reindeer. By accident I let a roll slip, and as I bent to pick it up I dropped a second roll. Behind me I heard a man's voice: 'I'll get them.' It was of course your man, John Coetzee. He picked up the two rolls, which were quite long, a metre maybe, and returned them to me, and as he did so, whether intentionally or not I still can't say, pressed them into my breast. For a second or two, through the length of the rolls, he could actually be said to have been prodding my breast.

It was outrageous, of course. At the same time it was not important. I tried to show no reaction: did not drop my eyes, did not blush, certainly did not smile. 'Thank you,' I said in a neutral voice, and turned away and went on with my business.

Nevertheless it was a personal act, no use pretending it wasn't. Whether it was going to fade away and be lost among all the other personal moments only time would tell. But not easily ignored, that intimate, unexpected nudge. In fact when I got home I went so far as to lift my bra and examine the breast in question. It was unmarked, of course. Just a breast, a young woman's innocent breast.

Then a couple of days later, driving home, I spotted him, Mister Prod, trudging along Tokai Road with his shopping bags. Without thinking twice I stopped and offered him a lift (you are too young to know, but in those days one still offered lifts).

Tokai of the 1970s was what you would call a new, upwardly mobile suburb. Though land was not cheap, there was a lot of building going on. But the house where John lived was from an earlier era. It was one of the cottages that had housed farm workers when Tokai was still farmland. Electricity and plumbing had been added, but as a home it was still fairly basic. I dropped him at the front gate; he did not ask me in.

Time passed. Then, happening one day to drive past the house, which was on Tokai Road itself, a major road, I caught sight of him. He was standing in the back of a pickup truck, shovelling sand into a wheelbarrow. He wore shorts; he looked pale and not particularly strong, but he seemed to be managing.

What was odd about the spectacle was that it was not usual in those days for a white man to do manual labour, unskilled labour. Kaffir work, it was generally called, work you paid someone else to do. If it was not exactly shameful to be seen shovelling sand, it certainly let the side down, if you know what I mean.

You asked me to give an idea of John as he was in those days, but I can't give you a picture without any background, otherwise there are things you will fail to understand.

I understand. I mean, I accept that.

I drove past, as I said, did not slow down, did not wave. The whole story could have ended there and then, the whole connection, and you would not be here listening to me, you would be in some other country listening to the ramblings of some other woman. But, as it happened, I had second thoughts, and turned back.

'Hello, what are you up to?' I called out.

'As you can see: shovelling sand,' he said.

'But to what end?'

'Construction work. Do you want a tour?' And he clambered down from the pickup.

'Not now,' I said. 'Some other day. Is that pickup yours?'

'Yes.'

'So you don't have to walk to the shops. You could drive.'

'Yes.' Then he said: 'Do you live around here?'

'Further out,' I replied. 'Beyond Constantiaberg. In the bush.'

It was a joke, the kind of little joke that passed between white South Africans in those days. Because of course it wasn't true that I lived in the bush. The only people who lived in the bush, the real bush, were blacks. What he was meant to understand was that I lived in one of the newer developments carved out of the ancestral bush of the Cape Peninsula.

'Well, I won't hold you up any longer,' I said. 'What are you constructing?'

'I'm not constructing, just concreting,' he said. 'I'm not clever enough to construct.' Which I took as a little joke on his part to answer the little joke on mine. Because if he was neither rich nor handsome nor appealing – none of which he was – then, if he was not clever, there was nothing left to be. But of course he had to be clever. He even looked clever, in the way that scientists who spend their lives hunched over microscopes look clever: a narrow, myopic kind of cleverness to go with the horn-rimmed glasses. You must believe me when I tell you that nothing – nothing! – could have been further from my mind than flirting with this man. For he had no sexual presence whatsoever. It was as though he had been sprayed from head to toe with a neutralizing spray, a neutering spray. Certainly he was guilty of nudging me in the breast with a roll of Christmas paper: I had not forgotten that, my breast retained the memory. But ten to one, I now told myself, it had been nothing but a clumsy accident, the act of a *Schlemiel*.

So why did I have second thoughts? Why did I turn back? Not an easy question to answer. If there is such a thing as taking to a person, I am not sure that I took to John, not for a long time. John was not easy to take to, his whole stance towards the world was too wary, too defensive for that. I presume his mother must have taken to him, when he was little, and loved him, because that is what mothers are there for. But it was hard to imagine anyone else doing so.

You don't mind a little frank talk, do you? So let me fill out the picture. I was twenty-six at the time, and had had carnal relations with only two men. Two. The first was a boy I met when I was fifteen. For years, until he was called up into the army, he and I were as tight as twins. After he went away I moped for a while, kept to myself, then found a new boyfriend. With the new boyfriend I remained as tight as twins throughout my student years; as soon as we graduated he and I married, with both families' blessing. In each case it was all or nothing. My nature has always been like that: all or nothing. So at the age of twenty-six I was in many respects an innocent. I had not the faintest idea, for instance, how one went about seducing a man.

Don't misunderstand me. It was not that I led a sheltered life. A sheltered life was not possible in the circles in which we, my husband and I, moved. More than once, at cocktail parties, some man or other, usually a business acquaintance of my husband's, had manoeuvred me into a corner and leant close and asked in a low voice whether I didn't feel lonely out in the suburbs, with Mark away so much of the time, whether I wouldn't like to get away one day next week for lunch. Of course I didn't play along, but this, I inferred, was how extramarital affairs were initiated. A strange man would take you to lunch and after lunch drive you to a beach cottage belonging to a friend to which he happened to have a key, or to a city hotel, and there the sexual part of the transaction would be carried out. Then the next day the man would phone to say how much he had enjoyed his time with you and would you like to meet again next Tuesday? And so it would proceed, Tuesday after Tuesday, the discreet lunches, the episodes in bed, until the man stopped calling or you stopped answering his calls; and the sum of it all was called having an affair.

In the world of business – I'll say more about my husband and his business in a moment – there was pressure on men – at least it was so in those days – to have presentable wives, and therefore on their wives to be presentable; to be presentable and to be accommodating too, within bounds. That is why, even though my husband would get upset when I told him about the overtures his colleagues were making to me, he and they continued to have cordial relations. No displays of outrage, no fisticuffs, no duels at dawn, just now and then a bout of quiet fuming and bad temper in the confines of the home.

The whole question of who in that little enclosed world was sleeping with whom seems to me now, as I look back, darker than anyone was prepared to admit, darker and more sinister. The men both liked and disliked it that their wives were coveted by other men. They felt threatened but they were nevertheless excited. And the women, the wives, were excited too: I would have had to be blind not to see that. Excitement all around, an envelope of libidinous excitement. From which I purposely excised myself. At the parties I mention I was as presentable as one was required to be but I was never accommodating.

As a result I made no friends among the wives, who accordingly put their heads together and decided I was cold and supercilious. What is more, they made certain their verdict got relayed to me. As for me, I would like to be able to say I could not have cared less, but that would not be true, I was too young and unsure of myself.

Mark did not want me to sleep with other men. At the same time he wanted other men to see what kind of woman he had married, and envy him. Much the same, I presume, held for his friends and colleagues: they wanted the wives of other men to succumb to their advances but they wanted their own wives to remain chaste – chaste and alluring. Logically it made no sense. As a social microsystem it was unsustainable. Yet these were businessmen, what the French call men of affairs, astute, clever (in another sense of the word clever), men who knew about systems, about which systems are sustainable and which are not. That is why I say that the system of the licit illicit in which they all participated was darker than they were prepared to admit. It could continue to function, in my view, only at considerable psychic cost to them, and only as long as they refused to acknowledge what at some level they must have known.

At the beginning of our marriage, Mark's and mine, when we were so sure of each other that we did not believe anything could shake us, we made a pact that we would have no secrets from each other. As far as I was concerned, that pact still held at the time I am telling you about. I hid nothing from Mark. I hid nothing because I had nothing to hide. Mark, on the other hand, had once transgressed. He had transgressed and had confessed his transgression, and been shaken by the consequences. After that jolt he privately concluded it was more convenient to lie than to tell the truth.

The field Mark was employed in was financial services. His firm identified investment opportunities for clients and managed their investments. The clients were for the most part wealthy South Africans trying to get their money out of the country before the country imploded (the word they used) or exploded (the word I preferred). For reasons that were never made clear to me – there were, after all, even in those days, such things as telephones – his job required him to travel once a week to their branch office in Durban for what he called consultations. If you added up the hours and days, it turned out he was spending as much time in Durban as at home.

One of the colleagues Mark needed to consult with at their Durban office was a woman named Yvette. She was older than he, Afrikaans, divorced. At first he used to speak freely of her. She even telephoned him at home, on business, he said. Then all mention of Yvette dried up. 'Is there some problem with Yvette?' I asked Mark. 'No,' he said. 'Do you find her attractive?' 'Not really.'

From his evasiveness I guessed something was brewing. I began to pay attention to odd details: messages that inexplicably didn't reach him, missed flights, things like that.

One day, when he came back from one of his lengthy absences, I confronted him head-on. 'I couldn't get hold of you last night at your hotel,' I said – 'Were you with Yvette?'

'Yes,' he said.

'Did you sleep with her?'

'Yes,' he replied (*I am sorry but I cannot tell a lie*).

'Why?' I said.

He shrugged.

'Why?' I said again.

'Because,' he said.

'Well, bugger you,' I said, and turned my back on him and locked myself in the bathroom, where I did not cry – the thought of crying did not so much as cross my mind – but on the contrary, choking with vengefulness, squeezed a full tube of toothpaste and a full tube of hair-mousse into the handbasin, flooded the mess with hot water, stirred it with a hairbrush, and flushed it down the sink.

That was the background. After that episode, after his confession did not win him the approval he was expecting, he turned to lying. 'Do you still see Yvette?' I asked after another of his trips.

'I have to see Yvette, I have no choice, we work together,' he replied.

'But do you still see her in *that* way?'

'What you call *that way* is over,' he said. 'It only happened once.'

'Once or twice,' I said.

'Once,' he repeated, cementing the lie.

'In fact, it was just one of those things,' I offered.

'Exactly. Just one of those things.' And therewith words ceased between Mark and me, words and everything else, for the night.

Each time Mark lied he would make sure he looked me straight in the eye. *Levelling with Julia*: that must be how he thought of it. It was from this level look of his that I could tell – infallibly – that he was lying. You won't believe how bad Mark was at lying – how bad men are in general. What a pity I had nothing to lie about, I thought. I could have shown Mark a thing or two, technique-wise.

Chronologically speaking, Mark was older than me, but that was not how I saw it. The way I saw it, I was the oldest in our family, followed by Mark, who was about thirteen, followed by our daughter Christina, who would be two at her next birthday. In respect of maturity my husband was therefore closer to the child than he was to me.

As for Mister Prod, Mister Nudge, the man shovelling sand from the back of the truck – to return to him – I had no idea how old he was. For all I knew, he might be another thirteen-year-old. Or he might actually, *mirabile dictu*, be a grown-up. I was going to have to wait and see.

'I was out by a factor of six,' he was saying (or maybe it was sixteen, I was only half listening). 'Instead of one ton of sand, six (or sixteen) tons of sand. Instead of one and a half tons of gravel, ten tons of gravel. I must have been out of my mind.'

'Out of your mind,' I said, playing for time while I caught up.

'To make a mistake like that.'

'I make mistakes with numbers all the time. I get the decimal point in the wrong place.'

'Yes, but a factor of six isn't like misplacing the decimal point. Not unless you are a Sumerian. Anyway, the answer to your question is, it is going to take for ever.'

What question, I asked myself? And what is this it that is going to take for ever?

'I have to go now,' I said. 'I have a child waiting for her lunch.'

'You have children?'

'Yes, I have a child. Why shouldn't I? I am a grown woman with a husband and a child whom I have to feed. Why are you surprised? Why else should I need to spend so much time in Pick n Pay?'

'For the music?' he offered.

'And you? Don't you have a family?'

'I have a father who lives with me. Or with whom I live. But no family in the conventional sense. My family has flown.'

'No wife? No children?'

'No wife, no children. I am back to being a son.'

They have always interested me, these exchanges between human beings when the words have nothing to do with the traffic of thoughts through the mind. As he and I were speaking, for instance, my memory threw up the visual image of the really quite repulsive stranger, with thick black hair sprouting from his earholes and over the top button of his shirt, who at the most recent barbecue had ever so casually placed a hand on my bottom as I stood dishing up salad for myself: not to stroke me or pinch me, just to cup my buttock in his big hand. If that image was filling my mind, what might be filling the mind of this other, less hirsute man? And how fortunate that most people, even people who are no good at straight-out lying, are at least competent enough at concealment not to reveal what is going on inside them, not by the slightest tremor of the voice or dilation of the pupil!

'Well, goodbye,' I said.

'Goodbye,' he said.

I went home, paid the house-help, gave Chrissie her lunch, and put her down for her nap. Then I baked two sheets of chocolate cookies. While the cookies were still warm I drove back to the house on Tokai Road. It was a beautiful, wind-still day. Your man (remember, I did not know his name at that point) was in the yard doing something with timber and a hammer and nails. He was stripped to the waist; his shoulders were red where the sun had caught them.

'Hello,' I said. 'You should wear a shirt, the sun isn't good for you. Here, I've brought some cookies for you and your father. They are better than the stuff you get at Pick n Pay.'

Looking suspicious, in fact looking quite irritated, he put aside his tools and took the parcel. 'I can't invite you in, too much of a mess,' he said. I was clearly not welcome.

'That's all right,' I said. 'I can't stay anyway, I have to get back to my child. I was just making a neighbourly gesture. Would you and your father like to come over for a meal one evening? A neighbourly meal?'

He gave a smile, the first smile I had had from him. Not an attractive smile, too tight-lipped. He was self-conscious about his teeth, which were in bad shape. 'Thank you,' he said, 'but I'll have to check with my father first. He isn't one for late nights.'

'Tell him it won't be a late night,' I said. 'You can eat and go, I won't be offended. It will just be the three of us. My husband is away.'

You must be getting worried, Mr Vincent. *What have I let myself in for?* you must be asking yourself. *How can this woman pretend to have total recall of mundane conversations dating back three or four decades? And when is she going to get to the point?* So let me be candid. I am making up the words, the dialogue, as I go along. Which I presume is permitted, since we are talking about a writer. What I am telling you may not be true to the letter, but it is true to the spirit, be assured of that. Can I proceed?

[Silence.]

I scribbled my phone number on the box of cookies. 'And let me tell you my name too,' I said, 'in case you were wondering. My name is Julia.'

'Julia. How sweetly flows the liquefaction of her clothes.'

'Really,' I said. Liquefaction. What did he mean?

He arrived as promised the next evening, but without his father. 'My father is not feeling well,' he said. 'He has taken an aspirin and gone to bed.'

We ate at the kitchen table, the two of us, with Chrissie on my lap. 'Say hello to the uncle,' I said to Chrissie. But Chrissie would have nothing to do with the strange man. A child knows when something is up. Feels it in the air.

In fact Christina never took to John, then or later. As a young child she was fair and blue-eyed, like her father and quite unlike me. I'll show you a picture. Sometimes I used to feel that, because she did not take after me in looks, she would never take to me. Strange. I was the one who did all the caring and caring-for in the household, yet compared with Mark I was the intruder, the dark one, the odd one out.

The uncle. That was what I called John in front of her. Afterwards I regretted it. Something sordid in passing off a lover as one of the family.

Anyway, we ate, we chatted, but the zest, the excitement was beginning to go out of me, leaving me flat. Aside from the wrapping paper incident in the supermarket, which I might or might not have misread, I was the one who had made all the overtures, issued the invitation. *Enough, no more, I said to myself. It is up to him now to push the button through the hole or else not push the button through the hole.* So to speak.

The truth is, I was not cut out to be a seductress. I did not even approve of the word, with its overtones of lacy underwear and French perfume. It was precisely in order not to fall into the role of seductress that I had not dressed up for the present occasion. I wore the same white cotton blouse and green Terylene slacks (yes, Terylene) that I had worn to the supermarket that morning. What you see is what you get.

Don't smile. I am perfectly aware how much I was behaving like a character in a book – like one of those high-minded young women in Henry James, say, determined, despite her better instincts, to do the difficult, the modern thing. Particularly when my peers, the wives of Mark's colleagues at the firm, were turning for guidance not to Henry James or George Eliot but to *Vogue* or *Marie Claire* or *Fair Lady*. But then, what are books for if not to change our lives? Would you have come all the way to far Ontario to hear what I have to say if you did not believe books are important?

No. No, I wouldn't.

Exactly. And John wasn't exactly a snappy dresser himself. One pair of good trousers, three plain white shirts, one pair of shoes: a real child of the Depression. But let me get back to my story.

For supper that night I made a simple lasagne. Pea soup, lasagne, ice cream: that was the menu, bland enough for a two-year-old. The lasagne was sloppier than it should have been because it was made with cottage cheese instead of ricotta. I could have made a second dash to the shops for ricotta, but on principle I did not, just as on principle I did not change my outfit.

What did we talk about over supper? Nothing much. I concentrated on feeding Chrissie – I didn't want her to feel neglected. And John was not a great talker, as you must know.

I don't know. I never met him in the flesh.

You never met him? I'm surprised to hear that.

I never sought him out. I never even corresponded with him. I thought it would be better if I had no sense of obligation towards him. It would leave me free to write what I wished.

But you sought me out. Your book is going to be about him yet you chose not to meet him. Your book is not going to be about me yet you asked to meet me. How do you explain that?

Because you were a figure in his life. You were important to him.

How do you know that?

I am just repeating what he said. Not to me, but to lots of people.

He said that I was an important figure in his life? I am surprised. I am gratified. Gratified not that he should have thought so – I agree, I did have an impact on his life – but that he should have said so to other people.

Let me make a confession. When you first contacted me, I nearly decided to turn you down, not to speak to you. I thought you would be some busybody, some academic newshound who had come upon a list of John's women, his conquests, and would now be going down the list, ticking off the names, hoping to get some dirt on him.

You don't have a high opinion of academic researchers.

No, I don't. Which is why I have tried to make it clear to you that I was not one of his conquests. If anything, he was one of mine. But tell me – I'm curious – to whom did he say that I was important?

To various people. In letters. He doesn't name you, but you are easy enough to identify. Also, he kept a photograph of you. I came across it among his papers.

A photograph! Can I see it? Do you have it with you?

I'll make a copy and send it.

Yes, of course I was important to him. He was in love with me, in his way. But there is an important way of being important, and an unimportant way, and I have my doubts that I made it to the important important level. I mean, he never wrote about me. I never entered his books. Which to me suggests that I never quite flowered within him, never quite came to life.

[Silence.]

No comment? You have read his books. Where in his books do you find traces of me?

I can't answer that. I don't know you well enough to say. Don't you recognize yourself in any of his characters?

No.

Perhaps you are in his books in a more diffuse way, not immediately detectable.

Perhaps. But I would have to be convinced of that. Shall we go on? Where was I?

Supper. Lasagne.

Yes. Lasagne. Conquests. I fed him lasagne and then I completed my conquest of him. How explicit do I need to be? Since he is dead, it can make no difference to him, any indiscreetness on my part. We used the marital bed. If I am going to desecrate my marriage, I thought, I may as well do so thoroughly. And a bed is more comfortable than the sofa or the floor.

As for the experience itself – I mean the experience of infidelity, which is what the experience was, predominantly, for me – it was stranger than I expected, and then over before I could get accustomed to the strangeness. Yet it was exciting, no doubt about that, from start to finish. My heart did not stop hammering. Not something I will forget, ever. I mentioned Henry James. There are plenty of betrayals in James, but I recall nothing about the sense of excitement, of heightened self-awareness, during the act itself – by which I mean the act of betrayal. James liked to present himself as a great betrayer, but I ask myself: Did he have any experience of the real thing, of real, bodily infidelity?

My first impressions? I found this new lover of mine bonier than my husband, and lighter. *Doesn't get enough to eat*, I remember thinking. He and his father together in that mean little cottage on Tokai Road, a widower and his celibate son, two incompetents, two of life's failures, supping on polony sausage and biscuits and tea. Since he didn't want to bring his father to me, would I have to start dropping in on them with baskets of nourishing goodies?

The image that has stayed with me is of him leaning over me with his eyes shut, stroking my body, frowning with concentration as if trying to memorize me through touch alone. Up and down his hand roamed, back and forth. I was, at the time, quite proud of my figure. The jogging, the callisthenics, the dieting: if there is no payoff when you undress for a man, when is there ever going to be a payoff? I may not have been a beauty, but at least I must have been a pleasure to handle: nice and trim, a good piece of woman-flesh.

If you find this kind of talk embarrassing, say so and I will restrain myself. I am in one of the intimate professions, so plain talk doesn't trouble me as long as it doesn't trouble you. No? No problem? Shall I go on?

That was our first time together. Interesting, an interesting experience, but not earth-shaking. But then, I never expected it to be earth shaking, not with him.

What I was determined to avoid was emotional entanglement. A casual fling would be one thing, an affair of the heart quite another.

Of myself I was fairly sure. I was not about to lose my heart to a man about whom I knew next to nothing. But what of him? Might he be the type to brood on what had passed between us, building it up into something bigger than it really was? Be on your guard, I told myself.

Days went by, however, without any word from him. Each time I drove past the house on Tokai Road I slowed down and peered, but caught no sight of him. Nor was he at the supermarket. There was only one conclusion I could come to: he was avoiding me. In a way that was a good sign; but it annoyed me nevertheless. In fact it hurt me. I wrote him a letter, an old-fashioned letter, and put a stamp on it and dropped it in the mailbox. 'Are you avoiding me?' I wrote. 'What need I do to reassure you I want us to be good friends, no more?' No response.

What I did not mention in the letter, and would certainly not mention when next I saw him, was how I passed the weekend immediately after his visit. Mark and I were at each other like rabbits, having sex in bed, on the floor, in the shower, everywhere, even when poor innocent Chrissie lay wide awake in her cot, wailing, calling for me.

Mark had his own ideas about why I was in such an inflamed state. Mark thought I could smell his girlfriend from Durban on him and wanted to prove to him how much better a – how shall I put it? – how much better a performer I was than she. On the Monday after the weekend in question he was booked to fly to Durban, but he pulled out – cancelled his flight, called the office to say he was sick. Then he and I went back to bed.

He could not have enough of me. He was positively enraptured with the institution of bourgeois marriage and the opportunities it afforded a man to rut both outside and inside the home.

As for me, I was – I choose my words with deliberation – I was unbearably excited at having two men so close to each other. To myself I said, in a rather shocked way, *You are behaving like a whore! Is that what you are, by nature?* But beneath it all I was quite proud of myself, of the effect I could have. That weekend I glimpsed for the first time the possibility of growth without end in the realm of the erotic. Until then I had had a rather trite picture of erotic life: you arrive at puberty, you spend a year or two or three hesitating on the brink of the pool, then you plunge in and splash around until you find a mate who satisfies you, and that is the end of it, the end of your quest. What dawned on me that weekend was that at the age of twenty-six my erotic life had barely begun.

Then at last I received a reply to my letter. A phone call from John. First some cautious probing: Was I alone, was my husband away? Then the invitation: Would I like to come over for supper, an early supper, and would I like to bring my child?

I arrived at the house with Chrissie in her pram. John was waiting at the door wearing one of those blue-and-white butcher's aprons. 'Come through to the back,' he said, 'we're having a braai.'

That was where I met his father for the first time. His father was sitting hunched over the fire as if he was cold, when in fact the evening was still quite warm. Somewhat creakily he got to his feet to greet me. He looked frail, though it turned out he was only sixty-odd. 'Pleased to meet you,' he said, and gave me a nice smile. He and I got on well from the start. 'And is this Chrissie? Hello, my girl! Come to visit us, eh?'

Unlike his son, he spoke with a heavy Afrikaans accent. But his English was perfectly passable. He had grown up on a farm in the Karoo, I discovered, with lots of siblings. They had learned their English from a tutor – there was no school nearby – a Miss Jones or Miss Smith, out from the Old Country.

In the walled estate where Mark and I lived each of the units came with a built-in barbecue in the back courtyard. Here on Tokai Road there was no such amenity, just an open fire with a few bricks around it. It seemed stupid beyond belief to have an unguarded fire when there was going to be a child around, particularly a child like Chrissie, not yet steady on her feet. I pretended to touch the wire grid, pretended to cry out with pain, whipped my hand away, sucked it. 'Hot!' I said to Chrissie. 'Careful! Don't touch!'

Why do I remember this detail? Because of the sucking. Because I was aware of John's eyes on me, and therefore purposely prolonged the moment. I had – excuse me for boasting – I had a nice mouth in those days, very kissable. My family name was Kiš, which in South Africa, where no one knew about funny diacritics, was spelled K-I-S. *Kiss-kiss*, the girls at school used to hiss when they wanted to provoke me. *Kiss-kiss*, and giggles, and a wet smacking of the lips. I could not have cared less. Nothing wrong with being kissable, I thought. End of digression. I am fully aware it is John you want to hear about, not me and my schooldays.

Grilled sausages and baked potatoes: that was the menu these two men had so imaginatively put together. For the sausages, tomato sauce from a bottle; for the potatoes, margarine. God knows what offal had gone into the making of the sausages. Fortunately I had brought along a couple of those little Heinz jars for the child.

I pleaded a ladylike appetite and took only a single sausage on my plate. With Mark away so much of the time, I found I was eating less and less meat. But for these two men it was meat and potatoes and nothing else. They ate in the same way, in silence, bolting down their food as if it might be whipped away at any moment. Solitary eaters.

'How is the concreting coming along?' I asked.

'Another month and it will be done, God willing,' said John.

'It's making a real difference to the house,' his father said. 'No doubt about that. Much less damp than there used to be. But it's been a big job, eh, John?'

I recognized the tone at once, the tone of a parent eager to boast about his child. My heart went out to the poor man. A son in his thirties, and nothing to be said for him but that he could lay concrete! How hard for the son too, the pressure of that longing in the parent, the longing to be proud! If there was one reason above all why I excelled at school, it was to give my parents, who lived such lonely lives in this strange country, something to be proud of.

His English – the father's – was perfectly passable, as I said, but it was clearly not his mother tongue. When he brought out an idiom, like *No doubt about that*, he did so with a little flourish, as if expecting to be applauded.

I asked him what he did. (*Did*: such an inane word; but he knew what I meant.) He told me he was a bookkeeper, that he worked in the city. 'It must be quite a schlep, getting from here to the city,' I said. 'Wouldn't it suit you better if you lived closer in?'

He mumbled some reply that I did not catch. Silence fell. Evidently I had touched on a sore spot. I changed the subject, but it did not help.

I had not expected much from the evening, but the flatness of the conversation, the long silences, and something else in the air too, discord or bad temper between the two of them – these were more than I was prepared to stomach. The food had been dreary, the coals were turning grey, I was feeling chilly, darkness had begun to fall, Chrissie was being attacked by mosquitoes. Nothing obliged me to go on sitting in this weed-infested backyard, nothing obliged me to participate in the family tensions of people I barely knew, even if in a technical sense one of them was or had been my lover. So I picked Chrissie up and put her back in her cart.

'Don't leave yet,' said John. 'I'll make coffee.'

'I must go,' I said. 'It's well past the child's bedtime.'

At the gate he tried to kiss me, but I wasn't in the mood for it.

The story I told myself after that evening, the story I settled on, was that my husband's infidelities had provoked me to such an extent that to punish him and salvage my own *amour propre* I had gone out and had a brief infidelity of my own. Now that it was evident what a mistake that infidelity had been, at least in the choice of accomplice, my husband's infidelity appeared in a new light, as probably a mistake too, and thus not worth getting upset about.

Over the weekends when my husband was at home I think I will at this point draw a modest veil. I have told you enough. Let me simply remind you that it was against the background of those weekends that my weekday relations with John played themselves out. If John became more than a little intrigued and even infatuated with me, it was because in me he encountered a woman at the peak of her womanly powers, living a heightened sexual life – a life that in truth had little to do with him.

Mr Vincent, I am perfectly aware it is John you want to hear about, not me. But the only story involving John that I can tell, or the only one I am prepared to tell, is this one, namely the story of my life and his part in it, which is quite different, quite another matter, from the story of his life and my part in that. My story, the story of me, began years before John arrived on the scene and went on for years after he made his exit. In the phase I am telling you about today, Mark and I were, properly speaking, the protagonists, John and the woman in Durban members of the supporting cast. So you have to choose. Will you accept what I have to offer you? Shall I go on with my recital, or shall I call it off here and now?

Go on.

You are sure? Because there is a further point I wish to make. It is this. You commit a grave error if you think to yourself that the difference between the two stories, the story you wanted to hear and the story you are getting from me, will be nothing more than a matter of perspective – that while from my point of view the story of John may have been just one episode among many in the long narrative of my marriage, nevertheless, by dint of a quick flip, a quick manipulation of perspective, followed by some clever editing, you can transform it into a story about John and one of the women who passed through his life. Not so. Not so. I warn you most earnestly: if you start playing around with your text, cutting out words here and adding in words there, the whole thing will turn to ash in your hands. I *really* was the main character. John *really* was a minor player. I am sorry if I seem to be lecturing you on your profession, but you will thank me in the end. Do you understand?

I hear what you are saying. I don't necessarily agree, but I hear.

Well, let it not be said I did not warn you.

As I told you, those were great days for me, a second honeymoon, sweeter than the first and longer-lasting too. Why else do you think I remember them so well? *Truly, I am coming into myself!* I said to myself. *This is what a woman can be; this is what a woman can do!*

Do I shock you? Probably not. You belong to an unshockable generation. But it would shock my mother, what I am revealing to you, if she were alive to hear it. My mother would never have dreamed of speaking to a stranger as I am speaking now.

From one of his trips to Singapore Mark had come back with an early-model video camera. Now he set it up in the bedroom to film the two of us making love. *As a record,* he said. *And as a turn-on.* I didn't mind. I let him go ahead. He probably still has the film; he may even watch it when he feels nostalgic about the old days. Or perhaps it is lying forgotten in a box in the attic, and will be found only after his death. The stuff we leave behind! Just imagine his grandchildren, eyes popping as they watch their youthful granddad frolicking in bed with his foreign wife.

Your husband . . .

Mark and I were divorced in 1988. He married again, on the rebound. I never met my successor. They live in the Bahamas, I think, or maybe Bermuda.

Shall we let it rest there? You have heard a lot, and it's been a long day.

But that isn't the end of the story, surely.

On the contrary, it is the end of the story. At least of the part that matters.

But you and Coetzee continued to see each other. For years you exchanged letters. So even if that is where the story ends, from your point of view — my apologies, even if that is the end of the part of the story that is of importance to you — there is still a long tail to follow, a long entailment. Can't you give me some idea of the tail end?

A short tail, not a long one. I will tell you about it, but not today. I have things to attend to. Come back next week. Fix a date with my receptionist.

Next week I will be gone. Can't we meet again tomorrow?

Tomorrow is out of the question. Thursday. I can give you half an hour on Thursday, after my last appointment.

YES, THE TAIL END. Where shall I begin? Let me start with John's father. One morning, not long after that dreary barbecue, I was driving down Tokai Road when I noticed someone standing by himself at a bus stop. It was the elder Coetzee. I was in a hurry, but it would have been too rude to simply drive past, so I stopped and offered him a ride.

He asked how Chrissie was getting on. I said she was missing her father, who was away from home much of the time. I asked about John and the concreting. He gave some vague answer.

Neither of us was really in the mood for talk, but I forced myself. If he didn't mind my asking, I asked, how long had it been since his wife passed away? He told me. Of his life with her, whether it had been happy or not, whether he missed her, he volunteered nothing.

'And is John your only child?' I asked.

'No, no, he has a brother, a younger brother.' He seemed surprised I did not know.

'That's curious,' I said, 'because John has the air of an only child.' Which I meant critically. I meant that he was preoccupied with himself, did not seem to make allowances for people around him.

He gave no answer – did not inquire, for instance, what air it was that an only child might have.

I asked about his second son, about where he lived. In England, replied Mr C. He had quit South Africa years ago and never come back. 'You must miss him,' I said. He shrugged. That was his characteristic response: the wordless shrug.

I must tell you, from the very first I found something unbearably sorrowful about this man. Sitting next to me in the car in his dark business suit, giving off a smell of cheap deodorant, he may have seemed the personification of stiff rectitude, but if he had suddenly burst into tears I would not have been surprised, not in the slightest. All alone save for that cold fish his elder son, trudging off each morning to what sounded like a soul-destroying job, coming back at night to a silent house – I felt more than a little pity for him.

'Well, one misses so much,' he said at last, when I thought he was not going to answer at all. He spoke in a whisper, gazing straight ahead.

I dropped him in Wynberg near the train station. 'Thanks for the lift, Julia,' he said, 'very kind of you.'

It was the first time he had actually used my name. I could have replied, *See you soon*. I could have replied, *You and John must come over for a bite*. But I didn't. I just gave a wave and drove off.

How mean! I berated myself. *How hard-hearted!* Why was I so hard on him, on both of them?

And indeed, why was I, why am I, so critical of John? At least he was looking after his father. At least, if something went wrong, his father would have a shoulder to lean on. That was more than could be said for me. My father – you are probably not interested, why should you be?, but let me tell you anyway – my father was at that very moment in a private sanatorium outside Port Elizabeth. His clothes were locked away, he had nothing to wear, day or night, but pyjamas and a dressing gown and slippers. And he was dosed to the gills with tranquillizers. Why so? Simply for the convenience of the nursing staff, to keep him tractable. Because when he neglected to take his pills he became agitated and started to shout.

[Silence.]

Did John love his father, do you think?

Boys love their mothers, not their fathers. Don't you know your Freud? Boys hate their fathers and want to supplant them in their mothers' affections. No, of course John did not love his father, he did not love anybody, he was not built for love. But he did feel guilty about his father. He felt guilty and therefore behaved dutifully. With certain lapses.

I was telling you about my own father. My father was born in 1905, so at the time we are talking about he was getting on for seventy, and his mind was going. He had forgotten who he was, forgotten the rudimentary English he picked up when he came to South Africa. To the nurses he spoke sometimes German, sometimes Magyar, of which they understood not a word. He was convinced he was in Madagascar, in a prison camp. The Nazis had taken over Madagascar, he thought, and turned it into a *Strafkolonie* for Jews. Nor did he always remember who I was. On one of my visits he mistook me for his sister Trudi, my aunt, whom I had never met but who looked a bit like me. He wanted me to go to the prison commandant and plead on his behalf. 'Ich bin der Erstgeborene,' he kept saying: I am the first-born. If *der Erstgeborene* was not going to be allowed to work (my father was a jeweller and diamond-cutter by trade), how would his family survive?

That's why I am here. That's why I am a therapist. Because of what I saw in that sanatorium. To save people from being treated as my father was treated there.

The money that kept my father in the sanatorium was supplied by my brother, his son. My brother was the one who religiously visited every week, even though my father recognized him only intermittently. In the sole sense that matters, my brother had taken on the burden of his care. In the sole sense that matters, I had abandoned him. And I was his favourite – I, his beloved Julischka, so pretty, so clever, so affectionate!

Do you know what I hope for, above all else? I hope that in the after-life we will be allowed a chance, each of us, to say our sorries to the people we have wronged. I will have plenty of sorries to say, believe you me.

Enough of fathers. Let me get back to the story of Julia and her adulterous dealings, the story you have travelled so far to hear.

One day my husband announced that he would be going to Hong Kong for discussions with the firm's overseas partners.

'How long will you be away?' I asked.

'A week,' he replied. 'Maybe a day or two longer if the discussions go well.'

I thought no more of it until, shortly before he was due to leave, I got a phone call from the wife of one of his colleagues: was I packing an evening dress for the Hong Kong trip? It's just Mark who is going to Hong Kong, I replied, I am not accompanying him. Oh, she said, I thought all the wives were invited.

When Mark came home I raised the subject. 'June just phoned,' I said. 'She says she is going with Alistair to Hong Kong. She says all the wives are invited.'

'Wives are invited but the firm isn't paying for them,' Mark said. 'Do you really want to come all the way to Hong Kong to sit in a hotel with a bunch of wives from the firm, bitching about the weather? Hong Kong is like a steam bath at this time of year. And what will you do with Chrissie? Do you want to take Chrissie along too?'

'I have no desire whatsoever to go to Hong Kong and sit in a hotel with a screaming child,' I said. 'I just want to know what's what. So that I don't have to be humiliated when your friends phone.'

'Well, now you know what's what,' he said.

He was wrong. I didn't know. But I could guess. Specifically I could guess that the girlfriend from Durban was going to be in Hong Kong too. From that moment I was as cold as ice to Mark. *Let this put paid, you bastard, to any idea you may have that your extramarital activities excite me!* That was what I thought to myself.

'Is this all about Hong Kong?' he said to me, when at last the message began to get through. 'If you want to come to Hong Kong, for God's sake just say the word, instead of stalking around the house like a tiger with indigestion.'

'And what might that word be?' I said. 'Is the word *Please*? No, I don't want to accompany you to Hong Kong of all places. I would only be bored, as you say, sitting and kvetching with the wives while the men are busy elsewhere deciding the future of the world. I will be happier here at home where I belong, looking after your child.'

That was how things stood between us the day Mark left.

Just a minute, I'm confused. Where are we in time? When did this trip to Hong Kong take place?

It must have been sometime in 1973, early 1973, I can't give you a precise date.

So you and John Coetzee had been seeing each other . . .

No. He and I had not been seeing each other. You asked at the beginning how I came to meet John, and I told you. That was the head of the tale. Now we are coming to the tail of the tale, namely, how our relationship drifted on and then came to an end.

But where is the body of the tale, you ask? There is no body. I can't supply a body because there was none. This is a tale without a body.

We return to Mark, to the fateful day he left for Hong Kong. No sooner was he gone than I jumped into the car, drove to Tokai Road, and pushed a note under the front door: 'Drop by this afternoon, if you feel like it, around 2.'

As two o'clock approached I could feel the fever mount in me. The child felt it too. She was restless, she cried, she clung to me, she would not sleep. Fever, but what kind of fever, I wondered to myself? A fever of madness? A fever of rage?

I waited but John did not come, not at two, not at three. He came at five-thirty, by which time I had fallen asleep on the sofa with Chrissie, hot and sticky, on my shoulder. The doorbell woke me; when I opened the door to him I was still groggy and confused.

'Sorry I couldn't come earlier,' he said, 'but I teach in the afternoons.'

It was too late, of course. Chrissie was awake, and jealous in her own way.

Later John returned, by arrangement, and we spent the night together. In fact while Mark was in Hong Kong, John spent every night in my bed, departing at the crack of dawn so as not to bump into the house-help. For the sleep I lost I compensated by napping in the afternoons. What he did to make up for lost sleep I have no idea. Maybe his students, his Portuguese girls – you know about them, about his scatterlings from the ex-Portuguese empire? No? Remind me to tell you – maybe his girls had to suffer for his nocturnal excesses.

My high summer with Mark had given me a new conception of sex: as a contest, a variety of wrestling in which you do your best to subject your opponent to your erotic will. For all his failings, Mark was a more than competent sex wrestler, though not as subtle as I, or as steely. Whereas my verdict on John – and here at last, at last, comes the moment you have been waiting for, Mr Biographer – my verdict on John Coetzee, after seven nights of testing, was that he was not in my league, not as I was then.

John had what I would call a sexual mode, into which he would switch when he took off his clothes. In sexual mode he could perform the male part perfectly adequately – adequately, competently, but – for my taste – too impersonally. I never had the feeling that he was with me, me in all my reality. Rather, it was as if he was engaged with some erotic image of me inside his head; perhaps even with some image of Woman with a capital W.

At the time I was simply disappointed. Now I would go further. In his lovemaking I now think there was an autistic quality. I offer this not as a criticism but as a diagnosis, if it interests you. The autistic type treats other people as automata, mysterious automata. In return he expects to be treated as a mysterious automaton too. So if you are autistic, falling in love translates as turning the other into the inscrutable object of your desire; and reciprocally, being loved translates as being treated as the inscrutable object of the other's desire. Two inscrutable automata having inscrutable commerce with each other's bodies: that was how it felt to be in bed with John. Two separate enterprises on the go, his and mine. What his enterprise was I can't say, it was opaque to me. But to sum up: sex with him lacked all thrill.

In my practice I have not had much experience of patients I would classify as clinically autistic. Nevertheless, regarding their sex lives, my guess is that they find masturbation more satisfying than the real thing.

As I think I told you, John was only the third man I had had. Three men, and I left them all behind, sex-wise. A sad story. After those three I lost interest in white South Africans, white South African men. There was some quality they had in common that I found it hard to put a finger on, but that I connected with the evasive flicker I caught in the eyes of Mark's colleagues when they spoke about the future of the country – as if there were some conspiracy they all belonged to that was going to create a fake, trompe-l'oeil future where no future had seemed possible before. Like a camera shutter flicking open for an instant to reveal the falseness at their core.

Of course I was a South African too, as white as white could be. I was born among the whites, was reared among them, lived among them. But I had a second self to fall back on: Julia Kiš, or even better Kiš Julia, of Szombathely. As long as I did not desert Julia Kiš, as long as Julia Kiš did not desert me, I could see things to which other whites were blind.

For instance, white South Africans in those days liked to think of themselves as the Jews of Africa, or at least the Israelis of Africa: cunning, unscrupulous, resilient, running close to the ground, hated and envied by the tribes they lorded it over. All false. All nonsense. It takes a Jew to know a Jew, as it takes a woman to know a man. Those people were not tough, they were not even cunning, or cunning enough. And they were certainly not Jews. In fact they were babes in the wood. That is how I think of them now: a great big family of babies looked after by slaves.

John used to twitch in his sleep, so much that it kept me awake. When I couldn't stand it any longer I would give him a shake. 'You were having a bad dream,' I would say. 'I never dream,' he would mumble in return, and go straight back to sleep. Soon he would be twitching and jerking again. It reached a point where I began to long to have Mark back in my bed. At least Mark slept like a log.

Enough of that. You get the picture. Not a sensual idyll. Far from it. What else? What else do you want to know?

Let me ask this. You are Jewish and John was not. Was there ever any tension because of that?

Tension? Why should there have been tension? Tension on whose side? I was not planning to marry John, after all. No, John and I got on perfectly well in that respect. It was Northerners he didn't get on with, particularly the English. The English stifled him, he said, with their good manners, their well-bred reserve. He preferred people who were ready to give more of themselves; then sometimes he would pluck up the courage to give a little of himself in return.

Any further questions before I conclude?

No.

One morning (I skip ahead, I would like to get this over with) John appeared at the front door. 'I won't stay,' he said, 'but I thought you might like this.' He was holding out a book. On the cover: *Dusklands*, by J M Coetzee.

I was taken completely aback. 'You wrote this?' I said. I knew he wrote, but then, lots of people write; I had no inkling that in his case it was serious.

'It's for you. It's a proof copy. I got two proof copies in the mail today.'

I flipped through the book. Someone complaining about his wife. Someone travelling by ox-cart. 'What is it?' I said. 'Is it fiction?'

'Sort of.'

Sort of. 'Thank you,' I said. 'I look forward to reading it. Is it going to make you a lot of money? Will you be able to give up teaching?'

He found that very funny. He was in a gay mood, because of the book. Not often that I saw that side of him.

'I didn't know your father was an historian,' I remarked the next time we met. I was referring to the preface to his book, in which the author, the writer, this man in front of me, claimed that his father, the little man who went off every morning to his bookkeeping job in the city, was also an historian who haunted the archives and turned up old documents.

'You mean the preface?' he said. 'Oh, that's all made up.'

'And how does your father feel about it,' I said – 'about having false claims made about him, about being turned into a character in a book?'

John looked uncomfortable. What he did not want to reveal, as I found out later, was that his father had not set eyes on *Dusklands*.

'And Jacobus Coetzee?' I said. 'Did you make up your estimable ancestor Jacobus Coetzee too?'

'No, there was a real Jacobus Coetzee,' he said. 'At least, there is a real, paper-and-ink document which claims to be a transcript of an oral deposition made by someone who gave his name as Jacobus Coetzee. At the foot of that document there is an X which the scribe attests was made by the hand of this same Coetzee, an X because he was illiterate. In that sense I did not make him up.'

'For an illiterate, your Jacobus strikes me as being very literary. For instance, I see he quotes Nietzsche.'

'Well, they were surprising fellows, those eighteenth-century frontiersmen. You never knew what they would come up with next.'

I can't say I like *Dusklands*. I know it sounds old-fashioned, but I prefer my books to have heroes and heroines, characters I can admire. I have never written stories, I have never had ambitions in that direction, but I suspect it is a lot easier to make up bad characters – untrustworthy characters, contemptible characters – than good ones. That is my opinion, for what it is worth.

Did you ever say so to Coetzee?

Did I say I thought he was going for the easy option? No. I was simply surprised that this intermittent lover of mine, this amateur handyman and part-time schoolteacher, had it in him to write a book-length book and, what is more, find a publisher for it, albeit only in Johannesburg. I was surprised, I was gratified for his sake, I was even a little proud. Reflected glory. In my student years I had hung around with numbers of would-be writers, but none had actually published a book.

I've never asked: What did you study? Psychology?

No, far from it. I studied German literature. As a preparation for my life as housewife and mother I read Novalis and Gottfried Benn. I graduated in literature, after which, for two decades, until Christina grew up and left home, I was – how shall I put it? – intellectually dormant. Then I went back to college. This was in Montreal. I started from scratch with basic science, followed by medical studies, followed by training as a therapist. A long road.

Would relations with Coetzee have been any different, do you think, if you had been trained in psychology rather than in literature?

What a curious question! The answer is no. If I had studied psychology in the South Africa of the 1960s I would have had to immerse myself in the neurological processes of rats and octopi, and John wasn't a rat or an octopus.

What kind of animal was he?

What odd questions you ask! He wasn't any kind of animal, and for a very specific reason: his mental capacities, and specifically his ideational faculties, were overdeveloped, at the cost of his animal self. He was Homo sapiens, or even Homo sapiens sapiens.

   Which leads me back to *Dusklands*. As a piece of writing I don't say *Dusklands* is lacking in passion, but the passion behind it is obscure. I read it as a book about cruelty, an exposé of the cruelty involved in various forms of conquest. But what was the actual source of that cruelty? Its locus, it now seems to me, lay within the author himself. The best interpretation I can give of the book is that writing it was a project in self-administered therapy. Which casts a certain light back over our time together, his and my conjoint time.

I am not sure I understand. Can you say more?

What don't you understand?

Are you saying he took out his cruelty on you?

No, not at all. John never behaved towards me with anything but the utmost gentleness. He was what I would call a gentle person, a gentleperson. That was part of his problem. His life project was to be gentle. Let me start again. In *Dusklands* you must recall how much killing there is – killing not only of human beings but of animals. Well, at about the time the book appeared, John announced to me he was becoming a vegetarian. I don't know how long he persisted in it, but I interpreted the vegetarian move as part of a larger project of self-reformation. He had decided he was going to block cruel and violent impulses in every arena of his life – including his love life, I might say – and channel them into his writing, which as a consequence was going to become a sort of unending cathartic exercise.

How much of this was visible to you at the time, and how much do you owe to later insights as a therapist?

I saw it all – it was on the surface, you didn't need to dig – but at the time I did not have the language to describe it. Besides, I was having an affair with the man. You can't be too analytic in the middle of a love affair.

A love affair. You haven't used that expression before.

Then let me correct myself. An erotic entanglement. Because, young and self-centred as I was then, it would have been hard for me to love, really love, someone as radically incomplete as John. So: I was in the midst of an erotic entanglement with two men, in one of whom I had made a deep investment – I had married him, he was the father of my child – and in the other of whom I had made no investment at all.

Why I made no deeper investment in John has much to do, I now suspect, with his project of turning himself into what I described to you, a gentle man, the kind of man who would do no harm, not even to dumb animals, not even to a woman. I should have made myself clearer to him, I now think. *If for some reason you are holding yourself back, I should have said, then don't, there is no need.* If I had told him that, if he had taken it to heart, if he had allowed himself to be a little more impetuous, a little more imperious, a little less thoughtful, then he might actually have yanked me out of a marriage that was already bad for me and would become worse later. He might actually have saved me, or saved the best years of my life for me, which, as it turned out, were wasted.

[Silence.]

I've lost track. What were we talking about?

Dusklands.

Yes, *Dusklands*. A word of caution. That book was actually written before he met me. Check the chronology. Don't be tempted to read it as about the two of us.

The thought did not cross my mind.

I remember asking John, after *Dusklands*, what new project he had on the go. His answer was vague. 'There is always something or other I am working on,' he said. 'If I yielded to the seduction of not working, what would I do with myself? What would there be to live for? I would have to shoot myself.'

That surprised me – his need to write, I mean. I knew hardly anything about his habits, about how he spent his time, but he had never struck me as an obsessive worker.

'Do you mean that?' I said.

'I get depressed if I am not writing,' he replied.

'Then why the endless house repairs?' I said. 'You could pay someone else to do the repairs, and devote the time you saved to writing.'

'You don't understand,' he said. 'Even if I had the money to employ a builder, which I don't, I would still feel the need to spend X hours a day digging in the garden or moving rocks or mixing concrete.' And he launched into another of his speeches about the need to overthrow the taboo on manual labour.

I wondered whether there might not be some criticism of myself hanging in the air: that the paid labour of my black domestic set me free to have idle affairs with strange men, for instance. But I let it pass. 'Well,' I said, 'you certainly don't understand economics. The first principle of economics is that if we all insisted on spinning our own thread and milking our own cows rather than employing other people to do it for us, we would be stuck for ever in the Stone Age. That is why we have invented an economy based on exchange, which has in turn made possible our long history of material progress. You pay someone else to lay the concrete, and in exchange you get the time to write the book that will justify your leisure and give meaning to your life. That may even give meaning to the life of the workman laying the concrete for you. So that we all prosper.'

'Do you really believe that?' he said. 'That books give meaning to our lives?'

'Yes.' I said. 'A book should be an axe to chop open the frozen sea inside us. What else should it be?'

'A gesture of refusal in the face of time. A bid for immortality.'

'No one is immortal. Books are not immortal. The entire globe on which we stand is going to be sucked into the sun and burnt to a cinder. After which the universe itself will implode and disappear down a black hole. Nothing is going to survive, not me, not you, and certainly not minority-interest books about imaginary frontiersmen in eighteenth-century South Africa.'

'I didn't mean immortal in the sense of existing outside time. I mean surviving beyond one's physical demise.'

'You want people to read you after you are dead?'

'It affords me some consolation to cling to that prospect.'

'Even if you won't be around to witness it?'

'Even if I won't be around to witness it.'

'But why should the people of the future bother to read the book you write if it doesn't speak to them, if it doesn't help them find meaning in their lives?'

'Perhaps they will still like to read books that are well written.'

'That's silly. It's like saying that if I build a good enough gram-radio then people will still be using it in the twenty-fifth century. But they won't. Because gram-radios, however well made, will be obsolete by then. They won't speak to twenty-fifth-century people.'

'Perhaps in the twenty-fifth century there will still be a minority curious to hear what a late-twentieth-century gram-radio sounded like.'

'Collectors. Hobbyists. Is that how you intend to spend your life: sitting at your desk handcrafting an object that might or might not be preserved as a curiosity?'

He shrugged. 'Have you a better idea?'

You think I am showing off. I can see that. You think I make up dialogue to show how smart I am. But that is how they were at times, conversations between John and myself. They were fun. I enjoyed them; I missed them afterwards, after I stopped seeing him. In fact our conversations were probably what I missed most. He was the only man I knew who would let me beat him in an honest argument, who wouldn't bluster or obfuscate or go off in a huff when he saw he was losing. And I always beat him, or nearly always.

The reason was simple. It wasn't that he couldn't argue; but he ran his life according to principles, whereas I have always been a pragmatist. Pragmatism beats principles; that is just the way things are. The universe moves, the ground changes under our feet; principles are always a step behind. Principles are the stuff of comedy. Comedy is what you get when principles bump into reality. I know he had a reputation for being dour, but John Coetzee was actually quite funny.

A figure of comedy. Dour comedy. Which, in an obscure way, he knew, even accepted. That is why I still look back on him with affection. If you want to know.

[Silence.]

I was always good at arguing. At school everyone used to be nervous around me, even my teachers. *A tongue like a knife,* my mother used to say half-reprovingly. *A girl should not argue like that, a girl should learn to be more soft.* But at other times she would say: *A girl like you should be a lawyer.* She was proud of me, of my spirit, of my sharp tongue. She came from a generation when a daughter was still married out of the father's home straight into the husband's, or the father-in-law's.

Anyway, 'Have you a better idea,' John said – 'a better idea for how to use one's life than writing books?'

'No. But I have an idea that might shake you up and help give direction to your life.'

'What is that?'

'Find yourself a good woman and marry her.'

He looked at me strangely. 'Are you making me a proposal?' he said.

I laughed. 'No,' I said, 'I am already married, thank you. Find a woman better suited to you, someone who will take you out of yourself.'

I am already married, therefore marriage to you would constitute bigamy: that was the unspoken part. Yet what was wrong with bigamy, come to think of it, aside from it being against the law? What made bigamy a crime when adultery was only a sin, or a recreation? I was already an adulteress; why should I not be a bigamist or *bigamiste* too? This was Africa, after all. If no African man was going to be hauled before a court for having two wives, why should I be forbidden to have two spouses, a public one and a private one?

'This is not, emphatically not, a proposal,' I repeated, 'but – just hypothetically – if I were free, would you marry me?'

It was only an inquiry, an idle inquiry. Nevertheless, without a word he took me in his arms and held me so tight that I could not breathe. It was the first act of his I could recollect that seemed to come straight from the heart. Certainly I had seen him worked on by animal desire – we did not spend our time in bed discussing Aristotle – but never before had I seen him in the grip of emotion. So, I asked myself in some wonderment, *does this cold fish have feelings after all?*

'What's up?' I said, disengaging myself from his grasp. 'Is there something you want to tell me?'

He was silent. Was he crying? I switched on the bedside lamp and inspected him. No tears, but he did wear a look of stricken mournfulness. 'If you can't tell me what's up,' I said, 'I can't help you.'

Later, when he had pulled himself together, we collaborated to make light of the moment. 'For the right woman,' I said, 'you would make a *prima* husband. Responsible. Hard-working. Intelligent. Quite a catch, in fact. Good in bed too,' though that was not strictly true. 'Affectionate,' I added as an afterthought, though that was not true either.

'And an artist to boot,' he said. 'You forgot to mention that.'

'And an artist to boot. An artist in words.'

[Silence.]

And?

That's all. A difficult passage between the two of us, which we successfully negotiated. My first inkling that he cherished deeper feelings for me.

Deeper than what?

Deeper than the feelings any man might cherish for his neighbour's attractive wife. Or his neighbour's ox or ass.

Are you saying he was in love with you?

In love . . . In love with me or with the idea of me? I don't know. What I do know is that he had reason to be thankful to me. I made things easy for him. There are men who find it hard to court a woman. They are afraid to expose their desire, to open themselves to rebuff. Behind their fear there often lies a childhood history. I never forced John to expose himself. I was the one who did the courting. I was the one who did the seducing. I was the one who managed the terms of the affair. I was even the one who decided when it was over. So you ask, Was he in love? and I reply, He was in gratitude.

[Silence.]

I often wondered, afterwards, what would have happened if instead of fending him off I had responded to his surge of feeling with a surge of feeling of my own. If I had had the courage to divorce Mark back then, rather than waiting another thirteen or fourteen years, and hitched up with John. Would I have made more of my life? Perhaps. Perhaps not. But then I would not be the ex-mistress talking to you. I would be the grieving widow.

Chrissie was the problem, the fly in the ointment. Chrissie was very attached to her father, and I was finding it more and more difficult to handle her. She was no longer a baby – she was getting on for two – and although her progress in speech was disturbingly slow (as it turned out, I needn't have worried, she made up for it in a burst later on), she was growing more agile by the day – agile and fearless. She had learned to clamber out of her cot; I had to hire a handyman to put in a gate at the head of the stairs in case she came tumbling down.

I remember one night Chrissie appeared without warning at my bedside, rubbing her eyes, whimpering, confused. I had the presence of mind to gather her up and whisk her back to her room before she registered that it wasn't Daddy in bed beside me; but what if I wasn't so lucky next time?

I was never quite sure what subterranean effect my double life might be having on the child. On the one hand I told myself that as long as I was physically fulfilled and at peace with myself, the beneficial effects ought to seep through to her too. If that strikes you as self-serving, let me remind you that at that time, in the 1970s, the progressive view, the *bien-pensant* view, was that sex was a force for the good, in any guise, with any partner. On the other hand it was clear that Chrissie was finding the alternation between Daddy and Uncle John in the household puzzling. What was going to happen when she began to speak? What if she got the two of them mixed and called her father Uncle John? There would be hell to pay.

I have always tended to regard Sigmund Freud as bunk, starting with the Oedipus complex and proceeding to his refusal to see that children were routinely being sexually abused, even in the homes of his middle-class clientele. Nevertheless I do agree that children, from a very early age, spend a lot of time trying to puzzle out their place in the family. In the case of Chrissie, the family had up to then been a simple affair: she herself, the sun at the centre of the universe, plus Mommy and Daddy, her attendant planets. I had put some effort into making it clear that Maria, who appeared at eight o'clock in the morning and disappeared at noon, was not part of the family set-up. 'Maria must go home now,' I would say to her in front of Maria. 'Say ta-ta to Maria. Maria has her own little girl to feed and look after.' (I referred to Maria's little girl in the singular in order not to complicate matters. I knew perfectly well that Maria had seven children to feed and clothe, five of her own and two passed on by a sister dead of tuberculosis.)

As for Chrissie's wider family, her grandmother on my side had passed away before she was born and her grandfather was tucked away in a sanatorium, as I told you. Mark's parents lived in the rural Eastern Cape in a farmhouse ringed by a two-metre-high electrified fence. They never spent a night away from home for fear the farm would be plundered and the livestock driven off, so they might as well have been in jail. Mark's elder sister lived thousands of miles away in Seattle; my own brother never visited the Cape. So Chrissie had the most stripped-down version of a family possible. The sole complication was the uncle who at midnight sneaked in at the back door and into Mommy's bed. How did this uncle fit in? Was he one of the family or on the contrary a worm eating away at the heart of the family?

And Maria – how much did Maria know? I could never be sure. Migrant labour was the norm in South Africa in those days, so Maria must have been all too familiar with the phenomenon of the husband who says goodbye to wife and children and goes off to the big city to find work. But whether Maria approved of wives fooling around in their husbands' absence was another matter. Though Maria never actually laid eyes on my night-time visitor, it was hardly likely that she was deceived. That kind of visitor leaves too many traces behind.

But what is this? Is it really six o'clock? I had no idea it was so late. We must stop. Can you come back tomorrow?

I'm afraid I am due to head home tomorrow. I fly from here to Toronto, from Toronto to London. I'd hate it if . . .

Very well, let's press on. There is not much more. I'll be quick.

One night John arrived in an unusually excited state. He had with him a little cassette player, and put on a tape, the Schubert string quintet. It was not what I would call sexy music, nor was I particularly in the mood, but he wanted to make love, and specifically – excuse the explicitness – wanted us to co-ordinate our activities to the music, to the slow movement.

Well, the slow movement in question may be very beautiful but I found it far from arousing. Added to which I could not shake off the image on the box containing the tape: Franz Schubert looking not like a god of music but like a harried Viennese clerk with a head-cold.

I don't know if you remember the slow movement, but there is a long violin aria with the viola throbbing below, and I could feel John trying to keep time with it. The whole business struck me as forced, ridiculous. Somehow or other my remoteness communicated itself to John. 'Empty your mind!' he hissed at me. 'Feel through the music!'

Well, there can be nothing more irritating than being told what you must feel. I turned away from him, and his little erotic experiment collapsed at once.

Later on he tried to explain himself. He wanted to demonstrate something about the history of feeling, he said. Feelings had natural histories of their own. They came into being within time, flourished for a while or failed to flourish, then died or died out. The kinds of feeling that had flourished in Schubert's day were by now, most of them, dead. The sole way left to us to re-experience them was via the music of the times. Because music was the trace, the inscription, of feeling.

Okay, I said, but why do we have to fuck while we listen to the music?

Because the slow movement of the quintet happens to be about fucking, he replied. If, instead of resisting, I had let the music flow into me and animate me, I would have experienced glimmerings of something quite unusual: what it had felt like to make love in post-Bonaparte Austria.

'What it felt like for post-Bonaparte man or what it felt like for post-Bonaparte woman?' I said. 'For Mr Schubert or for Mrs Schubert?'

That really annoyed him. He didn't like his pet theories to be made fun of.

'Music isn't about fucking,' I went on. 'That is where you lose the plot. Music is about foreplay. It is about courtship. You sing to the maiden *before* you are admitted to her bed, not while you are in bed with her. You sing to her to woo her, to win her heart. If you aren't happy with me in bed, maybe it is because you haven't won my heart.'

I should have called it a day at that point, but I didn't, I went further. 'The mistake the two of us made,' I said, 'was that we skimped the fore-play. I'm not blaming you, it was as much my fault as yours, but it was a fault nonetheless. Sex is better when it is preceded by a good, long courtship. More emotionally satisfying. More erotically satisfying too. If you are trying to improve our sex life, you won't achieve it by making me fuck in time to music.'

I expected him to fight back, to argue the case for musical sex. But he did not rise to the bait. Instead he put on a sullen, defeated look and turned his back on me.

I know I am contradicting what I said earlier, about him being a good sport and a good loser, but this time I really seemed to have touched a sore spot.

Anyway, there we were. I had gone on the offensive, I couldn't turn back. 'Go home and practise your wooing,' I said. 'Go on. Go away. Take your Schubert with you. Come again when you can do better.'

It was cruel; but he deserved it for not fighting back.

'Right – I'll go,' he said in a sulky voice. 'I have things to do anyway.' And he began to put on his clothes.

Things to do! I picked up the nearest object to hand, which happened to be a quite nice little baked-clay plate, brown with a painted yellow border, one of a set of six that Mark and I had bought in Swaziland. For an instant I could still see the comic side of it: the dark-tressed, bare-breasted mistress exhibiting her stormy central-European temperament by shouting abuse and throwing crockery. Then I hurled the plate.

It hit him on the neck and bounced to the floor without breaking. He hunched his shoulders and turned to me with a puzzled stare. Never before, I am sure, had he had a plate thrown at him. 'Go!' I shouted or perhaps even screamed, and waved him away. Chrissie woke up and began crying.

Strange to say, I felt no regret afterwards. On the contrary, I was aroused and excited and proud of myself. *Straight from the heart!* I said to myself. *My first plate!*

[Silence.]

Have there been others?

Other plates? Plenty.

[Silence.]

Was that how it ended, then, between you and him?

Not quite. There was a coda. I'll tell you the coda, then that will be that.

It was a condom that spelled the real end, a condom tied at the neck, full of dead sperm. Mark fished it out from under the bed. I was flabbergasted. How could I have missed it? It was as if I wanted it to be found, wanted to shout my infidelity from the rooftops.

Mark and I never used condoms, so there was no point in lying. 'How long has this been going on?' he demanded. 'Since last December,' I said. 'You bitch,' he said, 'you filthy, lying bitch! And I trusted you!'

He was about to storm out of the room, but then as if on afterthought he turned and – I am sorry, I am going to draw a veil over what happened next, it is too shameful to repeat, too shaming. I will simply say it left me surprised, shocked, but above all furious. 'For that, Mark, I will never forgive you,' I said when I recovered myself. 'There is a line, and you've just crossed it. I'm going. You look after Chrissie for a change.'

At the moment I uttered the words *I'm going, you look after Chrissie*, I swear I meant no more than that I was leaving the house and he could look after the child for the afternoon. But in the five paces it took to reach the front door it came to me in a blinding flash that this could actually be the moment of liberation, the moment when I walked out of an unfulfilling marriage and never came back. The clouds over my head, the clouds in my head, lightened, evaporated. *Don't think!* I told myself. *Just do it!* Without missing a step I turned, strode upstairs, stuffed some underwear into a carry-bag, and raced downstairs again.

Mark was barring the way. 'Where do you think you are going?' he demanded. 'Are you going to *him*?'

'Go to hell,' I said. I tried to push past, but he grabbed my arm.

'Let me go!' I said.

No screams, no snarls, just a simple, curt command, but it was as though out of the skies a crown and regal robes had descended upon me. Without a word he let go. When I drove off he was still standing in the doorway, dumbstruck.

So easy! I exulted. *So easy! Why didn't I do it before?*

What puzzles me about that moment – which was in fact one of the key moments of my life – what puzzled me then and continues to puzzle me to the present day, is the following. Even if some force within me – let us call it the unconscious, to make things easier, though I have my reservations about the classical unconscious – had held me back from checking under the bed – had held me back precisely in order to precipitate this marital crisis – why on earth did Maria leave the incriminating item lying there – Maria who was definitely not part of my unconscious, Maria whose job it was to clean, to clean up, to clean things away? Did Maria deliberately overlook the condom? Did she draw herself up, when she saw it, and say to herself, *This is going too far! Either I defend the sanctity of the marriage bed or I become complicit in an outrageous affair!*

Sometimes I imagine flying back to South Africa, the new, longed-for, democratic South Africa, with the sole purpose of seeking out Maria, if she is still alive, and having it out with her, getting an answer to that vexing question.

Well, I was certainly not running off to join the him of Mark's jealous rage, but where exactly was I heading? For I had no friends in Cape Town, none who were not Mark's in the first place and mine only in the second.

There was an establishment I had spotted while driving through Wynberg, a rambling old mansion with a sign outside: *Canterbury Hotel | Residential | Full or part board | Weekly and monthly rates.* I decided to try the Canterbury.

Yes, said the woman at the desk, there happened to be a room available, would I want it for a week or for a longer term? A week, I said, in the first place.

The room in question – be patient, this is not irrelevant – was on the ground floor. It was spacious, with a neat little bathroom en suite and a compact refrigerator and French doors giving onto a shady, vine-covered veranda. 'Very nice,' I said. 'I'll take it.'

'And your baggage?' said the woman.

'My baggage will be coming,' I said, and she understood. I am sure I was not the first runaway wife to pitch up on the doorstep of the Canterbury. I am sure they enjoyed quite a traffic in pissed-off spouses. And a nice little bonus to be made from the ones who paid for a week, spent a night, then, repentant or exhausted or homesick, checked out the next morning.

Well, I was not repentant and I was certainly not homesick. I was quite ready to make the Canterbury my home until the burden of childcare led Mark to sue for peace.

There was a rigmarole about security that I barely followed – keys for doors, keys for gates – plus rules for parking, rules for visitors, rules for this, rules for that. I would not be having visitors, I informed the woman.

That evening I dined in the lugubrious *salle à manger* of the Canterbury and had a first glimpse of my fellow residents, who seemed to come straight out of William Trevor or Muriel Spark. But no doubt I appeared much the same to them: another flushed escapee from a sour marriage. I went to bed early and slept well.

I had thought I would enjoy my newfound solitude. I drove in to the city, did some shopping, saw an exhibition at the National Gallery, had lunch in the Gardens. But the second evening, alone in my room after a wretched meal of wilted salad and poached sole with béchamel sauce, I was suddenly overcome with loneliness and, worse than loneliness, self-pity. From the public telephone in the lobby I called John and, in murmurs (the receptionist was eavesdropping), told him of my situation.

'Would you like me to come by?' he said. 'We could go to a late movie.'

'Yes,' I said; 'yes, yes, yes.'

I repeat as emphatically as I can, I did not run away from my husband and child in order to be with John. It was not that kind of affair. In fact, it was hardly an affair at all, more of a friendship, an extramarital friendship with a sexual component whose importance, at least on my side, was symbolic rather than substantial. Sleeping with John was my way of retaining my self-respect. I hope you understand that.

Nevertheless, *nevertheless*, within minutes of his arrival at the Canterbury he and I were in bed, and – what is more – our lovemaking was, for once, something truly to write home about. I even shed tears at its conclusion. 'I don't know why I am crying,' I sobbed, 'I am so happy.'

'It is because you didn't get any sleep last night,' he said, thinking he needed to console me. 'It is because you are overwrought.'

I stared at him. *Because you are overwrought*: he really seemed to believe that. It quite took my breath away, how stupid he could be, how insensitive. Yet in his wrongheaded way perhaps he was right. For my day of freedom had been coloured by a memory that kept creeping back, the memory of that humiliating face-off with Mark, which had left me feeling more like a spanked child than an erring spouse. Save for that, I would probably not have telephoned John, and would therefore not be in bed with him. So yes: I was upset, and why not? My world had been turned upside down.

There was another source too for my uneasiness, even harder to confront: shame at having been found out. Because really, if you regarded the situation with a cold eye, I, with my sordid little tit-for-tat affair in Constantiaberg, was behaving no better than Mark, with his sordid little liaison in Durban.

The fact was, I had come to some kind of moral limit. The fit of euphoria at leaving home had evaporated; my sense of outrage was seeping away; as for the solitary life, its allure was fading fast. Yet how could I repair the damage other than by returning to Mark with my tail between my legs, suing for peace, and resuming my duties as chastened wife and mother? And in the midst of all that confusion of spirit, this piercingly sweet lovemaking! What was my body trying to tell me? That when one's defences are down, the gateways to pleasure open up? That the marital bed is a bad place to commit adultery, hotels are better? What John felt I had no idea, he was never a forthcoming person; but for myself I knew without a doubt that the half hour I had just been through would endure as a landmark in my erotic life. Which it has. To this day. Why else would I still be talking about it?

[Silence.]

I'm glad I told you that story. Now I feel less guilty about the Schubert business.

[Silence.]

Anyway, I fell asleep in John's arms. When I awoke it was dark and I hadn't the faintest idea where I was. *Chrissie*, I thought – *I have completely forgotten to feed Chrissie!* I even groped for the light switch – in the wrong place – before it all came back to me. I was alone (no trace of John); it was six in the morning.

From the lobby I called Mark. 'Hello, it's me,' I said in my most neutral, most pacific voice. 'Sorry to call so early, but how is Chrissie?'

For his part, Mark was in no mood for conciliation. 'Where are you?' he demanded.

'I'm phoning from Wynberg,' I said. 'I have moved into a hotel. I thought we should take a break from each other until things cool down. How is Chrissie? What are your plans for the week? Are you going to be in Durban?'

'What I do with my time is none of your business,' he said. 'If you want to stay away, stay away.'

Even on the telephone I could hear he was still in a rage. When Mark was cross he would explode his plosives: *none of your business*, with a puff of infuriated air on the *b* that would make your eyeballs shrivel. Memories of everything I disliked about him came flooding back. 'Don't be silly, Mark,' I said, 'you don't know how to look after a child.'

'Nor do you, you filthy bitch!' he said, and slammed down the receiver.

Later that morning, when I went to the shops, I found my bank account had been blocked.

I drove out to Constantiaberg. My latchkey turned the latch, but the door was double-locked. I knocked and knocked. No reply. No sign of Maria either. I circled the house. Mark's car was gone, the windows were closed.

I telephoned his office. 'He's away at our Durban office,' said the girl at the switchboard.

'There's an emergency at his home,' I said. 'Could you contact Durban and leave a message? Ask him to give his wife a call as soon as he can, at the following number. Say it's urgent.' And I gave the hotel number.

For hours I waited. No call.

Where was Chrissie? That was what I needed to know most of all. It seemed beyond belief that Mark could have taken the child with him to Durban. But if he hadn't, what had he done with her?

I telephoned Durban direct. No, said the secretary, Mark was not in Durban, was not expected this week. Had I tried the firm's Cape Town office?

Distraught by now, I telephoned John. 'My husband has taken the child and decamped, vanished into thin air,' I said. 'I have no money. I don't know what to do. Do you have any suggestions?'

There was an elderly couple in the lobby, guests, openly listening to me. But I had ceased to care who knew of my troubles. I wanted to cry, but I think I laughed instead. 'He has absconded with my child, and because of what?' I said. 'Is this' – I gestured towards my surroundings, that is, towards the interior of the Canterbury Hotel (Residential) – 'is this what I am being punished for?' Then I really began to cry.

Being miles away, John could not have seen my gesture, therefore (it occurred to me afterwards) must have attached a quite different meaning to the word this. I must have seemed to be referring to my affair with him – to have been dismissing it as unworthy of such a fuss.

'Do you want to go to the police?' he said.

'Don't be ridiculous,' I said. 'You can't run away from your husband and then turn around and accuse him of stealing your child.'

'Would you like me to come over and fetch you?' I could hear the caution in his voice. And I could sympathize. I too would have been cautious in his position, with an hysterical female on the line. But I didn't want caution, I wanted my child back. 'No, I would not like to be fetched,' I snapped.

'Have you at least had something to eat?' he said.

'I don't want anything to eat,' I said. 'That's enough of this stupid conversation. I'm sorry, I don't know why I called. Goodbye.' And I put down the phone.

I didn't want anything to eat, though I wouldn't have minded something to drink: a stiff whisky, for instance, followed by a dead, dreamless sleep.

I had just slumped down in my room and covered my head with a pillow when there was a tapping at the French door. It was John. Words between us, which I won't repeat. To be brief, he took me back to Tokai and bedded me down in his room. He himself slept on the sofa in the living room. I was half expecting him to come to me during the night, but he didn't.

I was woken by murmured talk. The sun was up. I heard the front door close. A long silence. I was alone in this strange house.

The bathroom was primitive, the toilet not clean. An unpleasant smell of male sweat and damp towels hung in the air. Where John had gone, when he would be back, I had no idea. I made myself coffee and did some exploring. From room to room the ceilings were so low I felt I would suffocate. It was only a farm cottage, I understood that, but why had it been built for midgets?

I peered into the elder Coetzee's room. The light had been left on, a single dim bulb without a shade in the centre of the ceiling. The bed was unmade. On a table by the bedside, a newspaper folded open to the crossword puzzle. On the wall a painting, amateurish, of a whitewashed Cape Dutch farmhouse, and a framed photograph of a severe-looking woman. The window, which was small and covered with a lattice of steel bars, looked out onto a stoep empty but for a pair of canvas deckchairs and a row of withered ferns in pots.

John's room, where I had slept, was larger and better lit. A bookshelf: dictionaries, phrasebooks, teach yourself this, teach yourself that. Beckett. Kafka. On the table, a mess of papers. A filing cabinet. Idly I searched through the drawers. In the bottom drawer, a box of photographs, which I burrowed amongst. What was I looking for? I didn't know. For something I would recognize only when I found it. But it was not there. Most of the photographs were from his school years: sports teams, class portraits.

From the front I heard noises, and went outdoors. A beautiful day, the sky a brilliant blue. John was unloading sheets of galvanized iron roofing from his truck. 'I'm sorry if I forsook you,' he said. 'I needed to pick these up, and I didn't want to wake you.'

I drew up a deckchair in a sunny spot, closed my eyes, and indulged in a little day-dreaming. I wasn't about to abandon my child. I wasn't about to walk out on my marriage. Nevertheless, what if I did? What if I forgot about Mark and Chrissie, settled down in this ugly little house, became the third member of the Coetzee family, the adjunct, Snow White to the two dwarves, doing the cooking, the cleaning, the laundering, maybe even helping with roof repairs? How long before my wounds healed? And then how long before my true prince rode by, the prince of my dreams, who would recognize me for who I was, lift me onto his white stallion, and bear me off into the sunset?

Because John Coetzee was not my prince. Finally I come to the point. If that was the question at the back of your mind when you came to Kingston – Is this going to be another of those women who mistook John Coetzee for their secret prince? – then you have your answer now. John was not my prince. Not only that: if you have been listening carefully you will have understood by now how very unlikely it was that he could have been a prince, a satisfactory prince, to any maiden on earth.

You don't agree? You think otherwise? You think the fault lay with me, not with him – the fault, the deficiency? Well, cast your mind back to the books he wrote. What is the one theme that keeps recurring from book to book? It is that the woman doesn't fall in love with the man. The man may or may not love the woman; but the woman never loves the man. What do you think that theme reflects? My guess, my highly informed guess, is that it reflects his life experience. Women didn't fall for him – not women in their right senses. They inspected him, they sniffed him, maybe they even tried him out. Then they moved on.

They moved on as I did. I could have remained in Tokai, as I said, in the Snow White role. As an idea it was not without its seductions. But in the end I did not. John was a friend to me during a rough patch in my life, he was a crutch I sometimes leant on, but he was never going to be my lover, not in the real sense of the word. For real love you need two full human beings, and the two need to fit together, to fit into each other. Like Yin and Yang. Like an electrical plug and an electrical socket. Like male and female. He and I didn't fit.

Believe me, over the course of the years I have given plenty of thought to John and his type. What I am going to tell you now I offer with due consideration, and I hope without animus. Because, as I said, John was important to me. He taught me a lot. He was a friend who remained a friend even after I broke up with him. When I felt low I could always rely on him to joke with me and lift my spirits. He raised me once to unexpected erotic heights – once only, alas! But the fact is, John wasn't made for love, wasn't constructed that way – wasn't constructed to fit into or be fitted into. Like a sphere. Like a glass ball. There was no way to connect with him. That is my conclusion, my mature conclusion.

Which may not come as a surprise to you. You probably think it holds true for artists in general, male artists: that they aren't built for what I am calling love; that they can't or won't give themselves fully for the simple reason that there is a secret essence of themselves they need to preserve for the sake of their art. Am I right? Is that what you believe?

Do I believe that artists aren't built for love? No. Not necessarily. I try to keep an open mind on the subject.

Well, you can't keep your mind open indefinitely, not if you mean to get your book written. Consider. Here we have a man who, in the most intimate of human relations, cannot connect, or can connect only briefly, intermittently. Yet how did he make a living? He made a living writing reports, expert reports, on intimate human experience. Because that is what novels are about – isn't it? – intimate experience. Novels as opposed to poetry or painting. Doesn't that strike you as odd?

[Silence.]

I have been very open with you, Mr Vincent. For instance, the Schubert business: I never told anyone about that before you. Why not? Because I thought it would cast John in too ridiculous a light. Because who but a total dummy would order the woman he is supposed to be in love with to take lessons in lovemaking from some dead composer, some Viennese *Bagatellenmeister*? When a man and a woman are in love they create their own music, it comes instinctively, they don't need lessons. But what does our friend John do? He drags a third presence into the bedroom. Franz Schubert becomes number one, the master of love; John becomes number two, the master's disciple and executant; and I become number three, the instrument on whom the sex-music is going to be played. That – it seems to me – tells you all you need to know about John Coetzee. The man who mistook his mistress for a violin. Who probably did the same with every other woman in his life: mistook her for some instrument or other, violin, bassoon, timpani. Who was so dumb, so cut off from reality, that he could not distinguish between playing on a woman and loving a woman. A man who loved by numbers. One doesn't know whether to laugh or cry!

That is why he was never my Prince Charming. That is why I never let him bear me off on his white steed. Because he was not a prince but a frog. Because he was not human, not in the fullest sense.

I said I would be frank with you, and I have kept my promise. I will tell you one more frank thing, just one more, then I will stop, and that will be the end of it. It is about the night I tried to describe to you, the night at the Canterbury Hotel, when, after all our experimenting, the two of us finally hit on the right chemistry, the right combination. How could we have achieved that, you may ask – as I ask too – if John was a frog and not a prince?

Let me tell you how I now see that pivotal night. I was hurt and confused, as I said, and beside myself with worry. John saw or guessed what was going on in me and for once opened his heart, the heart he normally kept wrapped in armour. With open hearts, his and mine, we came together. For him that first opening of the heart could and should have marked a sea-change, the beginning of a new life for the two of us together. Yet what happened? In the middle of the night John woke up and saw me sleeping beside him with no doubt a look of peace on my face, even of bliss, bliss is not unattainable in this world. He saw me – saw me as I was at that moment – took fright, hurriedly strapped the armour back over his heart, with chains and a double padlock, and stole out into the darkness.

Do you think I find it easy to forgive him for that? Do you?

You are being a little hard on him, if I may say so.

No, I am not. I am just telling the truth. Without the truth, no matter how hard, there can be no healing. That's all. That's the end of my offering for your book. Look, it's nearly eight o'clock. Time for you to go. You have a plane to catch in the morning.

Just one question more, one brief question.

No, absolutely not, no more questions. You have had time enough. End. Fin. Go.

Interview conducted in Kingston, Ontario, May 2008.

Margot

Let me bring you up to date, Mrs Jonker, with what I have been doing since we met last December. After I got back to England I transcribed the tapes of our conversations. I asked a colleague who was originally from South Africa to check that I had all the Afrikaans words right. Then I did something fairly radical, which I am hoping you will approve of. I cut out my own interjections, my prompts and questions, and fixed up the prose to read as if it were an uninterrupted narrative spoken in your voice.

What I would like to do now is to read through the new text with you and give you a chance to comment. How does that sound?

All right.

One further point. Because the story you told was quite lengthy, longer than I expected, I decided to dramatize it here and there, for the sake of variety, letting the various people speak in their own voices. You will see what I mean once we get going.

All right.

Here goes then.

In the old days, at Christmas-time, there would be huge gatherings on the family farm. From far and wide the sons and daughters of Gerrit and Lenie Coetzee would converge on Voëlfontein, bringing with them their spouses and offspring, more and more offspring each year, for a week of laughing and joking and reminiscing and, above all, eating. For the menfolk it was a time for hunting too: game birds, antelope.

But by now, in the 1970s, those family gatherings are sadly dimin-
ished. Gerrit Coetzee is long in the grave, Lenie shuffles around a nursing
home in The Strand. Of their twelve sons and daughters, the firstborn
has already joined the multitudinous shades; in private moments –

Multitudinous shades?

Too grand-sounding? I'll change it. The firstborn has already departed
this life. In private moments the survivors have intimations of their own
end, and shudder.

No, I don't like that.

You mean the shuddering? No problem. I'll cut it out. Has already
departed this life. Among the survivors the joking has grown more
subdued, the reminiscing sadder, the eating more temperate. As for
hunting parties, there are no more of those: old bones are weary, and
anyway, after year upon year of drought, there is nothing left in the veld
worth shooting.

Of the third generation, the sons and daughters of the sons and daughters, most are by now too absorbed in their own affairs to attend, or too
indifferent to the larger family. This year only four of that generation are
present: her cousin Michiel, who has inherited the farm; her cousin John
from Cape Town; her sister Carol; and herself, Margot. And of the four,
she alone, she suspects, looks back to the old days with anything like
nostalgia.

I don't understand. Why do you call me she?

Of the four, Margot alone, she – Margot – suspects, looks back with
anything like nostalgia . . . You can hear how clumsy it sounds. It just
won't work that way. The *she* I have introduced is like *I* but is not *I*. Do
you really dislike it so much?

I find it confusing. But you know better than I. Go on.

John's presence on the farm is a source of unease. After years spent overseas – so many years it was concluded he was gone for good – he has suddenly reappeared among them under some cloud or other, some disgrace. One story being whispered about is that he has spent time in an American jail.

The family simply does not know how to behave towards him. Never yet have they had a criminal – if that is what he is, a criminal – in their midst. A bankrupt, yes: the man who married her aunt Marie, a braggart and heavy drinker of whom the family had disapproved from the start, declared himself bankrupt to avoid paying his debts and thereafter did not a stitch of work, loafing at home, living off his wife's earnings. But bankruptcy, while it may leave a bad taste in the mouth, is not a crime; whereas going to jail is going to jail.

Her own feeling is that the Coetzees ought to try harder to make the lost sheep feel welcome. She has a lingering soft spot for John. As young children they used to talk quite openly of marrying each other when they grew up. They assumed it would be allowed – why should it not be? They did not understand why the adults smiled, smiled and would not say why.

Did I really tell you that?

You did. Do you want me to cut it out? I like it. It's sweet.

All right, leave it in. [Laughs.] Go on.

Her sister Carol is of quite another mind. Carol is married to a German, an engineer, who has for years been trying to get the two of them out of South Africa and into the United States. Carol has made it plain she does not want it to appear in her American dossier that she is related to a man who, whether or not he is technically a criminal, has in some way fallen foul of the law, their law. But Carol's hostility to John goes deeper than that. She finds him affected and supercilious. From the heights of his *engelse* [English] education, says Carol, John looks down on the Coetzees, one and all. Why he has decided to favour them with his presence at Christmastide she cannot imagine.

She, Margot, is distressed by her sister's attitude. Her sister, she believes, has grown more and more hardhearted ever since she married and began to move in her husband's circle, a circle of German and Swiss expatriates who arrived in South Africa in the 1960s to make quick money and are preparing to abandon ship now that the country is going through stormy times.

I don't know. I don't know if I can let you say that.

Well, whatever you decide, I will abide by what you say. But that is what you told me, word for word. And bear in mind, it is not as if your sister is going to pick up an obscure book published by an academic press in England. Where is your sister now?

She and Klaus live in Florida, in a town called St Petersburg. I have never been there. As for your book, one of her friends might come across it and send it to her — you never know. But that is not the main point. When I spoke to you last year, I was under the impression you were simply going to transcribe our interview. I had no idea you were going to rewrite it completely.

That's not entirely fair. I have not actually rewritten it, I have merely recast it as a narrative, giving it a different form. Giving it new form has no effect on the content. If you feel I am taking liberties with the content itself, that is another question. Do you feel I am taking too many liberties?

I don't know. Something sounds wrong to me, but I can't put my finger on it yet. All I can say is, your version doesn't sound like what I said to you. But I am going to shut up now. I will wait until the end to make up my mind. So go on.

All right.

If Carol is too hard, she is too soft, she will admit to that. She is the one who cries when the new kittens have to be drowned, the one who blocks her ears when the slaughter-lamb bleats in fear, bleats and bleats. She used to mind, when she was younger, being scoffed at for it; but now, in her mid-thirties, she is not so sure she need be ashamed of being tender-hearted.

Carol claims not to understand why John is attending the family gathering, but to her the reason is obvious. To the haunts of his youth he has brought back his father, who though not much over sixty looks like an old man, looks to be on his last legs – has brought him back so that he can be renewed and fortified, or, if he cannot be renewed, so that he can at least say his farewells. It is, to her mind, an act of filial duty, one that she thoroughly approves of.

She tracks John down behind the packing-shed, where he is working on his car, or pretending to.

'Something wrong with the car?' she asks.

'It's overheating,' he says. 'We had to stop twice on Du Toit's Kloof to let the engine cool.'

'You should ask Michiel to have a look at it. He knows everything about cars.'

'Michiel is busy with his guests. I'll fix it myself.'

Her guess is that Michiel would welcome an excuse to escape his guests, but she does not press her case. She knows male stubbornness all too well, knows that a man will wrestle endlessly with a problem rather than undergo the humiliation of asking another man for help.

'Is this what you drive in Cape Town?' she says. By this she means this one-ton Datsun pickup, the kind of light truck she associates with farmers and builders. 'What do you need a truck for?'

'It's useful,' he replies curtly, not explaining what its use might be.

She could not help laughing when he made his arrival at the farm behind the wheel of this selfsame truck, he with his beard and his unkempt hair and his owl-glasses, his father beside him like a mummy, stiff and embarrassed. She wishes she could have taken a photograph. She wishes, too, she could have a quiet word with John about his hair-style. But the ice is not yet broken, intimate talk will have to wait.

'Anyway,' she says, 'I've been instructed to call you for tea, tea and melktert that Aunt Joy has baked.'

'I'll come in a minute,' he says.

They speak Afrikaans together. His Afrikaans is halting; she suspects her English is better than his Afrikaans, though, living in the back country, the *platteland*, she seldom has call to speak English. But they have spoken Afrikaans together since they were children; she is not about to embarrass him by offering to switch.

She blames the deterioration in his Afrikaans on the move he made years ago, first to Cape Town, to 'English' schools and an 'English' university, then to the world abroad, where not a word of Afrikaans is to be heard. *In 'n minuut*, he says: in a minute. It is the kind of solecism that Carol will latch onto at once and make fun of. '*In 'n minuut sal meneer sy tee kom geniet*,' Carol will say: in a minute his lordship will come and partake of tea. She must protect him from Carol, or at least plead with Carol to have mercy on him for the space of these few days.

At table that evening she makes sure she is seated beside him. The evening meal is simply a hotchpotch of leftovers from the midday meal, the main meal of the day: cold mutton, warmed-up rice, green beans with vinegar.

She notices that he passes on the meat platter without helping himself.

'Aren't you having mutton, John?' calls out Carol from the other end of the table in a tone of sweet concern.

'Not tonight, thanks,' John replies. '*Ek het my vanmiddag dik gevreet*': I stuffed myself like a pig this afternoon.

'So you are not a vegetarian. You didn't become a vegetarian while you were overseas.'

'Not a strict vegetarian. *Dis nie 'n woord waarvan ek hou nie. As 'n mens verkies om nie so veel vleis te eet nie . . .*' It is not a word he is fond of. If one chooses not to eat so much meat . . .

'*Ja?*' says Carol. '*As 'n mens so verkies, dan . . . ?*' If that is what you choose, then – what?

Everyone is by now staring at him. He has begun to blush. Clearly he has no idea how to deflect the benign curiosity of the gathering. And if he is paler and scrawnier than a good South African ought to be, might the explanation be, not just that he has tarried too long amid the snows of North America, but that he has indeed been starved too long of good Karoo mutton? *As 'n mens verkies . . .* – what is he going to say next?

His blush has grown desperate. A grown man, yet he blushes like a girl! Time to intervene. She lays a reassuring hand on his arm. '*Jy wil seker sê, John, ons het almal ons voorkeure,*' we all have our preferences.

'*Ons voorkeure,*' he says; '*ons fiemies.*' Our preferences; our silly little whims. He spears a green bean and pops it into his mouth.

It is December, and in December it does not get dark until well after nine. Even then – so pristinely clear is the air on the high plateau – the moon and stars are bright enough to light one's footsteps. So after supper she and he go for a walk, making a wide loop to avoid the cluster of cabins that house the farm workers.

'Thank you for saving me at the dinner table,' he says.

'You know Carol,' she says. 'She has always had a sharp eye. A sharp eye and a sharp tongue. How is your father?'

'Depressed. As you must surely know, he and my mother did not have the happiest of marriages. Even so, after my mother died he went into a decline – moped, didn't know what to do with himself. Men of his generation were brought up to be more or less helpless. If there isn't some woman on hand to cook and care for them, they simply fade away. If I hadn't offered my father a home he would have starved to death.'

'Is he still working?'

'Yes, he still has his job with the motor-parts dealer, though I think they have been hinting it may be time for him to retire. And his enthusiasm for sport is undimmed.'

'Isn't he a cricket umpire?'

'He was, but not any more. His eyesight has deteriorated too far.'

'And you? Didn't you play cricket too?'

'Yes. In fact I still play in the Sunday league. The standard is fairly amateurish, which suits me. Curious: he and I, two Afrikaners devoted to an English game that we aren't much good at. I wonder what that says about us.'

Two Afrikaners. Does he really think of himself as an Afrikaner? She doesn't know many real [*egte*] Afrikaners who would accept him as one of the tribe. Even his father might not pass scrutiny. To pass as an Afrikaner nowadays you need at the very least to vote National and attend church on Sundays. She can't imagine her cousin putting on a suit and tie and going off to church. Or indeed his father.

They have arrived at the dam. The dam used to be filled by a wind-pump, but during the boom years Michiel installed a diesel-driven pump and left the old wind-pump to rust, because that was what everyone was doing. Now that the oil price has gone through the roof, Michiel may have to think again. He may have to fall back on God's wind after all.

'Do you remember,' she says, 'When we used to come here as children . . .'

'And catch tadpoles in a sieve,' he picks up the story, 'and carry them back to the house in a bucket of water and the next morning they all would be dead and we could never figure out why.'

'And locusts. We caught locusts too.'

Having mentioned the locusts, she wishes she hadn't. For she has remembered the fate of the locusts, or of one of them. Out of the bottle in which they had trapped it John took the insect and, while she watched, pulled steadily at a long rear leg until it came off the body, dryly, without blood or whatever counts as blood among locusts. Then he released it and they watched. Each time it tried to launch itself into flight it toppled to one side, its wings scrabbling in the dust, the remaining rear leg jerking ineffectually. *Kill it!* she screamed at him. But he did not kill it, just walked away, looking disgusted.

'Do you remember,' she says, 'how once you pulled the leg off a locust and left me to kill it? I was so cross with you.'

'I remember it every day of my life,' he says. 'Every day I ask the poor thing's forgiveness. I was just a child, I say to it, just an ignorant child who did not know better. *Kaggen*, I say, forgive me.'

'*Kaggen*?'

'*Kaggen*. The name of mantis, the mantis god. Maybe not a locust, but the locust will understand. In the afterworld there are no language problems. It's like Eden all over again.'

The mantis god. He has lost her.

A night wind moans through the vanes of the dead wind-pump. She shivers. 'We must go back,' she says.

'In a minute. Have you read the book by Eugène Marais about the year he spent in the Waterberg observing a baboon troop? He claims that at nightfall, when the troop stopped their foraging and settled down to watch the sun set, he could detect in their eyes, or at least the eyes of the older baboons, stirrings of melancholy, the birth of a first aware-ness of their own mortality.'

'Is that what the sunset makes you think of – mortality?'

'No. But I can't help remembering the first conversation you and I had, the first meaningful conversation. We must have been six years old. What the actual words were I don't recall, but I know I was unbur-dening my heart to you, telling you everything about myself, all my hopes and longings. And at the same time I was thinking, *So this is what it means to be in love!* Because – let me confess it – I was in love with you in those days. And ever since then, being in love with a woman has meant being free to say everything on my heart.'

'Everything on your heart . . . What has that to do with Eugène Marais?'

'Simply that I understand what the old male baboon was thinking as he watched the sun go down, the troop leader, the one Marais was closest to. *Never again*, he was thinking: *Just one life and then never again. Never, never, never.* That is what the Karoo does to me too. It fills me with melancholy. It spoils me for life.'

She still does not see what baboons have to do with the Karoo or their childhood years, but she is not going to let on.

'This place wrenches my heart,' he says. 'It wrenched my heart when I was a child, and I have never been right since.'

His heart is wrenched. She had no inkling of that. It used to be, she thinks to herself, that she knew without being told what was going on in other people's hearts. Her own special talent: *meegevoel*, feeling-with. But not any more, alas, not any more! She grew up; and as she grew up she grew stiff, like a woman who never gets asked to dance, who spends her Saturday evenings waiting in vain on a bench in the church hall, who by the time some man remembers his manners and offers his hand has lost all pleasure, wants only to go home. What a shock! What a revelation! This cousin of hers carries within him memories of how as a child he used to love her! Has carried them all these years!

[Groans.] *Did I really say all that?*

[Laughs.] You did.

How indiscreet of me! [Laughs.] *Never mind, go on.*

'Don't reveal any of that to Carol,' he – John, her cousin – says. 'Don't tell her, with her satirical tongue, how I feel about the Karoo. If you do, I'll never hear the end of it.'

'You and the baboons,' she says. 'Carol has a heart too, believe it or not. But no, I won't tell her your secret. It's getting chilly. Shall we go back?'

They circle past the farm-workers' quarters, keeping a decent distance. Through the dark the coals of a cooking-fire glow in fierce points of red.

'How long will you be staying?' she asks. 'Will you still be here for New Year's Day?' *Nuwejaar:* for the *volk*, the people, a red letter day, quite overshadowing Christmas.

'No, I can't stay so long. I have things to attend to in Cape Town.'

'Then why don't you leave your father behind and come back later to fetch him? Give him time to relax and build up his strength. He doesn't look well.'

'He won't stay behind. My father has a restless nature. Wherever he happens to be, he wants to be somewhere else. The older he grows, the worse it gets. It's like an itch. He can't keep still. Besides, he has his job to get back to. He takes his job very seriously.'

The farmhouse is quiet. They slip in through the back door. 'Goodnight,' she says, 'sleep tight.'

In her room she hurries to get into bed. She would like to be asleep by the time her sister and brother-in-law come indoors, or at least to be able to pretend she is asleep. She is not keen to be interrogated on what passed during her ramble with John. Given half a chance, Carol will prise the story out of her. *I was in love with you when I was six; you set the pattern of my love for other women.* What a thing to say! Indeed, what a compliment! But what of herself? What was going on in her six-year-old heart when all that premature passion was going on in his? She consented to marry him, certainly, but did she accept that they were in love? If so, she has no recollection of it. And what of now – what does she feel for him now? His declaration has certainly made her heart glow. What an odd character, this cousin of hers! His oddness does not come from the Coetzee side, that she is sure of, she is after all half Coetzee herself, so it must come from his mother's, from the Meyers or whatever the name was, the Meyers from the Eastern Cape. Meyer or Meier or Meiring.

Then she is asleep.

'He is stuck up,' says Carol. 'He thinks too much of himself. He can't bear to lower himself to talk to ordinary people. When he isn't messing around with his car he is sitting in a corner with a book. And why doesn't he get a haircut? Every time I lay eyes on him I want to slap a pudding-bowl over his head and snip off those hideous greasy locks of his.'

'His hair isn't greasy,' she protests, 'it's just too long. I think he washes it with hand soap. That's why it is all over the place. And he is shy, not stuck up. That's why he keeps to himself. Give him a chance, he's an interesting person.'

'He is flirting with you. Anyone can see it. And you are flirting back. You, his cousin! You should be ashamed of yourself. Why isn't he married? Is he homosexual, do you think? Is he a *moffie*?'

She never knows whether Carol means what she says or is simply out to provoke her. Even here on the farm Carol goes about in modish white slacks and low-cut blouses, high-heeled sandals, heavy bracelets. She buys her clothes in Frankfurt, she says, on business trips with her husband. She certainly makes the rest of them look very dowdy, very staid, very country-cousin. She and Klaus live in Sandton in a twelve-room mansion owned by Anglo-American, for which they pay no rent, with stables and polo-ponies and a groom, though neither of them knows how to ride. They have no children yet; they will have children, Carol informs her, when they are properly settled. Properly settled means settled in America.

In the Sandton set in which she and Klaus move, Carol once confided, quite advanced things go on. She did not spell out what these advanced things might be, and she, Margot, did not want to ask, but they seemed to have to do with sex.

I won't let you write that. You can't write that about Carol.

It's what you told me.

Yes, but you can't write down every word I say and broadcast it to the world. I never agreed to that. Carol will never speak to me again.

All right, I'll cut it out or tone it down, I promise. Just hear me to the end. Can I go on?

Go on.

Carol has broken completely from her roots. She bears no resemblance to the *plattelandse meisie*, the country girl, she once used to be. She looks, if anything, German, with her bronzed skin and coiffeured blonde hair and emphatic eyeliner. Stately, big-busted, and barely thirty. Frau Dr Müller. If Frau Dr Müller decided to flirt in the Sandton manner with cousin John, how long would it be before cousin John succumbed? Love means being able to open your heart to the beloved, says John. What would Carol say to that? About love Carol could teach her cousin a thing or two, she is sure – at least about love in its more advanced version.

John is not a *moffie*: she knows enough about men to know that. But there is something cool or cold about him, something that if not neuter is at least neutral, as a young child is neutral in matters of sex. There must have been women in his life, if not in South Africa then in America, though he has said not a word about them. Did his American women get to see his heart? If he makes a practice of it, of opening his heart, then he is unusual: men, in her experience, find nothing harder.

She herself has been married for ten years. Ten years ago she said goodbye to Carnarvon, where she had a job as a secretary in a lawyer's office, and moved to her bridegroom's farm east of Middelpos in the Roggeveld where, if she is lucky, if God smiles on her, she will live out the rest of her days.

The farm is home to the two of them, home and *Heim*, but she cannot be at home as much as she wishes. There is no money in sheep-farming any more, not in the barren, drought-ridden Roggeveld. To help make ends meet she has had to go back to work, as a bookkeeper this time, at the one hotel in Calvinia. Four nights of the week, Monday through Thursday, she spends at the hotel; on Fridays her husband drives in from the farm to fetch her, delivering her back in Calvinia at the crack of dawn the next Monday.

Despite this weekly separation – it makes her heart ache, she hates her dreary hotel room, sometimes she cannot hold back her tears, but lays her head on her arms and sobs – she and Lukas have what she would call a happy marriage. More than happy: fortunate, blessed. A good husband, a happy marriage, but no children. Not by design but by fate: her fate, her fault. Of the two sisters, one barren, the other *not yet settled*.

A good husband but close with his feelings. Is a guarded heart an afflic-tion of men in general or just of South African men? Are Germans – Carol's husband, for instance – any better? At this moment Klaus is seated on the stoep with the troop of Coetzee kinsfolk he has acquired by marriage, smoking a cheroot (he freely offers his cheroots around, but his *rookgoed* is too strange, too foreign for the Coetzees), regaling them in his loud baby-Afrikaans, of which he is not in the slightest ashamed, with stories of the times he and Carol have gone skiing in Zermatt. Does Klaus, in the privacy of their Sandton home, open up his heart to Carol once in a while in his slick, easy, confident European manner? She doubts it. She doubts that Klaus has much of a heart to show. She has seen little evidence of one. Whereas of the Coetzees it can at least be said that they have hearts, to a man and to a woman. Too much heart, in fact, sometimes, some of them.

'No, he's not a *moffie*,' she says. 'Talk to him and you will see for yourself.'

'WOULD YOU LIKE TO go for a drive this afternoon?' John offers. 'We could do a grand tour of the farm, just you and I.'

'In what?' she says. 'In your Datsun?'

'Yes, in my Datsun. It's fixed.'

'Fixed so that it won't break down in the middle of nowhere?'

It is of course a joke. Voëlfontein is already the middle of nowhere. But it is not just a joke. She has no idea how big the farm is, measured in square miles, but she does know you cannot walk from one end of it to the other in a single day, not unless you take your walking seriously.

'It won't break down,' he says. 'But I'll bring spare water along just in case.'

Voëlfontein lies in the Koup region, and in the Koup it has rained not a drop in the past two years. What on earth inspired Grandpa Coetzee to buy land here, where every last farmer is struggling to keep his stock alive?

'What sort of word is *Koup*?' she says. 'Is it English? The place where no one can cope?'

'It's Khoi,' he says. 'Hottentot. *Koup*: dry place. It's a noun, not a verb. You can tell by the final –p.'

'Where did you learn that?'

'From books. From grammars put together by missionaries in the old days. There are no speakers of Khoi languages left, not in South Africa. The languages are, for all practical purposes, dead. In South-West Africa there are still a handful of old people speaking Nama. That's the sum of it. The sum of what is left.'

'And Xhosa? Do you speak Xhosa?'

He shakes his head. 'I am interested in the things we have lost, not the things we have kept. Why should I speak Xhosa? There are millions of people who can do that already. They don't need me.'

'I thought languages exist so that we can communicate with each other,' she says. 'What is the point of speaking Hottentot if no one else does?'

He presents her with what she is coming to think of as his secret little smile, betokening that he has an answer to her question, but since she will be too stupid to understand, he will not waste his breath revealing it. It is this Mister Know-All smile, above all, that sends Carol into a rage.

'Once you have learned Hottentot out of your old grammar books, who can you speak to?' she repeats.

'Do you want me to tell you?' he says. The little smile has turned into something else, something tight and not very nice.

'Yes, tell me. Answer me.'

'The dead. You can speak with the dead. Who otherwise' – he hesitates, as if the words might be too much for her and even for him – 'who otherwise are cast out into everlasting silence.'

She wanted an answer and now she has one. It is more than enough to shut her up.

They drive for half an hour, to the westernmost boundary of the farm. There, to her surprise, he opens the gate, drives through, closes the gate behind them, and without a word drives on along the rough dirt road. By four-thirty they have arrived at the town of Merweville, where she has not set foot in years.

Outside the Apollo Café he draws to a halt. 'Would you like a cup of coffee?' he says.

They enter the café with half a dozen barefoot children tagging along behind them, the youngest a mere toddler. Mevrou the proprietress has the radio on, playing Afrikaans pop tunes. They sit down, wave the flies away. The children cluster around their table, staring with unabashed curiosity. 'Middag, jongens,' says John. 'Middag, meneer,' says the eldest.

They order coffee and get a version of coffee: pale Nescafé with long-life milk. She takes a sip of hers and pushes it aside. He drinks his abstractedly.

A tiny hand reaches up and filches the cube of sugar from her saucer. 'Toe, loop!' she says: Run off! The child smiles merrily at her, unwraps the sugar, licks it.

It is by no means the first hint she has had of how far the old barriers between white and Coloured have come down. The signs are more obvious here than in Calvinia. Merweville is a smaller town and in decline, in such decline that it must be in danger of falling off the map. There can be no more than a few hundred people left. Half the houses they drove past seemed unoccupied. The building with the legend *Volkskas* [People's Bank] in white pebbles studded in the mortar over the door houses not a bank but a welding works. Though the worst of the afternoon heat is past, the sole living presence on the main street is provided by two men and a woman stretched out, along with a scrawny dog, in the shade of a flowering jacaranda.

Did I say all that? I don't remember.

I may have added a detail or two to bring the scene to life. I didn't tell you, but since Merweville figures so largely in your story, I actually paid a visit there to check it out.

You went to Merweville? How did it seem to you?

Much as you described it. But there is no Apollo Café any more. No café at all. Shall I go on?

John speaks. 'Are you aware that, among his other accomplishments, our grandfather used to be mayor of Merweville?'

'Yes, I am aware of that.' Their mutual grandfather had his finger in all too many pies. He was – the English word occurs to her – a *go-getter* in a land with few go-getters, a man with plenty of – another English word – *spunk*, more spunk probably than all his children put together. But perhaps that is the fate of the children of strong fathers: to be left with less than a full share of spunk. As with the sons, so with the daughters too: a little too self-effacing, the Coetzee women, blessed with too little of whatever the female equivalent of spunk might be.

She has only tenuous memories of their grandfather, who died when she was still a child: of a stooped, grouchy old man with a bristly chin. After the midday meal, she remembers, the whole house would freeze into silence: Grandpa was having his nap. Even at that age she was surprised to see how fear of the old man could make grown people creep about like mice. Yet without that old man she would not be here, nor would John: not just here on earth but here in the Karoo, on Voëlfontein or in Merweville. If her own life, from cradle to grave, has been and is still being determined by the ups and downs of the market in wool and mutton, then that is her grandfather's doing: a man who started out as a *smous*, a hawker peddling cotton prints and pots and pans and patent medicines to country folk, then when he had saved up enough money bought a share in a hotel, then sold the hotel and bought land and settled down as of all things a gentleman horse-breeder and sheep-farmer.

'You haven't asked what we are doing here in Merweville,' says John.

'Very well: what are we doing in Merweville?'

'I want to show you something. I am thinking of buying property here.'

She cannot believe her ears. 'You want to buy property? You want to live in Merweville? In *Merweville*? Do you want to be mayor too?'

'No, not live here, just spend time here. Live in Cape Town, come here for weekends and holidays. It's not impossible. Merweville is seven hours from Cape Town if you drive without stopping. You can buy a house for a thousand rand – a four-room house and half a morgen of land with peach trees and apricot trees and orange trees. Where else in the world will you get such a bargain?'

'And your father? What does your father think of this plan of yours?'

'It's better than an old-age home.'

'I don't understand. What is better than an old-age home?'

'Living in Merweville. My father can stay here, take up residence; I will be based in Cape Town but I will come up regularly to see that he is okay.'

'And what will your father do during the time he is here all by himself? Sit on the stoep and wait for the one car a day to drive past? There is a simple reason why you can buy a house in Merweville for peanuts, John: because no one wants to live here. I don't understand you. Why this sudden enthusiasm for Merweville?'

'It's in the Karoo.'

Die Karoo is vir skape geskape! The Karoo was made for sheep! She has to bite back the words. *He means it! He speaks of the Karoo as if it were para-dise!* And all of a sudden memories of those Christmastides of yore come flooding back, when they were children roaming the veld as free as wild animals. 'Where do you want to be buried?' he asked her one day, then without waiting for her answer whispered: 'I want to be buried here.' 'For ever?' she said, she, her child self – 'Do you want to be buried for ever?' 'Just till I come out again,' he replied.

Till I come out again. She remembers it all, remembers the very words.

As a child one can do without explanations. One does not demand that everything make sense. But would she be recalling those words of his if they had not puzzled her then and, deep down, continued to puzzle her all these years? *Come out again*: did her cousin really believe, does he really believe, that one comes back from the grave? Who does he think he is: Jesus? And what does he think this place is, this Karoo: the Holy Land?

'If you mean to take up residence in Merweville you will need to get a haircut first,' she says. 'The good folk of this town won't allow a wild man to settle in their midst and corrupt their sons and daughters.'

From Mevrou behind the counter come unmistakable hints that she would like to close up shop. He pays, and they drive off. On the way out of the town he slows down before a house with a TE KOOP sign at the gate: For Sale. 'That's the house I had in mind,' he says. 'A thousand rand plus the legal paperwork. Can you believe it?'

The house is a nondescript cube with a corrugated-iron roof, a shaded veranda running the length of the front, and a steep wooden staircase up the side leading to a loft. The paintwork is in a sorry state. In front of the house, in a bedraggled rockery, a couple of aloes struggle to stay alive. Does he really mean to dump his father here, in this dull house in this exhausted hamlet? An old man, trembly, eating out of tins, sleeping between dirty sheets?

'Would you like to take a look?' he says. 'The house is locked, but we can walk around the back.'

She shivers. 'Another time,' she says. 'I'm not in the mood today.'

What she is in the mood for today she does not know. But her mood ceases to matter twenty kilometres out of Merweville, when the engine begins to cough and John frowns and switches it off and coasts to a stop. A smell of burning rubber invades the cab. 'It's overheating again,' he says. 'I won't be a minute.'

From the back he fetches a jerry can of water. He unscrews the radiator cap, dodging a whoosh of steam, and refills the radiator. 'That should be enough to get us home,' he says. He tries to restart the engine. It turns over dryly without catching.

She knows enough about men never to question their competence with machines. She offers no advice, is careful not to seem impatient, not even to sigh. For an hour, while he fiddles with hoses and clamps and filthies his clothes and tries again and again to get the engine going, she maintains a strict, benign silence.

The sun begins to dip below the horizon; he continues to toil in what might as well be darkness.

'Do you have a torch?' she asks. 'Perhaps I can hold a torch for you.'

But no, he has not brought a torch. Furthermore, since he does not smoke, he does not even have matches. Not a Boy Scout, just a city boy, an unprepared city boy.

'I'll walk back to Merweville and get help,' he says at last. 'Or we can both walk.'

She is wearing light sandals. She is not going to stumble in sandals twenty kilometres across the veld in the dark.

'By the time you get to Merweville it will be midnight,' she says. 'You know no one there. There isn't even a service station. Who are you going to persuade to come out and fix your truck?'

'Then what do you suggest we do?'

'We wait here. If we are lucky, someone will drive past. Otherwise Michiel will come looking for us in the morning.'

'Michiel doesn't know we went to Merweville. I didn't tell him.'

He tries one last time to start the engine. When he turns the key there is a dull click. The battery is flat.

She gets out and, at a decent distance, relieves her bladder. A thin wind has come up. It is cold and is going to be colder. There is nothing in the truck with which to cover themselves, not even a tarpaulin. If they are going to wait out the night, they are going to have to do so huddled in the cab. And then, when they get back to the farm, they are going to have to explain themselves.

She is not yet miserable; she is still removed enough from their situation to find it grimly amusing. But that will soon change. They have nothing to eat, nothing even to drink save water from the can, which smells of petrol. Cold and hunger are going to gnaw away at her fragile good humour. Sleeplessness too, in due course.

She winds the window shut. 'Shall we just forget,' she says, 'that we are a man and a woman, and not be too embarrassed to keep each other warm? Because otherwise we are going to freeze.'

In the thirty-odd years they have known each other they have now and then kissed, in the way that cousins kiss, that is to say, on the cheek. They have embraced too. But tonight an intimacy of quite another order is on the cards. Somehow, on this hard seat, with the gear lever uncomfortably in the way, they are going to have to lie together, or slump together, give warmth to each other. If God is kind and they manage to fall asleep, they may in addition have to suffer the humiliation of snoring or being snored upon. What a test! What a trial!

'And tomorrow,' she says, allowing herself a single acid moment, 'when we get back to civilization, maybe you can arrange to have this truck fixed properly. There is a good mechanic at Leeuw Gamka. Michiel uses him. Just a friendly suggestion.'

'I am sorry. The fault is mine. I try to do things myself when I ought really to leave them to more competent hands. It's because of the country we live in.'

'The country we live in? Why is it the country's fault that your truck keeps breaking down?'

'Because of our long history of making other people do our work for us while we sit in the shade and watch.'

So that is the reason why they are here in the cold and the dark waiting for some passer-by to rescue them. To make a point, namely that white folk should do their own car repairs. How comical.

'The mechanic in Leeuw Gamka is white,' she says. 'I am not suggesting that you take your car to a Native.' She would like to add: *If you want to do your own repairs, for God's sake take a course in auto maintenance first.* But she holds her tongue. 'What other kind of work do you insist on doing,' she says instead, 'besides fixing cars?' *Besides fixing cars and writing poems.*

'I do garden work. I do repairs around the house. I am at present relaying the drainage. It may seem funny to you but to me it is not a joke. I am making a gesture. I am trying to break the taboo on manual labour.'

'The taboo?'

'Yes. Just as in India it is taboo for upper-caste people to clean up – what shall we call it? – human waste, so, in this country, if a white man touches a pickaxe or a spade he at once becomes unclean.'

'What nonsense you talk! That is simply not true! It's just anti-white prejudice!'

She regrets the words as soon as she has spoken them. She has gone too far, driven him into a corner. Now she is going to have this man's resentment to cope with, on top of the boredom and the cold.

'But I can see your point,' she goes on, helping him out, since he doesn't seem able to help himself. 'You are right in one sense: we have become too used to keeping our hands clean, our white hands. We should be more ready to dirty our hands. I couldn't agree more. End of subject. Are you sleepy yet? I'm not. I have a suggestion. To pass the time, why don't we tell each other stories.'

'You tell a story,' he says stiffly. 'I don't know any stories.'

'Tell me a story from America,' she says. 'You can make it up, it doesn't have to be true. Any story.'

'Given the existence of a personal God,' he says, 'with a white beard quaquaquaqua outside time without extension who from the heights of divine apathia loves us deeply quaquaquaqua with some exceptions.'

He stops. She has not the faintest idea what he is talking about.

'Quaquaquaqua,' he says.

'I give up,' she says. He is silent. 'My turn,' she says. 'Here follows the story of the princess and the pea. Once upon a time there is a princess so delicate that even when she sleeps on ten piled-up feather mattresses she is convinced she can feel a pea, one of those hard little dried peas, underneath the last mattress. She frets and frets all night – *Who put a pea there? Why?* – and as a result doesn't get a wink of sleep. She comes down to breakfast looking haggard. To her parents the king and queen she complains: "I couldn't sleep, and it's all the fault of that accursed pea!" The king sends a serving-woman to remove the pea. The woman searches and searches but can find nothing.

'"Let me hear no more of peas," says the king to his daughter. "There is no pea. The pea is just in your imagination."

'That night the princess reascends her mountain of feather mattresses. She tries to sleep but cannot, because of the pea, the pea that is either underneath the bottom-most mattress or else in her imagination, it does not matter which, the effect is the same. By daybreak she is so exhausted that she cannot even eat breakfast. "It's all the pea's fault!" she laments.

'Exasperated, the king sends an entire troop of serving-women to hunt for the pea, and when they return, reporting that there is no pea, has them beheaded. "Now are you satisfied?" he bellows at his daughter. "Now will you sleep?"'

She pauses for breath. She has no idea what is going to happen next in this bedtime story, whether the princess will at last manage to fall asleep or not; yet, strangely, she is convinced that, when she opens her lips, the right words will come.

But there is no need for more words. He is asleep. Like a child, this prickly, opinionated, incompetent, ridiculous cousin of hers has fallen asleep with his head on her shoulder. Fast asleep, undoubtedly: she can feel him twitching. No peas under him.

And what of her? Who is going to tell her stories to send her off to the land of nod? Never has she felt more awake. Is this how she is going to have to spend the night: bored, fretting, bearing the weight of a somnolent male?

He claims there is a taboo on whites doing manual labour, but what of the taboo on cousins of opposite sexes spending the night together? What are the Coetzees back on the farm going to say? Truly, she has no feeling towards John that could be called physical, not the faintest quiver of womanly response. Will that be enough to absolve her? Why is there no male aura about him? Does the fault lie with him; or on the contrary does it lie with her, who has so wholeheartedly absorbed the taboo that she cannot think of him as a man? If he has no woman, is that because he has no feeling for women, and therefore women, herself included, respond by having no feeling for him? Is her cousin, if not a *moffie*, then a eunuch?

The air in the cab is becoming stale. Taking care not to wake him, she opens the window a crack. What presences surround them – bushes or trees or perhaps even animals – she senses on her skin rather than sees. From somewhere comes the chirping of a lone cricket. *Stay with me tonight*, she whispers to the cricket.

But perhaps there is a type of woman who is attracted to a man like this, who is happy to listen without contradicting while he airs his opinions, and then to take on those opinions as her own, even the self-evidently silly ones. A woman indifferent to male silliness, indifferent even to sex, simply in search of a man to attach to herself and take care of and protect against the world. A woman who will put up with shoddy work around the house because what matters is not that the windows close and the locks work but that her man have the space in which to live out his idea of himself. And who will afterwards quietly call in hired help, someone good with his hands, to fix up the mess.

For a woman like that, marriage might well be passionless but it need not therefore be childless. She could give birth to a whole brood. Then of an evening they could all sit around the table, the lord and master at the head, his helpmeet at the foot, their healthy, well-behaved offspring down the two sides; and over the soup course the master could expatiate on the sanctity of labour. *What a man is my mate!* the wife could whisper to herself. *What a developed conscience he has!*

Why is she feeling so bitter towards John, and even bitterer towards this wife she has conjured up for him out of thin air? The simple answer: because due to his vanity and clumsiness she is stranded on the Merweville road. But the night is long, there is plenty of time to unfold a grander hypothesis and inspect that hypothesis to see if it has any virtue. The grander answer: she feels bitter because she had hoped for much from her cousin, and he has failed her.

What had she hoped for from him?

That he would redeem the Coetzee men.

Why did she desire the redemption of the Coetzee men?

Because the Coetzee men are so *slapgat*.

Why had she placed her hopes in John in particular?

Because of the Coetzee men he was the one blessed with the best chance. He had a chance and he did not make use of it.

Slapgat is a word she and her sister throw around rather easily, perhaps because it was thrown around rather easily in their hearing while they were children. It was only after she left home that she noticed the shocked looks that the word evoked, and began to use it more cautiously. A *slap gat*: a rectum, an anus, over which one has less than complete control. Hence *slapgat*: slack, spineless.

Her uncles have turned out *slapgat* because their parents, her grandparents, brought them up that way. While their father thundered and roared and made them quake in their boots, their mother tiptoed around like a mouse. The result was that they went out into the world lacking all fibre, lacking backbone, lacking belief in themselves, lacking courage. The life-paths they chose for themselves were without exception easy paths, paths of least resistance. Gingerly they tested the tide, then swam with it.

What made the Coetzees so easygoing and therefore so *gesellig*, such good company, was precisely their preference for the easiest available path; and their *geselligheid* was precisely what made the Christmas get-togethers such fun. They never quarrelled, never squabbled among themselves, got along famously, all of them. It was the next generation, her generation, who had to pay for their easygoingness, who went out into the world expecting the world to be just another *slap*, *gesellige* place, Voëlfontein writ large, and found that, behold, it was not!

She herself has no children. She cannot conceive. But if, blessedly, she had children, she would take it as her first duty to work the Coetzee blood out of them. How you work *slap* blood out of people she does not know offhand, short of taking them to a hospital and having their blood pumped out and replaced with the blood of some vigorous donor; but perhaps a strict training in self-assertion, starting at the earliest possible age, would do the trick. Because if there is one thing she knows about the world in which the child of the future will have to grow up, it is that there will be no room for the *slap*.

Even Voëlfontein and the Karoo are no longer Voëlfontein and the Karoo as they used to be. Look at those children in the Apollo Café. Look at cousin Michiel's work gang, who are certainly not the *plaasvolk* of yore. In the attitude of Coloured people in general towards whites there is a new and unsettling hardness. The younger ones regard one with a cold eye, refuse to call one *Baas* or *Miesies*. Strange men flit across the land from one settlement to another, *lokasie* to *lokasie*, and no one will report them to the police as in the old days. The police find it harder and harder to come up with information they can trust. People no longer want to be seen talking to them; sources have dried up. For the farmers, summons for commando duty come more often and for longer. Lukas complains about it all the time. If that is the way things are in the Roggeveld, it must certainly be the way things are here in the Koup.

Business is changing character too. To get on in business it is no longer enough to be friends with all and sundry, to do favours and be owed favours in return. No, nowadays you have to be as hard as nails and ruthless as well. What chance do *slapgat* men stand in such a world? No wonder her Coetzee uncles are not prospering: bank managers idling away the years in dying *platteland* towns, civil servants stalled on the ladder of promotion, penurious farmers, even in the case of John's father a disgraced, disbarred attorney.

If she had children, she would not only do her utmost to purge them of their Coetzee inheritance, she would think seriously of doing what Carol is doing: whisking them out of the country, giving them a fresh start in America or Australia or New Zealand, places where they can look forward to a decent future. But as a childless woman she is spared having to make that decision. She has another role prepared for her: to devote herself to her husband and to the farm; to live as good a life as the times allow, as good and as fair and as just.

The barrenness of the future that yawns before Lukas and herself – this is not a new source of pain, no, it returns again and again like a toothache, to the extent that it has by now begun to bore her. She wishes she could dismiss it and get some sleep. How is it that this cousin of hers, whose body manages to be both scrawny and soft at the same time, does not feel the cold, while she, who is undeniably more than a few kilos over her best weight, has begun to shiver? On cold nights she and her husband sleep tight and warm against each other. Why does her cousin's body fail to warm her? Not only does he not warm her, he seems to suck her own body heat away. Is he by nature as heatless as he is sexless?

A ripple of true anger runs through her; and, as if sensing it, this male being beside her stirs. 'Sorry,' he mumbles, sitting upright.

'Sorry for what?'

'I lost track.'

She has no idea what he is talking about and is not going to inquire. He slumps down and in a moment is asleep again.

Where is God in all of this? With God the Father she finds it harder and harder to have dealings. What faith she once had in Him and His providence she has by now lost. Godlessness: an inheritance from the godless Coetzees, no doubt. When she thinks of God, all she can picture is a bearded figure with a booming voice and a grand manner who inhabits a mansion on top of a hill with hosts of servants rushing around anxiously, doing things for Him. Like a good Coetzee, she prefers to steer clear of people like that. The Coetzees look askance at self-important folk, crack jokes about them *sotto voce*. She may not be as good at jokes as the rest of the family, but she does find God a bit of a trial, a bit of a bore.

Now I must protest. You are really going too far. I said nothing remotely like that. You are putting words of your own in my mouth.

I'm sorry, I must have got carried away. I'll fix it. I'll tone it down.

Cracking jokes *sotto voce*. Nevertheless, does God in His infinite wisdom have a plan for her and for Lukas? For the Roggeveld? For South Africa? Will things that look merely chaotic today, chaotic and purposeless, reveal themselves at some future date to be part of some vast, benign design? For instance: Is there a larger explanation for why a woman in the prime of her life must spend four nights a week sleeping alone in a dismal second-floor room in the Grand Hotel in Calvinia, month after month, perhaps even year after year, with no end in sight; and for why her husband, a born farmer, must spend most of his time trucking other people's livestock to the abattoirs in Paarl and Maitland – an explanation larger than that the farm would go under without the income these soul-destroying jobs bring in? And is there a larger explanation for why the farm that the two of them are slaving to keep afloat will in the fullness of time pass into the care not of a son of their loins but of some ignoramus nephew of her husband's, if it is not swallowed down by the bank first? If, in God's vast, benign design, it was never intended that this part of the world – the Roggeveld, the Karoo – should be profitably farmed, then what exactly is His intention for it? Is it meant to fall back into the hands of the *volk*, who will proceed, as in the old, old days, to roam from district to district with their ragged flocks in search of grazing, trampling the fences flat, while people like herself and her husband expire in some forgotten corner, disinherited?

Useless to put questions like that to the Coetzees. *Die boer saai, God maai, maar waar skuil die papegaai?* say the Coetzees, and cackle. Nonsense words. A nonsense family, flighty, without substance; clowns. *'n Hand vol vere*: a handful of feathers. Even the one member for whom she had had some slight hopes, the one beside her who has tumbled straight back into dreamland, turns out to be a lightweight. Who ran away to the big world and now comes creeping ignominiously back to the little world. Failed runaway, failed car mechanic too, for whose failure she is at this moment having to suffer. Failed son. Sitting in that dreary, dusty old house in Merweville looking out on the empty, sunstruck street, rattling a pencil between his teeth, trying to think up verses. *O droë land, o barre kranse* . . . O parched land, o barren cliffs . . . What next? Something about *weemoed* for sure, melancholy.

She wakes as first streaks of mauve and orange begin to extend across the sky. In her sleep she has somehow twisted her body and slumped down further in the seat, so that her cousin, still dormant, reclines not against her shoulder but against her rump. Irritably she frees herself. Her eyes are gummy, her bones creak, she has a raging thirst. Opening the door, she slides out.

The air is cold and still. Even as she watches, thornbushes and tufts of grass, touched by the first light, emerge out of nothing. It is as if she were present at the first day of creation. *My God*, she murmurs; she has an urge to sink to her knees.

There is a rustle nearby. She is looking straight into the dark eyes of an antelope, a little steenbok not twenty paces off, and it is looking straight back at her, wary but not afraid, not yet. *My kleintjie!* she says, my little one. More than anything she wants to embrace it, to pour out upon its brow this sudden love; but before she can take a first step the little one has whirled about and raced off with drumming hooves. A hundred yards away it halts, turns, inspects her again, then trots at less urgent pace across the flats and into a dry riverbed.

'What's that?' comes her cousin's voice. He has at last awoken; he clambers out of the truck, yawning, stretching.

'A steenbokkie,' she says curtly. 'What are we going to do now?'

'I'll head back to Merweville,' he says. 'You wait here. I should be back by ten o'clock, eleven at the latest.'

'If a car passes and offers me a lift, I'm taking it,' she says. 'Either direction, I'm taking it.'

He looks a mess, with his unkempt hair and beard sticking out at all angles. *Thank God I don't have to wake up with you in my bed every morning,* she thinks. *Not enough of a man. A real man would do better than this, sowaar!*

The sun is showing above the horizon; already she can feel the warmth on her skin. The world may be God's world, but the Karoo belongs first of all to the sun. 'You had better get going,' she says. 'It's going to be a hot day.' And watches as he trudges off, the empty jerry can slung over his shoulder.

An adventure: perhaps that is the best way to think of it. Here in the back of beyond she and John are having an adventure. For years to come the Coetzees will be reminiscing about it. *Remember the time when Margot and John broke down on that godforsaken Merweville road?* In the meantime, while she waits for her adventure to end, what has she for diversion? The tattered instruction manual for the Datsun; nothing else. No poems. Tyre rotation. Battery maintenance. Tips for fuel economy.

The truck, facing into the rising sun, grows stiflingly hot. She takes shelter in its lee.

On the crest of the road, an apparition: out of the heat-haze emerges first the torso of a man, then by degrees a donkey and donkey-cart. On the wind she can even hear the neat clip-clop of the donkey's hooves.

The figure grows clearer. It is Hendrik from Voëlfontein, and behind him, sitting on the cart, is her cousin.

Laughter and greetings. 'Hendrik has been visiting his daughter in

Merweville,' John explains. 'He will give us a ride back to the farm, that is, if his donkey consents. He says we can hitch the Datsun to the cart and he will tow it.'

Hendrik is alarmed. '*Nee, meneer!*' he says.

'*Ek jok maar net,*' says her cousin. Just joking.

Hendrik is a man of middle age. As the result of a botched operation for a cataract he has lost the sight of one eye. There is something wrong with his lungs too, such that the slightest physical effort makes him wheeze. As a labourer he is not of much use on the farm, but her cousin Michiel keeps him on because that is how things are done here.

Hendrik has a daughter who lives with her husband and children outside Merweville. The husband used to have a job in the town but seems to have lost it; the daughter does domestic work. Hendrik must have set off from their place before first light. About him there is a faint smell of sweet wine; when he climbs down from the cart, she notices, he stumbles. Sozzled by mid-morning: what a life!

Her cousin reads her thoughts. 'I have some water here,' he says, and proffers the full jerry can. 'It's clean. I filled it at a wind-pump.'

So they set off for the farm, John seated beside Hendrik, she in the back holding an old jute bag over her head to keep off the sun. A car passes them in a cloud of dust, heading for Merweville. If she had seen it in time she would have hailed it – got a ride to Merweville and from there telephoned Michiel to come and fetch her. On the other hand, though the road is rutted and the ride uncomfortable, she likes the idea of arriving at the farmhouse in Hendrik's donkey-cart, likes it more and more: the Coetzees assembled on the stoep for afternoon tea, Hendrik doffing his hat to them, bringing back Jack's errant son, dirty and sunburnt and chastened. '*Ons was so bekommerd!*' they will berate the miscreant. '*Waar was julle dan? Michiel wou selfs die polisie bel!*' From him, nothing but mumble-mumble. '*Die arme Margie! En wat het van die bakkie geword?*' We were so worried! Where were you? Michiel was on the point of phoning the police! Poor Margie! And where is the truck?

There are stretches of road where the incline is so steep that they have to get down and walk. For the rest the little donkey is up to its task, with no more than a touch of the whiplash to its rump now and again to remind it who is master. How slight its frame, how delicate its hooves, yet what staunchness, what powers of endurance! No wonder Jesus had a fondness for donkeys.

Inside the boundary of Voëlfontein they halt at a dam. While the donkey drinks she chats with Hendrik about the daughter in Merweville, then about the other daughter, the one who works in the kitchen at a home for the aged in Beaufort West. Discreetly she does not ask after Hendrik's most recent wife, whom he married when she was no more than a child and who ran away as soon as she could with a man from the railway camp at Leeuw Gamka.

Hendrik finds it easier to talk to her than to her cousin, she can see that. She and he share a language, whereas the Afrikaans John speaks is stiff and bookish. Half of what John says probably goes over Hendrik's head. *Which is more poetic, do you think, Hendrik: the rising sun or the setting sun? A goat or a sheep?*

'*Het Katryn dan nie vir padkos gesorg nie?*' she teases Hendrik: Hasn't your daughter packed lunch for us?

Hendrik goes through the motions of embarrassment, averting his gaze, shuffling. '*Ja-nee, mies,*' he wheezes. A *plaashotnot* from the old days, a farm Hottentot.

As it turns out, Hendrik's daughter has indeed provided *padkos*. From a jacket pocket Hendrik brings out, wrapped in brown paper, a leg of chicken and two slices of buttered white bread, which shame forbids him to divide with them yet equally forbids him to devour in front of them.

'*In Godsnaam eet, man!*' she commands. '*Ons is glad nie honger nie, ons is ook binnekort tuis*': We aren't hungry, and anyway we'll soon be home. And she draws John away on a circuit of the dam so that Hendrik, with his back to them, can hurriedly down his meal.

Ons is glad nie honger nie: a lie, of course. She is famished. The very smell of the cold chicken makes her salivate.

'Sit up front beside the driver,' John suggests. 'For our triumphal return.' And so she does. As they approach the Coetzees, assembled on the stoep exactly as she had foreseen, she takes care to put on a smile and even to wave in a parody of royalty. In response she is greeted with a light ripple of clapping. She descends, 'Dankie, Hendrik, eerlik dankie,' she says: Thank you sincerely. 'Mies,' says Hendrik. Later in the day she will go over to his house and leave some money: for Katryn, she will say, for clothing for her children, though she knows the money will go on liquor.

'En toe?' says Carol, in front of everyone. 'Sê vir ons: waar was julle?' Where were you?

Just for a second there is silence, and in that second she realizes that the question, on the face of it simply a prompt for her to come up with some flippant, amusing retort, has a serious core. The Coetzees really want to know where she and John have been; they want to be reassured that nothing truly scandalous has taken place. It takes her breath away, the cheek of it. That people who have known her and loved her all her life could think her capable of misconduct! 'Vra vir John,' she replies curtly – ask John – and stalks indoors.

When she rejoins them half an hour later the atmosphere is still uneasy.

'Where has John gone?' she asks.

John and Michiel, it turns out, set off just a moment ago in Michiel's pickup to recover the Datsun. They will tow it to Leeuw Gamka, to the mechanic who will fix it properly.

'We stayed up late last night,' says her aunt Beth. 'We waited and waited. Then we decided you and John must have gone to Beaufort and were spending the night there because the National Road is so dangerous at this time of the year. But you didn't phone, and that worried us. This morning Michiel phoned the hotel at Beaufort and they said they hadn't seen you. He phoned Fraserburg too. We never guessed you had gone to Merweville. What were you doing in Merweville?'

What indeed were they doing in Merweville? She turns to John's father. 'John says you and he are thinking of buying property in Merweville,' she says. 'Is that true, Uncle Jack?'

A shocked silence falls.

'Is it true, Uncle Jack?' she presses him. 'Is it true you are going to move from the Cape to Merweville?'

'If you put the question like that,' Jack says – the bantering Coetzee manner is gone, he is all caution – 'no, no one is actually going to move to Merweville. John has the idea – I don't know how realistic it is – of buying one of those abandoned houses and fixing it up as a holiday home. That's as far as we have gone in talking about it.'

A holiday home in Merweville! Who has ever heard of such a thing! Merweville of all places, with its snooping neighbours and its *diaken* [deacon] knocking at the door, pestering one to attend church! How can Jack, in his day the liveliest and most irreverent of them all, be planning a move to Merweville?

'You should try Koegenaap first, Jack,' says his brother Alan. 'Or Pofadder. In Pofadder the big day of the year is when the dentist from Upington comes visiting to pull teeth. They call it *die Groot Trek*, the Great Trek.'

As soon as their ease is threatened, the Coetzees come up with jokes. A family drawn up in a tight little *laager* to keep the world and its menaces at bay. But how long will the jokes go on doing their magic? One of these days the great foe himself will come knocking at the door, the Grim Reaper, whetting his scythe-blade, calling them out one by one. What power will their jokes have then?

'According to John, you are going to move to Merweville while he stays on in Cape Town,' she persists. 'Are you sure you will be able to cope by yourself, Uncle Jack, without a car?'

A serious question. The Coetzees don't like serious questions. '*Margie word 'n bietjie grim*,' they will say among themselves: Margie is becoming a bit grim. *Is your son planning to shunt you off to the Karoo and abandon you, she is asking, and if that is what is afoot, how come you don't raise your voice in protest?*

'No, no,' replies Jack. 'It won't be like you say. Merweville will just be somewhere quiet to take a break. If it goes through. It's just an idea, you know, an idea of John's. It's nothing definite.'

'IT'S A SCHEME TO get rid of his father,' says her sister Carol. 'He wants to dump him in the middle of the Karoo and wash his hands of him. Then it will be up to Michiel to take care of him. Because Michiel will be closest.'

'Poor old John!' she replies. 'You always believe the worst of him. What if he is telling the truth? He has promised he will visit Merweville every weekend, and spend the school holidays there as well. Why not give him the benefit of the doubt?'

'Because I don't believe a word he says. The whole plan sounds fishy to me. He has never got on with his father.'

'He looks after his father in Cape Town.'

'He lives with his father, but only because he has no money. He is thirty-something years old with no prospects. He ran away from South Africa to escape the army. Then he was thrown out of America because he broke the law. Now he can't find a proper job because he is too stuck-up. The two of them live on the pathetic salary his father gets from the scrapyard where he works.'

'But that's not true!' she protests. Carol is younger than she. Once Carol used to be the follower and she, Margot, the leader. Now it is Carol who stalks ahead, she who tails anxiously behind. How did it happen? 'John teaches in a high school,' she says. 'He earns his own money.'

'That's not what I hear. What I hear is that he coaches dropouts for their matric exams and is paid by the hour. It's part-time work, the sort of job students take to earn some pocket money. Ask him straight out. Ask him what school he teaches at. Ask him what he earns.'

'A big salary isn't all that counts.'

'It isn't just a matter of salary. It's a matter of telling the truth. Let him tell you the truth about why he wants to buy this house in Merweville. Let him tell you who is going to pay for it, he or his father. Let him tell you his plans for the future.' And then, when she looks blank: 'Hasn't he told you? Hasn't he told you his plans?'

'He doesn't have plans. He is a Coetzee, Coetzees don't have plans, they don't have ambitions, they only have idle longings. He has an idle longing to live in the Karoo.'

'His ambition is to be a poet, a full-time poet. Have you ever heard of such a thing? This Merweville scheme has nothing to do with his father's welfare. He wants a place in the Karoo where he can come when it suits him, where he can sit with his chin on his hands and contemplate the sunset and write poems.'

John and his poems again! She can't help it, she snorts with laughter. John sitting on the stoep of that ugly little house making up poems! With a beret on his head, no doubt, and a glass of wine at his elbow. And the little Coloured children clustered around him, pestering him with questions. *Wat maak oom? – Nee, oom maak gedigte. Op sy ou ramkiekie maak oom gedigte. Die wêreld is ons woning nie* . . . What is sir doing? – Sir is making poems. On his old banjo sir is making poems. This world is not our dwelling-place . . .

'I'll ask him,' she says, still laughing. 'I'll ask him to show me his poems.'

SHE CATCHES JOHN THE next morning as he is setting off on one of his walks. 'Let me come with you,' she says. 'Give me a minute to put on proper shoes.'

They follow the path that runs eastward from the farmstead along the bank of the overgrown riverbed towards the dam whose wall burst in the floods of 1943 and has never been repaired. In the shallow waters of the dam a trio of white geese float peacefully. It is still cool, there is no haze, they can see as far as the Nieuweveld Mountains.

'God,' she says, 'dis darem mooi. Dit raak jou siel aan, nè, dié ou wêreld.' Isn't it beautiful. It touches one's soul, this landscape.

They are in a minority, a tiny minority, the two of them, of souls that are stirred by these great, desolate expanses. If anything has held them together over the years, it is that. This landscape, this kontrei – it has taken over her heart. When she dies and is buried, she will dissolve into this earth so naturally it will be as if she never had a human life.

'Carol says you are still writing poems,' she says. 'Is that true? Will you show me?'

'I am sorry to disappoint Carol,' he replies stiffly, 'but I haven't written a poem since I was a teenager.'

She bites her tongue. She forgot: you do not ask a man to show you his poems, not in South Africa, not without reassuring him beforehand that it will be all right, he is not going to be mocked. What a country, where poetry is not a manly activity but a hobby for children and *oujongnooiens* [spinsters] – *oujongnooiens* of both sexes! How Totius or Louis

Leipoldt got by she cannot guess. No wonder Carol chooses John's poem-writing to attack, Carol with her nose for other people's weaknesses.

'If you gave up so long ago, why does Carol think you still write?'

'I have no idea. Perhaps she saw me marking student essays and jumped to the wrong conclusion.'

She does not believe him, but she is not going to press him further. If he wants to evade her, let him. If poetry is a part of his life he is too shy or too ashamed to talk about, then so be it.

She does not think of John as a *moffie*, but it continues to puzzle her that he has no woman. A man alone, particularly one of the Coetzee men, seems to her like a boat without oar or rudder or sail. And now two of them, two Coetzee men, living as a couple! While Jack still had the redoubtable Vera behind him he steered a more or less straight course; but now that she is gone he seems quite lost. As for Jack and Vera's son, he could certainly do with some level-headed guidance. But what woman with any sense would want to devote herself to the hapless John?

Carol is convinced John is a bad bet; and the rest of the Coetzee family, despite their good hearts, would probably agree. What sets her, Margot, apart, what keeps her confidence in John precariously afloat, is, oddly enough, the way in which he and his father behave towards each other: if not with affection, that would be saying too much, then at least with respect.

The pair used to be the worst of enemies. The bad blood between Jack and his elder son was the subject of much head-shaking. When the son disappeared overseas, the parents put on the best front they could. He had gone to pursue a career in science, his mother claimed. For years she put forward a story that John was working as a scientist in England, even as it became clear that she had no idea for whom he worked or what sort of work he did. *You know how John is*, his father would say: *always very independent. Independent*: what did that mean? Not without reason, the Coetzees took it to mean he had disowned his country, his family, his very parents.

Then Jack and Vera started putting out a new story: John was not in England after all but in America, pursuing ever higher qualifications.

Time passed; in the absence of hard news, interest in John and his doings waned. He and his younger brother became just two among thousands of young white men who had run away to escape military service, leaving an embarrassed family behind. He had almost vanished from their collective memory when the scandal of his expulsion from the United States burst upon them.

That terrible war, said his father: it was all the fault of a war in which American boys were sacrificing their lives for the sake of Asians who seemed to feel no gratitude at all. No wonder ordinary Americans were revolting. No wonder they took to the streets. John had been caught up willy-nilly in a street protest, the story proceeded; what ensued had just been a bad misunderstanding.

Was it his son's disgrace, and the untruths he had to tell as a consequence, that had turned Jack into a shaky, prematurely aged man? How can she even ask?

'You must be glad to see the Karoo again,' she says to John. 'Aren't you relieved you decided not to stay in America?'

'I don't know,' he replies. 'Of course, in the midst of this' – he does not gesture, but she knows what he means: this sky, this space, the vast silence enclosing them – 'I feel blessed, one of a lucky few. But practically speaking, what future do I have in this country, where I have never fitted in? Perhaps a clean break would have been better after all. Cut yourself free of what you love and hope that the wound heals.'

A frank answer. Thank heaven for that.

'I had a chat with your father yesterday, John, while you and Michiel were away. Seriously, I don't think he fully grasps what you are planning. I am talking about Merweville. Your father is not young any more, and he is not well. You can't dump him in a strange town and expect him to fend for himself. And you can't expect the rest of the family to step in and take care of him if things go wrong. That's all. That's what I wanted to say.'

He does not respond. In his hand is a length of old fencing-wire that he has picked up. Swinging the wire petulantly left and right, flicking off the heads of the waving grass, he descends the slope of the eroded dam wall.

'Don't behave like this!' she calls out, trotting after him. 'Speak to me, for God's sake! Tell me I am wrong! Tell me I am making a mistake!'

He halts and turns upon her a look of cold hostility. 'Let me fill you in on my father's situation,' he says. 'My father has no savings, not a cent, and no insurance. He has only a state pension to look forward to: forty-three rand a month when I last checked. So despite his age, despite his poor health, he has to go on working. Together the two of us earn in a month what a car salesman earns in a week. My father can give up his job only if he moves to a place where living expenses are lower than in the city.'

'But why does he have to move at all? And why to Merweville, to some rundown old ruin?'

'My father and I can't live together indefinitely, Margie. It makes us too miserable, both of us. It's unnatural. Fathers and sons were never meant to share a home.'

'Your father doesn't strike me as a difficult person to live with.'

'Perhaps; but I am a difficult person to live with. My difficulty consists in not wanting to share space with other people.'

'So is that what this Merweville business is all about – about you wanting to live by yourself?'

'Yes. Yes and no. I want to be able to be alone when I choose.'

THEY ARE CONGREGATED ON the stoep, all the Coetzees, having their morning tea, chatting, idly watching Michiel's three young sons play cricket on the open *werf*.

On the far horizon a cloud of dust materializes and hangs in the air.

'That must be Lukas,' says Michiel, who has the keenest eyes. 'Margie, it's Lukas!'

Lukas, as it turns out, has been on the road since dawn. He is tired but in good spirits nonetheless, full of vim. Barely has he greeted his wife and her family before he lets himself be roped into the boys' game. He may not be competent at cricket, but he loves being with children, and children adore him. He would be the best of fathers: it breaks her heart that he must be childless.

John joins in the game too. He is better at cricket than Lukas, more practised, one can see that at a glance, but children don't warm to him.

Nor do dogs, she has noticed. Unlike Lukas, not a father by nature. An *alleenloper*, as some male animals are: a loner. Perhaps it is as well he has not married.

Unlike Lukas; yet there are things she shares with John that she can never share with Lukas. Why? Because of the childhood times they spent together, the most precious of times, when they opened their hearts to each other as one can never do later, even to a husband, even to a husband whom one loves more than all the treasure in the world.

Best to cut yourself free of what you love, he had said during their walk — *cut yourself free and hope the wound heals.* She understands him exactly. That is what they share above all: not just a love of this farm, this *kontrei*, this Karoo, but an understanding that goes with the love, an understanding that love can be too much. To him and to her it was granted to spend their childhood summers in a sacred space. That glory can never be regained; best not to haunt old sites and come away from them mourning what is for ever gone.

Being wary of loving too much is not something that makes sense to Lukas. For Lukas, love is simple, wholehearted. Lukas gives himself over to her with all his heart, and in return she gives him all of herself. *With this body I thee worship.* Through his love her husband brings out what is best in her: even now, sitting here drinking tea, watching him at play, she can feel her body warming to him. From Lukas she has learned what love can be. Whereas her cousin . . . She cannot imagine her cousin giving himself wholeheartedly to anyone. Always a quantum held back, held in reserve. One does not need to be a dog to see that.

It would be nice if Lukas could take a break, if she and he could spend a night or two here on Voëlfontein. But no, tomorrow is Monday, they must be back at Middelpos by nightfall. So after lunch they say their goodbyes to the aunts and uncles. When John's turn comes she hugs him tight, feeling his body against her tense, resistant. 'Totsiens', she says: Goodbye. 'I'm going to write you a letter and I want you to write back.' 'Goodbye,' he says. 'Drive safely.'

She begins the promised letter that same night, sitting in her dressing gown and slippers at the table in her own kitchen, the kitchen she married into and has come to love, with its huge old fireplace and its ever-cool, windowless larder whose shelves still groan with jars of jam and preserves she laid in last autumn.

Dear John, she writes, I was so cross with you when we broke down on the Merweville road – I hope it didn't show too much, I hope you will forgive me. All that bad temper has now blown away, there is no trace left. They say you don't know a person properly until you have spent a night with him (or her). I am glad I had a chance to spend a night with you. In sleep our masks slip off and we are seen as we truly are.

The Bible looks forward to the day when the lion shall lie down with the lamb, when we will no longer need to be on our guard since we will have no more cause for fear. (Rest assured, you are not the lion, nor am I the lamb.)

I want to raise one last time the subject of Merweville.

We all grow old one day, and in the way we treat our parents we will surely be treated too. What goes around comes around, as they say. I am sure it is hard for you to live with your father when you have been used to living alone, but Merweville is not the right solution.

You are not alone in your difficulties, John. Carol and I face the same problem with our mother. When Klaus and Carol go off to America, the burden will fall squarely on Lukas and me.

I know you are not a believer, so I won't suggest that you pray for guidance. I am not much of a believer either, but prayer is a good thing. Even if there is no one above to listen, one at least brings out the words, which is better than bottling things up.

I wish we had had more time to talk. Do you remember how we used to talk when we were children? It is so precious to me, the memory of those times. How sad that when our turn comes to die our story, the story of you and me, will die too.

I cannot tell you what tenderness I feel for you at this moment. You were always my favourite cousin, but it is more than that. I long to protect you from the world, even though you probably don't need protecting (I am guessing). It is hard to know what to do with feelings like these. It has become such an old-fashioned relationship, hasn't it, cousinship. Soon all the rules we had to memorize about who is allowed to marry whom, first cousins and second cousins and third cousins, will just be anthropology.

Still, I am glad we did not act on our childhood vows (do you remember?) and marry each other. You are probably glad too. We would have made a hopeless couple.

John, you need someone in your life, someone to look after you. Even if you choose someone who is not necessarily the love of your life, married life will be better than what you have now, with just your father and yourself. It is not good to sleep alone night after night. Excuse me for saying this, but I speak from bitter experience.

I should tear up this letter, it's so embarrassing, but I won't. I say to myself, we have known each other a long time, you will surely forgive me if I tread where I should not tread.

Lukas and I are happy together in every possible way. I go down on my knees every night (so to speak) to give thanks that his path crossed mine. How I wish you could have the same!

As if summoned, Lukas comes into the kitchen, bends down over her, presses his lips to her head, slips his hands under the dressing gown, cups her breasts. 'My skat,' he says: my treasure.

You can't write that. You can't. You are just making things up.

I'll cut it out. Presses his lips to her head. 'My skat,' he says, 'when are you coming to bed?' 'Now,' she says, and lays down the pen. 'Now.'

Skat: an endearment she disliked until the day she heard it from his lips. Now, when he whispers the word, she melts. This man's treasure, into which he may dip whenever it pleases him.

They lie in each other's arms. The bed creaks, but she could not care less, they are at home, they can make the bed creak as much as they like.

Again!

I promise, when I have finished I will hand over the text to you, the entire text, and let you cut out whatever you wish.

'Was that a letter to John you were writing?' says Lukas.

'Yes. He is so unhappy.'

'Maybe that's just his nature. A melancholy type.'

'But he used not to be. He used to be such a happy soul in the old days. If he could only find someone to take him out of himself!'

But Lukas is asleep. That is his nature, his type: he falls asleep at once, like an innocent child.

She would like to be able to join him, but sleep is slow in coming. It is as if the ghost of her cousin still lurks, calling her back to the dark kitchen to complete what she was writing to him. *Have faith in me*, she whispers. *I promise I will return.*

But when she wakes it is Monday, there is no time for writing, no time for intimacies, they have to set off at once on the drive to Calvinia, she to the hotel, Lukas to the transport depot. In the windowless little office behind the reception desk she labours over the backlog of invoices; by evening she is too exhausted to pursue the letter she was writing, and anyhow she has lost touch with the feeling. *Am thinking of you*, she writes at the foot of the page. Even that is not true, she has not given John a thought all day, she has had no time. *Much love*, she writes. *Margie*. She addresses the envelope and seals it. So. It is done.

Much love, but exactly how much? Enough to save John, in a pinch? Enough to raise him out of himself, out of the melancholy of his type? She doubts it. And what if he does not want to be raised? If his grand plan is to spend weekends on the stoep of the house in Merweville writing poems with the sun beating down on the tin roof and his father coughing in a back room, he may need all the melancholy he can summon up.

That is her first moment of misgiving. The second moment comes as she is mailing the letter, as the envelope is trembling on the very lip of the slot. Is what she has written, what her cousin will be fated to read if she lets the letter go, truly the best she can offer him? *You need someone in your life*. What kind of help is it to be told that? *Much love.*

But then she thinks, *He is a grown man, why should it be up to me to save him?* and she gives the envelope a final nudge.

She has to wait ten days, until the Friday of the next week, for a reply.

Dear Margot,

Thank you for your letter, which was waiting for us when we got back from Voëlfontein, and thank you for the good if impracticable advice re marriage.

The drive back from Voëlfontein was incident-free. Michiel's mechanic friend did a first-class job. I apologize again for the night I made you spend in the open.

You write about Merweville. I agree, our plans were not properly thought through, and now that we are back in Cape Town begin to seem a bit crazy. It is one thing to buy a weekend shack on the coast, but who in his right mind would want to spend summer vacations in a hot Karoo town?

I trust that all is well on the farm. My father sends his love to you and Lukas, as do I.

John

Is that all? The cold formality of his response shocks her, brings an angry flush to her cheeks.

'What is it?' asks Lukas.

She shrugs, 'It's nothing,' she says, and passes the letter over. 'A letter from John.'

He reads it through swiftly. 'So they are dropping their plans for Merweville,' he says. 'That's a relief. Why are you so upset?'

'It's nothing,' she says. 'Just the tone.'

They are parked, the two of them, in front of the post office. This is what they do on Friday afternoons, it is part of the routine they have created for themselves: last thing, after they have done the shopping and before driving back to the farm, they fetch the week's mail and scan it sitting side by side in the pickup. Though she could fetch the mail herself any day of the week, she does not. She and Lukas do it together, as they do together whatever else they can.

For the moment Lukas is absorbed in a letter from the Land Bank, with a long attachment, pages of figures, more important by far than mere family matters. 'Don't hurry, I'll go for a stroll,' she says, and gets out and crosses the street.

The post office is newly built, squat and heavy, with glass bricks instead of windows and a heavy steel grille over the door. She dislikes it. It looks, to her eye, like a police station. She thinks back with fondness to the old post office that was demolished to make way for it, the building that had once upon a time been the Truter house.

Not half her lifespan gone, and already she is hankering for the past!

It was never just a question of Merweville, of John and his father, of who was going to be living where, in the city or in the country. *What are we doing here?*: that had been the unspoken question all the time. He had known it and she had known it. Her own letter, however cowardly, had at least hinted at the question: *What are we doing in this barren part of the world? Why are we spending our lives in dreary toil if it was never meant that people should live here, if the whole project of humanizing the place was misconceived from the start?*

This part of the world. The part she means is not Merweville or Calvinia but the whole Karoo, perhaps the whole country. Whose idea was it to lay down roads and railway lines, build towns, bring in people and then bind them to this place, bind them with rivets through the heart, so that they cannot get away? *Better to cut yourself free and hope the wound heals,* he said when they were out walking in the veld. But how do you cut through rivets like that?

It is long past closing time. The post office is closed, the shops are closed, the street is deserted. Meyerowitz Jeweller. Babes in the Wood – Laybyes Accepted. Cosmos Café. Foschini Modes.

Meyerowitz ('Diamonds are Forever') has been here longer than she can remember. Babes in the Wood used to be Jan Harmse Slagter. Cosmos Café used to be Cosmos Milk Bar. Foschini Modes used to be Winterberg Algemene Handelaars. All this change, all this busyness! *O droewige land!* O sorrowful land! Foschini Modes is confident enough to open a new branch in Calvinia. What can her cousin the failed emigrant, the poet of melancholy, claim to know about the future of this land that Foschini does not? Her cousin who believes that even baboons, as they stare out over the veld, are overcome with *weemoed.*

Lukas is convinced there will be a political accommodation. John may claim to be a liberal, but Lukas is a more practical liberal than John will ever be, and a more courageous one too. If they chose to, Lukas and she, *boer* and *boervrou,* man and wife, could scrape together a living on their farm. They might have to tighten their belt a notch or two or three, but they would survive. If Lukas chooses instead to drive trucks for the Co-op, if she keeps the books for the hotel, it is not because the farm is a doomed enterprise but because she and Lukas made up their minds long ago they would house their workers properly and pay them a decent wage and make sure their children went to school and support those same workers later when they grew old and infirm; and because all that decency and support costs money, more money than the farm as a farm brings in or ever will bring in, in the foreseeable future.

A farm is not a business: such was the premise she and Lukas agreed on long ago. The Middelpos farm is home not only to the two of them with the ghosts of their unborn children but to thirteen other souls as well. To bring in the money to maintain the whole little community, Lukas has to spend days at a time on the road and she to pass her nights alone in Calvinia. That is what *she* means when she calls Lukas a liberal: he has a generous heart, a liberal heart; and through him she has learned to have a liberal heart too.

And what is wrong with that, as a way of life? That is the question she would like to ask her clever cousin, the one who first ran away from South Africa and now talks of cutting himself free. From what does he mean to free himself? From love? From duty? *My father sends his love, as do I.* What kind of lukewarm love is that? No, she and John may share the same blood but, whatever it is he feels for her, it is not love. Nor does he love his father, not really. Does not even love himself. And what is the point, anyway, of cutting oneself free of everyone and everything? What is he going to do with his freedom? *Love begins at home* – isn't that an English saying? Instead of forever running away, he should find himself a decent woman and look her straight in the eye and say: *Will you wed me? Will you wed me and welcome my aged parent into our home and care for him faithfully until he dies? If you will take on that burden, I will undertake to love you and be faithful to you and find a proper job and work hard and bring home my money and be cheerful and stop kvetching about the droewige vlaktes, the mournful plains.* She wishes he were here this moment, in Kerkstraat, Calvinia, so that she could *raas* with him, give him an earful as the English say: she is in the mood.

A whistle. She turns. It is Lukas, leaning out of the car window. *Skattie, hoe mompel jy dan nou?* he calls out, laughing. How come you are mumbling to yourself?

NO FURTHER LETTERS PASS between herself and her cousin. Before long he and his problems have ceased to have any place in her thoughts. More pressing concerns have arisen. The visas have come through that Klaus and Carol have been waiting for, the visas for the Promised Land. With swift efficiency they are readying themselves for the move. One of their first steps is to bring her mother, who has been staying with them and whom Klaus too calls Ma though he has a perfectly good mother of his own in Düsseldorf, back to the farm.

They drive the sixteen hundred kilometres from Johannesburg in twelve hours, taking turns at the wheel of the BMW. This feat affords Klaus much satisfaction. He and Carol have completed advanced driving courses and have certificates to show for it; they are looking forward to driving in America, where the roads are so much better than in South Africa, though not of course as good as the German *Autobahnen*.

Ma is not at all well: she, Margot, can see that as soon as she is helped out of the back seat. Her face is puffy, she is not breathing easily, she complains that her legs are sore. Ultimately, Carol explains, the problem lies with her heart: she has been seeing a specialist in Johannesburg and has a new sequence of pills to take three times a day without fail.

Klaus and Carol stay overnight on the farm, then set off back to the city. 'As soon as Ma improves, you and Lukas must bring her to America for a visit,' says Carol. 'We will help with the air fares.' Klaus embraces her, kissing her on both cheeks ('It is warmer that way'). With Lukas he shakes hands.

Lukas detests his brother-in-law. There is not the faintest chance that Lukas will go and visit them in America. As for Klaus, he has never been shy of expressing his verdict on South Africa. 'Beautiful country,' he says, 'beautiful landscapes, rich resources, but, many, many problems. How you will solve them I cannot see. In my opinion things will get worse before they will get better. But that is just my opinion.'

She would like to spit in his eye, but does not.

Her mother cannot stay alone on the farm while she and Lukas are away, there is no question of that. So she arranges for a second bed to be moved into her room at the hotel. It is inconvenient, it means the end of all privacy for her, but there is no alternative. She is billed full board for her mother, though in fact her mother eats like a bird.

They are into the second week of this new regime when a member of the cleaning staff comes upon her mother slumped on a couch in the empty hotel lounge, unconscious and blue in the face. She is rushed to the district hospital and resuscitated. The doctor on duty shakes his head. Her heartbeat is very weak, he says, she needs more urgent and more expert care than she can get in Calvinia; Upington is an option, there is a decent hospital there, but it would be preferable if she went to Cape Town.

Within an hour she, Margot, has shut her office and is on the way to Cape Town, sitting in the cramped back of the ambulance, holding her mother's hand. With them is a young Coloured nurse named Aletta, whose crisp, starched uniform and cheerful air soon set her at ease.

Aletta, it turns out, was born not far away, in Wuppertal in the Cederberg, where her parents still live. She has made the trip to Cape Town more times than she can count. She tells of how, only last week, they had to rush a man from Loeriesfontein to Groote Schuur Hospital along with three fingers packed in ice in a cool box, fingers he had lost in a mishap with a bandsaw.

'Your mother will be fine,' says Aletta. 'Groote Schuur – only the best.'

At Clanwilliam they stop for petrol. The ambulance driver, who is even younger than Aletta, has brought along a thermos flask of coffee. He offers her, Margot, a cup, but she declines. 'I'm cutting down on coffee,' she says (a lie), 'it keeps me awake.'

She would have liked to buy the two of them a cup of coffee at the café, would have liked to sit down with them in a normal, friendly way, but of course one could not do that without causing a fuss. *Let the time come soon, O Lord,* she prays to herself, *when all this apartheid nonsense will be buried and forgotten.*

They resume their places in the ambulance. Her mother is sleeping. Her colour is better, she is breathing evenly beneath the oxygen mask.

'I must tell you how much I appreciate what you and Johannes are doing for us,' she says to Aletta. Aletta smiles back in the friendliest of ways, with not the faintest trace of irony. She hopes for her words to be understood in their widest sense, with all the meaning that for very shame she cannot express: *I must tell you how grateful I am for what you and your colleague are doing for an old white woman and her daughter, two strangers who have never done anything for you but on the contrary have participated in your humiliation in the land of your birth, day after day after day. I am grateful for the lesson you teach me through your actions, in which I see only human kindness, and above all through that lovely smile of yours.*

They reach the city of Cape Town at the height of the afternoon rush hour. Though theirs is not, strictly speaking, an emergency, Johannes nevertheless sounds his siren as he coolly threads his way through the traffic. At the hospital she trails behind as her mother is wheeled into the emergency unit. By the time she returns to thank Aletta and Johannes, they have left, taken the long road back to the Northern Cape.

When I get back! she promises herself, meaning *When I get back to Calvinia I will make sure I thank them personally!* but also *When I get back I will become a better person, that I swear!* She also thinks: *Who was the man from Loeriesfontein who lost the three fingers? Is it only we whites who are rushed by ambulance to a hospital — only the best! — where well-trained surgeons will sew our fingers back on or give us a new heart as the case may be, and all at no cost? Let it not be so, O Lord, let it not be so!*

When she sees her again, her mother is in a room by herself, awake, in a clean white bed, wearing the nightdress that she, Margot, had the good sense to pack for her. She has lost her hectic colouring, is even able to push aside the mask and mumble a few words: 'Such a fuss!'

She raises her mother's delicate, in fact rather babyish hand to her lips. 'Nonsense,' she says. 'Now Ma must rest. I'll be right here if Ma needs me.'

Her plan is to spend the night at her mother's bedside, but the doctor in charge dissuades her. Her mother is not in danger, he says;

her condition is being monitored by the nursing staff; she will be given a sleeping pill and will sleep until morning. She, Margot, the dutiful daughter, has been through enough, best if she gets a good night's sleep herself. Does she have somewhere to stay?

She has a cousin in Cape Town, she replies, she can stay with him.

The doctor is older than her, unshaven, with dark, hooded eyes. She has been told his name but did not catch it. He may be Jewish, but there are many other things he may be too. He smells of cigarette smoke; there is a blue cigarette pack peeking out of his breast pocket. Does she believe him when he says that her mother is not in danger? Yes, she does; but she has always had a tendency to trust doctors, to believe what they say even when she knows they are just guessing; therefore she mistrusts her trust.

'Are you absolutely sure there is no danger, doctor?' she says.

He gives her a tired nod. Absolutely indeed! What is *absolutely* in human affairs? 'In order to take care of your mother you must take care of yourself,' he says.

She feels a welling-up of tears, a welling-up of self-pity too. *Take care of both of us!* she wants to plead. She would like to fall into the arms of this stranger, to be held and comforted. 'Thank you, doctor,' she says.

Lukas is on the road somewhere in the Northern Cape, uncontactable. She calls her cousin John from a public telephone. 'I'll come and fetch you at once,' says John. 'Stay with us as long as you like.'

Years have passed since she was last in Cape Town. She has never been to Tokai, the suburb where he and his father live. Their house sits behind a high wooden fence smelling strongly of damp-rot and engine oil. The night is dark, the pathway from the gate unlit; he takes her arm to guide her. 'Be warned,' he says, 'it is all a bit of a mess.'

At the front door her uncle awaits her. He greets her distractedly; he is agitated in a way that she is familiar with among the Coetzees, talking rapidly, running his fingers through his hair. 'Ma is fine,' she reassures him, 'it was just an episode.' But he prefers not to be reassured, he is in the mood for drama.

John leads her on a tour of the premises. The house is small, ill-lit, stuffy; it smells of wet newspaper and fried bacon. If she were in charge she would tear down the dreary curtains and replace them with something lighter and brighter; but of course in this men's world she is not in charge.

He shows her into the room that is to be hers. Her heart sinks. The carpet is mottled with what look like oil stains. Against the wall is a low single bed, and beside it a desk on which books and papers lie piled higgledy-piggledy. Glaring down from the ceiling is the same kind of neon lamp they used to have in the office in the hotel before she had it removed.

Everything here seems to be of the same hue: a brown verging in one direction on dull yellow and in the other on dingy grey. She doubts very much that the house has been cleaned, properly cleaned, in years.

Normally this is his bedroom, John explains. He has changed the sheets on the bed; he will empty two drawers for her use. Across the passage are the necessary facilities.

She explores the necessary facilities. The bathroom is grimy, the toilet stained, smelling of old urine.

Since leaving Calvinia she has had nothing to eat but a chocolate bar. She is famished. John offers her what he calls French toast, white bread soaked in egg and fried, of which she eats three slices. He also gives her tea with milk that turns out to be sour (she drinks it anyway).

Her uncle sidles into the kitchen, wearing a pyjama top over his trousers. 'I'll say goodnight, Margie,' he says. 'Sleep tight. Don't let the fleas bite.' He does not say goodnight to his son. Around his son he seems distinctly tentative. Have they been having a fight?

'I'm restless,' she says to John. 'Shall we go for a walk? I've been cooped up in the back of an ambulance all day.'

He takes her on a ramble through the well-lit streets of suburban Tokai. The houses they pass are all bigger and better than his. 'This used to be farmland not long ago,' he explains. 'Then it was subdivided and sold in lots. Our house used to be a farm-labourer's cottage. That's why it is so shoddily built. Everything leaks: roof, walls. I spend all my free time doing repairs. I'm like the boy with his finger in the dyke.'

'Yes, I begin to see the attraction of Merweville. At least in Merweville it doesn't rain. But why not buy a better house here in the Cape? Write a book. Write a best-seller. Make lots of money.'

It is only a joke, but he chooses to take it seriously. 'I wouldn't know how to write a best-seller,' he says. 'I don't know enough about people and their fantasy lives. Anyway, I wasn't destined for that fate.'

'What fate?'

'The fate of being a rich and successful writer.'

'Then what is the fate you are destined for?'

'For exactly the present one. For living with an ageing parent in a house in the white suburbs with a leaky roof.'

'That's just silly, *slap* talk. That's the Coetzee in you speaking. You could change your fate tomorrow if you would just put your mind to it.'

The dogs of the neighbourhood do not take kindly to strangers roaming their streets by night, arguing. The chorus of barking grows clamorous.

'I wish you could hear yourself, John,' she plunges on. 'You are so full of nonsense! If you don't take hold of yourself you are going to turn into a sour old prune of a man who wants only to be left alone in his corner. Let's go back. I have to get up early.'

SHE SLEEPS BADLY ON the uncomfortable, hard mattress. Before first light she is up, making coffee and toast for the three of them. By seven o'clock they are on their way to Groote Schuur Hospital, crammed together in the cab of the Datsun.

She leaves Jack and his son in the waiting room, but then cannot locate her mother. Her mother had an episode during the night, she is informed at the nurses' station, and is back in intensive care. She, Margot, should return to the waiting room, where a doctor will speak to her.

She rejoins Jack and John. The waiting room is already filling up. A woman, a stranger, is slumped in a chair opposite them. Over her head, covering one eye, she has knotted a woollen pullover caked with blood. She wears a tiny skirt and rubber sandals; she smells of mouldy linen and sweet wine; she is moaning softly to herself.

She does her best not to stare, but the woman is itching for a fight. '*Waarna loer jy?*' she glares: What are you staring at? '*Jou moer!*'

She casts her eyes down, withdraws into silence.

Her mother, if she lives, will be sixty-eight next month. Sixty-eight blameless years, blameless and contented. A good woman, all in all: a good mother, a good wife of the distracted, fluttering variety. The kind of woman men find it easy to love because she so clearly needs to be protected. And now cast into this hell-hole! *Jou moer!* – filthy talk. She must get her mother out as soon as she can, and into a private hospital, no matter what the cost.

My little bird, that is what her father used to call her: *my tortelduifie*, my little turtledove. The kind of little bird that prefers not to leave its cage. Growing up she, Margot, had felt big and ungainly beside her mother. *Who will ever love me?* she had asked herself. *Who will ever call me his little dove?*

Someone is tapping her on the shoulder. 'Mrs Jonker?' A fresh young nurse. 'Your mother is awake, she is asking for you.'

'Come,' she says. Jack and John follow her.

Her mother is conscious, she is calm, so calm as to seem a little remote. The oxygen mask has been replaced with a tube into her nose. Her eyes have lost their colour, turned into flat grey pebbles. 'Margie?' she whispers.

She presses her lips to her mother's brow. 'I'm here, Ma,' she says.

The doctor enters, the same doctor as before, with the dark-rimmed eyes. *Kiristany* says the badge on his coat. On duty yesterday afternoon, still on duty this morning.

Her mother has had a cardiac episode, says Doctor Kiristany, but is now stable. She is very weak. Her heart is being stimulated electrically.

'I would like to move my mother to a private hospital,' she says to him, 'somewhere quieter than this.'

He shakes his head. Impossible, he says. He cannot give his consent. Perhaps in a few days' time, if she rallies.

She stands back. Jack bends over his sister, murmuring words she cannot hear. Her mother's eyes are open, her lips move, she seems to be replying. Two old people, two innocents, born in olden times, out of place in the loud, angry place this country has become.

'John?' she says. 'Do you want to speak to Ma?'

He shakes his head. 'She won't know me,' he says.

[Silence.]

And?

That's the end.

The end? But why stop there?

It seems a good place. She won't know me: a good line.

[Silence.]

Well, what is your verdict?

My verdict? I still don't understand: if it is a book about John why are you putting in so much about me? Who is going to want to read about me — me and Lukas and my mother and Carol and Klaus?

You were part of your cousin. He was part of you. That is plain enough, surely. What I am asking is, can it stand as it is?

Not as it is, no. I want to go over it again, as you promised.

Interviews conducted in Somerset West, South Africa,
December 2007 and June 2008.

Adriana

SENHORA NASCIMENTO, YOU ARE Brazilian by birth, but you spent several years in South Africa. How did that come about?

We went to South Africa from Angola, my husband and I and our two daughters. In Angola my husband worked for a newspaper and I had a job with the National Ballet. But then in 1973 the government declared an emergency and shut down his newspaper. They wanted to call him up into the army too – they were calling up all men under the age of forty-five, even those who were not citizens. We could not go back to Brazil, it was still too dangerous, we saw no future for ourselves in Angola, so we left, we took the boat to South Africa. We were not the first to do that, or the last.

And why Cape Town?

Why Cape Town? No special reason, except that we had a relative there, a cousin of my husband's who owned a fruit and vegetable shop. After we arrived we stayed with him and his family, it was difficult for all of us, nine people in three rooms, while we waited for our residence papers. Then my husband managed to find a job as a security guard and we could move into a flat of our own. That was in a place called Epping. A few months later, just before the disaster that ruined everything, we moved again, to Wynberg, to be nearer the children's school.

What disaster do you refer to?

My husband was working night shifts guarding a warehouse near the docks. He was the only guard. There was a robbery – a gang of men broke in. They attacked him, hit him with an axe. Maybe it was a machete, but more likely it was an axe. One side of his face was smashed in. I still don't find it easy to talk about. An axe. Hitting a man in the face with an axe because he is doing his job. I can't understand it.

What happened to him?

There were injuries to his brain. He died. It took a long time, nearly a year, but he died. It was terrible.

I'm sorry.

Yes. For a while the firm he worked for went on paying his wages. Then the money stopped coming. He was not their responsibility any more, they said, he was the responsibility of Social Welfare. Social Welfare! Social Welfare never gave us a cent. My older daughter had to leave school. She took a job as a packer in a supermarket. That brought in a hundred and twenty rands a week. I looked for work too, but I couldn't find a position in ballet, they weren't interested in my kind of ballet, so I had to teach classes at a dance studio. Latin American. Latin American was popular in South Africa in those days. Maria Regina stayed at school. She still had the rest of that year and the next year before she could matriculate. Maria Regina, my younger daughter. I wanted her to get her certificate, not follow her sister into the supermarket, putting cans on shelves for the rest of her life. She was the clever one. She loved books.

In Luanda my husband and I had made an effort to speak a little English at the dinner table, also a little French, just to remind the girls Angola wasn't the whole world, but they didn't really pick it up. In Cape Town English was Maria Regina's weakest school subject. So I enrolled her for extra lessons in English. The school ran these extra lessons in the afternoons for children like her, new arrivals. That was when I began to hear about Mr Coetzee, the man you are asking about, who, as it turned out, was not one of the regular teachers, no, not at all, but was hired by the school to teach these extra classes.

This Mr Coetzee sounds like an Afrikaner to me, I said to Maria Regina. Can't your school afford a proper English teacher? I want you to learn proper English, from an English person.

I never liked Afrikaners. We saw lots of them in Angola, working for the mines or as mercenaries in the army. They treated the blacks like dirt. I didn't like that. In South Africa my husband picked up a few words of Afrikaans – he had to, the security firm was all Afrikaners – but as for me, I didn't even like to listen to the language. Thank God the school did not make the girls learn Afrikaans, that would have been too much.

Mr Coetzee is not an Afrikaner, said Maria Regina. He has a beard. He writes poetry.

Afrikaners can have beards too, I told her, you don't need a beard to write poetry. I want to see this Mr Coetzee for myself, I don't like the sound of him. Tell him to come here to the flat. Tell him to come and drink tea with us and show he is a proper teacher. What is this poetry he writes?

Maria Regina started to fidget. She was at an age when children don't like you to interfere in their school life. But I told her, as long as I pay for extra lessons I will interfere as much as I want. What kind of poetry does this man write?

I don't know, she said. He makes us recite poetry. He makes us learn it by heart.

What does he make you learn by heart? I said. Tell me.

Keats, she said.

What is Keats? I said (I had never heard of Keats, I knew none of those old English writers, we didn't study them in the days when I was at school).

A drowsy numbness overtakes my sense, Maria Regina recited, as though of hemlock I had drunk. Hemlock is poison. It attacks your nervous system.

That is what this Mr Coetzee makes you learn? I said.

It's in the book, she said. It's one of the poems we have to learn for the exam.

My daughters were always complaining I was too strict with them.

But I never yielded. Only by watching over them like a hawk could I keep them out of trouble in this strange country where they were not at home, on a continent where we should never have come. Joana was easier, Joana was the good girl, the quiet one. Maria Regina was more reckless, more ready to challenge me. I had to keep Maria Regina on a tight rein, Maria with her poetry and her romantic dreams.

There was the question of the invitation, the correct way to phrase an invitation to your daughter's teacher to visit her parents' home and drink tea. I spoke to Mario's cousin, but he was no help. So in the end I had to ask the receptionist at the dance studio to write the letter for me. 'Dear Mr Coetzee,' she wrote, 'I am the mother of Maria Regina Nascimento, who is in your English class. You are invited to a tea at our residence' – I gave the address – 'on such-and-such a day at such-and-such a time. Transport from the school will be arranged. RSVP Adriana Teixeira Nascimento.'

By transport I meant Manuel, the eldest son of Mario's cousin, who used to give Maria Regina a lift home in the afternoons, in his van, after he had made his deliveries. It would be easy for him to pick up the teacher too.

Mario was your husband.

Mario. My husband, who died.

Please go on. I just wanted to be sure.

Mr Coetzee was the first person who was invited to our flat – the first one outside Mario's family. He was only a schoolteacher – we met plenty of schoolteachers in Luanda, and before Luanda in São Paulo, I had no special esteem for them – but to Maria Regina and even to Joana schoolteachers were gods and goddesses, and I saw no reason why I should disillusion them. The evening before his visit the girls baked a cake and iced it and even wrote on it (they wanted to write 'Welcome Mr Coetzee' but I made them write 'St Bonaventure 1974'). They also baked trayfuls of the little biscuits that in Brazil we call *brevidades*.

Maria Regina was very excited. *Come home early, please, please!* I heard her urging her sister. *Tell your supervisor you are feeling ill!* But Joana wasn't prepared to do that. It is not so easy to take time off, she said, they dock your pay if you don't complete your shift.

So Manuel brought Mr Coetzee to our flat, and I could see at once he was no god. He was in his early thirties, I estimated, badly dressed, with badly cut hair and a beard when he shouldn't have worn a beard, his beard was too thin. Also he struck me at once, I can't say why, as *célibataire*. I mean not just unmarried but also not suited to marriage, like a man who has spent his life in the priesthood and lost his manhood and become incompetent with women. Also his comportment was not good (I am telling you my first impressions). He seemed ill at ease, itching to get away. He had not learned to hide his feelings, which is the first step towards civilized manners.

'How long are you a teacher, Mr Coetzee?' I asked.

He squirmed in his seat, said something I don't remember any more about America, about being a teacher in America. Then, after more questions, it emerged that in fact he had never taught in a school before this one, and – what is worse – did not even have a teacher's certificate. Of course I was surprised. 'If you don't have a certificate, how come you are Maria Regina's teacher?' I said. 'I don't understand.'

The answer, which again took a long time to squeeze out of him, was that, for subjects like music and ballet and foreign languages, schools were permitted to hire persons who had no qualifications, or at least did not have certificates of competence. These unqualified persons would not be paid salaries like proper teachers, they would instead be paid by the school with money collected from parents like me.

'But you are not English,' I said. It was not a question this time, it was an accusation. Here he was, hired to teach the English language, paid out of my money and Joana's money, yet he was not a teacher, and moreover he was an Afrikaner, not an Englishman.

'I agree I am not of English descent,' he said. 'Nevertheless I have spoken English from an early age and have passed university examinations in English, therefore I believe I can teach English. There is nothing special about English. It is just one language among many.'

That is what he said. English is just one language among many. 'My daughter is not going to be like a parrot that mixes up languages, Mr Coetzee,' I said. 'I want her to speak English properly, and with a proper English accent.'

Fortunately for him, this was the moment when Joana arrived home. Joana was already twenty by then, but in the presence of a man she was still bashful. Compared with her sister she was not a beauty – look, here is a snapshot of her with her husband and their little boys, it was taken some time after we moved back to Brazil, you can see, not a beauty, all the beauty went to her sister – but she was a good girl and I always knew she would make a good wife.

Joana came into the room where we were sitting, still wearing her raincoat (I remember that long raincoat of hers). 'My sister,' said Maria Regina, as if she was explaining who this new person was rather than introducing her. Joana said nothing, just looked shy, and as for Mr Coetzee the teacher, he almost knocked over the coffee table trying to get to his feet.

Why is Maria Regina besotted with this foolish man? What does she see in him? That was the question I asked myself. It was easy enough to guess what a lonely *célibataire* might see in my daughter, who was turning into a real dark-eyed beauty though she was still only a child, but what made her learn poems by heart for this man, something she had never done for her other teachers? Had he perhaps been whispering words to her that had turned her head? Was that the explanation? Was there something going on between the two of them that she was keeping secret from me?

Now if this man were to become interested in Joana, I thought to myself, it would be a different story. Joana may not have a head for poetry, but at least she has her feet on the ground.

'Joana is working this year at Clicks,' I said. 'To get experience. Next year she will take a management course. To be a manager.'

Mr Coetzee nodded abstractedly. Joana said nothing at all.

'Take off your coat, my child,' I said, 'and drink some tea.' We did not normally drink tea, we drank coffee. Joana brought home some tea the day before for this guest of ours, Earl Grey tea it was called, very English but not very nice, I wondered what we were going to do with the rest of the packet.

'Mr Coetzee is from the school,' I repeated to Joana, as if she did not know. 'He is telling us how he is not English but is nevertheless the English teacher.'

'I am not, properly speaking, the English teacher,' Mr Coetzee interjected, addressing Joana. 'I am the Extra English teacher. That means I have been hired by the school to help students who are having difficulty with English. I try to get them through the examinations. So I am a kind of examination coach. That would be a better description of what I do, a better name for me.'

'Do we have to talk about school?' said Maria Regina. 'It is so boring.'

But what we were talking about was not boring at all. Painful, perhaps, for Mr Coetzee, but not boring. 'Go on,' I said to him, ignoring her.

'I do not intend to be an examination coach for the rest of my life,' he said. 'It is something I am doing for the present, something I happen to be qualified to do, in order to make a living. But it is not my vocation. It is not what I was called into the world to do.'

Called into the world. More and more strange.

'If you would like me to explain my philosophy of teaching I can do so,' he said. 'It is quite brief, brief and simple.'

'Go on,' I said, 'let us hear your brief philosophy.'

'What I call my philosophy of teaching is in fact a philosophy of learning. It comes out of Plato, modified. Before true learning can occur, I believe, there must be in the student's heart a certain yearning for the truth, a certain fire. The true student burns to know. In the teacher she recognizes, or apprehends, the one who has come closer than herself to the truth. So much does she desire the truth embodied in the teacher that she is prepared to burn her old self up to attain it. For his part, the teacher recognizes and encourages the fire in the student, and responds to it by burning with an intenser light. Thus together the two of them ascend to a higher realm. So to speak.'

He paused, smiling. Now that he had had his say he seemed more relaxed. *What a strange, vain man!* I thought. *Burn herself up! What nonsense he talks! Dangerous nonsense too! Out of Plato! Is he making fun of us?* But Maria Regina, I noticed, was leaning forward, devouring his face with her eyes. Maria Regina did not think he was joking. *This is not good! I* said to myself.

'That does not sound like philosophy to me, Mr Coetzee,' I said, 'it sounds like something else, I will not say what, since you are our guest. Maria, you can fetch the cake now. Joana, help her; and take off that raincoat. My daughters baked a cake last night in honour of your visit.'

The moment the girls were out of the room I went to the heart of the matter, speaking softly so that they would not hear. 'Maria is still a child, Mr Coetzee. I am paying for her to learn English and get a good certificate. I am not paying for you to play with her feelings. Do you understand?' The girls came back, bearing their cake. 'Do you understand?' I repeated.

'We learn what we most deeply want to learn,' he replied. 'Maria wants to learn – do you not, Maria?'

Maria flushed and sat down.

'Maria wants to learn,' he repeated, 'and she is making good progress. She has a feeling for language. Maybe she will become a writer one day. What a magnificent cake!'

'It is good when a girl can bake,' I said, 'but it is even better when she can speak good English and get good marks in her English examination.'

'Good elocution, good marks,' he said. 'I understand your wishes perfectly.'

When he had left, when the girls had gone to bed, I sat down and wrote him a letter in my bad English, I could not help that, it was not the kind of letter my friend at the studio should see.

Respected Mr Coetzee, I wrote, I repeat what I told you during your visit. You are employed to teach my daughter English, not to play with her feelings. She is a child, you are a grown man. If you wish to expose your feelings, expose them outside the classroom. Yours faithfully, ATN.

That is what I said. It may not be how you speak in English, but it is how we speak in Portuguese – your translator will understand. *Expose your feelings outside the classroom* – that was not an invitation to him to pursue me, it was a warning to him not to pursue my daughter.

I sealed up the letter in an envelope and wrote his name on it, Mr

Coetzee | Saint Bonaventure, and on the Monday morning I put it in Maria Regina's bag. 'Give it to Mr Coetzee,' I said, 'put it in his hand.'

'What is it?' said Maria Regina.

'It is a note from a parent to her daughter's teacher, it is not for your eyes. Now go, or you will miss your bus.'

Of course I made a mistake, I should not have said, *It is not for your eyes*. Maria Regina was beyond the age where, if your mother gives you a command, you obey. She was beyond that age but I did not know it yet. I was living in the past.

'Did you give the note to Mr Coetzee?' I asked when she came home.

'Yes,' she said, and nothing more. I did not think I needed to ask, *Did you open it in secret and read it before you gave it to him?*

The next day, to my surprise, Maria Regina brought back a note from this teacher of hers, not an answer to mine but an invitation: would we all like to come on a picnic with him and his father? At first I was going to refuse. 'Think,' I said to Maria Regina: 'Do you really want your friends at school to get the impression you are the teacher's favourite? Do you really want them to gossip behind your back?' But that weighed nothing with her, she *wanted* to be the teacher's favourite. She pressed me and pressed me to accept, and Joana backed her up, so in the end I said yes.

There was lots of excitement at home, and lots of baking, and Joana brought things from the shop too, so when Mr Coetzee came to fetch us on the Sunday morning we had a whole basket of cakes and biscuits and sweets with us, enough to feed an army.

He did not fetch us in a car, he did not have a car, no, he came in a truck, the kind that is open at the back, that in Brazil we call a *caminhonete*. So the girls, in their nice clothes, had to sit in the back with the firewood while I sat in the front with him and his father.

That was the only time I met his father. His father was quite old already, and unsteady, with hands that trembled. I thought he might be trembling because he found himself sitting next to a strange woman, but later I saw his hands trembled all the time. When he was introduced to us he said 'How do you do?' very nicely, very courteously, but after that he shut up. All the time we drove he did not speak, not to me, not to

410

his son either. A very quiet man, very humble, or perhaps just frightened of everything.

We drove up into the mountains – we had to stop to let the girls put on their coats, they were getting cold – to a park, I don't remember the name now, where there were pine trees and places where people could have picnics, white people only, of course – a nice place, almost empty because it was winter. As soon as we chose our place Mr Coetzee made himself busy unloading the truck and building a fire. I expected Maria Regina to help him, but she slipped away, she said she wanted to explore. That was not a good sign. Because if relations had been comme il faut between them, just a teacher and a student, she would not have been embarrassed to help. But it was Joana who came forward instead, Joana was very good that way, very practical and efficient.

So there I was, left behind with his father as if we were the two old people, the grandparents! I found it hard talking to him, as I said, he could not understand my English and was shy too, with a woman; or maybe he just didn't understand who I was.

And then, even before the fire was burning properly, clouds came over and it grew dark and started to rain. 'It is just a shower, it will soon pass,' said Mr Coetzee. 'Why don't the three of you get into the truck.' So the girls and I took shelter in the truck, and he and his father huddled under a tree, and we waited for the rain to pass. But of course it did not, it went on raining and gradually the girls lost their good spirits. 'Why does it have to rain today of all days?' whined Maria Regina, just like a baby. 'Because it is winter,' I told her: 'because it is winter and intelligent people, people with their feet on the ground, don't go out on picnics in the middle of winter.'

The fire that Mr Coetzee and Joana had built went out. All the wood was wet by now, so we would never be able to cook our meat. 'Why don't you offer them some of the biscuits you baked?' I said to Maria Regina. Because I had never seen a more miserable sight than those two Dutchmen, the father and the son, sitting together side by side under a tree trying to pretend they were not cold and wet. A miserable sight, but funny too. 'Offer them some biscuits and ask them what we are going to do next. Ask them if they would like to take us to the beach for a swim.'

I said this to make Maria Regina smile, but all I did was make her more cross; so in the end it was Joana who went out in the rain and talked to them and came back with the message that we would leave as soon as it stopped raining, we would go back to their house and they would make tea for us. 'No,' I said to Joana. 'Go back and tell Mr Coetzee no, we cannot come to tea, he must take us straight back to the flat, tomorrow is Monday and Maria Regina has homework that she hasn't even started on.'

Of course it was an unhappy day for Mr Coetzee. He had hoped to make a good impression on me; maybe he also wanted to show off to his father the three attractive Brazilian ladies who were his friends; and instead all he got was a truck full of wet people driving through the rain. But to me it was good that Maria Regina should see what her hero was like in real life, this poet who could not even make a fire.

So that is the story of our expedition into the mountains with Mr Coetzee. When at last we got back in Wynberg, I said to him, in front of his father, in front of the girls, what I had been waiting to say all day. 'It was very kind of you to invite us out, Mr Coetzee, very gentlemanly,' I said, 'but maybe it is not a good idea for a teacher to be favouring one girl in his class above all others just because she is pretty. I am not admonishing you, just asking you to reflect.'

Those were the words I used: *just because she is pretty*. Maria Regina was furious with me for speaking like that, but as for me, I did not care as long as I was understood.

Later that night, when Maria Regina had already gone to bed, Joana came to my room. 'Mamãe, must you be so hard on Maria?' she said. 'Truly, there is nothing bad going on.'

'Nothing bad?' I said. 'What do you know of the world? What do you know of badness? What do you know of what men will do?'

'He is not a bad man, mamãe,' she said. 'Surely you can see that.'

'He is a weak man,' I said. 'A weak man is worse than a bad man. A weak man does not know where to stop. A weak man is helpless before his impulses, he follows wherever they lead.'

'Mamãe, we are all weak,' said Joana.

'No, you are wrong, I am not weak,' I said. 'Where would we be, you and Maria Regina and I, if I allowed myself to be weak? Now go to bed. And don't repeat any of this to Maria Regina. Not a word. She will not understand.'

I hoped that would be the end of Mr Coetzee. But no, a day or two later there arrived a letter from him, not via Maria Regina this time but through the mail, a formal letter, typed, the envelope typed too. In it he first apologized for the picnic that had been a failure. He had hoped to speak to me in private, he said, but had had no chance. Could he come and see me? Could he come to the flat, or would I prefer to meet him elsewhere, perhaps have lunch with him? The matter that weighed on him was not Maria Regina, he wanted to stress. Maria was an intelligent young woman, with a good heart; it was a privilege to teach her; I could be assured he would never, *never* betray the trust I had put in him. Intelligent and beautiful too – he hoped I would not mind if he said that. For beauty, true beauty, was more than skin-deep, it was the soul showing through the flesh; and where could Maria Regina have got her beauty but from me?

[Silence.]

And?

That was all. That was the substance. Could he meet me alone.

Of course I asked myself where he had got the idea that I would want to meet him, even want to receive a letter from him. Because I never said a word to encourage him.

So what did you do? Did you meet him?

What did I do? I did nothing and hoped he would leave me alone. I was a woman in mourning, though my husband was not dead, I did not want the attentions of other men, particularly of a man who was my daughter's teacher.

Do you still have that letter?

I don't have any of his letters. I did not keep them. When we left South Africa I did a clean-out of the flat and threw away all the old letters and bills.

And you did not reply?

No.

You did not reply and you did not allow relations to develop any further — relations between yourself and Coetzee?

What is this? Why these questions? You come all the way from England to talk to me, you tell me you are writing a biography of a man who happened many years ago to be my daughter's English teacher, and now suddenly you feel you are permitted to interrogate me about my 'relations'? What kind of biography are you writing? Is it like Hollywood gossip, like secrets of the rich and famous? If I refuse to discuss my so-called relations with this man, will you say I am keeping them secret? No, I did not have, to use your word, *relations* with Mr Coetzee. I will say more. For me it was not natural to have feelings for a man like that, a man who was so soft. Yes, soft.

Are you suggesting he was homosexual?

I am not suggesting anything. But there was a quality he lacked that a woman looks for in a man, a quality of strength, of manliness. My husband had that quality. He always had it, but his time in prison here in Brazil, under the *militares*, brought it out more clearly, even though he was not in prison a long time, only six months. After those six months, he used to say, nothing that human beings did to other human beings could come as a surprise to him. Coetzee had no such experience behind him to test his manhood and teach him about life. That is why I say he was soft. He was not a man, he was still a boy.

[Silence.]

414

As for homosexual, no, I do not say he was homosexual, but he was, as I told you, *célibataire* – I don't know the word for that in English.

A bachelor type? Sexless? Asexual?

No, not sexless. Solitary. Not made for conjugal life. Not made for the company of women.

[Silence.]

You mentioned that there were further letters.

Yes, when I did not reply he wrote again. He wrote many times. Perhaps he thought that if he wrote enough words they would eventually wear me down, like the waves of the sea wear down a rock. I put his letters away in the bureau; some I did not even read. But I thought to myself, *Among the many things this man lacks, the many many things, one is a tutor to give him lessons in love.* Because if you have fallen in love with a woman you do not sit down and type her one long letter after another, pages and pages, each one ending 'Yours sincerely'. No, you write a letter in your own hand, a proper love-letter, and have it delivered to her with a bouquet of red roses. But then I thought, perhaps this is how these Dutch Protestants behave when they fall in love: prudently, long-windedly, without fire, without grace. And no doubt that is how his lovemaking would be too, if he ever got a chance.

I put his letters away and said nothing of them to the children. That was a mistake. I could easily have said to Maria Regina, *That Mr Coetzee of yours has written me a note to apologize for Sunday. He mentions that he is pleased with your progress in English.* But I was silent, which in the end led to much trouble. Even today, I think, Maria Regina has not forgotten or forgiven.

Do you understand such things, Mr Vincent? Are you married? Do you have children?

Yes, I am married. We have one child, a boy. He will be four next month.

Boys are different. I don't know about boys. But I will tell you one thing, *entre nous*, which you must not repeat in your book. I love both my daughters, but I loved Maria in a different way from Joana. I loved her but I was also very critical of her as she grew up. Joana I was never critical of. Joana was always very simple, very straightforward. But Maria was a charmer. She could – do you use the expression? – twist a man around her finger. If you could have seen her, you would know what I mean.

What has become of her?

She is in her second marriage now. She is living in North America, in Chicago, with her American husband. He is a lawyer in a law firm. I think she is happy with him. I think she has made her peace with the world. Before that she had personal problems, which I will not go into.

Do you have a picture of her that I could perhaps use in the book?

I don't know. I will look. I will see. But it is getting late. Your colleague must be exhausted. Yes, I know how it is, being a translator. It looks easy from the outside, but the truth is you have to pay attention all the time, you cannot relax, the brain gets fatigued. So we stop here. Switch off your machine.

Can we speak again tomorrow?

Tomorrow is not convenient. Wednesday, yes. It is not such a long story, the story of myself and Mr Coetzee. I am sorry if it is a disappointment to you. You come all this way, and now you find there was no grand love affair with a dancer, just a brief infatuation, that is the word I would use, a brief, one-sided infatuation that never grew into anything. Come again on Wednesday at the same hour. I will give you tea.

You asked, last time, about pictures. I searched, but it is as I thought, I have none from those years in Cape Town. However, let me show you this one. It was taken at the airport the day we arrived back in São Paulo, by my sister, who came to meet us. See, there we are, the three of us. That is Maria Regina. The date was 1977, she was eighteen, getting on for nineteen. As you can see, a very pretty girl with a nice figure. And that is Joana, and that is me.

They are quite tall, your daughters. Was their father tall?

Yes, Mario was a big man. The girls are not so tall, it is just that they look tall when they are standing next to me.

Well, thank you for showing me. Can I take it away and have a copy made?

For your book? No, I cannot allow that. If you want Maria Regina in your book you must ask her yourself, I cannot speak for her.

I would like to include it as a picture of the three of you together.

No. If you want pictures of the girls you must ask them. As for me, no, I have decided no. It will be taken the wrong way. People will assume I was one of the women in his life, and it was never so.

Yet you were important to him. He was in love with you.

That is what you say. But the truth is, if he was in love, it was not with me, it was with some fantasy that he dreamed up in his own brain and gave my name to. You think I should feel flattered that you want to put me in your book as his lover? You are wrong. To me this man was not a famous writer, he was just a schoolteacher, a schoolteacher who didn't even have a diploma. Therefore no. No picture. What else? What else do you want me to tell you?

You were telling me last time about the letters he wrote you. I know you said you did not always read them; nevertheless, do you by any chance recall more of what he said in them?

One letter was about Franz Schubert – you know Schubert, the musician. He said that listening to Schubert had taught him one of the great secrets of love: how we can sublime love as chemists in the old days sublimed base substances. I remember the letter because of the word *sublime*. Sublime base substances: it made no sense to me. I looked up *sublime* in the big English dictionary I bought for the girls. To sublime: to heat something and extract its essence. We have the same word in Portuguese, *sublimar*, though it is not common. But what did it all mean? That he sat with his eyes closed listening to the music of Schubert while in his mind he heated his love for me, his *base substance*, into something higher, something more spiritual? It was nonsense, worse than nonsense. It did not make me love him, on the contrary it made me recoil.

It was from Schubert that he had learned to sublime love, he said. Not until he met me did he understand why in music movements are called movements. *Movement in stillness, stillness in movement*. That was another phrase I puzzled my head over. What did he mean, and why was he writing these things to me?

You have a good memory.

Yes, there is nothing wrong with my memory. My body is another story. I have arthritis of the hips, that is why I use a stick. The dancer's curse, they call it. And the pain – you will not believe the pain! But I remember South Africa very well. I remember the flat where we lived in Wynberg, where Mr Coetzee came to drink tea. I remember the mountain, Table Mountain. The flat was right under the mountain, so it got no sun in the afternoons. I hated Wynberg. I hated the whole time we spent there, first when my husband was in hospital and then after he died. It was very lonely for me, I cannot tell you how lonely. Worse than Luanda, because of the loneliness. If your Mr Coetzee had offered us his friendship I would not have been so hard on him, so cold. But I was not interested in love, I was still too close to my husband, still grieving for him. And he was just a boy, this Mr Coetzee. I was a woman and he was a boy. He was a boy as a priest is always a boy until suddenly one day he is an old man. The sublimation of love! He was offering to teach me about love, yet what could a boy like him teach me, a boy who knew nothing about life? I could have taught him, perhaps, but I was not interested in him. I just wanted him to keep his hands off Maria Regina.

You say, if he had offered you friendship it would have been different. What kind of friendship did you have in mind?

What kind of friendship? I will tell you. For a long time after the disaster that came over us, the disaster I told you about, I had to struggle with the bureaucracy, first over compensation, then over Joana's papers – Joana was born before we were married, so legally she was not my husband's daughter, she was not even his step-daughter, I will not bore you with the details. I know, in every country the bureaucracy is a labyrinth, I am not saying South Africa was the worst in the world, but whole days I would spend waiting in a line to get a rubber stamp – a rubber stamp for this, a rubber stamp for that – and always, *always* it would be the wrong office or the wrong department or the wrong line.

If we had been Portuguese it would have been different. There were many Portuguese who came to South Africa in those days, from Moçambique and Angola and even Madeira, there were organizations to help the Portuguese. But we were from Brazil, and there were no regulations for Brazilians, no precedents, to the bureaucrats it was as if we arrived in their country from Mars.

And there was the problem of my husband. You cannot sign for this, your husband must come and sign, they would say to me. My husband cannot sign, he is in hospital, I would say. Then take it to him in the hospital and get him to sign it and bring it back, they would say. My husband cannot sign anything, I would say, he is in Stikland, don't you know Stikland? Then let him make his mark, they would say. He cannot make his mark, sometimes he cannot even breathe, I would say. Then we cannot help you, they would say. Go to such-and-such an office and tell them your story – perhaps they can help you there.

And all of this pleading and petitioning I had to do alone, unaided, with my bad English that I had learned in school out of books. In Brazil it would have been easy, in Brazil we have these people, we call them *despachantes*, facilitators: they have contacts in the government offices, they know how to steer your papers through the maze, you pay them a fee and they do all the unpleasant business for you one-two-three. That was what I needed in Cape Town: a facilitator, someone to make things easier for me. Mr Coetzee could have offered to be my facilitator. A facilitator for me and a protector for my girls. Then, just for a minute, just for a day, I could have allowed myself to be weak, an ordinary, weak woman. But no, I dared not relax, or what would have become of us, my daughters and me?

Sometimes, you know, I would be trudging the streets of that ugly, windy city from one government office to another and I would hear this little cry come from my throat, yi-yi-yi, so soft that no one around me could hear. I was in distress. I was like an animal calling out in distress.

Let me tell you about my poor husband. When they opened the warehouse the morning after the attack and found him lying there in his blood, they were sure he was dead. They wanted to take him straight to the morgue. But he was not dead. He was a strong man, he fought and fought against death and held death at bay. In the city hospital, I forget its name, the famous one, they did one operation after another on his brain. Then they moved him from there to the hospital I mentioned, the one called Stikland, which was outside the city, an hour by train. Sunday was the only day you were allowed to visit Stikland. So every Sunday morning I would catch the train from Cape Town, and then the train back in the afternoon. That is another thing I remember as if it were yesterday: those sad journeys back and forth.

There was no improvement in my husband, no change. Week after week I would arrive and he would be lying in exactly the same position as before, with his eyes closed and his arms at his sides. They kept his head shaved, so you could see the stitch marks in his scalp. Also for a long time his face was covered with a wire mask where they had done a skin graft.

In all that time in Stikland my husband never opened his eyes, never saw me, never heard me. He was alive, he was breathing, though in a coma so deep he might as well have been dead. Formally I may not have been a widow, yet as far as I was concerned I was already in mourning, for him and for all of us, stranded and helpless in this cruel land.

I asked to bring him back to the flat in Wynberg, so that I could look after him myself, but they would not release him. They had not yet given up, they said. They were hoping that the electric currents they ran through his brain would all of a sudden *do the trick* (those were the words they used).

So they kept him in Stikland, those doctors, to do their tricks on him. Otherwise they cared nothing for him, a stranger, a man from Mars who should have died yet did not.

I promised myself, when they gave up on their electric currents I would bring him home. Then he could die properly, if that was what he wanted. Because though he was unconscious, I knew that deep inside him he felt the humiliation of what was happening to him. And if he could be allowed to die properly, in peace, then we would be released too, I and my daughters. Then we could spit on this atrocious earth of South Africa and be gone. But they never let him go, to the end.

So I sat by his bedside, Sunday after Sunday. *Never again will a woman look with love on this mutilated face,* I told myself, *so let me at least look, without flinching.*

In the next bed, I remember (there were at least a dozen beds crammed into a ward that should have held six), there was an old man so meagre, so cadaverous that his wristbones and the beak of his nose seemed to want to break through his skin. Though he had no visitors, he was always awake at the times when I came. He would roll his watery blue eyes towards me. *Help me, please,* he seemed to say, *help me to die!* But I could not help him.

Maria Regina never, thank God, visited that place. A psychiatric hospital is not a place for children. On the first Sunday I asked Joana to accompany me to help with the unfamiliar trains. Even Joana came away disturbed, not just by the spectacle of her father but also by things she saw in that hospital, things no girl should have to witness.

Why does he have to be here? I said to the doctor, the one who spoke about doing tricks. He is not mad – why does he have to be among mad people? Because we have the facilities for his kind of case, said the doctor. Because we have the equipment. I should have asked what equipment he meant, but I was too upset. Later I found out. He meant shock equipment, equipment to send my husband's body into convulsions, in the hope of doing the trick and bringing him back to life.

If I had been forced to spend an entire Sunday in that crowded ward I swear I would have gone mad myself. I used to take breaks, wander around the hospital grounds. There was a favourite bench I had, under a tree in a secluded corner. One day I arrived at my bench and found a woman sitting there with her baby beside her. In most places – in public gardens and on station platforms and so forth – benches used to be marked Whites or Non-whites; however, this one was not. I said to the woman, What a pretty baby or something like that, wanting to be friendly. A frightened look came over her face. Dankie, mies, she whispered, which meant Thank you, miss, and she picked up her baby and crept away.

I am not one of them, I wanted to call out to her. But of course I did not.

I wanted time to pass and I did not want time to pass. I wanted to be by Mario's side and I wanted to be away, free of him. At the beginning I would bring a book with me, intending to sit beside him and read. But I could not read in that place, could not concentrate. I thought to myself, I should take up knitting. I could knit whole bedspreads while I wait for this thick, heavy time to pass.

When I was young, in Brazil, there was never enough time for all I wanted to do. Now time was my worst enemy, time that would not pass. How I longed for it all to end, this life, this death, this living death! What a fatal mistake when we took the ship to South Africa!

So. That is the story of Mario.

He died in the hospital?

He died there. He could have lived longer, he had a strong constitution, he was like a bull. When they saw their tricks would not work, however, they stopped paying attention to him. Perhaps they stopped feeding him too, I can't say for sure, he always looked the same to me, he did not get thinner. Yet to tell the truth I did not mind, we wanted to be released, all of us, he and I and the doctors too.

We buried him in a cemetery not far from the hospital, I forget the name of the place. So his grave is in Africa. I have never been back, but I think of him sometimes, lying there all alone.

What is the time? All of a sudden I feel so tired, so sad. It always depresses me to be reminded of those days.

Shall we stop?

No, we can go on. There is not much more to say. Let me tell you about my dance classes, because that was where he pursued me, your Mr Coetzee. Then maybe you can answer one question for me. Then we will be finished.

I could not get proper work in those days. There were no professional openings for someone like me, coming from the *balet folclórico*. In South Africa the companies danced nothing but *Swan Lake* and *Giselle*, to prove how European they were. So I took the job I told you about, in a dance studio, teaching Latin American dance. Most of my students were what they called Coloured. By day they worked in shops or offices, then in the evenings they came to the studio to learn the latest Latin American steps. I liked them. They were nice people, friendly, gentle. They had romantic illusions about Latin America, Brazil above all. Lots of palm trees, lots of beaches. In Brazil, they thought, people like themselves would feel at home. I said nothing to disappoint them.

Each month there was a new intake, that was the system at the studio. No one was turned away. As long as a student paid, I had to teach them. One day when I walked in to meet my new class, there he was among the students, and there his name was on the list: *Coetzee, John.*

Well, I cannot tell you how upset I was. It is one thing, if you are a dancer who performs in public, to be pursued by admirers. I was used to that. Now, however, it was different. I was no longer putting myself on show, I was just a teacher now, I had a right not to be harried.

I did not greet him. I wanted him to see at once that he was not welcome. What did he think – that if he danced before me the ice in my heart would melt? How crazy! And all the crazier because he had no feeling for dance, no aptitude. I could see that from the first moment, from the way he walked. He was not at ease in his body. He moved as though his body were a horse that he was riding, a horse that did not like its rider and was resisting. Only in South Africa did I meet men like that, stiff, intractable, unteachable. Why did they ever come to Africa, I wondered – to Africa, the birthplace of dance? They would have been better off staying in Holland, sitting in their counting-houses behind their dykes counting money with cold fingers.

I taught my class as I was paid to do, then when the hour was over left the building at once by the back exit. I did not want to speak to Mr Coetzee. I hoped he would not return.

However, the next evening there he was again, doggedly following instructions, performing steps for which he had no feel. I could see he was not popular with the rest of the students. They tried to avoid him as a partner. As for me, his presence in the room took away all my pleasure. I tried to ignore him, but he would not be ignored, watching me, devouring my life.

At the end of the class I called to him to stay behind. 'Please stop this,' I said to him as soon as we were alone. He stared back at me without protest, mute. I could smell the cold sweat on his body. I felt an urge to strike him, lash him across the face. 'Stop this!' I said. 'Stop following me. I do not want to see you here again. And stop looking at me like that. Stop forcing me to humiliate you.'

There was more I could have said, but I was afraid I would lose control and start shouting.

Afterwards I spoke to the man who owned the studio, his name was Mr Anderson. There is a student in my class who is spoiling it for the other students, I said – please give him his money back and tell him to leave. But Mr Anderson would not. If there is a student disrupting your class it is up to you to put a stop to it, he said. This man is not doing anything wrong, I said, he is simply a bad presence. You cannot eject a student because he has a bad presence, said Mr Anderson. Find another solution.

The next evening I again called him back. There was nowhere private to go, I had to speak to him in the corridor. 'This is my work, you are disrupting my work,' I said. 'Go away from here. Leave me alone.'

He did not answer, but reached out a hand and touched my cheek.

That was the one and only time he ever touched me. The anger inside me boiled over. I knocked his hand aside. 'This is not a love-game!' I hissed. 'Don't you see I detest you? Leave me alone and leave my child alone too or I will report you to the school!'

It was true: if he had not begun filling my daughter's head with dangerous nonsense I would never have summoned him to our flat, and his miserable pursuit of me would never have begun. What was a grown man doing in a girls' school anyway, Saint Bonaventure, that was supposed to be a nuns' school, only there were no nuns?

And it was true too that I detested him. I was not afraid to say so. He forced me to detest him.

But when I pronounced the word *detest* he stared back at me in confusion as if he could not believe his ears – that a woman to whom he was offering himself could actually be refusing him. He did not know what to do, just as he did not know what to do with himself on the dance floor. It gave me no pleasure to see such bewilderment, such helplessness. It was as if he was dancing naked before me, this man who did not know how to dance. I wanted to shout at him. I wanted to beat him. I wanted to cry.

[Silence.]

This is not the story you wanted to hear, is it? You wanted a different kind of story for your book. You wanted to hear of the romance between your hero and the beautiful foreign ballerina. Well, I am giving you truth, not romance. Maybe too much truth. Maybe so much truth that there will be no place for it in your book. I don't know. I don't care.

Go on. It is not a very dignified picture of Coetzee that emerges from your story, I won't deny that, but I will change nothing, I promise.

Not dignified, you say. Well, maybe that is what you risk when you fall in love. You risk losing your dignity.

[Silence.]

Anyway, I went back to Mr Anderson. Get this man out of my class or I will resign, I said. I will see what I can do, said Mr Anderson. We all have difficult students to cope with, you are not the only one. He is not difficult, I said, he is mad.

Was he mad? I don't know. But he certainly had an *idée fixe* about me.

The next day I went to my daughter's school, as I had warned him I would, and asked to see the principal. The principal was busy, I was told. I will wait, I said. For an hour I waited in the secretary's office. Not one friendly word. No *Would you like a cup of tea, Mrs Nascimento?* Then at last, when it became plain I would not go away, they capitulated and let me see the principal.

'I have come to speak to you about my daughter's English lessons,' I said to her. 'I would like my daughter to go on with her lessons, but I want her to have a proper English teacher with a proper qualification. If I must pay more I will pay.'

The principal fetched a folder out of a filing cabinet. 'According to Mr Coetzee, Maria Regina is making good progress in English,' she said. 'That is confirmed by her other teachers. So what exactly is the problem?'

'I cannot tell you what is the problem,' I said. 'I just want her to have another teacher.'

This principal was not a fool. When I said I could not tell her what was the problem, she knew at once what was the problem. 'Mrs Nascimento,' she said, 'if I understand what you are saying, you are making a very serious complaint. But I can't act on such a complaint unless you are prepared to be more specific. Are you complaining about Mr Coetzee's actions towards your daughter? Are you telling me there has been something untoward in his behaviour?'

She was not a fool, but I am not a fool either. *Untoward:* what does that mean? Did I want to make an accusation against Mr Coetzee and sign my name to it, and then find myself in a court of law being interrogated by a judge? No. 'I am not making a complaint against Mr Coetzee,' I said, 'I am only asking you, if there is a proper English teacher, can Maria Regina take lessons from her instead.'

The principal did not like that. She shook her head. 'That is not possible,' she said. 'Mr Coetzee is the only teacher, the only person on

426

our staff, who teaches extra English. There is no other class into which Maria Regina can move. We don't have the luxury, Mrs Nascimento, of offering our girls a range of teachers to choose among. And further-more, with all respect, may I ask you to reflect, are you in the best posi-tion to judge Mr Coetzee's teaching, if it is simply the standard of his teaching we are discussing today?'

I know you are an Englishman, Mr Vincent, so don't take this personally, but there is a certain English manner that infuriates me, that infuriates many people, where the insult comes coated in pretty words, like sugar on a pill. *Dago*: you think I don't know that word, Mr Vincent? *You Portugoose dago!* she was saying – *How dare you come here and criticize my school! Go back to the slums where you came from!*

'I am Maria Regina's mother,' I said, 'I alone will say what is good for my daughter and what is not. I do not come to make trouble for you or Mr Coetzee or anyone else, but I tell you now, Maria Regina will not continue in that man's class. That is my word and it is final. I pay for my daughter to attend a good school, a school for girls, I do not want her in a class where the teacher is not a proper teacher, he has no qualification, he is not even English, he is a Boer.'

Maybe I should not have used that word, it was like *Dago*, but I was angry, I was provoked. *Boer*: in that little office of hers it was like a bomb. A bomb-word. But not as bad as *mad*. If I had said Maria Regina's teacher, with his incomprehensible poems and his wish to make his students burn with an intenser light, was mad, then the room would truly have exploded.

The woman's face grew stiff. 'It is up to me and to the school committee, Mrs Nascimento,' she said, 'to decide who is and who is not qualified to teach here. In my judgment and in the judgment of the committee Mr Coetzee, who holds a university degree in English, is adequately qualified for the work he does. You may remove your daughter from his class if you so wish, indeed you may remove her from the school, that is your right. But bear it in mind, it will be your daughter who will suffer in the end.'

'I will remove her from that man's class, I will not remove her from the school,' I replied. 'I want her to have a good education. I will myself find an English teacher for her. Thank you for seeing me. You think I am just some poor refugee woman who doesn't understand anything. You are wrong. If I were to tell you the whole story of our family you would see how wrong you are. Goodbye.'

Refugee. They kept calling me a refugee in that country of theirs, when all I desired was to escape from it.

When Maria Regina came home from school the next day a veritable storm burst over my head. 'How could you do it, mãe?' she shouted at me. 'How could you do this behind my back? Why do you always have to interfere in my life?'

For weeks and months, ever since Mr Coetzee made his appearance, relations had been strained between Maria Regina and myself. But never before had my daughter used such words to me. I tried to calm her. We are not like other families, I told her. Other girls do not have a father in hospital and a mother who has to humiliate herself to earn a few pennies so that a child who never lifts a finger in the home, or says thank you, can have extra classes in this and extra classes in that.

It was not true, of course. I could not have wished for better daughters than Joana and Maria Regina, serious, hard-working girls. But sometimes it is necessary to be a little harsh, even with those we love.

Maria Regina heard nothing that I said, she was in such a fury. 'I hate you!' she shouted. 'You think I don't know why you are doing this! It is because you are jealous, because you don't want me to see Mr Coetzee, because you want him for yourself!'

'I am jealous of you? What nonsense! Why should I want this man for myself, this man who is not even a real man? Yes, I say he is not a real man! What do you know about men, you, a child? Why do you think this man wants to be among young girls? Do you think that is normal? Why do you think he encourages your dreaming, your fantasies? Men like that should not be allowed near a school. And you – you should be thankful I am saving you. But instead you shout abuse and make accusations against me, your mother!'

I saw her lips move soundlessly, as though there were no words bitter enough for what was in her heart. Then she turned and ran out of the room. A moment later she was back, waving the letters that this man, this teacher of hers, had sent me, that I had put away in the bureau for no special reason, I certainly did not treasure them. 'He writes love-letters to you!' she screamed. 'And you write love-letters back to him! It's disgusting! If he is not normal why are you writing love-letters to him?'

Of course what she was saying was untrue. I wrote him no love-letters, not one. But how could I make the poor child believe that? 'How dare you!' I said. 'How dare you pry into my private papers!'

How I wished, at that moment, that I had burnt those letters of his, letters I never asked for!

Maria Regina was crying now. 'I wish I had never listened to you,' she sobbed. 'I wish I had never let you invite him here. You just spoil every-thing.'

'My poor child!' I said, and took her in my arms. 'I never wrote letters to Mr Coetzee, you must believe me. Yes, he wrote letters to me, I don't know why, but I never wrote back. I am not interested in him in that way, not in the slightest. Don't let him come between us, my darling. I am just trying to protect you. He is not right for you. He is a grown man, you are still a child. I will get you another teacher. I will get you a private teacher who will come here to the flat and help you. We will manage. A teacher is not expensive. We will get someone who has proper qualifi-cations and knows how to prepare you for the examinations. Then we can put this whole unhappy business behind us.'

So that is the story, the full story, of his letters and the trouble his letters caused me.

There were no more letters?

There was one more, but I did not open it. I wrote RETURN TO SENDER on the envelope and left it in the foyer for the postman to pick up. 'See?' I said to Maria Regina. 'See what I think of his letters?'

And what of the dance classes?

He stopped coming. Mr Anderson spoke to him and he stopped coming. Maybe he even gave back his money, I don't know.

Did you find another teacher for Maria Regina?

Yes, I found another teacher, a lady, a retired teacher. It cost money, but what is money when your child's future is at stake?

Was that the end, then, of your dealings with John Coetzee?

Yes. Absolutely.

You never saw him again, never heard from him?

I never saw him. I made sure Maria Regina never saw him. He may have been full of romantic nonsense, but he was too Dutch to be reckless. When he realized I was serious, not playing some love-game with him, he gave up his pursuit. He left us alone. His grand passion turned out to be not so grand after all. Or maybe he found someone else to be in love with.

Maybe. Maybe not. Maybe he kept you alive in his heart. Or the idea of you.

Why do you say that?

[Silence.]

Well, perhaps he did. You are the one who has studied his life, you will know better. With some people it does not matter who they are in love with as long as they are in love. Perhaps he was like that.

[Silence.]

In retrospect, how do you see the whole episode? Do you still feel anger towards him?

Anger? No. I can see how a lonely and eccentric young man like Mr Coetzee, who spent his days reading old philosophers and making up

430

poems, could fall for Maria Regina, who was a real beauty and would break many hearts. It is not so easy to see what Maria Regina saw in him; but then, she was young and impressionable, and he flattered her, made her think she was different from the other girls and had a great future.

Then when she brought him home and he laid eyes on me, I can see he might change his mind and decide to make me his true love instead. I am not claiming I was a great beauty, and of course I was not young any more, but Maria Regina and I were the same type: same bones, same hair, same dark eyes. And it is more practical – is it not? – to love a woman than to love a child. More practical, less dangerous.

What did he want from me, from a woman who did not respond to him and gave him no encouragement? Did he hope to sleep with me? What pleasure can there be for a man in sleeping with a woman who does not want him? Because, truly, I did not want this man, for whom I had not the slightest flicker of feeling. And what would it have been like anyway if I had taken up with my daughter's teacher? Could I have kept it secret? Certainly not from Maria Regina. I would have brought shame on myself before my children. Even when I was alone with him I would have been thinking, It is not me he desires, it is Maria Regina, who is young and beautiful but is forbidden to him.

But perhaps what he really wanted was both of us, Maria Regina and me, mother and daughter – perhaps that was his fantasy, I can't say, I can't look into his mind.

I remember, in the days when I was a student, existentialism was the fashion, we all had to be existentialists. But to be accepted as an existentialist you had first to prove you were a libertine, an extremist. Obey no restraints! Be free! – that was what we were told. But how can I be free, I asked myself, if I am obeying someone else's order to be free?

Coetzee was like that, I think. He had made up his mind to be an existentialist and a romantic and a libertine. The trouble was, it did not come from inside him, therefore he did not know how. Freedom, sensuality, erotic love – it was all just an idea in his head, not an urge rooted in his body. He had no gift for it. He was not a sensual being. And anyway, I suspect he secretly liked it when a woman was cold and distant.

You say you decided not to read his last letter. Do you ever regret that decision?

Why? Why should I regret it?

Because Coetzee was a writer, who knew how to use words. What if the letter you did not read contained words that would have moved you or even changed your feelings about him?

Mr Vincent, in your eyes John Coetzee is a great writer and a hero, I accept that, why else would you be here, why else would you be writing this book? To me, on the other hand – pardon me for saying this, but he is dead, so I cannot hurt his feelings – to me he is nothing. He is nothing, was nothing, just an irritation, an embarrassment. He was nothing and his words were nothing. I can see you are cross because I make him look like a fool. Nevertheless, to me he really was a fool.

As for his letters, writing letters to a woman does not prove you love her. This man was not in love with me, he was in love with some idea of me, some fantasy of a Latin mistress that he made up in his own mind. I wish, instead of me, he had found some other writer, some other fantasist, to fall in love with. Then the two of them could have been happy, making love all day to their ideas of each other.

You think I am cruel when I talk like this, but I am not, I am just a practical person. When my daughter's language teacher, a complete stranger, sends me letters full of his ideas about this and his ideas about that, about music and chemistry and philosophy and angels and gods and I don't know what else, page after page, poems too, I don't read it and memorize it for future generations, all I want to know is one simple, practical thing, which is, *What is going on between this man and my daughter who is only a child?* Because – forgive me for saying this – beneath all the fine words what a man wants from a woman is usually very basic and very simple.

You say there were poems too?

I did not understand them. Maria Regina was the one who liked poetry.

You recall nothing about them?

They were very modernistic, very intellectual, very obscure. That is why I say it was all a big mistake. He thought I was the kind of woman you lie in bed with in the dark, discussing poetry; but I was not like that at all. I was a wife and mother, the wife of a man locked up in a hospital that might as well have been a prison or a graveyard and the mother of two girls whom I had somehow to keep safe in a world where when people want to steal your money they bring along an axe. I had no time to take pity on this ignorant young man who was throwing himself at my feet and humiliating himself in front of me. And, frankly, if I had wanted a man, it would not be a man like him.

Because, let me assure you – I am keeping you late, I apologize – let me assure you, I was not without feeling, far from it. You must not go away with a false impression of me. I was not dead to the world. In the mornings, when Joana was at work and Maria Regina was at school and the sun shone its rays into that little flat of ours, which was usually so dark and gloomy, I would sometimes stand in the sunlight by the open window listening to the birds and feeling the warmth on my face and my breast; and at times like that I would long to be a woman again. I was not too old, I was just waiting. So. Enough. Thank you for listening.

You said last time that you had a question for me.

Yes, I forgot, I have a question. It is this. I am not usually wrong about people; so tell me, am I wrong about John Coetzee? Because to me, frankly, he was not anybody. He was not a man of substance. Maybe he could write well, maybe had a certain talent for words, I don't know, I never read his books, I was never curious to read them. I know he won a big reputation later; but was he really a great writer? Because to my mind, a talent for words is not enough if you want to be a great writer. You have also to be a great man. And he was not a great man. He was a little man, an unimportant little man. I can't give you a list of reasons A-B-C-D why I say so, but that was my impression from the beginning, from the moment I set eyes on him, and nothing that happened afterwards

433

changed it. So I turn to you. You have studied him deeply, you are writing a book about him. Tell me: What is your estimation of him? Was I wrong?

My estimation of him as a writer or my estimation of him as a human being?

As a human being.

I can't say. I would be reluctant to pronounce a judgment on anyone without ever meeting him face to face. Him or her. But I think that, at the time he met you, Coetzee was lonely, unnaturally lonely. Perhaps that explains certain – what shall I say? – certain extravagances of behaviour.

How do you know that?

From the record he left behind. From putting two and two together. He was a little lonely and a little desperate.

Yes, but we are all a little desperate, that is life. If you are strong you conquer the despair. That is why I ask: how can you be a great writer if you are just an ordinary little man? Surely you must have a certain flame in you that sets you apart from the man in the street. Maybe in his books, if you read them, you can see that flame. But for me, in the times I was with him I never felt any fire. On the contrary, he seemed to me – how shall I express it? – tepid.

To an extent I would agree with you. Fire is not the first word that comes to mind when one thinks of his writings. But he had other virtues, other strengths. For instance, I would say he was steady. He had a steady gaze. He was not easily fooled by appearances.

For a man who was not fooled by appearances, he fell in love rather easily, don't you think?

[Laughter.]

But maybe, when he fell in love, he was not fooled. Maybe he saw things that other people do not see.

In the woman?

Yes, in the woman.

[Silence.]

You tell me he was in love with me even after I sent him away, even after I forgot he even existed. Is that what you mean by steadiness? Because to me it just seems stupid.

I think he was dogged. A very English word. Whether there is an equivalent in Portuguese I don't know. Like a bulldog that grips you with his teeth and does not let go.

If you say so, then I must believe you. But being like a dog – is that admirable, in English?

[Laughter.]

You know, in my profession, rather than just listen to what people say, we prefer to watch the way they move, the way they carry themselves. That is our way to get to the truth, and it is not a bad way. Your Mr Coetzee may have had a talent for words but, as I told you, he could not dance. He could not dance – here is one of the phrases I remember from South Africa, Maria Regina taught it to me – he could not dance to save his life.

[Laughter.]

But seriously, Senhora Nascimento, there have been many great men who were not good dancers. If you must be a good dancer before you can be a great man, then Gandhi was not a great man, Tolstoy was not a great man.

No, you are not listening to what I say. I too am serious. You know the word *disembodied*? This man was disembodied. He was divorced from his body. To him, the body was like one of those wooden puppets that you move with strings. You pull this string and the left arm moves, you pull that string and the right leg moves. And the real self sits up above, where you cannot see him, like the puppet-master pulling the strings.

Now this man comes to me, to the mistress of the dance. *Show me how to dance!* he implores. So I show him, show him how we move in the dance. So, I say to him – *move your feet so and then so*. And he listens and tells himself, *Aha, she means pull the red string followed by the blue string!* – *Turn your shoulder so,* I say to him, and he tells himself, *Aha, she means pull the green string!*

But that is not how you dance! That is not how you dance! Dance is incarnation. In dance it is not the puppet-master in the head that leads and the body that follows, it is the body itself that leads, the body with its soul, its body-soul. Because the body knows! It knows! When the body feels the rhythm inside it, it does not need to think. That is how we are if we are human. That is why the wooden puppet cannot dance. The wood has no soul. The wood cannot feel the rhythm.

So I ask: How could this man of yours be a great man when he was not human? It is a serious question, not a joke any more. Why do you think I, as a woman, could not respond to him? Why do you think I did everything I could to keep my daughter away from him while she was still young, with no experience to guide her? Because from such a man no good can come. Love: how can you be a great writer when you know nothing about love? Do you think I can be a woman and not know in my bones what kind of lover a man will be? I tell you, I shiver with cold when I think of, you know, intimacy with a man like that. I don't know if he ever married, but if he did I shiver for the woman who married him.

Yes. It is getting late, it has been a long afternoon, my colleague and I must be on our way. Thank you, Senhora Nascimento, for the time you have so generously given us. It has been most gracious of you. Senhora Gross will transcribe our conversation and tidy up the translation, after which I will send it to you to see if there is anything you would like to change or add or cut out.

I understand. Of course you offer to me that I can change the record, I can add or cut out. But how much can I change? Can I change the label I wear around my neck that says I was one of Coetzee's women? Will you let me take off that label? Will you let me tear it up? I think not. Because it would destroy your book, and you would not allow that.

But I will be patient. I will wait to see what you send me. Perhaps – who knows? – you will take seriously what I have told you. Also – let me confess – I am curious to see what the other women in this man's life have told you, the other women with labels around their necks – whether they too found this lover of theirs to be made of wood. Because, you know, that is what I think you should call your book: *The Wooden Man*.

[Laughter.]

But tell me, seriously again, did this man who knew nothing about women ever write about women, or did he just write about dogged men like himself? I ask because, as I say, I have not read him.

He wrote about men and he wrote about women too. For example – this may interest you – there is a book named Foe *in which the heroine spends a year shipwrecked on an island off the coast of Brazil. In the final version she is an Englishwoman, but in the first draft he made her a Brasileira.*

And what kind of woman is this *Brasileira* of his?

What shall I say? She has many good qualities. She is attractive, she is resourceful, she has a will of steel. She hunts all over the world to find her young daughter, who has disappeared. That is the substance of the novel: her quest to recover her daughter, which overrides all other concerns. To me she seems an admirable heroine. If I were the original of a character like that, I would feel proud.

I will read this book and see for myself. What is the title again?

Foe, *spelled F-O-E. It was translated into Portuguese, but the translation is probably out of print by now. I can send you a copy in English if you like.*

Yes, send it. It is a long time since I read an English book, but I am interested to see what this man of wood made of me.

[Laughter.]

Interview conducted in São Paulo, Brazil,
in December 2007.

Martin

IN ONE OF HIS *late notebooks Coetzee gives an account of his first meeting with you, on the day in 1972 when you were both being interviewed for a position at the University of Cape Town. The account is only a few pages long – I'll read it to you if you like. I suspect it was intended to fit into the third memoir, the one that never saw the light of day. As you will hear, he follows the same convention as in* Boyhood *and* Youth, *where the subject is called 'he' rather than 'I'.*

This is what he writes.

'He has had his hair cut for the interview. He has trimmed his beard. He has put on a jacket and tie. If he is not yet Mr Sobersides, at least he no longer looks like the Wild Man of Borneo.

'In the waiting room are the two other candidates for the job. They stand side by side at the window overlooking the gardens, conversing softly. They seem to know each other, or at least to have struck up an acquaintance.'

You don't recall who this third person was, do you?

He was from the University of Stellenbosch, but I don't remember his name.

He goes on: 'This is the British way: to drop the contestants into the pit and watch to see what will happen. He will have to reaccustom himself to British ways of doing things, in all their brutality. A tight ship, Britain, crammed to the gunwales. Dog eat dog. Dogs snarling and snapping at one another, each guarding its little territory. The American way, by comparison, decorous, even gentle. But then there is more space in America, more room for urbanity.

'The Cape may not be Britain, may be drifting further from Britain every day,

yet what is left of British ways it clutches tight to its chest. Without that saving connection, what would the Cape be? A minor landing on the way to nowhere; a place of savage idleness.

'In the order paper pinned to the door, he is Number Two to appear before the committee. Number One, when summoned, rises calmly, taps out his pipe, stores it away in what must be a pipe case, and passes through the portal. Twenty minutes later he re-emerges, his face inscrutable.

'It is his turn. He enters and is waved to a seat at the foot of a long table. At the far end sit his inquisitors, five in number, all men. Because the windows are open, because the room is above a street where cars are continually passing by, he has to strain to hear them, and raise his own voice to make himself heard.

'Some polite feints, then the first thrust: If appointed, what authors would he most like to teach?

'"I can teach pretty much across the board," he replies. "I am not a specialist. I think of myself as a generalist."

'As an answer it is at least defensible. A small department in a small university might be happy to recruit a jack of all trades. But from the silence that falls he gathers he has not answered well. He has taken the question too literally. That has always been a fault of his: taking questions too literally, responding too briefly. These people don't want brief answers. They want something more leisurely, more expansive, something that will allow them to work out what kind of fellow they have before them, what kind of junior colleague he would make, whether he would fit in in a provincial university that is doing its best to maintain standards in difficult times, to keep the flame of civilization burning.

'In America, where they take job-hunting seriously, people like him, people who don't know how to read the agenda behind a question, can't speak in rounded paragraphs, don't put themselves over with conviction – in short, people deficient in people skills – attend training sessions where they learn to look the interrogator in the eye, smile, respond to questions fully and with every appearance of sincerity. Presentation of the self: that is what they call it in America, without irony.

'What authors would he prefer to teach? What research is he currently engaged in? Would he feel competent to offer tutorials in Middle English? His answers sound more and more hollow. The truth is, he does not really want this job. He does not want it because in his heart he knows he is not cut out to be a teacher. Lacks the temperament. Lacks zeal.

'He emerges from the interview in a state of black dejection. He wants to get away from this place at once, without delay. But no, first there are forms to be filled in, travel expenses to be collected.

"'How did it go?"

'The speaker is the candidate who was interviewed first, the pipe-smoker.' That is you, if I am not mistaken.

Yes. But I have given up the pipe.

'He shrugs. "Who knows?" he says. "Not well."

"'Shall we get a cup of tea?"

'He is taken aback. Are the two of them not supposed to be rivals? Is it permitted for rivals to fraternize?

'It is late afternoon, the campus is deserted. They make for the Student Union in quest of their cup of tea. The Union is closed. MJ' – that is what he calls you – 'takes out his pipe. "Ah well," he says. "Do you smoke?"

'How surprising: he is beginning to like this MJ, with his easy, straightforward manner! His gloom is fading fast. He likes MJ and, unless it is all just an exercise in self-presentation, MJ seems inclined to like him too. And this mutual liking has grown up in a flash!

'Yet should he be surprised? Why have the two of them (or the three of them, if the shadowy third is included) been selected to be interviewed for a lectureship in English literature, if not because they are the same kind of person, with the same formation behind them (formation: not the customary English word, he must remember that); and because both, finally and most obviously, are South Africans, white South Africans?'

That is where the fragment ends. It is undated, but I am pretty sure he wrote it in 1999 or 2000. So . . . a couple of questions relating to it. First question: You were the successful candidate, the one who was awarded the lectureship, while Coetzee was passed over. Why do you think he was passed over? And did you detect any resentment on his part?

None at all. I was from inside the system – the colonial university system as it was in those days – while he was from outside, insofar as he had gone off to America for his graduate education. Given the nature of all systems, namely to reproduce themselves, I was always going to have the edge over him. He understood that, in theory and in practice. He certainly didn't put the blame on me.

Very well. Another question: He suggests that in you he has found a new friend, and goes on to list traits that you and he have in common. But when he gets to your white South Africanness he stops and writes no more. Have you any idea why he should have stopped just there?

Why he should have raised the topic of white South African identity and then dropped it? There are two explanations I can offer. One is that it might have seemed too complex a topic to be explored in a memoir or diary – too complex or too close to the bone. The other is simpler: that the story of his adventures in the academy was becoming too boring to go on with, too short of narrative interest.

And which explanation do you incline towards?

Probably the first, with an admixture of the second. John left South Africa in the 1960s, came back in the 1970s, for decades hovered between South Africa and the United States, then finally decamped to Australia and died there. I left South Africa in the 1970s and never returned. Broadly speaking, he and I shared a common stance towards South Africa, namely that our presence there was illegitimate. We may have had an abstract right to be there, a birthright, but the basis of that right was fraudulent. Our existence was grounded in a crime, specifically colonial conquest, perpetuated by apartheid. Whatever the opposite is of *native* or *rooted*, that was what we felt ourselves to be. We thought of ourselves as sojourners, temporary residents, and to that extent without a home, without a homeland. I don't think I am misrepresenting John. It was something he and I talked about a great deal. I am certainly not misrepresenting myself.

Are you saying that you and he commiserated together?

Commiserated is the wrong word. We had too much going for us to regard our fate as a miserable one. We had our youth – I was still in my twenties at the time, he was only slightly older – we had a not-bad education behind us, we even had modest material assets. If we had been whisked away and set down somewhere else in the world – the civilized world, the First World – we would have prospered, flourished. (About the Third World I would not be so confident. We were not Robinson Crusoes, either of us.)

Therefore no, I did not regard our fate as tragic, and I am sure he did not either. If anything, it was comic. His ancestors in their way, and my ancestors in theirs, had toiled away, generation after generation, to clear a patch of wild Africa for their descendants, and what was the fruit of all their labours? Doubt in the hearts of those descendants about title to the land; an uneasy sense that it belonged not to them but, inalienably, to its original owners.

Do you think that if he had gone on with the memoir, if he had not abandoned it, that is what he would have said?

More or less. Let me elaborate a little further on our stance vis-à-vis South Africa. We both cultivated a certain provisionality in our feelings towards the country, he perhaps more so than I. We were reluctant to invest too deeply in the country, since sooner or later our ties to it would have to be cut, our investment in it annulled.

And?

That's all. We had a certain style of mind in common, a style that I attribute to our origins, colonial and South African. Hence the commonality of outlook.

In his case, would you say that the habit you describe, of treating feelings as provisional, of not committing himself emotionally, extended beyond relations with the land of his birth into personal relations too?

I wouldn't know. You are the biographer. If you find that train of thought worth following up, follow it.

Can we now turn to his teaching? He writes that he was not cut out to be a teacher. Would you agree?

I would say that one teaches best what one knows best and feels most strongly about. John knew a fair amount about a range of things, but not a great deal about anything in particular. I would count that as one strike against him. Second, though there were writers who mattered deeply to him – the nineteenth-century Russian novelists, for instance – the real depth of his involvement did not come out in his teaching, not in any obvious way. Something was always being held back. Why? I don't know. All I can suggest is that a strain of secretiveness that seemed to be engrained in him, part of his character, extended to his teaching too.

Do you feel then that he spent his working life, or most of it, in a profession for which he had no talent?

That is a little too sweeping. John was a perfectly adequate academic. A perfectly adequate academic but not a notable teacher. Perhaps if he had taught Sanskrit it would have been different, Sanskrit or some other subject in which the conventions permit you to be a little dry and reserved.

He told me once that he had missed his calling, that he should have been a librarian. I can see the sense in that.

I haven't been able to lay my hands on course descriptions from the 1970s – the University of Cape Town doesn't seem to archive material like that – but among Coetzee's papers I did come across an advertisement for a course that you and he offered jointly in 1976, to extramural students. Do you remember that course?

Yes, I do. It was a poetry course. I was working on Hugh McDiarmid at the time, so I used the occasion to give McDiarmid a close reading. John had the students read Pablo Neruda in translation. I had never read Neruda, so I sat in on his sessions.

A strange choice, don't you think, for someone like him: Neruda?

No, not at all. John had a fondness for lush, expansive poetry: Neruda, Whitman, Stevens. You must remember that he was, in his way, a child of the 1960s.

In his way – what do you mean by that?

I mean within the confines of a certain rectitude, a certain rationality. Without being a Dionysian himself, he approved in principle of Dionysianism. Approved in principle of letting oneself go, though I don't recall that he ever let himself go – he would probably not have known how to. He had a need to believe in the resources of the unconscious, in the creative force of unconscious processes. Hence his inclination towards the more vatic poets.

You must have noted how rarely he discussed the sources of his own creativity. In part that came out of the native secretiveness I mentioned. But in part it also suggests a reluctance to probe the sources of his inspiration, as if being too self-aware might cripple him.

Was the course a success – the course you and he taught together?

I certainly learned from it – learned about the history of surrealism in Latin America, for instance. As I said, John knew a little about a lot of things. As for what our students came away with, that I can't say. Students, in my experience, soon work out whether what you are teaching matters to you. If it does, then they are prepared to consider letting it matter to them too. But if they conclude, rightly or wrongly, that it doesn't, then, curtains, you may as well go home.

And Neruda didn't matter to him?

No, I'm not saying that. Neruda may have mattered a great deal to him. Neruda may even have been a model – an unattainable model – of how a poet can respond creatively to injustice and repression. But – and this is my point – if you treat your connection with the poet as a personal secret to be closely guarded, and if moreover your classroom manner is somewhat stiff and formal, you are never going to acquire a following.

You are saying he never acquired a following?

Not as far as I am aware. Perhaps he smartened up his act in his later years. I just don't know.

At the time when you met him, in 1972, he had a rather precarious position teaching at a high school. It wasn't until some time later that he was actually offered a position at the University. Even so, for almost all of his working life, from his mid-twenties until his mid-sixties, he was employed as a teacher of one kind or another. I come back to my earlier question: Doesn't it seem strange to you that a man who had no talent as a teacher should have made teaching his career?

Yes and no. The ranks of the teaching profession are, as you must know, full of refugees and misfits.

And which was he: a refugee or a misfit?

He was a misfit. He was also a cautious soul. He liked the security of a monthly salary cheque.

You sound critical.

I am only pointing to the obvious. If he hadn't wasted so much of his life correcting students' grammar and sitting through boring meetings, he might have written more, perhaps even written better. But he was not a child. He knew what he was doing. He made his accommodation with society and lived with the consequences.

On the other hand, being a teacher allowed him contact with a younger generation. Which he might not have had, had he withdrawn from the world and devoted himself wholly to writing.

True.

Did he have any special friendships that you know of among students?

Now you sound as if you are angling. What do you mean, special friendships? Do you mean, did he overstep the mark? Even if I knew, which I don't, I would not comment.

Yet the theme of the older man and the younger woman keeps coming back in his fiction.

It would be very, very naïve to conclude that because the theme was present in his writing it had to be present in his life.

In his inner life, then.

His inner life. Who can say what goes on in people's inner lives?

Is there any other aspect of him that you would like to bring forward? Any stories worth recounting?

Stories? I don't think so. John and I were colleagues. We were friends. We got on well together. But I can't say I knew him intimately. Why do you ask if I have stories?

Because in biography one has to strike a balance between narrative and opinion. I have no shortage of opinion – people are more than ready to tell me what they think or thought of Coetzee – but one needs more than that to bring a life-story to life.

Sorry, I can't help you. Perhaps your other sources will be more forthcoming. Who else will you be speaking to?

I have five names on my list, including yours.

Only five? Don't you think that is a bit risky? Who are we lucky five? How did you come to choose us?

I'll give you the names. From here I travel to South Africa — it will be my second trip — to speak to Coetzee's cousin Margot, with whom he was close. Then on to Brazil to meet a woman named Adriana Nascimento who lived in Cape Town for some years during the 1970s. After that — but the date isn't fixed yet — I go to Canada to see someone named Julia Frankl, who in the 1970s would have gone under the name Julia Smith. And I will also be seeing Sophie Denoël in Paris.

Sophie I knew, but not the others. How did you come up with these names?

Basically I let Coetzee himself do the choosing. I followed up on clues he dropped in his notebooks — clues as to who was important to him at the time, in the 1970s.

It seems a peculiar way of selecting biographical sources, if you don't mind my saying so.

Perhaps. There are other names I would have wanted to add, of people who knew him well, but alas they are dead now. You call it a peculiar way of going about a biography. Perhaps. But I am not interested in delivering a final judgment on Coetzee. I am not writing that kind of book. Final judgments I leave to history. What I am doing is telling the story of a stage in his life, or if we can't arrive at a single story then several stories from different perspectives.

And the sources you have selected have no axes to grind, no ambitions of their own to pronounce final judgment on Coetzee?

[Silence.]

Let me ask: Leaving aside Sophie, and leaving aside the cousin, was either of the women you mention emotionally involved with Coetzee?

Yes. Both. In different ways. Which I have yet to explore.

Shouldn't that give you pause? With your very narrow roster of sources, will you not inevitably come out with an account or set of accounts that are slanted towards the personal and the intimate at the expense of the man's actual achievements as a writer? Worse: do you not run the risk of allowing your book to become no more than – forgive me for putting it in this way – no more than a settling of scores, personal scores?

Why? Because my informants are women?

Because it is not in the nature of love affairs for the lovers to see each other whole and steady.

[Silence.]

I repeat, it seems to me strange to be putting together a biography of a writer that will ignore his writing. But perhaps I am wrong. Perhaps I am out of date. Perhaps that is what literary biography has become. I must go. One final thing: if you are planning to quote me, would you make sure I have a chance to check the text first?

Of course.

Interview conducted in Sheffield, England,
in September 2007.

Sophie

MME DENOËL, TELL ME *how you came to know John Coetzee.*

He and I were for years colleagues at the University of Cape Town. He was in the Department of English, I was in French. We collaborated to offer a course in African literature. This was in 1976. He taught the Anglophone writers, I the Francophone. That was how our acquaintance began.

And how did you yourself come to be in Cape Town?

My husband was sent there to run the Alliance Française. Before that we had been living in Madagascar. During our time in Cape Town our marriage broke up. My husband returned to France, I stayed on. I took a position at the University, a junior position teaching French language.

And in addition you taught the joint course that you mention, the course in African literature.

Yes. It may seem odd, two whites offering a course in black African literature, but that is how it was in those days. If we two had not offered it, no one would have.

Because blacks were excluded from the University?

No, no, by then the system had started to crack. There were black students, though not many; some black lecturers too. But very few specialists in Africa, the wider Africa. That was one of the surprising things I discovered about South Africa: how insular it was. I went back on a visit last year, and it was the same: little or no interest in the rest of Africa. Africa was a dark continent to the north, best left unexplored.

And you? Where did your interest in Africa come from?

From my education. From France. Remember, France was once a great colonial power. Even after the colonial era officially ended, France had other means at its disposal to maintain its influence – economic means, cultural means. *La Francophonie* was the new name we invented for the old empire. Writers from *Francophonie* were promoted, fêted, studied. For my *agrégation* I worked on Aimé Césaire.

And the course you taught in collaboration with Coetzee – was that a success, would you say?

Yes, I believe so. It was an introductory course, no more than that, but students found it, as you say in English, an eye-opener.

White students?

White students plus a few black. We did not attract the more radical black students. Our approach would have been too academic for them, not *engagé* enough. We thought it sufficient to offer students a glimpse of the riches of the rest of Africa.

And you and Coetzee saw eye to eye on this approach?

I believe so. Yes.

You were a specialist in African literature, he was not. His training was in the literature of the metropolis. How did he come to be teaching African literature?

It is true, he had no formal training in the field. But he had a good

general knowledge of Africa, admittedly just book knowledge, not practical knowledge, he had not travelled in Africa, but book knowledge is
not worthless – right? He knew the anthropological literature better than
I did, including the francophone materials. He had a grasp of the history,
the politics. He had read the important figures writing in English and
in French (of course in those days the body of African literature was not
large – things are different now). There were gaps in his knowledge –
the Maghreb, Egypt, and so forth. And he didn't know the diaspora,
particularly the Caribbean, which I did.

What did you think of him as a teacher?

He was good. Not spectacular but competent. Always well prepared.

Did he get on well with students?

That I can't say. Perhaps if you track down old students of his they will
be able to help you.

And yourself? Compared with him, did you get on well with students?

[Laughs.] What is it you want me to say? Yes, I suppose I was the more
popular one, the more enthusiastic. I was young, remember, and it was
a pleasure for me to be talking about books for a change, after all the
language classes. We made a good pair, I thought, he more serious,
more reserved, I more open, more flamboyant.

He was considerably older than you.

Ten years. He was ten years older than me.

[Silence.]

*Is there anything you would like to add on the subject? Other aspects of him you
would like to comment on?*

We had a liaison. I presume you are aware of that. It did not endure.

Why not?

It was not sustainable.

Would you like to say more?

Would I like to say more for your book? Not before you tell me what kind of book it is. Is it a book of gossip or a serious book? Do you have authorization for it? Who else are you speaking to besides me?

Does one need authorization to write a book? If one wanted authorization, where would one seek it? From the executors of Coetzee's estate? I don't think so. But I can give you my assurance, the book I am writing is a serious book, a seriously intended biography. I concentrate on the years from Coetzee's return to South Africa in 1971/72 until his first public recognition in 1977. That seems to me an important period of his life, important yet neglected, a period when he was still finding his feet as a writer.

As for whom I have chosen to interview, let me put the situation before you candidly. I made two trips to South Africa, one last year, one the year before. Those trips were not as fruitful as I had hoped they would be. Of the people who knew Coetzee best, a number had died. In fact, the whole generation to which he belonged was on the point of dying out. And the memories of the survivors were not always to be trusted. In one or two cases, people who claimed to have known him turned out, after a little scratching, to have the wrong Coetzee (as you are aware, the name Coetzee is not uncommon in that country). The upshot is, the biography will rest on interviews with a handful of friends and colleagues, including, I would hope, yourself. Is that enough to reassure you?

No. What of his diaries? What of his letters? What of his notebooks? Why so much reliance on interviews?

Mme Denoël, I have been through the letters and diaries that are available to me. What Coetzee writes there cannot be trusted, not as a factual record — not because he was a liar but because he was a fictioneer. In his letters he is making up a fiction of himself for his correspondents; in his diaries he is doing much the same for his own eyes, or perhaps for posterity. As documents they have their value, of course; but if you want the truth, the full truth, then surely you need to set beside them the testimony of people who knew him in the flesh, who participated in his life.

Yes; but what if we are all fictioneers, as you call Coetzee? What if we are all continually making up the stories of our lives? Why should what I tell you about Coetzee be any more worthy of credence than what he writes in his own person?

Of course we are all fictioneers, more or less, I do not deny that. But which would you rather have: a range of independent reports from independent perspectives, from which you can then attempt to synthesize a whole; or the massive, unitary self-projection comprised by his oeuvre? I know which I would prefer.

Yes, I can see that. There remains the other question I raised, the question of discretion. I am not one of those who believe that once a person is dead all restraint falls away. What existed between myself and John Coetzee I am not necessarily prepared to share with the world.

I accept that. Discretion is your privilege, your right. Nevertheless, I ask you to pause and reflect. A great writer is the property of all the world. You knew John Coetzee closely. One of these days you too will no longer be with us. Do you think it good that your memories should pass away with you?

A great writer? How John would laugh if he could hear you! The day of the great writer is long gone, he would say.

The day of the writer as oracle – yes, I would agree, that day is past. But would you not accept that a well-known writer – let us call him that instead – a well-known figure in our common cultural life, is to some extent public property?

On that subject my opinion is irrelevant. What is relevant is what he himself believed. And there the answer is clear. He believed our life-stories are ours to construct as we wish, within or even against the constraints imposed by the real world – as you yourself acknowledged a moment ago. That is why I specifically used the term *authorization*. It was not the authorization of his family or his executors that I had in mind, it was his own authorization. If you were not authorized by him to expose the private side of his life, then I will certainly not assist you.

Coetzee cannot have authorized me for the simple reason that he and I never had any contact. But on that point let us agree to differ, and move on. I return to the course you mentioned, the course on African literature that you and he taught together. One remark you made intrigues me. You said you and he did not attract the more radical African students. Why do you think that was so?

Because we were not radicals ourselves, not by their standards. We had both, obviously, been affected by 1968. In 1968 I was still a student at the Sorbonne, where I took part in the manifestations, the days in May. John was in the United States at the time, and fell foul of the American author-ities, I don't remember all the details, but I know it became a turning point in his life. Yet I stress we were not Marxists, either of us, and certainly not Maoists. I was probably to the left of him, but I could afford that because I was shielded by my status within the French diplomatic enclave. If I had gotten into trouble with the South African security police I would have been discreetly put on a plane to Paris, and that would have been the end of the matter. I would not have ended up in a prison cell.

Whereas Coetzee . . .

Coetzee would not have ended up in a prison cell either. He was not a militant. His politics were too idealistic, too Utopian for that. In fact he was not political at all. He looked down on politics. He didn't like political writers, writers who espoused a political programme.

Yet he published some quite left-leaning commentary in the 1970s. I think of his essays on Alex La Guma, for example. He was sympathetic to La Guma, and La Guma was a communist.

La Guma was a special case. He was sympathetic to La Guma because La Guma was from Cape Town, not because he was a communist.

You say he was not political. Do you mean that he was apolitical? Because some people would say that the apolitical is just one variety of the political.

No, not apolitical, I would rather say anti-political. He thought that politics brought out the worst in people. It brought out the worst in people and also brought to the surface the worst types in society. He preferred to have nothing to do with it.

Did he preach this anti-political politics in his classes?

Of course not. He was very scrupulous about not preaching. His political beliefs you discovered only after you got to know him better.

You say his politics were Utopian. Are you implying they were unrealistic?

He looked forward to the day when politics and the state would wither away. I would call that Utopian. On the other hand, he did not invest a great deal of himself in these Utopian longings. He was too much of a Calvinist for that.

Please explain.

You want me to say what lay behind Coetzee's politics? You can best get that from his books. But let me try anyway.

In Coetzee's eyes, we human beings will never abandon politics because politics is too convenient and too attractive as a theatre in which to give rein to our baser emotions. Baser emotions meaning hatred and rancour and spite and jealousy and bloodlust and so forth. In other words, politics as we know it is a symptom of our fallen state and expresses that fallen state.

Even the politics of liberation?

If you refer to the politics of the South African liberation struggle, the answer is yes. As long as liberation meant national liberation, the liberation of the black nation of South Africa, John had no interest in it.

Was he then hostile to the liberation struggle?

Was he hostile? No, he was not hostile. Hostile, sympathetic – as a biographer you above all ought to be wary of putting people in neat little boxes with labels on them.

I hope I am not putting Coetzee in a box.

Well, that is how it sounds to me. No, he was not hostile to the liberation struggle. If you are a fatalist, as he tended to be, there is no point in being hostile to the course that history takes, however much you may regret it. To the fatalist, history is fate.

Very well, did he then regret the liberation struggle? Did he regret the form the liberation struggle took?

He accepted that the liberation struggle was just. The struggle was just, but the new South Africa towards which it strove was not Utopian enough for him.

What would have been Utopian enough for him?

The closing down of the mines. The ploughing under of the vineyards. The disbanding of the armed forces. The abolition of the automobile. Universal vegetarianism. Poetry in the streets. That sort of thing.

In other words, poetry and the horse-drawn cart and vegetarianism are worth fighting for, but not liberation from apartheid?

Nothing is worth fighting for. You compel me into the role of defending his position, a position I do not happen to share. Nothing is worth fighting for because fighting only prolongs the cycle of aggression and retaliation. I merely repeat what Coetzee says loud and clear in his writings, which you say you have read.

Was he at ease with his black students – with black people in general?

Was he at ease with anyone? He was not an at-ease person (can you say that in English?). He never relaxed. I witnessed that with my own eyes. So: Was he at ease with black people? No. He was not at ease among people who were at ease. The ease of others made him ill at ease. Which sent him off – in my opinion – in the wrong direction.

What do you mean?

He saw Africa through a romantic haze. He thought of Africans as embodied, in a way that had been lost long ago in Europe. What do I mean? Let me try to explain. In Africa, he used to say, body and soul were indistinguishable, the body was the soul. He had a whole philosophy of the body, of music and dance, which I can't reproduce, but which seemed to me, even then – how shall I say? – unhelpful. Politically unhelpful.

Please continue.

His philosophy ascribed to Africans the role of guardians of the truer, deeper, more primitive being of humankind. He and I argued quite strenuously about this. What his position boiled down to, I said, was old-fashioned Romantic primitivism. In the context of the 1970s, of the liberation struggle and the apartheid state, it was unhelpful to look at Africans in his way. And anyway, it was a role they were no longer prepared to fulfil.

Was this the reason why black students avoided his course, your joint course, in African literature?

It was a viewpoint that he did not openly propagate. He was always very careful in that respect, very correct. But if you listened carefully it must have come across.

There was one further circumstance, one further bias to his thinking, that I must mention. Like many whites, he regarded the Cape, the western Cape and perhaps the northern Cape along with it, as standing apart from the rest of South Africa. The Cape was a country of its own, with its own geography, its own history, its own languages and culture. In this mythical Cape, haunted by the ghosts of what we used to call the Hottentots, the Coloured people were rooted, and to a lesser extent the Afrikaners too, but black Africans were aliens, latecomers, outsiders, as were the English.

Why do I mention this? Because it suggests how he could justify the rather abstract, rather anthropological attitude he took up towards black South Africa. He had no *feeling* for black South Africans. That was my private conclusion. They might be his fellow citizens but they were not his countrymen. History – or fate, which was to him the same thing – might have cast them in the role of inheritors of the land, but at the back of his mind they continued to be *they* as opposed to *us*.

If Africans were they, who were us? The Afrikaners?

No. *Us* was principally the Coloured people. It is a term I use only reluctantly, as shorthand. He – Coetzee – avoided it as far as he could. I mentioned his Utopianism. This avoidance was another aspect of his Utopianism. He longed for the day when everyone in South Africa would call themselves nothing, neither African nor European nor white nor black nor anything else, when family histories would have become so tangled and intermixed that people would be ethnically indistinguishable, that is to say – I utter the tainted word again – Coloured. He called that the Brazilian future. He approved of Brazil and the Brazilians. He had of course never been to Brazil.

But he had Brazilian friends.

He had met a few Brazilian refugees in South Africa.

[Silence.]

You mention an intermixed future. Are we talking here about biological mixture? Are we talking about intermarriage?

Don't ask me. I am just delivering a report.

Then why, instead of contributing to the future by – legitimately or illegitimately – fathering Coloured children – why was he having a liaison with a young white colleague from France?

[Laughs.] Don't ask me.

What did you and he talk about?

About our teaching. About colleagues and students. In other words, we talked shop. We also talked about ourselves.

Go on.

You want me to tell you if we discussed his writing? The answer is no. He never spoke to me about what he was writing, nor did I press him.

This was around the time when he was writing In the Heart of the Country.

He was just completing In the Heart of the Country.

Did you know that In the Heart of the Country *would be about madness and parricide and so forth?*

I had absolutely no idea.

Did you read it before it was published?

Yes.

What did you think of it?

[Laughs.] I must tread carefully. I presume you do not mean, what was my considered critical judgment, I presume you mean how did I respond? Frankly, I was at first nervous. I was nervous that I would find myself in the book in some embarrassing guise.

Why did you think that might be so?

Because – so it seemed to me at the time, now I realize how naïve this was – I believed you could not be closely involved with another person and yet exclude her from your imaginative universe.

And did you find yourself in the book?

No.

Were you upset?

What do you mean – was I upset not to find myself in his book?

Were you upset to find yourself excluded from his imaginative universe?

No. I was learning. My exclusion was part of my education. Shall we leave it at that? I think I have given you enough.

Well, I am certainly grateful to you. But, Mme Denoël, let me make one further appeal. Coetzee was never a popular writer. By that I do not simply mean that his books did not sell widely. I also mean that the public never took him to their collective heart. There was an image of him in the public realm as a remote and supercilious intellectual, an image he did nothing to dispel. Indeed one might even say he encouraged it.

Now, I don't believe that image does him justice. The conversations I have had with people who knew him well reveal a very different person, not necessarily warmer in temperament but more unsure of himself, more confused, more human, if I can use that word.

I wonder if you would be prepared to comment on the human side of him. I value what you have said about his politics, but are there stories of a more personal nature that you would be prepared to share, stories that might shed a better light on his character?

You mean stories that would show him in a more attractive, more endearing light – stories of kindness towards animals, for instance, animals and women? No, stories like that I will be saving for my own memoirs.

[Laughter.]

All right, I will tell you one story. It may not seem all that personal, it may again seem to be political, but you must remember, in those days politics thrust its way into everything.

A journalist from Libération, the French newspaper, came on an assignment to South Africa, and asked whether I could set up an interview with John. I went back to John and persuaded him to accept: I told him Libération was a good paper, I told him French journalists were not like South African journalists, they would never arrive for an interview without having done their homework.

We held the interview in my office on the campus. I thought I would assist in case there were language problems, John's French was not good.

Well, it soon became clear that the journalist was not interested in John himself but in what John could tell him about Breyten Breytenbach, who was at the time in trouble with the South African authorities. Because in France there was a lively interest in Breytenbach – he was a romantic figure, he had lived in France for many years, he had connections in the French intellectual world.

John's response was that he could not help: he had read Breytenbach but that was all, he did not know him personally, had never met him. All of which was true.

But the journalist, who was used to literary life in France, where everything is so much more incestuous, would not believe him. Why would one writer refuse to comment on another writer from the same little tribe, the Afrikaner tribe, unless there was some personal grudge between them or some political animosity?

So he kept pressing John, and John kept trying to explain how hard it was for a foreigner, an outsider, to appreciate Breytenbach's achievement as a poet, since his poetry was so deeply rooted in the *volksmond*, the language of the people.

'Are you referring to his dialect poems?' said the journalist. And then, when John failed to understand, he remarked, very disparagingly, 'Surely you would agree one cannot write great poetry in dialect.'

That remark really infuriated John. But, since his way of being angry was, rather than shouting and creating a scene, to turn cold and retreat into silence, the man from *Libération* was nonplussed. He had no idea of what he had provoked.

Afterwards, when John had left, I tried to explain that Afrikaners became very emotional when their language was insulted, that Breytenbach himself would probably have responded in the same way. But the journalist just shrugged. It made no sense, he said, to write in dialect when one had a world language at one's disposal (actually he didn't say a dialect, he said an obscure dialect, and he didn't say a world language, he said a proper language, *une vraie langue*). At which point it began to dawn on me that he was putting Breytenbach and John in the same category, as vernacular or dialect writers.

Well, of course John did not write in Afrikaans at all, he wrote in English, very good English, and had written in English all his life. Even so, he responded in the prickly fashion I have described to what he saw as an insult to the dignity of Afrikaans.

He did translations from Afrikaans, didn't he? I mean, translated Afrikaans writers.

Yes. He knew Afrikaans well, I would say, though in much the same fashion as he knew French, that is, better on the page than spoken. I was not competent to judge his Afrikaans, of course, but that was the impression I got.

So we have the case of a man who spoke the language only imperfectly, who stood outside the national religion or at least the state religion, whose outlook was cosmopolitan, whose politics was – what shall we say? – dissident, yet who was prepared to embrace an Afrikaner identity. Why do you think that was so?

My opinion is that under the gaze of history he felt there was no way in which he could separate himself off from the Afrikaners while retaining his self-respect, even if that meant being associated with all that the Afrikaners were responsible for, politically.

Was there nothing that drew him more positively to embrace an Afrikaner identity – nothing at a more personal level, for example?

Perhaps there was, I can't say. I never got to meet his family. Perhaps they would provide a clue. But John was by nature very cautious, very much the tortoise. When he sensed danger, he would withdraw into his shell. He had been rebuffed by the Afrikaners too often, rebuffed and humiliated – you have only to read his book of childhood memories to see that. He was not going to take the risk of being rejected again.

So he preferred to remain an outsider.

I think he was happiest in the role of outsider. He was not a joiner. He was not a team player.

You say you were never introduced to his family. Did you not find that strange?

No, not at all. His mother had passed away by the time he and I met, his father was not well, his brother had left the country, he was on strained terms with the wider family. As for me, I was a married woman, therefore our relationship, as far as it went, had to be clandestine.

But he and I talked, of course, about our families, our origins. What distinguished his family, I would say, is that they were cultural Afrikaners but not political Afrikaners. What do I mean by that? Reflect for a moment on the Europe of the nineteenth century. All over the continent you see ethnic or cultural identities transforming themselves into political identities. That process commences in Greece and spreads rapidly through the Balkans and central Europe. Before long the wave hits the colonies. In the Cape Colony, Dutch-speaking Creoles begin to reinvent themselves as a separate nation, the Afrikaner nation, and to agitate for national independence.

Well, somehow or other that wave of romantic nationalist enthusiasm passed John's family by. Or else they decided not to swim with it.

They kept their distance because of the politics associated with nationalist enthusiasm – I mean, the anti-imperialist, anti-English politics?

Yes. First they were disturbed by the whipped-up hostility to everything English, by the mystique of *Blut und Boden*; then later they recoiled from the ideological baggage that the nationalists took over from the radical right in Europe – scientific racism, for example – and the policies that went with it: the policing of culture, militarization of the youth, a state religion, and so forth.

So, all in all, you see Coetzee as a conservative, an anti-radical.

A cultural conservative, yes, as many of the modernists were cultural conservatives – I mean the modernist writers from Europe who were his models. He was deeply attached to the South Africa of his youth, a South Africa which by 1976 was starting to look like a never-never land. For proof you have only to turn to the book I mentioned, *Boyhood*, where you find a palpable nostalgia for the old feudal relations between white and

Coloured. To people like him, the National Party with its policy of apartheid represented not backwoods conservatism but on the contrary new-fangled social engineering. He was all in favour of the old, complex, feudal social textures which so offended the tidy minds of the *dirigistes* of apartheid.

Did you ever find yourself at odds with him over questions of politics?

That is a difficult question. Where, after all, does character end and politics begin? At a personal level, I saw him as rather too fatalistic and therefore too passive. Did his mistrust of political activism express itself in passivity in the conduct of his life, or did an innate fatalism express itself in mistrust of political action? I cannot decide. But yes, at a personal level there was a certain tension between us. I wanted our relationship to grow and develop, whereas he wanted it to remain the same, without change. That was what caused the breach, in the end. Because between a man and a woman there is no standing still, in my view. Either you are going up or you are going down.

When did the breach occur?

In 1980. I left Cape Town and returned to France.

Did you and he have no further contact?

For a while he wrote to me. He sent me his books as they came out. Then the letters stopped coming. I presumed he had found someone else.

And when you look back over the relationship, how do you see it?

How do I see our relationship? John was a marked Francophile of the kind who believes that if he can acquire for himself a French mistress then supreme felicity will be his. Of the French mistress it will be expected that she recite Ronsard and play Couperin on the clavecin while simultaneously inducting her lover into the amatory mysteries, French style. I exaggerate, of course.

Was I the French mistress of his fantasy? I doubt it very much. Looking back, I now see our relationship as comical in its essence. Comico-sentimental. Based on a comic premise. Yet with a further element that I must not minimize, namely, that he helped me escape from a bad marriage, for which I remain grateful to this day.

Comico-sentimental . . . You make it sound rather light. Did Coetzee not leave a deeper imprint on you, and you on him?

As to what imprint I may have left on him, that I am not in a position to judge. But in general I would say that unless you have a strong presence you do not leave a deep imprint; and John did not have a strong presence. I don't mean to sound flippant. I know he had many admirers; he was not awarded the Nobel Prize for nothing; and of course you would not be here today, pursuing these researches, if you did not think he was important as a writer. But – to be serious for a moment – in all the time I was with him I never had the feeling I was with an exceptional person, a truly exceptional human being. It is a cruel thing to say, I know, but regrettably it is true. I experienced no flash of lightning from him that suddenly illuminated the world. Or if there were flashes, I was blind to them.

I found John clever, I found him knowledgeable, I admired him in many ways. As a writer he knew what he was doing, he had a certain style, and in style lies the beginning of distinction. But he had no special sensitivity that I could detect, no original insight into the human condition. He was just a man, a man of his time, talented, maybe even gifted, but, frankly, not a giant. I am sorry if I disappoint you. From other people who knew him you will get a different picture, I am sure.

Turning to his writings: speaking objectively, as a critic, what is your estimation of his books?

I liked the early work best. In a book like *In the Heart of the Country* there is a certain daring, a certain wildness, that I can still admire. In *Foe* as well, which is not so early. But after that he became more respectable, and in my view more tame. After *Disgrace* I lost interest. I did not read the later stuff.

In general I would say his work lacks ambition. Control over the elements of the fiction is too tight. You do not sense you are in the presence of a writer who is deforming his medium in order to say what has never been said before, which is to me the mark of great writing. Too cool, too neat, I would say. Too easy. Too lacking in passion, creative passion. That's all.

Interview conducted in Paris in January 2008.

Notebooks: Undated fragments

Undated fragment

IT IS A SATURDAY afternoon in winter, ritual time for the game of rugby. With his father he catches a train to Newlands in time for the 2.15 curtain-raiser. The curtain-raiser will be followed at 4.00 by the main match. After the main match they will catch a train home again.

He goes with his father to Newlands because sport – rugby in winter, cricket in summer – is the strongest surviving bond between them, and because it went through his heart like a knife, the first Saturday after his return to the country, to see his father put on his coat and without a word go off to Newlands like a lonely child.

His father has no friends. Nor has he, though for a different reason. He had friends when he was younger; but these old friends are by now dispersed all over the world, and he seems to have lost the knack, or perhaps the will, to make new ones. So he is cast back on his father, as his father is cast back on him. As they live together, so on Saturdays they take their pleasure together. That is the law of the family.

It surprised him, when he came back, to discover that his father knew no one. He had always thought of his father as a convivial man. But either he was wrong about that or his father has changed. Or perhaps it is simply one of the things that happen to men as they grow older: they withdraw into themselves. On Saturdays the stands at Newlands are full of them, solitary men in grey gabardine raincoats in the twilight of their lives, keeping to themselves as if their loneliness were a shameful disease.

He and his father sit side by side on the north stand, watching the curtain-raiser. Over the day's proceedings hangs an air of melancholy. This is the last season when the stadium will be used for club rugby. With the belated arrival of television in the country, interest in club rugby has dwindled away. Men who used to spend their Saturday afternoons at Newlands now prefer to stay at home and watch the game of the week. Of the thousands of seats in the north stand no more than a dozen are occupied. The railway stand is entirely empty. In the south stand there is still a bloc of diehard Coloured spectators who come to cheer for UCT and Villagers and boo Stellenbosch and Van der Stel. Only the grand-stand holds a respectable number, perhaps a thousand.

A quarter of a century ago, when he was a child, it was different. On a big day in the club competition – the day when Hamiltons played Villagers, say, or UCT played Stellenbosch – one would struggle to find standing-room. Within an hour of the final whistle *Argus* vans would be racing through the streets dropping off bundles of the Sports Edition for the vendors on the street corners, with eyewitness accounts of all the first-league games, even the games played in far-off Stellenbosch and Somerset West, together with scores from the lesser leagues, 2A and 2B, 3A and 3B.

Those days are gone. Club rugby is on its last legs. One can sense it today not just in the stands but on the field itself. Depressed by the booming space of the empty stadium, the players seem merely to be going through the motions. A ritual is dying out before their eyes, an authentic petit-bourgeois South African ritual. Its last devotees are gath-ered here today: sad old men like his father; dull, dutiful sons like himself.

A light rain begins to fall. Over the two of them he raises an umbrella. On the field thirty half-hearted young men blunder about, groping for the wet ball.

The curtain-raiser is between Union, in sky-blue, and Gardens, in maroon and black. Union and Gardens are at the bottom of the first-league table and in danger of relegation. It used not to be like that. Once upon a time Gardens was a force in Western Province rugby. At home there is a framed photograph of the Gardens third team as it was in 1938, with his father seated in the front row in his freshly laundered hooped jersey with its Gardens crest and its collar turned up fashionably around

470

his ears. But for certain unforeseen events, World War II in particular, his father might even – who knows? – have made it into the second team.

If old allegiances counted, his father would cheer for Gardens over Union. But the truth is, his father does not care who wins, Gardens or Union or the man in the moon. In fact he finds it hard to detect what his father cares about, in rugby or anything else. If he could solve the mystery of what in the world his father wants, he might perhaps be a better son.

The whole of his father's family is like that – without any passion that he can put a finger on. They do not even seem to care about money. All they want is to get along with everyone and have a bit of a laugh in the process.

In the laughing department he is the last companion his father needs. In laughing he comes bottom of the class. A gloomy fellow: that must be how the world sees him, when it sees him at all. A gloomy fellow; a wet blanket; a stick in the mud.

And then there is the matter of his father's music. After Mussolini capitulated in 1944 and the Germans were driven north, the Allied troops occupying Italy, including the South Africans, were allowed to relax briefly and enjoy themselves. Among the recreations mounted for them were free performances in the big opera houses. Young men from America, Britain, and the far-flung British dominions across the seas, wholly innocent of Italian opera, were plunged into the drama of *Tosca* or *The Barber of Seville* or *Lucia di Lammermoor*. Only a handful took to it, but his father was among that handful. Brought up on sentimental Irish and English ballads, he was entranced by the lush new music and overwhelmed by the spectacle. Day after day he went back for more.

So when Corporal Coetzee returned to South Africa at the end of hostilities, it was with a newfound passion for opera. 'La donna è mobile,' he would sing in the bath. 'Figaro here, Figaro there,' he would sing, 'Figaro, Figaro, Feeegaro!' He went out and bought a gramophone, their family's first; over and over again he would play a 78 rpm recording of Caruso singing 'Your tiny hand is frozen'. When long-playing records were invented he acquired a new and better gramophone, together with an album of Renata Tebaldi singing well-loved arias.

Thus in his adolescent years there were two schools of vocal music at war with each other in the house: an Italian school, his father's, manifested by Tebaldi and Tito Gobbi in full cry; and a German school, his own, founded on Bach. All of Sunday afternoon the household would drown in choruses from the B-minor Mass; then in the evenings, with Bach at last silenced, his father would pour himself a glass of brandy, put on Renata Tebaldi, and sit down to listen to real melodies, real singing.

For its sensuality and decadence – that was how, at the age of sixteen, he saw it – he resolved he would for ever hate and despise Italian opera. That he might despise it simply because his father loved it, that he would have resolved to hate and despise anything in the world that his father loved, was a possibility he would not admit.

One day, while no one was around, he took the Tebaldi record out of its sleeve and with a razor blade drew a deep score across its surface.

On Sunday evening his father put on the record. With each revolution the needle jumped. 'Who has done this?' he demanded. But no one, it seemed, had done it. It had just happened.

Thus ended Tebaldi; now Bach could reign unchallenged.

For that mean and petty deed of his he has for the past twenty years felt the bitterest remorse, remorse that has not receded with the passage of time but on the contrary grown keener. One of his first actions when he returned to the country was to scour the music shops for the Tebaldi record. Though he failed to find it, he did come upon a compilation in which she sang some of the same arias. He brought it home and played it through from beginning to end, hoping to lure his father out of his room as a hunter might lure a bird with his pipes. But his father showed no interest.

'Don't you recognize the voice?' he asked.

His father shook his head.

'It's Renata Tebaldi. Don't you remember how you used to love Tebaldi in the old days?'

He refused to accept defeat. He continued to hope that one day, when he was out of the house, his father would put the new, unblemished record on the player, pour himself a glass of brandy, sit down in his armchair, and allow himself to be transported to Rome or Milan or wherever it was that as a young man his ears were first opened to the sensual beauties of the human voice. He wanted his father's breast to swell with that old joy; if only for an hour, he wanted him to relive that lost youth, forget his present crushed and humiliated existence. Above all he wanted his father to forgive him. *Forgive me!* he wanted to say to his father. *Forgive you? Heavens, what is there to forgive?* he wanted to hear his father reply. Upon which, if he could summon up the courage, he would at last make full confession: *Forgive me for deliberately and with malice aforethought scratching your Tebaldi record. And for more besides, so much more that the recital would take all day. For countless acts of meanness. For the meanness of heart in which those acts originated. In sum, for all I have done since the day I was born, and with such success, to make your life a misery.*

But no, there was no indication, not the faintest, that during his absences from the house Tebaldi was being set free to sing. Tebaldi had, it seemed, lost her charms; or else his father was playing a terrible game with him. *My life a misery? What makes you think my life has been a misery? What makes you think you have ever had it in your power to make my life a misery?*

Intermittently he plays the Tebaldi record for himself; and as he listens the beginnings of some kind of transformation seem to take place inside him. As it must have been with his father in 1944, his heart too begins to throb in time with Mimi's. As the great rising arc of her voice must have called out his father's soul, so it now calls out his soul too, urging it to join hers in passionate, soaring flight.

What has been wrong with him all these years? Why has he not been listening to Verdi, to Puccini? Has he been deaf? Or is the truth worse than that: did he, even as a youth, hear and recognize perfectly well the call of Tebaldi, and then with tight-lipped primness ('I won't!') refuse to heed it? *Down with Tebaldi, down with Italy, down with the flesh!* And if his father must go down too in the general wreck, so be it!

Of what is going on inside his father he has no idea. His father does not talk about himself, does not keep a diary or write letters. Only once, by accident, has the door opened a chink. In the Lifestyle supplement to the weekend *Argus* he has come upon a Yes-No quiz that his father has filled in and left lying around, a quiz titled 'Your Personal Satisfaction Index'. Next to the third question – 'Have you known many members of the opposite sex?' – his father has ticked the box No. 'Have relations with the opposite sex been a source of satisfaction to you?' reads the fourth. No, is the answer again.

Out of a possible twenty, his father scores six. A score of fifteen or above, says the creator of the Index, one Ray Schwarz, MD, PhD, author of *How to Succeed in Life and Love*, a best-selling guide to personal development, means that the respondent has lived a fulfilled life. A score of less than ten, on the other hand, suggests that he or she needs to cultivate a more positive outlook, to which end joining a social club or taking up ballroom dancing might be a first step.

Theme to carry further: his father and why he lives with him. The reaction of the women in his life (bafflement).

Undated fragment

Over the airwaves come denunciations of the communist terrorists, together with their dupes and cronies in the World Council of Churches. The terms of the denunciations may change from day to day, but their hectoring tone does not. It is a tone familiar to him from the Worcester of his schooldays, where once a week all the children, from youngest to oldest, were herded into the school hall to have their brains washed. So familiar is the voice that at its first breath a visceral loathing rises in him and he dives for the off switch.

He is the product of a damaged childhood, that he long ago worked out; what surprises him is that the worst damage was done not in the seclusion of the home but out in the open, at school.

He has been reading here and there in educational theory, and in the writings of the Dutch Calvinist school he begins to recognize what underlay the form of schooling that was administered to him. The purpose of education, say Abraham Kuyper and his disciples, is to form the child as congregant, as citizen, and as parent to be. It is the word *form* that gives him pause. During his years at school in Worcester, his teachers, themselves formed by followers of Kuyper, had all the time been labouring to form him and the other little boys in their charge – form them as a craftsman forms a clay pot; while he, using what paltry, pathetic, inarticulate means he had at his disposal, had tried to resist them – to resist them then as he resists them now.

But why had he so stubbornly resisted? Where did that resistance of his come from, that refusal to accept that the end goal of education should be to form him in some predetermined image, who would otherwise have no form but wallow instead in a state of nature, unsaved, savage? There can be only one answer: the kernel of his resistance, his counter-theory to their Kuyperism, must have come from his mother. Somehow or other, either from her own upbringing as the daughter of the daughter of an Evangelical missionary, or more likely from her sole year in college, a year from which she emerged with no more than a diploma licensing her to teach in primary schools, she must have picked up an alternative ideal of the educator and the educator's task, and then somehow impressed that ideal on her children. The task of the educator, according to his mother, should be to identify and foster the natural talents of the child, the talents with which the child is born and which make the child unique. If the child is to be pictured as a plant, then the educator should feed the roots of the plant and watch over its growth, rather than – as the Kuyperians preached – prune its branches and shape it.

But what grounds does he have for thinking that in bringing him up – him and his brother – his mother followed any theory at all? Why should the truth not be that his mother let the two of them grow up wallowing in savagery simply because she herself had grown up savage – she and her brothers and sisters on the farm in the Eastern Cape where they were born? The answer is given in names he dredges up from the recesses of memory: Montessori; Rudolf Steiner. The names meant nothing when he heard them as a child. But now, in his readings in education, he comes across them again. Montessori, the Montessori Method: so that is why he was given blocks to play with, wooden blocks that he would at first fling hither and thither across the room, thinking that was what they were for, then later pile one on top of the other until the tower (always a tower!) came crashing down and he would howl with frustration.

Blocks to make castles with, and plasticine to make animals with (plasticine which, at first, he would try to chew); and then, before he was ready for it, a Meccano set with plates and rods and bolts and pulleys and cranks.

My little architect; my little engineer. His mother departed the world before it became incontrovertibly clear that he was going to become neither of these, and therefore that the blocks and the Meccano set had not worked their magic, perhaps not the plasticine either (*my little sculptor*). Did his mother wonder: *Was it all a big mistake, the Montessori Method?* Did she even, in darker moments, think to herself: *I should have let those Calvinists form him, I should never have backed him in his resistance?*

If they had succeeded in forming him, those Worcester schoolteachers, he would more than likely have become one of their number himself, patrolling rows of silent children with a ruler in his hand, rapping on their desks as he passed to remind them who was boss. And at the end of the day he would have had a Kuyperian family of his own to go home to, a well-formed, obedient wife and well-formed, obedient children – a family and a home within a community within a homeland. Instead of which he has – what? A father to look after, a father not very good at looking after himself, smoking a little in secret, drinking a little in secret, with a view of their joint domestic situation no doubt at variance with his own: the view, for instance, that it has fallen to him, the unlucky father, to look after the grown-up son, since the son is not very good at looking after himself, as is all too evident from his recent history.

To be developed: his own, home-grown theory of education, its roots in (a) Plato and (b) Freud, its elements (a) discipleship (the student aspiring to be like the teacher) and (b) ethical idealism (the teacher striving to be worthy of the student), its perils (a) vanity (the teacher basking in the student's worship) and (b) sex (bodily intercourse as shortcut to knowledge).

His attested incompetence in matters of the heart; transference (Freudian style) in the classroom and his repeated failures to manage it.

Undated fragment

His father works as a bookkeeper for a firm that imports and sells components for Japanese cars. Because most of these components are made not in Japan but in Taiwan, South Korea, or even Thailand, they cannot be called authentic parts. On the other hand, because they do not come in forged manufacturers' packaging but proclaim (in small print) their country of origin, they are not pirate parts either.

The owners of the firm are two brothers, now in late middle age, who speak English with eastern European inflections and pretend to be innocent of Afrikaans though in fact they were born in Port Elizabeth and understand street Afrikaans perfectly well. They employ a staff of five: three counter hands, a bookkeeper, and a bookkeeper's assistant. The bookkeeper and his assistant have a little wood and glass cubicle of their own to insulate them from the activities around them. As for the hands, they spend their time bustling back and forth between the counter and the racks of auto parts that stretch into the shadowy recesses of the store. The chief counter hand, Cedric, had been with them from the start. No matter how obscure a part may be – a fan housing for a 1968 Suzuki three-wheeler, a kingpin bush for an Impact five-ton truck – Cedric will unerringly know where to find it.

Once a year the firm does a stocktaking during which every part bought or sold, down to the last nut and bolt, is accounted for. It is a major undertaking: most dealers would shut their doors for the duration. But Acme Auto Parts has got where it has got, say the brothers, by staying open from 8 a.m. until 5 p.m. five days of the week, plus 8 a.m. until 1 p.m. on Saturdays, come hell or high water, fifty-two weeks of the year, Christmas and New Year excepted. Therefore the stocktaking has to be done after hours.

As bookkeeper his father is at the centre of operations. During the stocktaking period he sacrifices his lunch hour and works late into the evening. He works alone, without help: working overtime, and therefore catching a late train home, is something that neither Mrs Noerdien, his father's assistant, nor even the counter hands is prepared to do. Riding the trains after dark has become too dangerous, they say: too many commuters are being attacked and robbed. So after closing time it is only the brothers, in their office, and his father, in his cubicle, who stay behind, poring over documents and ledgers.

'If I had Mrs Noerdien for just one extra hour a day,' says his father, 'we could be finished in no time. I could call out the figures and she could check. Doing it by myself is hopeless.'

His father is not a qualified bookkeeper; but during the years he spent running his own legal practice he picked up at least the rudiments. He has been the brothers' bookkeeper for twelve years, ever since he gave up the law. The brothers, it must be presumed – Cape Town is not a big city – are cognisant of his chequered past in the legal profession. They are cognisant of it and therefore – it must be presumed – keep a close watch on him, in case, even so close to retirement, he should think of trying to diddle them.

'If you could bring the ledgers home with you,' he suggests to his father, 'I could give you a hand with the checking.'

His father shakes his head, and he can guess why. When his father refers to the ledgers, he does so in hushed tones, as though they were holy books, as though keeping them were a priestly function. There is more to keeping books, his attitude would seem to suggest, than applying elementary arithmetic to columns of figures.

'I don't think I can bring the ledgers home,' his father says. 'Not on the train. The brothers would never allow it.'

He can appreciate that. What would become of Acme if his father were mugged and the sacred books stolen?

'Then let me come in to the city at the end of the day, at closing time, and take over from Mrs Noerdien. You and I could work together from five till eight, say.'

His father is silent.

'I'll just help with the checking,' he says. 'If anything confidential comes up, I promise not to look.'

By the time he arrives for his first stint, Mrs Noerdien and the counter hands have gone home. He is introduced to the brothers. 'My son John,' says his father, 'who has offered to help with the checking.'

He shakes their hands: Mr Rodney Silverman, Mr Barrett Silverman.

'I'm not sure we can afford you on the payroll, John,' says Mr Rodney.

He turns to his brother. 'Which do you think is more expensive, Barrett, a PhD or a CA? We may have to take out a loan.'

They all laugh together at the joke. Then they offer him a rate. It is precisely the same rate he earned as a student, sixteen years ago, for copying household data onto cards for the municipal census.

With his father he settles down in the bookkeepers' glass cubicle. The task that faces them is simple. They have to go through file after file of invoices, confirming that the figures have been transcribed correctly to the books and to the bank ledger, ticking them off one by one in red pencil, checking the addition at the foot of the page.

They set to work and make steady progress. Once every thousand entries they come across an error, a piddling five cents one way or the other. For the rest the books are in exemplary order. As defrocked clergymen make the best proofreaders, so debarred lawyers seem to make good bookkeepers – debarred lawyers assisted if need be by their over-educated, under-employed sons.

The next day, on his way to Acme, he is caught in a rain-shower. He arrives sodden. The glass of the cubicle is fogged; he enters without knocking. His father is hunched over his desk. There is a second presence in the cubicle, a woman, young, gazelle-eyed, softly curved, in the act of putting on her raincoat.

He halts in his tracks, transfixed.

His father rises from his seat. 'Mrs Noerdien, this is my son John.'

Mrs Noerdien averts her gaze, does not offer a hand. 'I'll go now,' she says in a low voice, addressing not him but his father.

An hour later the brothers too take their leave. His father boils the kettle and makes them coffee. Page after page, column after column they press on with the work, until ten o'clock, until his father is blinking with exhaustion.

The rain has stopped. Down a deserted Riebeeck Street they head for the station: two men, able-bodied more or less, safer at night than a single man, many times safer than a single woman.

'How long has Mrs Noerdien been working for you?' he asks.

'She came last February.'

He waits for more. There is no more. There is plenty he could ask.

For instance: How does it happen that Mrs Noerdien, who wears a head-scarf and is presumably Muslim, comes to be working for a Jewish firm, one where there is no male relative to keep a protective eye on her?

'Is she good at her job? Is she efficient?'

'Very good. Very meticulous.'

Again he waits for more. Again, that is the end of it.

The question he cannot bring himself to ask is: What does it do to the heart of a lonely man like yourself to be sitting side by side, day after day, in a cubicle no larger than many prison cells, with a woman who is not only as good at her job and as meticulous as Mrs Noerdien, but also as feminine?

For that is the chief impression he carries away from his brush with Mrs Noerdien. He calls her feminine because he has no better word: the feminine, a higher rarefaction of the female, to the point of becoming spirit. Married to such a woman, what would it take for a man to traverse each day the space from the exalted heights of the feminine to the earthly body of the female? To sleep with a being like that, to embrace her, to smell and taste her – what would it do to the soul? And to be beside her all day, conscious of her slightest stirring: did his father's sad response to Dr Schwarz's lifestyle quiz – 'Have relations with the opposite sex been a source of satisfaction to you?' – 'No' – have something to do with coming face to face, in the wintertime of his life, with beauty such as he has not known before and can never hope to possess?

Query: Why ask whether his father is in love with Mrs Noerdien when he has so obviously fallen for her himself?

Undated fragment

Idea for a story.

A man, a writer, keeps a diary. In it he notes down thoughts, ideas, significant occurrences.

Things take a turn for the worse in his life. 'Bad day,' he writes in his diary, without elaboration. 'Bad day . . . Bad day,' he writes, day after day.

Tiring of calling each day a bad day, he decides to simply mark bad days with an asterisk, as some people (women) mark with a red cross days when they will bleed, or as other people (men, womanizers) mark with an X days when they have notched up a success.

The bad days pile up; the asterisks multiply like a plague of flies.

Poetry, if he could write poetry, might take him to the root of his malaise, this malaise that blossoms in the form of asterisks. But the spring of poetry in him seems to have dried up.

There is prose to fall back on. In theory prose can perform the same cleansing trick as poetry. But he has doubts about that. Prose, in his experience, calls for many more words than poetry. There is no point in embarking on an adventure in prose if one lacks confidence that one will be alive the next day to carry on with it.

He plays with thoughts like these – the thought of poetry, the thought of prose – as a way of not writing.

In the back pages of his diary he makes lists. One of them is headed *Ways of Doing Away with Oneself*. In the left-hand column he lists *Methods*, in the right-hand column *Drawbacks*.

Of the ways of doing away with oneself he has listed, the one he favours, on mature consideration, is drowning, that is to say, driving to Fish Hoek one night, parking near the deserted end of the beach, undressing in the car and putting on his swimming trunks (but why?), crossing the sand (it will have to be a moonlit night), breasting the waves, striking out into the dark, swimming until his physical powers are exhausted, then letting fate take its course.

All of his intercourse with the world seems to take place through a membrane. Because the membrane is there, fertilization (of himself, by the world) will not take place. It is an interesting metaphor, full of potential, but it does not take him anywhere that he can see.

Undated fragment

His father grew up on a farm in the Karoo drinking artesian water high in fluoride. The fluoride turned the enamel of his teeth brown and hard as stone. His boast used to be that he never needed to see a dentist. Then in mid-life his teeth began to go rotten, one after another, and he had to have them all extracted.

Now, in his mid-sixties, his gums are giving him trouble. Abscesses are forming that will not heal. His throat becomes infected. He finds it painful to swallow, to speak.

He goes first to a dentist, then to an ear, nose and throat specialist, who sends him for X-rays. The X-rays reveal a cancerous tumour on the larynx. He is advised to submit to surgery urgently.

He visits his father in the male ward at Groote Schuur Hospital. He is wearing general-issue pyjamas and his eyes are frightened. Inside the too-large jacket he is like a bird, all skin and bone.

'It is a routine operation,' he reassures his father. 'You will be out in a few days.'

'Will you explain to the brothers?' his father whispers with painful slowness.

'I will phone them.'

'Mrs Noerdien is very capable.'

'I am sure Mrs Noerdien is very capable. I am sure she will manage until you come back.'

There is nothing more to say. He could stretch out and take his father's hand and hold it, to comfort him, to convey to him that he is not alone, that he is loved and cherished. But he does no such thing. Save in the case of small children, children not yet old enough to be formed, it is not the practice in their family for one person to reach out and touch another. Nor is that the worst. If on this one extreme occasion he were to ignore family practice and grasp his father's hand, would what that gesture implied be true? Is his father truly loved and cherished? Is his father truly not alone?

He takes a long walk, from the hospital to the Main Road, then along the Main Road as far as Newlands. The south-easter is howling, whipping up trash from the gutters. He walks fast, conscious of the vigour of his limbs, the steadiness of his heartbeat. The air of the hospital is still in his lungs; he must expel it, get rid of it.

When he arrives in the ward the next day, his father is flat on his back, his chest and throat swathed in a dressing with tubes running out of it. He looks like a corpse, the corpse of an old man.

He has been prepared for the spectacle. The larynx, which was tumorous, had to be excised, says the surgeon, there was no avoiding that. His father will no longer be able to speak in the normal way. However, in due course, after the wound has healed, he will be fitted with a prosthesis that will permit vocal communication of a kind. A more urgent task is to ensure the cancer has not spread, which will mean further tests, plus radiotherapy.

'Does my father know that?' he asks the surgeon. 'Does he know what he is in for?'

'I tried to fill him in,' says the surgeon, 'but I am not sure how much he absorbed. He is in a state of shock. Which is to be expected, of course.'

He stands over the figure in the bed. 'I phoned Acme,' he says. 'I spoke to the brothers and explained the situation.'

His father opens his eyes. Generally he is sceptical about the capacity of the ocular orbs to express complex feelings, but this time he is shaken. The look his father gives him speaks of utter indifference: indifference to him, indifference to Acme Auto, indifference to everything but the fate of his own soul in the prospect of eternity.

'The brothers send their best wishes,' he continues. 'For a speedy recovery. They say not to worry, Mrs Noerdien will hold the fort until you are ready to come back.'

It is true. The brothers, or whichever of the brothers he spoke to, could not be more solicitous. Their bookkeeper may not be of the faith, but the brothers are not cold people. 'A jewel' – that is what the brother in question called his father. 'Your father is a jewel, his job will always be open for him.'

It is of course a fiction, all of it. His father will never go back to work. In a week or two or three he will be sent home, cured or part cured, to commence the next and final phase of his life, during which he will depend for his daily bread on the charity of the Automotive Industry Benefit Fund, of the South African state through its Department of Pensions, and of his surviving family.

'Is there anything I can bring you?' he inquires.

His father makes tiny scrabbling motions with his left hand, whose fingernails, he notes, are not clean. 'Do you want to write?' he says. He brings out his pocket diary, opens it to the page headed Telephone Numbers, and proffers it together with a pen.

The fingers cease moving, the eyes lose focus.

'I don't know what you mean,' he says. 'Try again to tell me what you mean.'

Slowly his father shakes his head, left to right.

On the stands beside the other beds in the ward there are vases of flowers, magazines, in some cases framed photographs. The stand beside his father's bed is bare save for a glass of water.

'I must go now,' he says. 'I have a class to teach.'

At a kiosk near the front entrance he buys a packet of sucking sweets and returns to his father's bedside. 'I got these for you,' he says. 'To hold in your mouth if your mouth gets dry.'

Two weeks later his father comes home in an ambulance. He is able to walk in a shuffling way with the aid of a stick. He makes his way from the front door to his bedroom and shuts himself in.

One of the ambulancemen hands him a cyclostyled sheet of instructions titled Laryngectomy – Care of Patients, and a card with a schedule of times when the clinic is open. He glances over the sheet. There is an outline sketch of a human head with a dark circle low in the throat. Care of Wound, it says.

He draws back. 'I can't do this,' he says. The ambulancemen exchange glances, shrug. It is not their business, taking care of the wound, taking care of the patient. Their business is to convey the patient to his or her place of residence. After that it is the patient's business, or the patient's family's business, or else no one's business.

It used to be that he, John, had too little employment. Now that is about to change. Now he will have as much employment as he can handle, as much and more. He is going to have to abandon some of his personal projects and be a nurse. Alternatively, if he will not be a nurse, he must announce to his father: I cannot face the prospect of ministering to you day and night. I am going to abandon you. Goodbye. One or the other: there is no third way.